MICHAEL DIBDIN, EDITOR

THE VINTAGE BOOK OF
CLASSIC CRIME

Michael Dibdin is the author of eleven novels, including *Cosí Fan Tutti, Dark Specter, The Dying of the Light, Dead Lagoon,* and *Ratking,* which won the Crime Writers Association Gold Dagger Award. He lives in Seattle, Washington.

THE VINTAGE BOOK OF
CLASSIC CRIME

THE VINTAGE BOOK OF
CLASSIC CRIME

EDITED BY

MICHAEL DIBDIN

Vintage Crime/Black Lizard

Vintage Books

A Division of Random House, Inc.

New York

Library of Congress Cataloging-in-Publication Data
The Vintage book of classic crime / edited by Michael Dibdin.
  p.   cm.—(Vintage crime/Black Lizard)
Originally published: Picador, 1993.
Includes bibliographical references.
ISBN 0-679-76855-6
1. Detective and mystery stories.
I. Dibdin, Michael.
II. Series.
PN6071.D45V56   1997
808.83'872—dc20   96-9620
CIP

THOMAS DE QUINCEY
ON MURDER CONSIDERED AS ONE OF THE FINE ARTS

When a murder is in the paulo-post-futurum tense – not done, not even (according to modern purism) *being* done, but only going to be done – and a rumour of it comes to our ears, by all means let us treat it morally. But suppose it over and done, and that you can say of it, Τετέλεσται, It is finished, or (in that adamantine molossus of *Medea*) εἴργασται, Done it is: it is a *fait accompli*; suppose the poor murdered man to be out of his pain, and the rascal that did it off like a shot, nobody knows whither; suppose, lastly, that we have done our best, by putting out our legs, to trip up the fellow in his flight, but all to no purpose – 'abiit, evasit, excessit, erupit,' etc. – why, then, I say, what's the use of any more virtue? Enough has been given to morality; now comes the turn of Taste and the Fine Arts. A sad thing it was, no doubt, very sad; but *we* can't mend it. Therefore let us make the best of a bad matter; and, as it is impossible to hammer anything out of it for moral purposes, let us treat it aesthetically, and see if it will turn to account in that way. Such is the logic of a sensible man, and what follows? We dry up our tears, and have the satisfaction, perhaps, to discover that a transaction, which, morally considered, was shocking, and without a leg to stand upon, when tried by principles of Taste, turns out to be a very meritorious performance. Thus all the world is pleased; the old proverb is justified, that it is an ill wind which blows nobody good; the amateur, from looking bilious and sulky, by too close an attention to virtue, begins to pick up his crumbs; and general hilarity prevails. Virtue has had her day; and henceforward, *Virtù*, so nearly the same thing as to differ only by a single letter (which surely is not worth haggling or higgling about) – *Virtù,* I repeat, and Connoisseurship, have leave to provide for themselves. Through this great gallery of murder, therefore, together let us wander hand in hand, in delighted admiration; while I endeavour to point your attention to the objects of profitable criticism.

CONTENTS

....

CONTENTS

PART THREE
SENTENCE FIRST, VERDICT AFTERWARDS
A CRITICAL INTERLUDE

CONTENTS

PART FOUR
UNCOMMON MURDERERS

CONTENTS

PART FIVE
THE DANGEROUS EDGE OF THINGS

THE VINTAGE BOOK OF
CLASSIC CRIME

INTRODUCTION

This anthology is dedicated to the proposition that good crime writing is good writing.

It is a sobering comment on perceptions of the genre that this statement, which in another context would risk sounding feebly tautologous, is likely to strike some readers as controversial if not deliberately provocative. It also begs the question of what constitutes good writing.

The answer is likely to emerge more lucidly from the examples and commentary which follow than from any attempt at definition, but let us be clear at the outset what it is *not*. For a start, good crime writing has nothing whatever in common with 'fine writing'. Raymond Chandler famously defined the pulp thriller's rule of thumb: 'When in doubt, have a man come through a door with a gun in his hand.' If Chandler transcended this formula to produce some of the greatest works of crime fiction, it was not by spending half a page describing the door, nor by giving the man artistic attributes and a taste for the finer things in life.

But for every writer who pads out a two-hundred-page detective story to twice that length with decorative frills and flounces there are ten whose work might have been written not just on but *by* a word processor. Here language is conceived as a neutral, 'natural', low-tech medium, wholly transparent to producer and user alike, in which the story-line may be conveniently packaged for provisional consumption pending its definitive incarnation as a Major Motion Picture.

Good crime writing has nothing to do with either of these. It does not seek to draw attention to the writer's erudition or taste, nor does it patronize prose as a cheap and cheerful form of communicating a pre-existing and independent 'idea'. Like any other form of literature, crime fiction at its best puts words to work to profuce effects which cannot be achieved – still less improved on – in any other way. It thus offers a unique set of opportunities and challenges to its practitioners.

This anthology seeks to illustrate some of the very different ways in which they have responded. Given the constraints of space, the selection cannot and does not pretend to be comprehensive. The playwright David Hare, admitting to an 'indiscriminate' enthusiasm for crime fiction, goes on to say: 'If I have a preference at all, it is for those who work against the form to make it do something to which it is not apparently suited.' If some of my selections appear eccentric this is because, like Hare, I believe that the best crime writing *is* eccentric – the product of a creative struggle against the overwhelming centripetal force of the genre.

I have exercised a measure of positive discrimination in favour of those British writers who tried to maintain an alternative tradition of crime writing at a time when readers and critics (and publishers) were hypnotized by the facile contrivances of the 'Golden Age' whodunnit. By extension, I have sought throughout to stress the diversity of work achievable within the constraints of a genre which has traditionally been bedevilled by rules, regulations, and rituals reminiscent of a third-rate Masonic cult.

As long ago as 1944, Chandler noted that 'the detective or mystery story as an art form has been so thoroughly explored that the real problem for a writer now is to avoid writing a mystery story while appearing to do so'. Substitute 'challenge' for 'problem' and you have a manifesto for crime writing based not on prescriptive lists of dos and dont's but on a celebration of the variety and scope of the opportunities on offer to writers of widely differing backgrounds, interests and approaches.

The presence of such names as Kafka and Zola, to say nothing of a clutch of poets, might look like a bid to gentrify the genre by demonstrating that the great and the good have gone slumming there from time to time; or even to suggest that any attempt to discriminate between crime and 'literary' fiction is a highbrow plot, and that at the end of the day *Crime and Punishment* is just a murder mystery with knobs on. I would argue, on the contrary, that it is precisely the fact that crime writing is a distinctive genre, with flexible but fixed parameters and a limited repertoire of themes, which has tempted so many mainstream writers to indulge in acts of homage, pastiche or cross-reference.

One of the most interesting aspects of our subject is the quantity and quality of comment it has attracted. The enduring popularity of the genre for over a century and a half, together with its social and cultural implications, has made crime fiction a phenomenon which even its detractors have found almost impossible to ignore. The result has been a degree of critical attention, much of it from very eminent figures, such as has been lavished on no other form of popular literature. A representative selection of these judgements, some taking the form of parody, has been included here to provoke reflection and discussion.

When all is said and done a book such as this is necessarily a reflection of the enthusiasms and prejudices of its compiler. One of our leading wine merchants introduces their catalogue with a disclaimer: 'We only sell what we would like to drink ourselves.' As a critic has pointed out, this can mean disappointing bottles if your tastes don't happen to coincide with theirs, but it can also lead to wonderful discoveries and eye-openers. I only hope that for most readers the latter will outweigh the former.

ACKNOWLEDGEMENTS

....

I am specially indebted to T. J. Binyon for lending me several works of reference, and to Jeff Morrison for translating a long essay by Brecht. Carmen Calill, J. A. Flanders, Peter Hainsworth, H. R. F. Keating, Alex King, Craig Raine, Helena Reckitt, Christopher Reid, Mike Ripley, Michael Sheringham, Clive Sinclair, Joan Smith, Peter Straus and Julian Symons were all helpful in suggesting passages for inclusion or tracing sources. Finally, I would like to thank the staff of the London Library, and of the Taylor Institute and the Bodleian Library, Oxford.

....

PART ONE

SERIOUS BUSINESS

MICHAEL DIBDIN

....

'It was not until several weeks after he had decided to murder his wife that Dr Bickleigh took any active steps in the matter. Murder is a serious business.' The opening lines of *Malice Aforethought* are perhaps the most famous in crime fiction, but it is difficult now to recapture their effect in an era when, as Brecht wrote, 'The crime novel, like the world itself, is ruled by the English.' In 1931 the whodunnit seemed as absolute and eternal a fact of life as the British Empire, yet here was Francis Iles giving away what was supposedly the crime writer's unique stock-in-trade in his opening line.

'In a detective story nothing should happen,' wrote T. S. Eliot. 'The crime has already been committed, and the rest of the tale consists of the collection, selection and combination of evidence.' Stories which infringed this rule risked losing their genteel status as, in V. S. Pritchett's phrase, 'the art for art's sake of our yawning Philistinism', and being degraded to the level of a mere thriller, as read by colonials and the servant class. Iles stood this logic on its head. By putting the murder itself – its preparation, execution and aftermath – at the centre of his book, he not only created an enduring classic but made crime writing itself a 'serious business' once more.

Every era has an emblematic transgression which addresses its intimate fears and fantasies. Victorian crime fiction did not always resort to murder, since theft or deceit incurred a fate which, socially, was worse than death. If the cult crime in recent years has been serial killing – a death which says a lot about the lives we think we lead – then uxoricide held an apparently endless fascination for the pre-war generation of British writers. Julian Symons treated the theme twice, the first time as tragedy and the second as farce. The later version features a henpecked suburban husband who creates a second life for himself as a womanizing cad, and then uses this *alter ego* to kill his wife The resulting confrontation is filled with ironies of all kinds, but remains perfectly credible.

As a critic, Symons has done more than anyone else to resurrect unjustly neglected titles and authors. One of his major coups was the publication in a readable translation of Chekhov's early (and only) novel, *The Shooting Party*. Like Henry James's 'crime' novel *The Other House*, this was not included in the standard collected edition of the author's works and has hence been overlooked or disparaged. The narrator is an investigating magistrate in an isolated provincial district who becomes involved with a debauched and alcoholic count whose wife is subsequently brutally murdered. The basic plot device anticipates one for which Agatha Christie was to be admired and censured almost half a century later, but the real power of the novel lies in the depiction of the hard-drinking rough-spoken rural nobility and the corrupt and tortured personality of the narrator.

Where the male lead in British crime novels used to murder his wife, his American counterpart fell prey to the siren charms of a *blonde fatale* who then induced him to kill her husband. The classic statement of this theme is James M. Cain's *The Postman Always Rings Twice*. For a time Cain was mentioned in the same critical breath as Steinbeck and Hemingway, and he has suffered for it ever since. Despite his mannerisms, he remains the only crime writer of his generation who can stand comparison with Hammett and Chandler, and the only one who can depict sexual behaviour convincingly. He also never patronizes his characters: the vagrant Nick, his lover Cora and her elderly Greek immigrant husband are equally real, equally human, equally doomed.

Cain's model for *Postman* may well have been Émile Zola's novel *Thérèse Raquin*, an extract from which is published here in the first anonymous, English translation of 1886. Here too the murder is staged as an accident during a pleasure-outing, this time at one of the picturesque villages on the Seine just outside Paris, and both scenes end with a ghostly reappearance by the victim – in Cain a literal echo, in Zola an uneaten meal.

The first section of Ira Levin's only crime novel is a stunning *tour de force*: at once a psychological study in the manner of Patricia Highsmith and a diabolically clever piece of deceit which tells us everything there is to know about the murderer except his identity. Wisely, perhaps, Levin never tried to repeat the performance, but his portrait of the All-American psychopath has been widely copied by less skilful hands.

In an article on Wilkie Collins, Eliot looked back to a golden age when there was no distinction between 'high-brow fiction' and crime novels. Because of the unique circumstances of his cultural milieu the Yiddish writer Isaac Bashevis Singer preserved that lost innocence to a greater degree than any other major twentieth-century figure. In *Under The Knife*, a drunken self-pitying brute plots the murder of an ex-girlfriend who has married a rich barber; the extract opens with his preliminary visit to a prostitute. If the stench of moral and psychological disintegration suggests Dostoyevsky, the final twist is a surprise ending any crime writer would be proud of.

The lower depths of the Polish ghetto where Singer sets his story in many ways resemble the early nineteenth century London dockland setting of *The Maul and the Pear Tree*, in which P. D. James and T. A. Critchley study the Ratcliffe Highway murders of 1811, which had already served De Quincey as the prime example of 'Murder Considered as One of the Fine Arts'. The interesting conclusions they come to are outside the scope of this anthology, but the account of the killings themselves is a fine example of P. D. James's descriptive prose: evocative but precisely detailed, leisurely yet compelling, confronting horrors without ever losing its balance and control.

The next piece might also seem to be a newspaper description of a real-life crime, judging by the journalistic rhetoric ('The enigmas of human nature!'). But the doorbell in the sixth paragraph sounds an alarm which is echoed by a series of other dreamlike distortions, until our suspicions are confirmed by the discovery of the author's identity. A passage from one of Joseph Conrad's letters perhaps throws some light on the title: 'Fraternity means nothing unless the Cain–Abel business. That's your true fraternity.'

American crime fiction has never been divorced from the

mainstream to the extent it has in Britain. While the work of John Dickson Carr or Agatha Christie bears no resemblance to that of Graham Greene or Elizabeth Bowen, the distinction between Hammett and Hemingway, although real, is mainly a question of register and range. This remains true today, with the work of the 'dirty realists' such as Richard Ford or Andre Dubus often bordering very closely on crime writing. Dubus's story *Killings*, gritty yet deeply felt, recounts the aftermath of a small-town *crime passionel*. The Simon Armitage poem which follows is even bleaker and sparer – the complete story of an everyday atrocity in just twenty-five lines.

Sanctuary and *Intruder in the Dust* can both be considered as crime novels, but William Faulkner also wrote a number of straightforward detective stories, one of which was awarded second prize in a competition in *Ellery Queen's Mystery Magazine*! The opening of 'Smoke' is such rich, seamless Faulkner prose that it is a double shock to find that it has been leading up to a classic Locked Room mystery.

At the height of his fame, Raymond Chandler was fairly dismissive of the stories he had written in the 1930s for the pulp magazine *Black Mask*, and critics have tended to follow suit. Certainly there are dull and clumsy passages, but at its best – as in this scene at the aptly named Surprise Hotel – the writing has an extraordinary vigour and freshness, and Chandler's delight in the jazzy rhythms of American slang was never keener.

Los Angeles in the nineties is not only infinitely more violent than the city Chandler knew, but even more racially complex. Alex Abella's novel is set in the Latino community, and specifi-cally among the Cuban-American *marielitos*. The opening scene is one of the longest and most detailed accounts of carnage in all crime fiction, but Abella's humane and ironic narrative voice precludes any hint of comic-book mannerism or voyeuristic sensation-seeking.

THE MAN WHO KILLED HIMSELF

He had not decided upon the method and manner of committing the act without thought. It was tempting to play with the idea of planning some deliberate deception about the time of death. 'It is not possible to be certain about the rate of cooling of a body': those encouraging words had been written by no less a medico-legal expert than Sir Sydney Smith, and books of medical jurisprudence all spoke with delightful uncertainty about estab-lishing the precise time of death. Suppose that one placed an electric fire near to a body, the time of death would appear to be an hour or two later than was actually the case. Or suppose – more ingenious and interesting – that one took ice cubes from the refrigerator and placed them in plastic non-leaking containers at various points about the body, the normal cooling process should be speeded up. He reluctantly rejected such ideas, partly because of the distaste that he felt for having anything to do with a dead body, but chiefly (or so he felt) because such ingenuity was in itself to be deprecated. If the police happened to notice that the electric fire, although turned off, was still curiously warm, if ice water somehow leaked out of the plastic packs, if in fact the police thought that deliberate deception was being attempted, might they not immediately suspect him? The strength of his position was that Arthur Brownjohn and Easonby Mellon were two wholly separate characters, and that there was no reason in the world why they should be associated. This was what he must remember. The act should be simple, quick and obvious. His plan was simple, and entailed practically no risk.

At Euston Station, on his return from Birmingham he telephoned Clare, and cut short a burst of recriminatory phrases by saying that he was coming home and wanted to see her.

There must have been something strange in his tone, for she checked abruptly as a horse coming to a jump. 'What about?'

'I can't explain now, but—'

'You can't explain,' she said incredulously.

'You're alone, aren't you?'

'Of course I am alone. I am just finishing my lunch.'

'I shall be back soon. Don't tell anybody I'm coming, will you?'

'Arthur, have you been drinking?'

'I'll be there soon after three.' He put down the telephone. His hand was shaking.

In the station lavatory he changed into Easonby Mellon's clothes, and carefully adjusted the wig and beard. He went out carrying Arthur Brownjohn's clothes and diary in his suitcase. He caught the two thirty train from Waterloo for the half-hour journey to Fraycut.

This time Major Mellon made his way straight out of the station in the direction of Livingstone Road. Phil Silvers was not on duty, and the man at the barrier took his ticket without a glance. The Laurels stood foursquare in exurban dignity. The rest of Livingstone Road appeared to sleep. He opened the gate, which gave its accustomed small squeak, walked up the path, inserted the key in the lock, turned it, was inside. Mr Slattery stared at him accusingly, as though aware of the revolver in his jacket pocket. The door of the living room opened, and Clare came out. 'What—' she said, and stopped. He found himself holding his breath, as if something important depended on her words. Then she completed the sentence.

'What are you doing in those ridiculous clothes, and that—' She seemed to find it impossible to specify the wig and beard. 'Take it all off immediately.'

She had known him at once. It was awful. His fists were clenched into tight balls. 'I can explain.'

'Your telegram, what was the meaning of that? I waited for more than an hour at Waterloo. And now this fancy dress.'

'I said I could explain.'

'I doubt it very much. I cannot think what possible explanation there can be.'

He heard himself saying that it was quite simple, and knew with dismay that the tones were those of Arthur Brownjohn, not of Easonby Mellon. How could boldness have so speedily and humiliatingly abandoned him? One hand went into a pocket and drew out the revolver.

'What is the *meaning* of this masquerade?' Clare was becoming angry, it could be seen in the thickening of her neck muscles and the spot of colour in her cheeks. He was near the door of the living room and she stood in the middle of it just beside the mottled grey sofa. She saw what was in his hand, and her reaction was one of pure exasperation. She spoke like a mother to a misbehaving child. 'Arthur, what are you doing? Put it *down*.'

'No.' He found it impossible to speak, then swallowed and managed it. 'I really must explain.'

She took a step towards him. He retreated. 'If you could see how silly you look.'

'Silly!' he cried out. The word moved him to anger. He raised the revolver, squeezed the trigger. Nothing happened.

'Of course you do. Just get that stuff off and wash your face and you'll feel better.'

'I am not silly,' he shouted. Why didn't she realize that he was a dangerous man? He realized that he had not moved the safety catch and did so. Suddenly the revolver went off, making a tremendous noise. The kickback jolted his arm severely. What happened to the bullet? He became aware that Clare was strangely pale.

She took another step towards him and said in a low voice, 'What is the matter with you, Arthur?'

He retreated. He had his back to the door. The revolver went off again, almost deafening him. This time she put her hands to her stomach, so evidently the bullet had hit her, but she did not fall down. Instead she put out a hand, and he felt that if she succeeded in touching him something terrible would happen. He cried out something, he could not have said what, and fired again and again, he did not know how many times or where the bullets went. There was a ping of glass and he thought: Heavens, I've broken the french window. He looked and saw the window starred at one point, and with a deep crack down the centre. He was so much distressed by this time that his attention was temporarily distracted from Clare. He saw, however, that she was badly hurt. She appeared to be trying to speak to him, but failed to do so. Blood shot in a stream from her mouth – he jumped back hurriedly so that it should not touch him – and she fell over the back of the sofa and then down the side of it to the floor, clawing at the sofa for support and making unintelligible noises in her throat. She seemed still to be trying to say something to him, but he could not imagine what it was. She lay on the carpet groaning. Blood continued to trickle from her mouth. He found it unendurable that she was not dead, perhaps would not die. The revolver was empty, but in any case he could not have fired it again. He stood and watched helplessly as she tried to inch her way across the carpet to – what would it be? – of course, the telephone. There was blood on her face now, and she moved more slowly. He could not have said whether it was seconds or minutes before he realized that she was not moving at all.

It would have been impossible for him to touch her with his gloved hands, but he moved across with the caution he would have used in approaching a squashed but possibly still dangerous insect, and rolled her over with his foot. She lay still, staring at the ceiling with her eyes open. She was, she must be, dead.

He felt that he could no longer bear to be in the house. He dropped the revolver to the floor, looked round him without seeing anything, and ran out of the room. His case stood in the hall. He picked it up, opened the front door, and began to run down the path. Then he checked himself. In the garden of Endholme old Mr Lillicrapp was at work with his fork and trowel. He straightened up and said, 'Afternoon. Some boys been breaking windows round here. Heard the glass go. Thought it might be mine, but it wasn't. Not next door, I hope.' He laughed heartily, but the man leaving The Laurels in a hurry made no reply. Mr Lillicrapp leaned on his fork and stood looking after the man as he walked down the road. Discourtesy was rampant nowadays. He ascribed it less to rudeness than to the hustle and bustle of modern life.

ANTON CHEKHOV

....

THE SHOOTING PARTY

About seven o'clock in the morning the village elder and his assistants, whom I had sent for, arrived. It was impossible to drive to the scene of the crime: the rain that had begun in the night was still pouring down in buckets. Little puddles had become lakes. The grey sky looked gloomy, and there was no promise of sunlight. The soaked trees appeared dejected with their drooping branches, and sprinkled a whole shower of large drops at every gust of wind. It was impossible to go there. Besides, it might have been useless. The trace of the crime, such as bloodstains, human footprints, etc., had probably been washed away during the night. But the formalities demanded that the scene of the crime should be examined, and I deferred this visit until the arrival of the police, and in the mean time I made out a draft of the official report of the case, and occupied myself with the examination of witnesses. First of all I examined the gypsies. The poor singers had passed the whole night sitting up in the ballrooms expecting horses to be sent round to convey them to the station. But horses were not provided; the servants, when asked, only sent them to the devil, warning them at the same time that his Excellency had forbidden anybody to be admitted to him. They were also not given the samovar they asked for in the morning. The perplexing and ambiguous situation in which they found themselves in a strange house in which a corpse was lying, the uncertainty as to when they could get away, and the damp melancholy weather had driven the gypsies, both men and women, into such a state of distress that in one night they had become thin and pale. They wandered about from room to room, evidently much alarmed and expecting some serious issue. By my examination I only increased their anxiety. First because my lengthy examination delayed their departure from the accursed house indefinitely, and secondly because it alarmed them. The simple people, imagining that they were seriously suspected of the murder, began to assure me with tears in their eyes, that they were not guilty and knew nothing about the matter. Tina, seeing me as an official personage, quite forgot our former connection, and while speaking to me trembled and almost fainted with fright like a little girl about to be whipped. In reply to my request not to be excited, and my assurance that I saw in them nothing but witnesses, the assistants of justice, they informed me in one voice that they had never been witnesses, that they knew nothing, and that they trusted that in future God would deliver them from all close acquaintance with ministers of the law.

I asked them by what road they had driven from the station, had they not passed through that part of the forest where the murder had been committed, had any member of their party quitted it for even a short time, and had they not heard Olga's heart-rending shriek. This examination led to nothing. The gypsies, alarmed by it, only sent two members of the chorus to the village to hire vehicles. The poor people wanted terribly to get away. Unfortunately for them there was already much talk in the village about the murder in the forest, and these swarthy messengers were looked at with suspicion; they were arrested and brought to me. It was only towards evening that the harassed chorus was able to get free from this nightmare and breathe freely, as having hired five peasants' carts at three times the proper fare, they drove away from the Count's house. Afterwards they were paid for their visit, but nobody paid them for the moral suffering that they had endured in the Count's apartments . . .

Having examined them, I made a search in the Scops-Owl's room. In her trunks I found quantities of all sorts of old woman's rubbish, but although I looked through all the old caps and darned stockings, I found neither money nor valuables that the old woman had stolen from the Count or his guests . . . Nor did I find the things that had been stolen from Tina some time before . . . Evidently the old witch had another hiding-place only known to herself.

I will not give here the preliminary report I drafted about the information I had obtained or the searches I had made . . . It was long; besides, I have forgotten most of it. I will only give a general idea of it. First of all I described the condition in which I found Olga, and I gave an account of every detail of my examination of her. By this examination it was evident that Olga was quite conscious when she answered me and purposely concealed the name of the murderer. She clearly did not *want* the murderer to suffer the penalty, and this inevitably led to the supposition that the criminal was near and dear to her.

The examination of her clothes, which I made together with the commissary of the rural police who had arrived post-haste, was highly revealing . . . The jacket of her riding habit, made of velvet with a silk lining, was still moist. The right side in which there was the hole made by the dagger was saturated with blood and in places bore marks of clotted blood . . . The loss of blood had been very great, and it was astonishing that Olga had not died on the spot. The left side was also bloodstained. The left sleeve was torn at the shoulder and at the wrist . . . The two upper buttons were torn off, and at our examination we did not find them. The skirt of the riding habit, made of black cashmere, was found to be terribly crumpled; it had been crumpled when they had carried Olga out of the wood to the vehicle and from the vehicle to her bed. Then it had been pulled off, rolled into a disorderly heap, and flung under the bed. It was torn at the waistband. This tear was about ten inches in length, and had probably been made while she was being carried or when it was pulled off; it might also have been made during her lifetime. Olga, who did not like mending, and not knowing to whom to give the habit to be mended, might have hidden away the tear under her bodice. I don't think any signs could be seen in this of the savage rage of the criminal, on which the assistant public prosecutor laid such special emphasis in his speech at the trial. The right side of the belt and the right-hand pocket were saturated with blood. The pocket handkerchief and the gloves, that were in this pocket, were like two formless lumps of a rusty colour. The whole of the riding habit, to the very end of the skirt, was bespattered with spots of blood of various forms and sizes ... Most of them, as it was afterwards explained, were the impressions of the bloodstained fingers and palms belonging to the coachmen and lackeys who had carried Olga ... The chemise was bloody, especially on the right side on which there was a hole produced by the cut of an instrument. There, as also on the left shoulder of the bodice, and near the wrists there were rents, and the wristband was almost torn off.

The things that Olga had worn, such as her gold watch, a long gold chain, a diamond brooch, earrings, rings and a purse containing silver coins, were found with the clothes. It was clear the crime had not been committed with the intent of robbery.

The results of the post-mortem examination, made by 'Screw' and the district doctor in my presence on the day after Olga's death, were set down in a very long report, of which I give here only a general outline. The doctors found that the external injuries were as follows: on the left side of the head, at the juncture of the temporal and the parietal bones, there was a wound of about one and a half inches in length that went as far as the bone. The edges of the wound were not smooth or rectilinear ... It had been inflicted by a blunt instrument, probably as we subsequently decided by the haft of the dagger. On the neck at the level of the lower cervical vertebrae a red line was visible that had the form of a semicircle and extended across the back half of the neck. On the whole length of this line there were injuries to the skin and slight bruises. On the left arm, an inch and a half above the wrist, four blue spots were found. One was on the back of the hand and the three others on the lower side. They were caused by pressure, probably of fingers ... This was confirmed by the little scratch made by a nail that was visible on one spot. The reader will remember that the place where these spots were found corresponds with the place where the left sleeve and the left cuff of the bodice of the riding habit were torn ...

Between the fourth and fifth ribs on an imaginary vertical line drawn from the centre of the armpit there was a large gaping wound of an inch in length. The edges were smooth, as if cut and steeped with liquid and clotted blood . . . The wound was deep . . . It was made by a sharp instrument, and as it appeared from the preliminary information, by the dagger which exactly corresponded in width with the size of the wound.

The interior examination revealed a wound in the right lung and the pleura, inflammation of the lung and haemorrhage in the cavity of the pleura.

As far as I can remember, the doctors arrived approximately at the following conclusion: (*a*) death was caused by anaemia consequent on a great loss of blood; the loss of blood was explained by the presence of a gaping wound on the right side of the breast; (*b*) the wound on the head must be considered a serious injury, and the wound in the breast was undoubtedly mortal; the latter must be reckoned as the immediate cause of death; (*c*) the wound on the head was given with a blunt instrument; the wound in the breast by a sharp and probably a double-edged one; (*d*) the deceased could not have inflicted all the above-mentioned injuries upon herself with her own hand; and (*e*) there probably had been no offence against feminine honour.

In order not to put it off till Doomsday and then repeat myself, I will give the reader at once the picture of the murder I sketched while under the impression of the first inspections, two or three examinations, and the perusal of the report of the post-mortem examination.

Olga, having left the rest of the party, walked about the wood. Lost in a reverie or plunged in her own sad thoughts – the reader will remember her mood on that ill-fated evening – she wandered deep into the forest. There she was met by the murderer. When she was standing under a tree, occupied with her own thoughts, the man came up and spoke to her . . . This man did not awaken suspicions in her, otherwise she would have called for help, but that cry would not have been heart-rending. While talking to her the murderer seized hold of her left arm with such strength that he tore the sleeve of her bodice and her chemise and left a mark in the form of four spots. It was at that moment probably that she shrieked, and this was the shriek heard by the party . . . She shrieked from pain and evidently because she read in the face and movements of the murderer what his intentions were. Either wishing that she should not shriek again, or perhaps acting under the influence of wrathful feelings, he seized the bodice of her dress near the collar, which is proved by the two upper buttons that were torn off and the red line the doctors found on her body. The murderer in clutching at her breast and shaking her, had tightened the gold watch-chain she wore round her neck . . . The friction and the pressure of the chain produced the red line. Then the murderer dealt her a blow on the head with some blunt weapon, for example, a stick or even the scabbard of the dagger that hung from Olga's girdle. Then flying into a passion, or finding that one wound was insufficient, he drew the dagger and plunged it into her right side with force – I say with force, because the dagger was blunt.

This was the gloomy aspect of the picture that I had the right to draw on the strength of the above-mentioned data. The question who was the murderer was evidently not difficult to determine and seemed to resolve itself naturally. First the murderer was not guided by covetous motives but something else . . . It was impossible therefore to suspect some wandering vagabond or ragamuffin, who might be fishing in the lake. The shriek of his victim could not have disarmed a robber: to take off the brooch and the watch was the work of a second.

Secondly, Olga had purposely not told me the name of the murderer, which she would have done if he had been a common thief. Evidently the murderer was dear to her, and she did not wish that he should suffer severe punishment on her account . . . Such people could only have been her mad father; her husband, whom she did not love, but before whom she felt herself guilty; or the Count, to whom perhaps in her soul she felt under a certain obligation . . . Her mad father was sitting at home in his little house in the forest on the evening of the murder, as his servant affirmed afterwards, composing a letter to the chief of the district police, requesting him to overcome the imaginary robbers who surrounded his house day and night . . . The Count had never left his guests before and at the moment the murder was committed. Therefore, the whole weight of suspicion fell on the unfortunate Urbenin. His unexpected appearance, his mien, and all the rest could only serve as good evidence.

Thirdly, during the last months Olga's life had been one continuous romance. And this romance was of the sort that usually ends with crime and capital punishment. An old, doting husband, unfaithfulness, jealousy, blows, flight to the lover-Count two months after the marriage . . . If the beautiful heroine of such a romance is killed, do not look for robbers or rascals, but search for the heroes of the romance. On this third count the most likely hero – or murderer – was again Urbenin.

....

THE POSTMAN ALWAYS RINGS TWICE

She got in, and took the wheel again, and me and the Greek kept on singing, and we went on. It was all part of the play. I had to be drunk, because that other time had cured me of this idea we could pull a perfect murder. This was going to be such a lousy murder it wouldn't even be a murder. It was going to be just a regular road accident, with guys drunk, and booze in the car, and all the rest of it. Of course, when I started to put it down, the Greek had to have some too, so he was just like I wanted him. We stopped for gas so there would be a witness that she was sober, and didn't want to be with us anyhow, because she was driving, and it wouldn't do for her to be drunk. Before that, we had had a piece of luck. Just before we closed up, about nine o'clock, a guy stopped by for something to eat, and stood there in the road and watched us when we shoved off. He saw the whole show. He saw me try to start, and stall a couple of times. He heard the argument between me and Cora, about how I was too drunk to drive. He saw her get out, and heard her say she wasn't going. He saw me try to drive off, just me and the Greek. He saw her when she made us get out, and switched the seats, so I was behind, and the Greek up front, and then he saw her take the wheel and do the driving herself. His name was Jeff Parker and he raised rabbits at Encino. Cora got his card when she said she might try rabbits in the lunch-room, to see how they'd go. We knew right where to find him, whenever we'd need him.

Me and the Greek sang 'Mother Machree', and 'Smile, Smile, Smile', and 'Down by the Old Mill Stream', and pretty soon we came to this sign that said To Malibu Beach. She turned off there. By rights, she ought to have kept on like she was going. There's two main roads that lead up the coast. One, about ten miles inland, was the one we were on. The other, right alongside the ocean, was off to our left. At Ventura they meet, and follow the sea right on up to Santa Barbara, San Francisco, and wherever you're going. But the idea was, she had never seen Malibu Beach, where the movie stars live, and she wanted to cut over on this road to the ocean, so she could drop down a couple of miles and look at it, and then turn around and keep right on up to Santa Barbara. The real idea was that this connection is about the worst piece of road in Los Angeles County, and an accident there wouldn't surprise anybody, not even a cop. It's dark, and has no traffic on it hardly, and no houses or anything, and suited us for what we had to do.

The Greek never noticed anything for a while. We passed a little summer colony that they call Malibu Lake up in the hills, and there was a dance going on at the clubhouse, with couples out on the lake in canoes. I yelled at them. So did the Greek. 'Give a one f' me.' It didn't make much difference, but it was one more mark on our trail, if somebody took the trouble to find it.

We started up the first long up-grade, into the mountains. There were three miles of it. I had told her how to run it. Most of the time she was in second. That was partly because there were sharp curves every fifty feet, and the car would lose speed so quick going around them that she would have to shift up to second to keep going. But it was partly because the motor had to heat. Everything had to check up. We had to have plenty to tell.

And then, when he looked out and saw how dark it was, and what a hell of a looking country those mountains were, with no light, or house, or filling station, or anything else in sight, the Greek came to life and started an argument.

'Hold on, hold on. Turn around. By golly, we off the road.'

'No we're not. I know where I am. It takes us to Malibu Beach. Don't you remember? I told you I wanted to see it.'

'You go slow.'

'I'm going slow.'

'You go plenty slow. Maybe all get killed.'

We got to the top and started into the down-grade. She cut the motor. They heat fast for a few minutes, when the fan stops. Down at the bottom she started the motor again. I looked at the temp gauge. It was 200. She started into the next up-grade and the temp gauge kept climbing.

'Yes sir, yes sir.'

It was our signal. It was one of those dumb things a guy can say any time, and nobody will pay any attention to it. She pulled off to one side. Under us was a drop so deep you couldn't see the bottom of it. It must have been five hundred feet.

'I think I'll let it cool off a bit.'

'By golly, you bet. Frank, look a that. Look what it says.'

'Whassit say?'

'Two hundred a five. Would be boiling in minute.'

'Letta boil.'

I picked up the wrench. I had it between my feet. But just then, away up the grade, I saw the lights of a car. I had to stall. I had to stall for a minute, until that car went by.

'C'mon, Nick. Sing's a song.'

He looked out on those bad lands, but he didn't seem to feel like singing. Then he opened the door and got out. We could hear him back there, sick. That was where he was when the car went by. I looked at the number to burn it in my brain. Then I burst out laughing. She looked back at me.

'S all right. Give them something to remember. Both guys alive when they went by.'

'Did you get the number?'

'2R-58-01.'

'2R-58-01. 2R-58-01. All right. I've got it too.'

'OK.'

He came around from behind, and looked like he felt better. 'You hear that?'

'Hear what?'

'When you laugh. Is a echo. Is a fine echo.'

He tossed off a high note. It wasn't any song, just a high note, like on a Caruso record. He cut it off quick and listened. Sure enough, here it came back, clear as anything, and stopped, just like he had.

'Is a sound like me?'

'Jus' like you, kid. Jussa same ol' toot.'

'By golly. Is swell.'

He stood there for five minutes, tossing off high notes and listening to them come back. It was the first time he ever heard what his voice sounded like. He was as pleased as a gorilla that seen his face in the mirror. She kept looking at me. We had to get busy. I began to act sore. 'Wot th' hell? You think we got noth'n t' do but lis'n at you yod'l at y'self all night? C'me on, get in. Le's get going.'

'It's getting late, Nick.'

'Hokay, hokay.'

He got in, but shoved his face out to the window and let go one. I braced my feet, and while he still had his chin on the window sill I brought down the wrench. His head cracked, and I felt it crush. He crumpled up and curled on the seat like a cat on a sofa. It seemed a year before he was still. Then Cora, she gave a funny kind of gulp that ended in a moan. Because here came the echo of his voice. It took the high note, like he did, and swelled, and stopped, and waited.

THÉRÈSE RAQUIN

The three excursionists came back to the waterside, and looked out for a restaurant. They selected a table on a sort of platform-terrace, in an eating-house that reeked of cooking and drink. The place re-echoed with screams, with choruses, with the rattle of crockery; in every room, public and private, there were people talking at the top of their voice, and the thin partitions gave the fullest scope to all this noise; while the waiters running up and down made the staircase shake again.

Up above, on the terrace, the river breeze dispelled the smell of grease. Thérèse was leaning against the balustrade and looking down at the quay. To the right and left extended two rows of drinking-shops and booths; under the arbours, among the scanty yellow foliage, you could see the white tablecloths, the black coats of the men, and the gay dresses of the women; people were coming and going, bare-headed, running and laughing; and with the uproar of the crowd were blended the dolorous tunes of the barrel-organs. A smell of fried fish and dust pervaded the calm air.

Below Thérèse, some girls from the Quartier-Latin were dancing in a ring on the trodden grass-plot to the words of a nursery rhyme. With their hats dangling over their shoulders, their hair flying loose, and holding each other by the hand, they were playing like little children. Their voices seemed to have regained a touch of freshness, and a maidenly blush suffused their pale cheeks – which bore the traces of brutish caresses – with a tender rose. An unwonted diffidence softened the fire of their bold, big eyes. Some students, smoking clay pipes, were watching them as they danced and cracked coarse jokes about them.

And beyond, over the Seine, over the distant hills, the sweetness of eventide was falling in a bluish impalpable mist which hung about the trees in a transparent haze.

'Well!' cried Laurent leaning over the banisters on the staircase, 'how about dinner, waiter?'

And then – as if with a happy thought – he added:

'I say, Camille, supposing we went for a row before dining? That will give them time to roast a chicken for us. It would be a bore to stop here an hour waiting for it.'

'Just as you please,' answered Camille, carelessly. 'But Thérèse is hungry.'

'No, no, I can wait,' hastily put in the young woman, upon whom Laurent was fixing his eyes.

All three of them went down again. As they passed the counter they engaged a table, they ordered the dinner, and they left word that they would be back in an hour's time. As the landlord had boats to let, they asked him to come and unmoor one. Laurent chose an outrigger of such light build that Camille took fright.

'The deuce!' he said, 'we mustn't move about too much in that cockle-shell. We should get a soaking.'

The fact was that Camille was awfully afraid of the water. At Vernon, when he was a boy, his many ailments prevented him from taking a dip in the Seine; and, while his school-fellows were off for a swim in deep water, he would be getting between two hot blankets. Laurent had become a bold swimmer, and a first-rate oar; Camille had never lost that horror of being out of his depth that is common to women and children. He touched the end of the boat with his foot as though doubtful of its stability.

'Come, get in,' laughed Laurent. 'You are always so nervous.'

Camille stepped over the side, and stumblingly went and sat

down in the stern. When he felt the boards beneath him he began to take his ease and to joke to prove his courage.

Thérèse had remained on the bank and, grave and motionless, was standing at the side of her lover who was holding the painter. He bent towards her and, in low, hurried tones:

'Look out,' he murmured, 'I'm going to chuck him into the water. Do as I tell you. I'll be answerable for everything.'

The young woman turned horribly pale. She stood as if rooted to the earth. She grew quite stiff, her eyes wide open.

'Get into the boat, can't you?' repeated Laurent.

She did not move. A terrible struggle was going on within her. She had to exercise all her strength of will in order not to burst out crying or swoon away.

'Ha! ha!' laughed Camille. 'Why, Laurent, just look at Thérèse! It's she who's afraid! She will – she won't! She will – she won't!'

He had stretched himself out in the stern-sheets, resting his elbows on the gunwale, and was trying to look quite at home. Thérèse gave him a strange glance. This poor fellow's giggle stung her like a whiplash, and drove her to desperation. She suddenly sprang into the boat, and sat down in the bows. Laurent took the oars, and, rowing slowly, made for the islands.

It was becoming twilight. The trees were casting great shadows, and the stream flowed as black as ink against the banks. In the middle of the river there were long streaks of pale silvery light. Very soon the boat had reached mid-channel. There, all the clamour of the quay died away; the choruses and the shouting sounded vague and melancholy, full of a languishing sadness. The smell of dust and fried fish was no longer perceptible. The night air was chilly; it was getting quite cold.

Laurent stopped rowing, and allowed the boat to drift with the current.

Opposite him rose the ruddy mass of islands. The two banks, clad in sombre brown flaked with grey, seemed like two broad belts which stretched and met in the far distance. The water and the sky were of the same leaden hue. There is nothing more painfully calm than an autumn twilight. The sun's rays turn pale in the shivering air; the senile trees shed their leaves about them. Burnt up by the hot glare of summer, the whole country side feels the impending death of its beauty in every cold wind. And in the breeze you can hear piteous sighs of despair. Then night descends from on high with its shroud-laden shadow.

The excursionists spoke never a word. From the drifting boat they were watching the last gleams of light vanishing among the foliage. They were nearing the islands. The big ruddy clumps were darkening; the whole landscape was becoming blurred in the twilight; the Seine, the sky, the islands, the hills, were by this time nothing more than patches of brown and grey, fast disappearing in the midst of a dull white mist.

Camille, who had subsided in the bottom of the boat, with his head craned over the side, fell to dipping his hands in the stream.

'Gad! it's cold enough!' he cried; 'I shouldn't care about taking a header into that bowl of broth!'

Laurent vouchsafed no answer. For the last minute or so he had been anxiously scanning the two banks, he was gripping his knees with both hands, and his lips were tightly compressed. Thérèse, erect and motionless, her head slightly thrown back, was waiting.

The boat was drifting into a narrow branch of the river between two islands, deep in the shadow. Behind one of these islands, the voices of some rowing-men who were going up the river, resounded through the still air, mellowed by their surroundings. As far as one could see ahead, the Seine was deserted.

Then Laurent got up, and twined his arms about Camille's waist. The clerk burst out laughing.

'Oh, don't! you're tickling me,' he cried. 'None of your larks! Come, chuck it up! You'll send me overboard.'

Laurent tightened his grip, and gave a jerk. Camille turned his head, and caught sight of his friend's terrible features, all convulsed. He could not make it out; a vague terror came over him. He would have screamed, but he felt a rough hand at his throat. With the instinct of an animal on the defensive, he got on to his knees and clutched at the boat's gunwale. In this position, he carried on the struggle for a few seconds.

'Thérèse! Thérèse!' he screamed at last in a choked and hissing voice.

The young woman was looking on, both hands clutching one of the seats of the wherry, which was pitching and creaking on the water. She was unable to close her eyes; a frightful fascination kept them wide open, fixed upon the ghastly sight of the struggle. She was petrified – speechless.

'Thérèse! Thérèse!' again yelled the poor wretch in his death-rattle.

At this last appeal Thérèse burst into sobs. Her nerves were unstrung. In the presence of the crisis she had been dreading, she dropped down into the bottom of the boat, trembling in every limb. There she remained in a heap, swooned away, like a corpse.

Laurent was still struggling with Camille, with one hand at his throat. At last, he managed to shake loose his hold with the help of his other hand. He held him up in his powerful arms as he might a child. As he bent his head towards him, he exposed his neck, and his victim, mad with rage and terror, twisted himself round and fixed his teeth in it. And when the murderer, smothering a howl of pain, suddenly hurled the clerk into the river, those teeth carried away a piece of his flesh between them.

Camille sank with a yell. He came up two or three times; but his cries grew fainter and fainter.

Laurent did not lose a moment. He raised the collar of his coat to conceal his wound. Then he caught up the unconscious Thérèse in his arms, capsized the boat with one heavy lurch, and let himself fall into the Seine with his mistress. He held her above water, and called for help with a dolorous voice.

The rowers, whose choruses he had heard from the other side of the island, came up at full speed. They understood that an accident had happened; they fished out Thérèse, and laid her on a seat; they helped in Laurent, who fell to bewailing his friend's fate. He leapt back into the water; he hunted for Camille wherever it was impossible to find him, he got in again, weeping bitterly, wringing his hands, tearing his hair. The crew tried to calm him, to comfort him.

'It's all my fault,' he howled; 'I oughtn't to have allowed the poor fellow to dance about and play the fool like that. Of course the minute we all happened to be on one side of the boat – over we went! His last words as he sank were, "Save my wife!"'

As is always the case at any accident, two or three of the new-comers would have it that they were eye-witnesses of the occurrence.

'We saw the whole affair,' said they. 'What can you expect, a boat isn't the floor of a room! Poor little woman – what a terrible awakening she will have!'

They took the wherry in tow, made play with their oars, and brought Thérèse and Laurent back to the restaurant, where dinner was ready and waiting. Every detail of the accident was known in Saint-Ouen within five minutes. The salvage crew spoke as though they had been eye-witnesses of the whole affair. A sympathizing crowd swarmed outside the eating-house.

The landlord and his wife were a couple of good souls, who soon supplied their half-drowned guests with dry clothing. When Thérèse recovered from her swoon, she had an attack of hysteria, and burst into agonizing sobs; they had to put her to bed. Nature was assisting the diabolical comedy that had just been performed.

When the young woman had grown calmer, Laurent left her in charge of the host. He wanted to get back to Paris alone, in order to break the dreadful news to Madame Raquin as carefully as possible. The truth of it was that Thérèse's nervous state alarmed him. He preferred to give her time to think over it all, and to study her rôle.

Camille's dinner was eaten by the rowing-men.

A KISS BEFORE DYING

He wasn't nervous at all. There had been a moment of near-panic when he couldn't get the door open, but it had dissolved the instant the door had yielded to the force of his shoulder, and now he was calm and secure. Everything was going to be perfect. No mistakes, no intruders. He just *knew* it. He hadn't felt so good since – Jesus, since high school!

He swung the door partly closed, leaving a half-inch between it and the jamb, so that it wouldn't give him any trouble when he left. He would be in a hurry then. Bending over, he moved the valise so that he would be able to pick it up with one hand while opening the door with the other. As he straightened up he felt his hat shift slightly with the motion. He took it off, looked at it, and placed it on the valise. Christ, he was thinking of everything! A little thing like the hat would probably louse up somebody else. They would push her over and then a breeze or the force of the movement might send their hat sailing down to land beside her body. Bam! They might as well throw themselves over after it. Not he, though; he had anticipated, prepared. An act of God, the crazy kind of little thing that was always screwing up perfect plans – and he had anticipated it. Jesus! He ran a hand over his hair, wishing there were a mirror.

'Come look at this.'

He turned. Dorothy was standing a few feet away, her back towards him, the alligator purse tucked under one arm. Her hands rested on the waist-high parapet that edged the roof. He came up behind her. 'Isn't it something?' she said. They were at the back of the building, facing south. The city sprawled before them, clear and sharp in the brilliant sunlight. 'Look,' Dorothy pointed to a green spot far away, 'I think that's the campus.' He put his hands on her shoulders. A white-gloved hand reached up to touch his.

He had planned to do it quickly, as soon as he got her up there, but now he was going to take it slow and easy, drawing it out as long as he safely could. He was entitled to that, after a week of nerve-twisting tension. Not just a week – years. Ever since high school it had been nothing but strain and worry and self-doubt. There was no need to rush this. He looked down at the top of her head against his chest, the dark green veiling buoyant in the yellow hair. He blew, making the fine net tremble. She tilted her head back and smiled up at him.

When her eyes returned to the panorama, he moved to her side, keeping one arm about her shoulders. He leaned over the parapet. Two storeys below, the red-tiled floor of a wide balcony extended like a shelf across the width of the building. The top of the twelfth-storey setback. It would be on all four sides. That was bad; a two-storey drop wasn't what he wanted. He turned and surveyed the roof.

It was perhaps a hundred and fifty feet square, edged by the brick parapet whose coping was flat white stone, a foot wide. An identical wall rimmed the airshaft, a square hole some thirty feet across, in the centre of the roof. On the left side of the roof was a vast stilt-supported water storage tank. On the right, the KBRI tower reared up like a smaller Eiffel, its girdered pattern black against the sky. The staircase entrance, a slant-roofed shed, was in front of him and a bit to his left. Beyond the airshaft, at the north side of the building, was a large rectangular structure, the housing of the elevator machinery. The entire roof was dotted with chimneys and ventilator pipes that stuck up like piers from a tarry sea.

Leaving Dorothy, he walked across to the parapet of the

airshaft. He leaned over. The four walls funnelled down to a tiny area fourteen storeys below, its corners banked with trash cans and wooden crates. He looked for a moment, then stooped and pried a rain-faded match-book from the gummy surface of the roof. He held the folder out beyond the parapet – and dropped it, watching as it drifted down, down, down, and finally became invisible. He glanced at the walls of the shaft. Three were striped with windows. The fourth, which faced him and evidently backed on the elevator shafts, was blank, windowless. This was the spot. The south side of the airshaft. Right near the stairway, too. He slapped the top of the parapet, his lips pursed thoughtfully. Its height was greater than he had anticipated.

Dorothy came up behind him and took his arm. 'It's so quiet,' she said. He listened. At first there seemed to be absolute silence, but then the sounds of the roof asserted themselves: the throbbing of the elevator motors, a gentle wind strumming the cables that guyed the radio tower, the squeak of a slow-turning ventilator cap . . .

They began walking slowly. He led her around the airshaft and past the elevator housing. As they strolled she brushed his shoulder clean of the dust from the door. When they reached the northern rim of the roof they were able to see the river, and with the sky reflected in it, it was really blue, as blue as the rivers painted on maps. 'Do you have a cigarette?' she asked.

He reached into his pocket and touched a pack of Chesterfields. Then his hands came out empty. 'No, I don't. Do you have any?'

'They're buried in here someplace.' She dug into her purse, pushing aside a gold compact and a turquoise handkerchief, and finally produced a crushed pack of Herbert Tareytons. They each took one. He lit them and she returned the pack to her purse.

'Dorrie, there's something I want to tell you' – she was blowing a stream of smoke against the sky, hardly listening – 'about the pills.'

Her face jerked around, going white. She swallowed. 'What?'

'I'm glad they didn't work,' he said, smiling. 'I really am.'

She looked at him uncomprehendingly. 'You're glad?'

'Yes. When I called you last night, I was going to tell you

not to take them, but you already had.' Come on, he thought, confess. Get it off your chest. It must be killing you.

Her voice was shaky. 'Why? You were so . . . what made you change your mind?'

'I don't know. I thought it over. I suppose I'm as anxious to get married as you are.' He examined his cigarette. 'Besides, I guess it's really a sin to do something like that.' When he looked up again her cheeks were flushed and her eyes glistened.

'Do you mean that?' she asked breathlessly. 'Are you really glad?'

'Of course I am. I wouldn't say it if I weren't.'

'Oh, thank God!'

'What's the matter, Dorrie?'

'Please, don't be angry. I – I didn't take them.' He tried to look surprised. The words poured from her lips: 'You said you were going to get a night job and I knew we could manage, everything would work out, and I was counting on it so much, *so* much. I knew I was right.' She paused. 'You aren't angry, are you?' she beseeched. 'You understand?'

'Sure, baby. I'm not angry. I told you I was glad they didn't work.'

Her lips made a quivering smile of relief. 'I felt like a criminal, lying to you. I thought I would never be able to tell you. I – I can't believe it!'

He took the neatly folded handkerchief from his breast pocket and touched it to her eyes. 'Dorrie, what did you do with the pills?'

'Threw them away.' She smiled shamefacedly.

'Where?' he asked casually, replacing the handkerchief.

'The john.'

That was what he wanted to hear. There would be no questions about why she had taken such a messy way out when she had already gone to the trouble of obtaining poison. He dropped his cigarette and stepped on it.

Dorothy, taking a final puff, did the same with hers. 'Oh, gee,' she marvelled, 'everything's perfect now. Perfect.'

He put his hands on her shoulders and kissed her gently on the lips. 'Perfect,' he said.

He looked down at the two stubs, hers edged with lipstick, his clean. He picked his up. Splitting it down the middle with his thumbnail, he let the tobacco blow away and rolled the paper into a tiny ball. He flicked it out over the parapet. 'That's the way we used to do it in the army,' he said.

She consulted her watch. 'It's ten to one.'

'You're fast,' he said, glancing at his. 'We've got fifteen minutes yet.' He took her arm. They turned and walked leisurely away from the edge of the roof.

'Did you speak to your landlady?'

'Wha—? Oh, yes. It's all set.' They passed the elevator housing. 'Monday we'll move your stuff from the dorm.'

Dorothy grinned. 'Will they be surprised, the girls in the dorm.' They strolled around the parapet of the airshaft. 'Do you think your landlady'll be able to give us some more closet space?'

'I think so.'

'I can leave some of my stuff, the winter things, in the attic at the dorm. There won't be too much.'

They reached the south side of the airshaft. He stood with his back against the parapet, braced his hands on the top of it, and hitched himself up. He sat with his heels kicking against the side of the wall.

'Don't sit there,' Dorothy said apprehensively.

'Why not?' he asked, glancing at the white stone coping. 'It's a foot wide. You sit on a bench a foot wide and you don't fall off.' He patted the stone on his left. 'Come on.'

'No,' she said.

'Chicken.'

She touched her rear. 'My suit—'

He took out his handkerchief, whipped it open and spread it on the stone beside him. 'Sir Walter Raleigh,' he said.

She hesitated a moment, then gave him her purse. Turning her back to the parapet, she gripped the top on either side of the handkerchief and lifted herself up. He helped her. 'There,' he said, putting his arm around her waist. She turned her head slowly, peeking over her shoulder. 'Don't look down,' he warned. 'You'll get dizzy.'

He put the purse on the stone to his right and they sat in

silence for a moment, her hands still fastened upon the front of the coping. Two pigeons came out from behind the staircase shed and walked around, watching them cautiously, their claws ticking against the tar.

'Are you going to call or write when you tell your mother?' Dorothy asked.

'I don't know.'

'I think I'll write Ellen and father. It's an awfully hard thing to just say over the phone.'

A ventilator cap creaked. After a minute, he took his arm from her waist and put his hand over hers, which gripped the stone between them. He braced his other hand on the coping and eased himself down from the parapet. Before she could do likewise he swung around and was facing her, his waist against her knees, his hands covering both of hers. He smiled at her and she smiled back. His gaze dropped to her stomach. 'Little mother,' he said. She chuckled.

His hands moved to her knees, cupped them, his fingertips caressing under the hem of her skirt.

'We'd better be going, hadn't we, darling?'

'In a minute, baby. We still have time.'

His eyes caught hers, held them, as his hands descended and moved behind to rest curving on the slope of her calves. At the periphery of his field of vision he could make out her white-gloved hands; they still clasped the front of the coping firmly.

'That's a beautiful blouse,' he said, looking at the fluffy silk bow at her throat. 'Is it new?'

'New? It's as old as the hills.'

His gaze became critical. 'The bow is a little off centre.'

One hand left the stone and rose to finger the bow. 'No,' he said, 'now you've got it worse.' Her other hand detached itself from the top of the parapet.

His hands moved down over the silken swell of her calves, as low as he could reach without bending. His right foot dropped back, poised on the toe in readiness. He held his breath.

She adjusted the bow with both hands. 'Is that any bett—'

With cobra speed he ducked – hands streaking down to catch her heels – stepped back and straightened up, lifting her legs high. For one frozen instant, as his hands shifted from cupping her heels to a flat grip against the soles of her shoes, their eyes met, stupefied terror bursting in hers, a cry rising in her throat. Then, with all his strength, he pushed against her fear-rigid legs.

Her shriek of petrified anguish trailed down into the shaft like a burning wire. He closed his eyes. The scream died. Silence, then a god-awful deafening crash. Wincing, he remembered the cans and crates piled far below.

UNDER THE KNIFE

Her room was in the basement. The passageway to it was so narrow that only one person could pass at a time. The girl walked ahead and Leib followed. On both sides brick walls hemmed them in; the ground was uneven; and Leib had to bend down in order not to hit his head. He felt as if he were already dead, wandering somewhere in subterranean caves amid devils from the nether world. A lamp glimmered in her room and the walls were painted pink. In the stove the coals glowed; on top a teakettle bubbled. A cat sat on a footstool squinting its green eyes. The bed had only a straw mattress with a dirty sheet, no other bedding. But that was for the guests. A pillow and a blanket were set on a chair in the corner. On the table lay half a loaf of bread. Leib saw himself reflected in the mirror: a large man with a pockmarked face, a long nose, a sunken mouth, a hole and a slit in place of a left eye. In the greenish glass, cracked, covered with dust, his image was refracted as if the glass were a murky pool. He hadn't shaved in over a week and a straw-colored beard covered his chin. The girl took off her shawl and for the first time Leib could really see her. She was small, flat-chested, with scrawny arms and bony shoulders. Her neck, too long, had a white spot on it. She had yellow eyebrows, yellow eyes, a crooked nose, a pointed chin. Her face was still youthful, but around her mouth there were two deep wrinkles, as though the mouth had aged all by itself. From her accent, she came from the country. Leib stared, vaguely recognizing her.

'Are you the only one here?' he asked.

'The other one is in the hospital.'

'Where's the madame?'

'Her brother died. She's sitting *shiva*.'

'You could steal everything.'

'There's nothing to steal.'

Leib sat down on the edge of the bed. He no longer looked at the girl, but at the bread. Though he was not hungry, he could not take his eyes off the loaf. The girl took off her boots but left on her red stockings.

'I wouldn't let a dog stay out in such weather,' she said.

'Are you going back out in front of the gate tonight?' Leib asked.

'No, I'll stay here.'

'Then we can talk.'

'What is there to talk about with me? I've ruined my life. My father was an honorable man. Do you really want to stab Rooshke?'

'She doesn't deserve anything better.'

'If I wanted to stab everyone who'd hurt me, I'd have to go around with six knives in each hand.'

'Women are different.'

'Yes? One should wait and let God judge. Half of my enemies are already rotting in their graves and the other half will end badly too. Why spill blood? God waits a long time but he punishes well.'

'He doesn't punish Rooshke.'

'Just wait. Nothing lasts for ever. She'll get hers sooner than you think.'

'Sooner than *you* think,' he answered with a laugh like a bark. Then he said: 'As long as I'm here, give me something to chew on.'

The girl blinked.

'Here. Have some bread. Pull up a chair to the table.'

Leib sat down. She brought him a glass of watery tea and

with her bony fingers dug out two cubes of sugar from a tin box. She busied herself about him like a wife. Leib took the knife from his boot top and cut off a piece of bread. The girl, watching him, laughed, showing her sparse teeth that were rusty and crooked. In her yellow eyes shone something sisterly and cunning as if she were an accomplice of his.

'The knife is not for bread,' she observed.

'What is it for then, eh? Flesh?'

She brought him a piece of salami from a cupboard and he sliced it in half with his knife. The cat jumped off her footstool and began to rub against his leg, meowing.

'Don't give her any. Let her eat the mice.'

'Are there enough mice?'

'Enough for ten cats.'

Leib cut his piece of salami in two and threw a slice to the cat. The girl looked at him crookedly, half-curiously, half-mockingly as though his whole visit were nothing but a joke. For a long while both of them were silent. Then Leib opened his mouth and asked without thinking:

'Would you like to get married?'

The girl laughed.

'I'll marry the Angel of Death.'

'I'm not joking.'

'As long as a woman breathes she wants to get married.'

'Would you marry me?'

'Even you—'

'Well then, let's get married.'

The girl was pouring water into the teakettle.

'Do you mean in bed or at the rabbi's?'

'First in bed, then at the rabbi's.'

'Whatever you want. I don't believe anybody any more, but what do I care if they pull my leg? If you say so, it's so. If you back out, nothing is lost. What's a word? Every third guest wants to marry me. Afterwards, they don't even want to pay the twenty kopecks.'

'I'll marry you. I've got nothing left to lose.'

'And what have I got to lose? Only my life.'

'Don't you have any money?'

The girl smiled familiarly, grimacing slightly as though she had expected Leib to ask this. Her whole face became aged, knowing, good-naturedly wrinkled like that of an old crone. She hesitated, glanced about, looked up at the small window covered with a black curtain. Her face seemed to laugh and at the same time to ponder something sorrowful and ancient. Then she nodded.

'My whole fortune is here in my stocking.'

She pointed with her finger to her knee.

Next morning Leib waited until the janitor opened the gates. Then he walked outside. Everything had gone smoothly. It was still dark but on this side of the Vistula, in the east, a piece of sky showed pale blue with red spots. Smoke was rising from chimneys. Peasant carts with meat, fruit, vegetables came by, the horses plodding along still half asleep. Leib breathed deeply. His throat felt dry. His guts were knotted up. Where could he get food and drink at this hour? He remembered Chaim Smetene's restaurant, which opened up when God was still asleep. Leib, shaking his head like a horse, set off in that direction. Well, it's all destined: I'm fulfilling my fate, he thought. Chaim Smetene's restaurant, smelling of tripe, beer, and goose gravy, was already open, its gaslights lit. Men who had been awake all night were sitting there eating but whether a meat breakfast or the remains of last night's supper was hard to know. Leib sat down at an empty table and ordered a bottle of vodka, onions with chicken fat, and an omelette. He drank three shots straight off on his empty stomach. Well, it's my last meal, he muttered to himself. Tomorrow by this time I'll be a martyr . . . ! The waiters were suspicious of him, thought maybe he was trying to get a free meal. The owner Chaim Smetene himself came over and asked:

'Leib, have you any money?'

Leib wanted to swing the bottle and hit him in his fat stomach which was draped with a chain of silver rubles.

'I'm no beggar.'

And Leib took a packet of banknotes tied with a red string from his pocket.

'Well, don't get mad.'

'Drop dead!'

Leib wanted to forget the insult. He tossed off one shot after another, became so engrossed in his drinking that he even forgot about the omelette. He took out a paper bill, gave it to the waiter for a tip, and ordered another bottle of vodka, not forty or sixty proof this time but ninety proof. The place was filling up with customers, growing thick with haze, noisy with voices. Someone threw sawdust over the stone floor. Near Leib men were talking, but though he heard the separate words, he could not grasp the connections between them. His ears felt as if filled with water. He leaned his head on the chair, snored, but at the same time kept his hand on the bottle to make sure it was not taken away. He was not asleep, but neither was he awake. He dreamed but the dream itself seemed far away. Someone was making a long speech to him, without interruption, like a preacher's sermon, but who was speaking and what he was saying, Leib could not understand. He opened his one eye, then closed it again.

After a while he sat up. It was bright day and the gaslights were out. The clock on the wall showed a quarter to nine. The room was full of people, but although he knew everyone on the street, he didn't recognize anyone. There was still some vodka in the bottle and he drank it. He tasted the cold omelette, grimaced, and began to bang his spoon on the plate for the waiter. Finally he left, walking out with unsteady legs. In front of his one eye hung a fog with something in the middle of it tossing about like jelly. I'm going completely blind, Leib said to himself. He went into Yanosh's bazaar, looking for Tsipeh, Rooshke's maid, who he knew came there every morning to shop. The bazaar was already packed with customers. Market women shouted their wares; fishmongers bent over tubs filled with fish; three slaughterers were killing fowl over a marble sink that glowed from the light of a kerosene lamp, handing them to pluckers who plucked and packed them, still alive, into baskets. Whoever has a knife uses it, Leib thought. God doesn't mind. Going towards the exit he spotted Tsipeh. She had just arrived with an empty basket. Well, now's the time!

He walked out of the bazaar and turned towards Rooshke's

yard. He was not afraid of being seen. He entered the gate, climbed up the stairs to the second floor where an engraved plaque said, 'Lemkin – Master Barber.' What will I do if the key doesn't fit? Leib asked himself. I'll break down the door, he answered. He could feel his strength; he was like Samson now. Taking the key from his breast pocket as if he were the owner of the flat, he put it into the keyhole and opened the door. The first thing he saw was a gas meter. A top hat was hanging on a hatrack and he tapped it playfully. Through the half-open kitchen door he saw a coffee grinder, a brass mortar and pestle. Smells of coffee grounds and fried onions came from there. Well, Rooshke, your time is up! He stepped quietly along the carpet in the corridor, moving, head forward, as adroitly and carefully as a dogcatcher trying to catch a dog. Something like laughter seized him as he drew out the knife leaving the sheath in his boot top. Leib threw open the bedroom door. There was Rooshke, asleep under a red blanket, her bleached blonde hair spread out on a white pillow, her face yellowish, flabby, smeared with cream. Eyeballs protruded against her closed lids and a double chin covered her wrinkled throat. Leib stood gaping. He almost didn't recognize her. In the few months since he had last seen her, she had grown fat and bloated, had lost her girlish looks, become a matron. Gray hair was visible near the scalp. On a night table a set of false teeth stood in a glass of water. So that's it, Leib muttered. She was right. She really has become an old hag. He recalled her words before they parted: 'I've been used enough. I'm not getting any younger, only older . . .'

He couldn't go on standing there. Any minute someone would knock at the door. But neither could he leave. What must be must be, Leib said to himself. Approaching the bed, he pulled off the blanket. Rooshke was not sleeping naked, but in an unbuttoned nightgown which exposed a pair of flabby breasts like pieces of dough, a protruding stomach, thick, unusually wide hips. Leib would never have imagined Rooshke could have such a fat belly, that her skin could have become so yellowish, withered, and scarred. Leib expected her to scream, but she opened her eyes slowly as if, until now, she had been only pretending she was asleep. Her eyes stared at him seriously, sadly, as if she were saying: Woe unto you, what has become of you? Leib trembled. He wanted to say the words he had rehearsed to himself so often, but he had forgotten them. They hung on the tip of his tongue. Rooshke herself had apparently lost her voice. She examined him with a strange calmness.

Suddenly she let out a scream. Leib raised the knife.

Well, it's really very easy, Leib muttered to himself. He closed the door and walked down the stairs slowly, banging his heels, as if he were looking for a witness, but he met no one either on the stairs or in the yard. Leaving, he stood for a while at the gates. The sky, which at sunrise had started out so blue, had turned dark and rainy. A porter passed by carrying a sack full of coal on his back. A hunchback shouted out, peddling pickled herring. At the dairy they were unloading milk cans. At the grocery a delivery man was piling loaves on his arm. The two horses in harness had put their heads together as if sharing a secret. Yes, it's the same street, nothing has changed, Leib thought. He yawned, shook himself. Then he remembered the words he had forgotten: Well, Rooshke, are you still tough, eh? He felt no fear, only an emptiness. It is morning but it looks like dusk, he mused. He felt in his pocket for cigarettes but had lost them somewhere. He passed the stationery shop. At the butcher's he looked in. Standing at his block, Leizer the butcher was cutting a side of beef with a wide cleaver. A throng of pushing, shoving women were bargaining and stretching out their hands for marrowbones. He'll cut off some woman's finger yet, Leib muttered. Suddenly he found himself in front of Lemkin's barber shop and he looked in through the glass door. The assistant hadn't arrived yet. Lemkin was alone, a small man, fat and pink, with a naked skull, short legs, and a pointed stomach. He was wearing striped pants, shoes with spats, a collar and bowtie, but no jacket, and his suspenders were short like those of a child. Standing there, he was thumbing through a Polish newspaper. He doesn't even know yet that he is a widower, Leib said to himself. He watched him, baffled. It was hard to believe that he, Leib, had brooded about this swinish little man for so long and had hated him so terribly. Leib pushed open the door and Lemkin looked at him sideways, startled, even frightened. I'll fix him too, Leib decided. He bent down to draw the knife from his boot top, but some force held him back. An invisible power seemed to have grabbed his wrist. Well, he's destined to live, Leib decided. He spoke:

'Give me a shave.'

'What? Sure, sure . . . sit down.'

Cheerfully, Lemkin put on his smock which lay ready on a chair, wrapped Leib in a fresh sheet, and poured warm water into a bowl. Soaping Leib, he half patted, half tickled his throat. Leib leaned his head back, closed the lid on his one eye, relaxed in the darkness. I think I'll take a nap, he decided. I'll tell him to cut my hair too. Leib felt a little dizzy and belched. A chill breeze ran through the barber shop and he sneezed. Lemkin wished him *Gesundheit*. The chair was too high and Lemkin lowered it. Taking a razor from its sheath, he stropped it on a leather strap and then began to scrape. Tenderly, as if they were relatives, he pinched Leib's cheek between his thick fingertips. Leib could feel the barber's breath as Lemkin said confidentially:

'You're a friend of Rooshke's . . . I know, I know . . . she told me everything.'

Lemkin waited for a reply from Leib. He even stopped scraping with his razor. After a while he began again.

'Poor Rooshke is sick.'

Leib was silent for a time.

'What's wrong with her?'

'Gallstones. The doctors say she should have an operation. She's been in the hospital two weeks now. But you don't go under the knife so easily.'

Leib lifted his head.

'In the hospital? Where?'

'In Chista. I go there every day.'

'Who's at home then?'

'A sister from Praga.'

'An older one, eh?'

'A grandmother already.'

Leib lowered his head. Lemkin lifted it up again.

'Believe me, Rooshke's not your enemy,' he whispered in

Leib's ear. 'She talks about you all the time. After all, what happened happened. We would like to do something for you, but you keep yourself a stranger . . .'

Lemkin was bending so near Leib as almost to touch him with his forehead. He smelled of mouth rinse and a brotherly warmth. Leib wanted to say something, but outside there was a scream and people began to run. Lemkin straightened up.

'I'll see what all the excitement's about.'

He walked outside, still in his smock, with the razor in his right hand and the left smeared with soap and beard. He lingered a minute or two, questioning someone. He came back in cheerfully.

'A whore's dead. Ripped open with a knife. The little redhead at Number 6.'

P. D. JAMES AND

T. A. CRITCHLEY

....

THE MAUL AND THE
PEAR TREE

A little before midnight on the last night of his life Timothy
Marr, a linen draper of Ratcliffe Highway, set about tidying up
the shop, helped by the shop-boy, James Gowen. Lengths of
cloth had to be folded and stacked away, rough worsted, dyed
linen, canvas for seamen's trousers and serge for their jackets,
cheap rolls of printed cotton at fourpence a yard, and bales of silk
and muslin laid in to attract the wealthier customers from
Wellclose Square and Spitalfields. It was Saturday, 7 December
1811; and Saturday was the busiest day of the week. The shop
opened at eight o'clock in the morning and remained open until
ten o'clock or eleven o'clock at night. The clearing up would take
the pair of them into the early hours of Sunday.

Marr was twenty-four years old. He had been a seafaring
man, employed by the East India Company, and had sailed on
his last voyage in the *Dover Castle* three years earlier, in 1808. It
was also Marr's most prosperous voyage. He did not sail before
the mast with the crew, but was engaged by the captain as his
personal servant. He seems to have been an agreeable young man,
conscientious, anxious to please and ambitious to better himself.
During the long return voyage this ambition took shape. He
knew precisely what he wanted. There was a girl waiting for him
at home. Captain Richardson had held out the promise of help

and patronage if Marr continued to serve him well. If he came safely home he would take his discharge, marry his Celia, and open a little shop. Life on shore might be difficult and uncertain, but at least it would be free from danger; and, if he worked hard, it would hold the sure promise of security and fortune. When the *Dover Castle* docked at Wapping Marr was signed off with enough money to start him in a modest way of business. He married, and in April 1811 the young couple found what they were looking for. Property in the riverside parishes of East London was cheap, and Marr understood the ways of sailors. He took a shop at 29 Ratcliffe Highway, in the parish of St George's-in-the-East, on the fringes of Wapping and Shadwell.

In the few months since he had been in business he had already gained a reputation for industry and honesty. Trade was brisk, and for the past few weeks he had been employing a carpenter, Mr Pugh, to modernise the shop and improve its layout. The whole of the shop front had been taken down and the brickwork altered to enlarge the window for a better display of goods. And on 29 August 1811, a son had been born to increase his joy and fortify his ambition. He could look forward to the day when his shop front – perhaps the front of many shops, stretching from Bethnal Green through Hackney, Dalston, the Balls Pond Road to Stamford Hill and beyond – would bear the inscription 'Marr and Son'.

The first shop, though, was a very modest start. It was one of a terrace of mean houses fronting on to Ratcliffe Highway. The shop, with its counter and shelves, took up most of the ground floor. Behind the counter a door led into a back hall from which ran two flights of stairs – downwards to the kitchen, in the basement, and upwards to a first-floor landing and two bedrooms. A second floor served as a warehouse to store silk, lace, pelisse, mantles and furs. It was a plain house, saved from drabness by the fine new bay window, freshly painted in olive green. The terrace in which the shop stood was one of four similar terraces that formed the sides of a square. Within the block each house had its own fenced-in back yard, accessible by a back-door in the hall. The ground inside the square was common to the inhabitants of the whole block. The terrace on the side of the square opposite to Marr's shop faced Pennington Street, and here the houses were overshadowed by a huge brick wall, twenty feet high. This was the wall of the London Dock, built six years earlier, and designed like a fortress by the architect of Dartmoor Prison to protect the hundreds of vessels moored inside. To build the dock eleven acres of shacks and hovels had been levelled and their inhabitants crammed into the slums alongside. Most of them were cut off from the only living they knew, since the ships they had once plundered were now protected by the monstrous black wall of the dock. Baulked of this easy living they preyed on the inhabitants of the riverside parishes, and added to London's growing army of thieves and beggars. The wall that made London's shipping more secure did nothing to increase the safety of Ratcliffe Highway.

And it was a bad time, as well as an unsavoury district, in which to set up shop. In 1811 Napoleon's blockade of the continental ports had almost halted European trade. In the industrial midlands the activities of machine-breakers fed fears of revolution. The harvest had been a disaster; and, appropriately for a year of violence and confusion, it was in 1811 that the old king was finally pronounced by his doctors to be irrevocably mad, and the Prince of Wales became Regent.

Now though, as he tidied his shop at the end of a busy week, Marr's mind would be occupied with more personal worries: the health of his wife, who was recovering only slowly from her confinement; the wisdom of the alteration of the shop (had he perhaps over-reached himself?); the irritating matter of a lost ripping chisel which Pugh, the carpenter, had been loaned by a neighbour and now insisted was still in Marr's shop, but which a thorough search had failed to recover; his own hunger at the end of a long day. The draper paused in his work and called to the servant girl, Margaret Jewell. Late though it then was (about ten minutes to midnight, as Margaret Jewell afterwards told the Coroner) he gave the girl a pound note and sent her out to pay the baker's bill and to buy some oysters. At a penny a dozen, supplied fresh from the oyster boats from Whitstable, they would be a cheap, tasty supper after a long day. And they would be a welcome surprise for Marr's young wife, Celia, who was then in the basement kitchen, feeding her baby. Timothy Marr junior was three and a half months old.

As she closed the shop door and went out into the night Margaret Jewell saw her master still at work, busy behind the counter with James Gowen.

Margaret Jewell made her way along Ratcliffe Highway to Taylor's oyster shop, but she found it shut. She retraced her steps to Marr's house, glanced through the window, and saw her master still at work behind the counter. It was the last time she saw him alive. The time would then be about midnight. It was a mild, cloudy night, following a wet day, and the girl may have been glad of an excuse to stay out longer. She continued past Marr's shop and turned off the Highway down John's Hill to pay the baker's bill.

And now she was turning her back on safety. Round the corner from John's Hill ran Old Gravel Lane, the historic land link with Wapping shore, winding down to the river seventy yards east of Execution Dock, where the pirates swung. Between the wharves the water heaved under a scum of sludge and sewage; behind them the tides of centuries had washed up deposits of old decaying hovels like barnacles on a ship's hulk. They conformed to no plan. The old custom had been to build in courts and alleys at right angles to the roads. Courts were built within courts, alleys behind alleys. And more recently the girl had seen whole areas walled in, dwarfed and darkened even in daylight by the eyeless walls of warehouses, the bleak soaring walls of sailors' tenements, and the cliff of the London Dock, sheltering its alien floating city. She would have heard chilling tales of life in the dark labyrinths taken over by squatters, men and women crammed into derelict property that offered a perpetual fire risk to the dens and warrens where Old Gravel Lane twisted down to the Thames – Gun Alley, Dung Wharf, Hangman's Gains, Pear Tree Alley. The starving people were quiet for the most part, with the sullen fortitude of despair, but to respectable Londoners they constituted a perpetual menace. Occasionally it erupted into reality, when savage mobs surged West to riot and plunder, or roared out for the festival of a public hanging.

'The baker's shop was shut,' Margaret Jewell later told the

Coroner. 'I then went to another place to get the oysters but I found no shop open. I was out about twenty minutes.' She did not venture down towards riverside Wapping, but returned to the familiar safety of Ratcliffe Highway.

But now it was past midnight, and the street noises were dying down. Public houses were closing, shutters were being fastened, bolts shot. And as the street fell silent Margaret Jewell would begin to hear her own footsteps echoing on the cobble-stones. Overhead, the rickety parish lamps of crude fish-blubber oil cast a flickering light on the wet pavement, animating and deepening the shadows; and between the lamps were pools of total darkness. Nor, when Margaret Jewell reached 29 Ratcliffe Highway, was any light shining in Marr's shop either. It, too, was dark, the door shut tightly against her. The girl stood alone in the silent street and pulled the bell.

Immediately the jangling seemed unnaturally loud to the waiting girl. There was no one about at this late hour, except George Olney, the watchman, who passed by without speaking on the other side of the street, taking a person in charge to the lock-up. Margaret Jewell rang again, more loudly, pressing herself close to the door, listening for any sound from within. She was not yet seriously worried. The master was taking his time. Probably he was with her mistress, in the comfort of the downstairs kitchen. Perhaps the family, despairing of their oysters, had even made their way to bed. The girl hoped that her master would not chide her for taking so long on a fruitless errand; that her ringing wouldn't waken the child. She pulled again, more vigorously; listened: and this time heard a sound which, to the end of her life, she would never recall without a *frisson* of horror. For the moment, though, it brought only relief, and the comforting assurance that she would soon gain the warmth of the familiar kitchen. There was a soft tread of footsteps on the stairs. Someone – surely her master? – was coming down to open the door. Then came another familiar sound. The baby gave a single low cry.

But no one came. The footsteps ceased and again there was silence. It was an absolute silence, eerie and frightening. The girl seized the bell and rang again; then, torn between panic and frustration, began to kick the door. She was cold and beginning to be very frightened. As she rang and kicked a man came up to her. His drunken senses irritated by the noise, or imagining the girl was causing a nuisance, he began to abuse her. Margaret Jewell gave up knocking. There was nothing to be done but wait for the next appearance of the watchman. To continue with her useless ringing now would only expose her to fresh insults.

She waited about thirty minutes. Promptly at one o'clock George Olney came calling the hour. Seeing the girl at Marr's door and not knowing who she was he told her to move on. She explained that she belonged to the house, and thought it very strange that she should be locked out. Olney agreed. He said he had no doubt but that the family were within. He had passed when calling the hour at twelve o'clock, and had himself seen Mr Marr putting up his shutters. A little after midnight he had examined the window, as was his custom, and had noted that the shutters were not fastened. He had called out to Marr at the time, and a strange voice had answered, 'We know of it.' Now, holding his lantern high against the window, he examined the shutter again. The pin was still unfastened. Seizing the bell he rang vigorously. There was no reply. He rang again, pounded on the knocker, then bent down and called through the keyhole, 'Mr Marr! Mr Marr!'

The renewed ringing, rising now to a crescendo, roused John Murray, pawnbroker, who lived next door. He was not a man to interfere with his neighbours, but he had been disturbed by Margaret Jewell's earlier assault on the door. Now, at a quarter-past-one, he and his wife were ready for bed, and hoping for sleep. There had been mysterious noises earlier in the night. Shortly after twelve o'clock he and his family had been disturbed at their late supper by a heavy sound from next door, as if a chair were being pushed back. It had been followed by the cry of a boy, or of a woman. These noises had made little impression at the time. Probably Marr, irritated and tired at the end of the longest and busiest trading day, was chastising his apprentice or his maid. This was his business. But the continued din was another matter. Murray made his way out into the street.

The situation was rapidly explained in a confused babble from Margaret Jewell of oysters, baker's bills and baby's cries, and George Olney's quieter explanation of the unfastened pin, and the fruitless knocking. John Murray took charge. He told the watchman to continue pulling hard at the bell, and he would go into his backyard and see if he could rouse the family from the back of the house. He did so, calling out 'Mr Marr', three or four times. Still there was no answer. Then he saw a light at the back of the house. Returning to the street he told the watchman to ring yet louder, while he tried to get into the house by the back door.

It was easy enough to get over the flimsy fence dividing the two properties, and he was soon in Marr's backyard. He found the door of the house was open. It was very quiet and very still inside, but there was a faint light from a candle burning on the landing of the first floor. Murray made his way up the stairs and took the candlestick in his hand. He found himself opposite the door of the Marrs' bedroom. Then, inhibited by delicacy, as habit sometimes does impose itself against all reason, he paused irresolutely at the door and called softly, as if the young people, oblivious of the clamour from the street, were sleeping quietly in each other's arms. 'Marr, Marr, your window shutters are not fastened.'

No one answered. Murray, still reluctant to invade the privacy of his neighbour's bedroom, held the candle high and made his way carefully down the stairs and into the shop.

It was then that he found the first body. The apprentice boy, James Gowen, was lying dead just inside the door which led to the shop and within six feet of the foot of the stairs. The bones of his face had been shattered by blow after blow. His head, from which the blood was still flowing, had been beaten to a pulp, and blood and brains splattered the shop as high as the counter, and even hung, a ghastly excrescence, from the low ceiling. Petrified with shock and horror Murray for a moment could neither cry out nor move. The candle shook in his hand, throwing shadows and a soft fitful light over the thing at his feet. Then, with a groan the pawnbroker stumbled towards the door, and found his path blocked by the body of Mrs Marr. She was lying face downwards with her face close against the street door, blood still draining from her battered head.

Somehow Murray got the door opened and gasped out his news incoherently. 'Murder! Murder! Come and see what murder is here!' The small crowd outside, swollen now by the arrival of neighbours and a second watchman, pressed into the shop. They stood aghast with horror. Margaret Jewell began to scream. The air was loud with groans and cries. It took only a moment for fresh tragedy to be revealed. Behind the counter, and also face downwards, with his head towards the window, was the body of Timothy Marr. Someone called out 'The child, where's the child?' and there was a rush for the basement. There they found the child, still in its cradle, the side of its mouth laid open with a blow, the left side of the face battered, and the throat slit so that the head was almost severed from the body.

Sickened by the horror and brutality and almost fainting with fright, the little group in the kitchen staggered upstairs. The shop was becoming crowded now and there was light from many candles. Huddled together for protection they looked around the room. There on that part of the counter which was free of Gowen's blood and brains they saw a carpenter's ripping chisel. With shaking and reluctant hands they took it up. It was perfectly clean.

FRANZ KAFKA

'A CASE OF FRATRICIDE'

It has been proved that the murder happened as follows:

Around nine in the evening of that moonlit night Schmar, the murderer, positioned himself at the corner round which Wese, the victim, must come in passing from the street in which his office was situated into the street where he lived.

Cold night air, enough to chill anyone to the bone. Yet Schmar had on only a thin blue coat; and the skirt was even unbuttoned. He did not feel the cold; also he was in constant movement. The murder weapon, half bayonet, half kitchen knife, was in full view and he kept a firm grip on it. Held it up to the moonlight and examined it; the cutting edge gleamed; not enough for Schmar; he struck it against the brick pavement till it gave off sparks; perhaps had second thoughts; and to repair the damage drew it like a violin bow across the sole of his boot while standing on one leg, leaning forward, listening simultaneously to the ring of the knife on his boot and for any sound from the fateful side street.

Why did private-eye Pallas, who saw everything from his nearby second-floor window, permit all this? The enigmas of human nature! With his collar turned up, his dressing-gown belted round his ample body, he looked down on the scene and shook his head.

And five houses farther on, across the street from him at an angle, Frau Wese, wearing a fox fur over her nightgown, stood looking out for her husband, who was unusually late today.

At last the doorbell of Wese's office rings, too loudly for a doorbell, out over the city, upwards at the sky, and Wese the industrious nightworker, emerges from the building invisible from this street as yet, heralded only by the bell's signal; the pavement begins to register his quiet footsteps.

Pallas leans right out; he must not miss anything. Frau Wese, reassured by the bell, rattles her window shut. Schmar, however, kneels down; having no other parts exposed at the moment, he presses only his face and hands to the stones; with everyone else freezing, Schmar is aglow.

Right on the borderline between the two streets Wese comes to a halt, with only his stick planted in the street beyond for support. A whim. His attention has been caught by the night sky, the dark blue and the gold. He gazes at it, unsuspecting; unsuspecting, he lifts his hat and smooths his hair; nothing up there shifts together to show him the immediate future; everything remains in its absurd, inscrutable place. Very reasonable, taken all round, that Wese should walk on, but he walks into Schmar's knife.

'Wese!' screams Schmar, standing on tiptoe, arm upraised, knife pointing downwards, 'Wese! Julia waits in vain!' And Schmar stabs him in the throat, once from the right and again from the left, with a third stab deep in the belly. Water rats, when you gut them, make the kind of sound Wese made.

'Done,' says Schmar, and he hurls the knife – superfluous, bloody encumbrance – at the nearest house front. 'The bliss of murder! The release, the wings lent by the pouring out of the other's blood! Wese, old man, friend of my nights and boozing companion, away you seep in the dark gutter. Why aren't you just a bladder filled with blood, then I could sit on you and you'd disappear altogether. All is not fulfilled, not every blossom cluster opened out, your heavy remains lie here, already impervious to kicks; asking a wordless question, but what does it mean?'

Pallas, choking all his rage into a confused mass in his body, stands in the doorway of his house, the two leaves of the door having sprung open. 'Schmar! Schmar! Saw everything, missed nothing.' Pallas and Schmar examine each other. Pallas is satisfied; Schmar fails to reach a conclusion.

Frau Wese, a crowd on either side of her, comes hurrying up; horror has put years on her face. The fur flies open, she throws herself on Wese, her body in its nightgown is his, the fur closing over the couple like grass over a grave is for the crowd.

Schmar, stifling the last waves of nausea with an effort, his lips pressed to the shoulder of the policeman who nimbly leads him away.

....

'KILLINGS'

Richard Strout shot Frank in front of the boys. They were sitting on the living-room floor watching television, Frank sitting on the couch, and Mary Ann just returning from the kitchen with a tray of sandwiches. Strout came in the front door and shot Frank twice in the chest and once in the face with a 9mm automatic. Then he looked at the boys and Mary Ann, and went home to wait for the police.

It seemed to Matt that from the time Mary Ann called weeping to tell him until now, a Saturday night in September, sitting in the car with Willis, parked beside Strout's car, waiting for the bar to close, that he had not so much moved through his life as wandered through it, his spirit like a dazed body bumping into furniture and corners. He had always been a fearful father: when his children were young, at the start of each summer he thought of them drowning in a pond or the sea, and he was relieved when he came home in the evenings and they were there; usually that relief was his only acknowledgement of his fear, which he never spoke of and which he controlled within his heart. As he had when they were very young and all of them in turn, Cathleen too, were drawn to the high oak in the backyard, and had to climb it. Smiling, he watched them, imagining the fall: and he was poised to catch the small body before it hit the earth. Or his legs were poised; his hands were in his pockets or his arms were folded and, for the child looking down, he appeared relaxed and confident while his heart beat with the two words he wanted to call out but did not: *Don't fall*. In winter he was less afraid: he made sure the ice would hold him before they skated, and he brought or sent them to places where they could sled without ending in the street. So he and his children had survived their childhood, and he only worried about them when he knew they were driving a long distance, and then he lost Frank in a way no father expected to lose his son, and he felt that all the fears he had borne while they were growing up, and all the grief he had been afraid of, had backed up like a huge wave and struck him on the beach and swept him out to sea. Each day he felt the same and when he was able to forget how he felt, when he was able to force himself not to feel that way, the eyes of his clerks and customers defeated him. He wished those eyes were oblivious, even cold; he felt he was withering in their tenderness. And beneath his listless wandering, every day in his soul he shot Richard Strout in the face; while Ruth, going about town on errands, kept seeing him. And at nights in bed she would hold Matt and cry, or sometimes she was silent and Matt would touch her tightening arm, her clenched fist.

As his own right fist was now, squeezing the butt of the revolver, the last of the drinkers having left the bar, talking to each other, going to their separate cars which were in the lot in front of the bar, out of Matt's vision. He heard their voices, their cars, and then the ocean again, across the street. The tide was in and sometimes it smacked the sea wall. Through the windscreen he looked at the dark red side wall of the bar, and then to his left, past Willis, at Strout's car, and through its windows he could see the now-emptied parking lot, the road, the sea wall. He could smell the sea.

The front door of the bar opened and closed again and Willis looked at Matt then at the corner of the building; when Strout came around it alone Matt got out of the car giving up the hope he had kept all night (and for the past week) that Strout would come out with friends, and Willis would simply drive away; thinking: *All right then. All right*; and he went around the front of Willis's car, and at Strout's he stopped and aimed over the hood at Strout's blue shirt ten feet away. Willis was aiming too, crouched on Matt's left, his elbow resting on the hood.

'Mr Fowler,' Strout said. He looked at each of them, and at the guns. 'Mr Trottier.'

Then Matt, watching the parking lot and the road, walked quickly between the car and the building and stood behind Strout. He took one leather glove from his pocket and put it on his left hand.

'Don't talk. Unlock the front and back and get in.'

Strout unlocked the front door, reached in and unlocked the back, then got in, and Matt slid into the back seat, closed the door with his gloved hand, and touched Strout's head once with the muzzle.

'It's cocked. Drive to your house.'

When Strout looked over his shoulder to back the car, Matt aimed at his temple and did not look at his eyes.

'Drive slowly,' he said. 'Don't try to get stopped.'

They drove across the empty front lot and on to the road, Willis's headlights shining into the car; then back through town, the sea wall on the left hiding the beach, though far out Matt could see the ocean; he uncocked the revolver; on the right were the places, most with their neon signs off, that did so much business in summer: the lounges and cafés and pizza houses, the street itself empty of traffic, the way he and Willis had known it would be when they decided to take Strout at the bar rather than knock on his door at two o'clock one morning and risk that one insomniac neighbor. Matt had not told Willis he was afraid he could not be alone with Strout for very long, smell his smells, feel the presence of his flesh, hear his voice, and then shoot him. They left the beach town and then were on the high bridge over the channel: to the left the smacking curling white at the breakwater and beyond that the dark sea and the full moon, and down to his right the small fishing boats bobbing at anchor in the cove. When they left the bridge, the sea was blocked by abandoned beach cottages, and Matt's left hand was sweating in the glove. Out here in the dark in the car he believed Ruth knew. Willis had come to his house at eleven and asked if he wanted a nightcap; Matt went to the bedroom for his wallet, put the gloves in one trouser pocket and the .38 in the other and went back to the living-room, his hand in his pocket covering the bulge of the cool cylinder pressed against his fingers, the butt against his palm. When Ruth said goodnight she looked at his face, and he felt she could see in his eyes the gun, and the night he was going to. But he knew he couldn't trust what he saw. Willis's wife had taken her sleeping pill, which gave her eight hours – the reason, Willis had told Matt, he had the alarms installed, for nights when he was late at the restaurant – and when it was all done and Willis got home he would leave ice and a trace of Scotch and soda in two glasses in the game room and tell Martha in the morning that he had left the restaurant early and brought Matt home for a drink.

'He was making it with my wife.' Strout's voice was careful, not pleading.

Matt pressed the muzzle against Strout's head, pressed it harder than he wanted to, feeling through the gun Strout's head flinching and moving forward; then he lowered the gun to his lap.

'Don't talk,' he said.

Strout did not speak again. They turned west, drove past the Dairy Queen closed until spring, and the two lobster restaurants that faced each other and were crowded all summer and were now also closed, on to the short bridge crossing the tidal stream, and over the engine Matt could hear through his open window the water rushing inland under the bridge; looking to his left he saw its swift moonlit current going back into the marsh which, leaving the bridge, they entered: the salt marsh stretching out on both sides, the grass tall in patches but mostly low and leaning earthward as though windblown, a large dark rock sitting as though it rested on nothing but itself, and shallow pools reflecting the bright moon.

Beyond the marsh they drove through woods, Matt thinking now of the hole he and Willis had dug last Sunday afternoon after telling their wives they were going to Fenway Park. They listened to the game on a transistor radio, but heard none of it as they dug into the soft earth on the knoll they had chosen because elms and maples sheltered it. Already some leaves had fallen. When the hole was deep enough they covered it and the piled earth with dead branches, then cleaned their shoes and pants and went to a restaurant farther up in New Hampshire where they ate sandwiches and drank beer and watched the rest of the game on television. Looking at the back of Strout's head he thought of Frank's grave; he had not been back to it; but he would go before winter, and its second burial of snow.

He thought of Frank sitting on the couch and perhaps talking to the children as they watched television, imagined him feeling young and strong, still warmed from the sun at the beach, and feeling loved, hearing Mary Ann moving about the kitchen, hearing her walking into the living-room; maybe he looked up at her and maybe she said something, looking at him over the tray of sandwiches, smiling at him, saying something the way women do when they offer food as a gift, then the front door opening and this son of a bitch coming in and Frank seeing that he meant the gun in his hand, this son of a bitch and his gun the last person and thing Frank saw on earth.

When they drove into town the streets were nearly empty: a few slow cars, a policeman walking his beat past the darkened fronts of stores. Strout and Matt both glanced at him as they drove by. They were on the main street, and all the stoplights were blinking yellow. Willis and Matt had talked about that too: the lights changed at midnight, so there would be no place Strout had to stop and where he might try to run. Strout turned down the block where he lived and Willis's headlights were no longer with Matt in the back seat. They had planned that too, had decided it was best for just the one car to go to the house, and again Matt had said nothing about his fear of being alone with Strout, especially in his house: a duplex, dark as all the houses on the street were, the street itself lit at the corner of each block. As Strout turned into the driveway Matt thought of the one insomniac neighbor, thought of some man or woman sitting alone in the dark living-room, watching the all-night channel from Boston. When Strout stopped the car near the front of the house, Matt said: 'Drive it to the back.'

He touched Strout's head with the muzzle.

'You wouldn't have it cocked, would you? For when I put on the brakes.'

Matt cocked it, and said: 'It is now.'

Strout waited a moment; then he eased the car forward, the engine doing little more than idling, and as they approached the garage he gently braked. Matt opened the door, then took off the glove and put it in his pocket. He stepped out and shut the door with his hip and said: 'All right.'

Strout looked at the gun, then got out, and Matt followed him across the grass, and as Strout unlocked the door Matt looked quickly at the row of small backyards on either side, and scattered tall trees, some evergreens, others not, and he thought of the red and yellow leaves on the trees over the hole, saw them falling soon, probably in two weeks, dropping slowly, covering. Strout stepped into the kitchen.

'Turn on the light.'

Strout reached to the wall switch, and in the light Matt looked at his wide back, the dark blue shirt, the white belt, the red plaid pants.

'Where's your suitcase?'

'My suitcase?'

'Where is it?'

'In the bedroom closet.'

'That's where we're going then. When we get to a door you stop and turn on the light.'

They crossed the kitchen, Matt glancing at the sink and stove and refrigerator: no dishes in the sink or even the dish rack beside it, no grease splashings on the stove, the refrigerator door clean and white. He did not want to look at any more but he looked quickly at all he could see: in the living-room magazines and newspapers in a wicker basket, clean ashtrays, a record player, the records shelved next to it, then down the hall where, near the bedroom door, hung a color photograph of Mary Ann and the two boys sitting on a lawn – there was no house in the picture – Mary Ann smiling at the camera or Strout or whoever held the camera, smiling as she had on Matt's lawn this summer while he waited for the charcoal and they all talked and he looked at her brown legs and at Frank touching her arm, her shoulder, her hair; he moved down the hall with her smile in his mind, wondering: Was that when they were both playing around and she was smiling like that at him and they were happy, even sometimes, making it worth it? He recalled her eyes, the pain in them, and he was conscious of the circles of love he was touching with the hand that held the revolver so tightly now as Strout stopped at the door at the end of the hall.

'There's no wall switch.'

'Where's the light?'

'By the bed.'

'Let's go.'

Matt stayed a pace behind, then Strout leaned over and the room was lighted: the bed, a double one, was neatly made; the ashtray on the bedside table clean, the bureau top dustless, and no photographs; probably so the girl – who *was* she? – would not have to see Mary Ann in the bedroom she believed was theirs. But because Matt was a father and a husband, though never an ex-husband, he knew (and did not want to know) that this bedroom had never been theirs alone. Strout turned around; Matt looked at his lips, his wide jaw, and thought of Frank's doomed and fearful eyes looking up from the couch.

'Where's Mr Trottier?'

'He's waiting. Pack clothes for warm weather.'

'What's going on?'

'You're jumping bail.'

'Mr Fowler—'

He pointed the cocked revolver at Strout's face. The barrel trembled but not much, not as much as he had expected. Strout went to the closet and got the suitcase from the floor and opened it on the bed. As he went to the bureau, he said: 'He was making it with my wife. I'd go pick up the kids and he'd be there. Sometimes he spent the night. My boys told me.'

He did not look at Matt as he spoke. He opened the top drawer and Matt stepped closer so he could see Strout's hands: underwear and socks, the socks rolled, the underwear folded and stacked. He took them back to the bed, arranged them neatly in the suitcase, then from the closet he was taking shirts and trousers and a jacket; he laid them on the bed and Matt followed him to the bathroom and watched from the door while he packed his shaving kit; watched in the bedroom as he folded and packed those things a person accumulated and that became part of him so that at times in the store Matt felt he was selling more than clothes.

'I wanted to try to get together with her again.' He was bent over the suitcase. 'I couldn't even talk to her. He was always with her. I'm going to jail for it; if I ever get out I'll be an old man. Isn't that enough?'

'You're not going to jail.'

Strout closed the suitcase and faced Matt, looking at the gun. Matt went to his rear, so Strout was between him and the lighted hall; then using his handkerchief he turned off the lamp and said: 'Let's go.'

They went down the hall, Matt looking again at the photograph, and through the living-room and kitchen, Matt turning off the lights and talking, frightened that he was talking, that he was telling this lie he had not planned: 'It's the trial. We can't go through that, my wife and me. So you're leaving. We've got you a ticket, and a job. A friend of Mr Trottier's. Out west. My wife keeps seeing you. We can't have that anymore.'

Matt turned out the kitchen light and put the handkerchief in his pocket, and they went down the two brick steps and across the lawn. Strout put the suitcase on the floor of the back seat, then got into the front seat and Matt got in the back and put on his glove and shut the door.

'They'll catch me. They'll check passenger lists.'

'We didn't use your name.'

'They'll figure that out too. You think I wouldn't have done it myself if it was that easy?'

He backed into the street, Matt looking down the gun barrel but not at the profiled face beyond it.

'You were alone,' Matt said. 'We've got it worked out.'

'There's no planes this time of night, Mr Fowler.'

'Go back through town. Then north on 125.'

They came to the corner and turned, and now Willis's headlights were in the car with Matt.

'Why north, Mr Fowler?'

'Somebody's going to keep you for a while. They'll take you to the airport.' He unlocked the hammer and lowered the revolver to his lap and said wearily: 'No more talking.'

As they drove back through town, Matt's body sagged, going limp with his spirit and its new and false bond with Strout, the hope his lie had given Strout. He had grown up in this town whose streets had become places of apprehension and pain for Ruth as she drove and walked, doing what she had to do; and for him too, if only in his mind as he worked and chatted six days a week in his store; he wondered now if his lie would have worked, if sending Strout away would have been enough; but then he knew that just thinking of Strout in Montana or whatever place lay at the end of the lie he had told, thinking of him walking the streets there, loving a girl there (who *was* she?) would be enough slowly to rot the rest of his days. And Ruth's. Again he was certain that she knew, that she was waiting for him.

They were in New Hampshire now, on the narrow highway, passing the shopping center at the state line, and then houses and small stores and sandwich shops. There were few cars on the road. After ten minutes he raised his trembling hand, touched Strout's neck with the gun, and said: 'Turn in up here. At the dirt road.'

Strout flicked on the indicator and slowed.

'Mr Fowler?'

'They're waiting here.'

Strout turned very slowly, easing his neck away from the gun. In the moonlight the road was light brown, lighter and yellowed where the headlights shone; weeds and a few trees grew on either side of it, and ahead of them were the woods.

'There's nothing back here, Mr Fowler.'

'It's for your car. You don't think we'd leave it at the airport, do you?'

He watched Strout's large, big-knuckled hands tighten on the wheel, saw Frank's face that night: not the stitches and bruised eye and swollen lips, but his own hand gently touching Frank's jaw, turning his wounds to the light. They rounded a bend in the road and were out of sight of the highway: tall trees all around them now, hiding the moon. When they reached the abandoned gravel pit on the left, the bare flat earth and steep pale embankment behind it, and the black crowns of trees at its top, Matt said: 'Stop here.'

Strout stopped but did not turn off the engine. Matt pressed the gun hard against his neck, and he straightened in the seat and looked in the rear-view mirror, Matt's eyes meeting his in the glass for an instant before looking at the hair at the end of the gun barrel.

'Turn it off.'

Strout did, then held the wheel with two hands, and looked in the mirror.

'I'll do twenty years, Mr Fowler; at least. I'll be forty-six years old.'

'That's nine years younger than I am,' Matt said, and got out and took off the glove and kicked the door shut. He aimed at Strout's ear and pulled back the hammer. Willis's headlights were off and Matt heard him walking on the soft thin layer of dust, the hard earth beneath it. Strout opened the door, sat for a moment in the interior light, then stepped out on to the road. Now his face was pleading. Matt did not look at his eyes, but he could see it in the lips.

'Just get the suitcase. They're right up the road.'

Willis was beside him now, to his left. Strout looked at both guns. Then he opened the back door, leaned in, and with a jerk brought the suitcase out. He was turning to face them when Matt said: 'Just walk up the road. Just ahead.'

Strout turned to walk, the suitcase in his right hand, and Matt and Willis followed; as Strout cleared the front of his car he dropped the suitcase and, ducking, took one step that was the beginning of a sprint to his right. The gun kicked in Matt's hand, and the explosion of the shot surrounded him, isolated him in a nimbus of sound that cut him off from all his time, all his history, isolated him standing absolutely still on the dirt road with the gun in his hand, looking down at Richard Strout squirming on his belly, kicking one leg behind him, pushing himself forward, toward the woods. Then Matt went to him and shot him once in the back of the head.

'HITCHER'

I'd been tired, under
the weather, but the ansaphone kept screaming:
one more sick-note, mister, and you're finished. Fired.
I thumbed a lift to where the car was parked.
A Vauxhall Astra. It was hired.

I picked him up in Leeds.
He was following the sun to west from east
with just a toothbrush and the good earth for a bed. The truth,
he said, was blowin' in the wind,
or round the next bend.

I let him have it
on the top road out of Harrogate: once
with the head, then six times with an elbow
in the face, and didn't even swerve.
I dropped it into third

and leant across
to let him out, and saw him in the mirror
bouncing off the kerb then disappearing down the verge.
We were the same age, give or take a week.
He'd said he liked the breeze

to run its fingers
through his hair. It was twelve noon.
The outlook for the day was moderate to fair.
Stitch that, I remember thinking,
you can walk from there.

WILLIAM FAULKNER

'SMOKE'

Anselm Holland came to Jefferson many years ago. Where from, no one knew. But he was young then and a man of parts, or of presence at least, because within three years he had married the only daughter of a man who owned two thousand acres of some of the best land in the county, and he went to live in his father-in-law's house, where two years later his wife bore him twin sons and where a few years later still the father-in-law died and left Holland in full possession of the property, which was now in his wife's name. But even before that event, we in Jefferson had already listened to him talking a trifle more than loudly of 'my land, my crops'; and those of us whose fathers and grandfathers had been bred here looked upon him a little coldly and a little askance for a ruthless man and (from tales told about him by both white and negro tenants and by others with whom he had dealings) for a violent one. But out of consideration for his wife and respect for his father-in-law, we treated him with courtesy if not with regard. So when his wife, too, died while the twin sons were still children, we believed that he was responsible, that her life had been worn out by the crass violence of an underbred outlander. And when his sons reached maturity and first one and then the other left home for good and all, we were not surprised. And when one day six months ago he was found dead, his foot fast in the stirrup of the saddled horse which he rode, and his body pretty badly broken where the horse had apparently dragged him through a rail fence (there still showed at the time on the horse's back and flanks the marks of the blows which he had dealt it in one of his fits of rage), there was none of us who was sorry, because a short time before that he had committed what to men of our town and time and thinking was the unpardonable outrage. On the day he died it was learned that he had been digging up the graves in the family cemetery where his wife's people rested, among them the grave in which his wife had lain for thirty years. So the crazed, hate-ridden old man was buried among the graves which he had attempted to violate, and in the proper time his will was offered for probate. And we learned the substance of the will without surprise. We were not surprised to learn that even from beyond the grave he had struck one final blow at those alone whom he could now injure or outrage: his remaining flesh and blood.

At the time of their father's death the twin sons were forty. The younger one, Anselm, Junior, was said to have been the mother's favorite – perhaps because he was the one who was most like his father. Anyway, from the time of her death, while the boys were still children almost, we would hear of trouble between Old Anse and Young Anse, with Virginius, the other twin, acting as mediator and being cursed for his pains by both father and brother; he was that sort, Virginius was. And Young Anse was his sort too; in his late teens he ran away from home and was gone ten years. When he returned he and his brother were of age, and Anselm made formal demand upon his father that the land which we now learned was held by Old Anse only in trust be divided and he – Young Anse – be given his share. Old Anse refused violently. Doubtless the request had been as violently made, because the two of them, Old Anse and Young Anse, were so much alike. And we heard that, strange to say, Virginius had taken his father's side. We heard that, that is. Because the land remained intact, and we heard how, in the midst of a scene of unparalleled violence even for them – a scene of such violence that the negro servants all fled the house and scattered for the night – Young Anse departed, taking with him the team of mules which he did own; and from that day until his father's death, even after Virginius also had been forced to leave home, Anselm never spoke to his father and brother again. He did not leave the county this time, however. He just moved back into the hills ('Where he can watch what the old man and Virginius are doing,' some of us said and all of us thought); and for the next fifteen years he lived alone in a dirt-floored, two-room cabin, like a hermit, doing his own cooking, coming into town behind his two mules not four times a year. Some time earlier he had been arrested and tried for making whiskey. He made no defence, refusing to plead either way, was fined both on the charge and for contempt of court, and flew into a rage exactly like his father when his brother Virginius offered to pay the fine. He tried to assault Virginius in the courtroom and went to the penitentiary at his own demand and was pardoned eight months later for good behavior and returned to his cabin – a dark, silent, aquiline-faced man whom both neighbors and strangers let severely alone.

The other twin, Virginius, stayed on, farming the land which his father had never done justice to even while he was alive. (They said of Old Anse, 'Wherever he came from and whatever he was bred to be, it was not a farmer.' And so we said among ourselves, taking it to be true, 'That's the trouble between him and Young Anse: watching his father mistreat the land which his mother aimed for him and Virginius to have.') But Virginius stayed on. It could not have been much fun for him, and we said later that Virginius should have known that such an arrangement could not last. And then later than that we said, 'Maybe he did know.' Because that was Virginius. You didn't know what he was thinking at the time, any time. Old Anse and Young Anse were like water. Dark water, maybe; but men could see what they were about. But no man ever knew what Virginius was thinking or doing until afterward. We didn't even know what happened that time when Virginius, who had stuck it out alone for ten years while Young Anse was away, was driven away at last; he didn't tell it, not even to Granby Dodge, probably. But we knew Old Anse and we knew Virginius, and we could imagine it, about like this:

We watched Old Anse smoldering for about a year after Young Anse took his mules and went back into the hills. Then one day he broke out: maybe like this, 'You think that, now your brother is gone, you can just hang around and get it all, don't you?'

'I don't want it all,' Virginius said. 'I just want my share.'

'Ah,' Old Anse said. 'You'd like to have it parcelled out right now too, would you? Claim like him it should have been divided up when you and him came of age.'

'I'd rather take a little of it and farm it right than to see it all in the shape it's in now,' Virginius said, still just, still mild – no man in the county ever saw Virginius lose his temper or even get ruffled, not even when Anselm tried to fight him in the court-room about that fine.

'You would, would you?' Old Anse said. 'And me that's kept it working at all, paying the taxes on it, while you and your brother have been putting money by every year, tax-free.'

'You know Anse never saved a nickel in his life,' Virginius said. 'Say what you want to about him, but don't accuse him of being forehanded.'

'Yes, by heaven! He was man enough to come out and claim what he thought was his and get out when he never got it. But you. You'll just hang around, waiting for me to go, with that damned meal mouth of yours. Pay me the taxes on your half back to the day your mother died, and take it.'

'No,' Virginius said. 'I won't do it.'

'No,' Old Anse said. 'No. Oh, no. Why spend your money for half of it when you can set down and get all of it some day without putting out a cent.' Then we imagined Old Anse (we thought of them as sitting down until now, talking like two civilized men) rising, with his shaggy head and his heavy eyebrows. 'Get out of my house!' he said. But Virginius didn't move, didn't get up, watching his father. Old Anse came toward him, his hand raised. 'Get. Get out of my house. By heaven, I'll . . .'

Virginius went, then. He didn't hurry, didn't run. He packed up his belongings (he would have more than Anse; quite a few little things) and went four or five miles to live with a cousin, the son of a remote kinsman of his mother. The cousin lived alone, on a good farm too, though now eaten up with mortgages, since the cousin was no farmer either, being half a stock-trader and half a lay preacher – a small, sandy, nondescript man whom you would not remember a minute after you looked at his face and then away – and probably no better at either of these than at farming. Without haste Virginius left, with none of his brother's foolish and violent finality; for which, strange to say, we thought none the less of Young Anse for showing, possessing. In fact, we always looked at Virginius a little askance too; he was a little too much master of himself. For it is human nature to trust quickest those who cannot depend on themselves. We called Virginius a deep one; we were not surprised when we learned how he had used his savings to disencumber the cousin's farm. And neither were we surprised when a year later we learned how Old Anse had refused to pay the taxes on his land and how, two days before the place would have gone delinquent, the sheriff received anonymously in the mail cash to the exact penny of the Holland assessment. 'Trust Virginius,' we said, since we believed we knew that the money needed no name to it. The sheriff had notified Old Anse.

'Put it up for sale and be damned,' Old Anse said. 'If they think that all they have to do is set there waiting, the whole brood and biling of them . . .'

The sheriff sent Young Anse word. 'It's not my land,' Young Anse sent back.

The sheriff notified Virginius. Virginius came to town and looked at the tax books himself. 'I got all I can carry myself, now,' he said. 'Of course, if he lets it go, I hope I can get it. But I don't know. A good farm like that won't last long or go cheap.' And that was all. No anger, no astonishment, no regret. But he was a deep one; we were not surprised when we learned how the sheriff had received that package of money, with the unsigned note: *Tax money for Anselm Holland farm. Send receipt to Anselm Holland, Senior.* 'Trust Virginius', we said. We thought about Virginius quite a lot during the next year, out there in a strange house, farming strange land, watching the farm and the house where he was born and that was rightfully his going to ruin. For the old man was letting it go completely now: year by year the good broad fields were going back to jungle and gully, though still each January the sheriff received that anonymous money in the mail and sent the receipt to Old Anse, because the old man had stopped coming to town altogether now, and the very house was falling down about his head, and nobody save Virginius ever stopped there. Five or six times a year he would ride up to the front porch, and the old man would come out and bellow at him in savage and violent vituperation, Virginius taking it quietly, talking to the few remaining negroes once he had seen with his own eyes that his father was all right, then riding away again. But nobody else ever stopped there, though now and then from a distance someone would see the old man going about the mournful and shaggy fields on the old white horse which was to kill him.

Then last summer we learned that he was digging up the graves in the cedar grove where five generations of his wife's people rested. A negro reported it, and the county health officer went out there and found the white horse tied in the grove, and the old man himself came out of the grove with a shotgun. The health officer returned, and two days later a deputy went out there and found the old man lying beside the horse, his foot fast in the stirrup, and on the horse's rump the savage marks of the stick – not a switch: a stick – where it had been struck again and again and again.

So they buried him, among the graves which he had violated. Virginius and the cousin came to the funeral. They were the funeral, in fact. For Anse, Junior, didn't come. Nor did he come near the place later, though Virginius stayed long enough to lock the house and pay the negroes off. But he too went back to the cousin's, and in due time Old Anse's will was offered for probate to Judge Dukinfield. The substance of the will was no secret; we all learned of it. Regular it was, and we were surprised neither at its regularity nor at its substance nor its wording: . . . *with the exception of these two bequests, I give and bequeath . . . my property to my elder son Virginius, provided it be proved to the satisfaction of the . . . Chancellor that it was the said Virginius who has been paying the taxes on my land, the . . . Chancellor to be the sole and unchallenged judge of the proof.*

The other two bequests were:

To my younger son Anselm, I give ... two full sets of mule harness, with the condition that this ... harness be used by ... Anselm to make one visit to my grave. Otherwise this ... harness to become and remain part ... of my property as described above.

To my cousin-in-law Granby Dodge I give ... one dollar in cash, to be used by him for the purchase of a hymn book or hymn books, as a token of my gratitude for his having fed and lodged my son Virginius since ... Virginius quitted my roof.

That was the will. And we watched and listened to hear or see what Young Anse would say or do. And we heard and saw nothing. And we watched to see what Virginius would do. And he did nothing. Or we didn't know what he was doing, what he was thinking. But that was Virginius. Because it was all finished then, anyway. All he had to do was to wait until Judge Dukinfield validated the will, then Virginius could give Anse his half – if he intended to do this. We were divided there. 'He and Anse never had any trouble,' some said. 'Virginius never had any trouble with anybody,' others said. 'If you go by that token, he will have to divide that farm with the whole county.' 'But it was Virginius that tried to pay Anse's fine,' the first ones said. 'And it was Virginius that sided with his father when Young Anse wanted to divide the land, too,' the second ones said.

So we waited and we watched. We were watching Judge Dukinfield now; it was suddenly as if the whole thing had sifted into his hands; as though he sat godlike above the vindictive and jeering laughter of that old man who even underground would not die, and above these two irreconcilable brothers who for fifteen years had been the same as dead to each other. But we thought that in his last coup, Old Anse had overreached himself; that in choosing Judge Dukinfield, the old man's own fury had checkmated him; because in Judge Dukinfield we believed that Old Anse had chosen the one man among us with sufficient probity and honor and good sense – that sort of probity and honor which has never had time to become confused and self-doubting with too much learning in the law. The very fact that the validating of what was a simple enough document appeared to be taking him an overlong time, was to us but fresh proof that

Judge Dukinfield was the one man among us who believed that justice is fifty per cent legal knowledge and fifty per cent unhaste and confidence in himself and in God.

So as the expiration of the legal period drew near, we watched Judge Dukinfield as he went daily between his home and his office in the courthouse yard. Deliberate and unhurried he moved – a widower of sixty and more, portly, white-headed, with an erect and dignified carriage which the negroes called 'rear-backted.' He had been appointed Chancellor seventeen years ago; he possessed little knowledge of the law and a great deal of hard common sense; and for thirteen years now no man had opposed him for re-election, and even those who would be most enraged by his air of bland and affable condescension voted for him on occasion with a kind of childlike confidence and trust. So we watched him without impatience, knowing that what he finally did would be right, not because he did it, but because he would not permit himself or anyone else to do anything until it was right. So each morning we would see him cross the Square at exactly ten minutes past eight o'clock and go on to the courthouse, where the negro janitor had preceded him by exactly ten minutes, with the clocklike precision with which the block signal presages the arrival of the train, to open the office for the day. The Judge would enter the office, and the negro would take his position in a wire-mended splint chair in the flagged passage which separated the office from the courthouse proper where he would sit all day long and doze, as he had done for seventeen years. Then at five in the afternoon the negro would wake and enter the office and perhaps wake the Judge too, who had lived long enough to have learned that the onus of any business is usually in the hasty minds of those theoreticians who have no business of their own; and then we would watch them cross the Square again in single file and go on up the street toward home, the two of them, eyes front and about fifteen feet apart, walking so erect that the two frock coats made by the same tailor and to the Judge's measure fell from the two pairs of shoulders in single boardlike planes, without intimation of waist or of hips.

Then one afternoon, a little after five o'clock, men began to run suddenly across the Square, toward the courthouse. Other men saw them and ran too, their feet heavy on the paving, among the wagons and the cars, their voices tense, urgent, 'What? What is it?' 'Judge Dukinfield,' the word went; and they ran on and entered the flagged passage between the courthouse and the office, where the old negro in his cast-off frock coat stood beating his hands on the air. They passed him and ran into the office. Behind the table the Judge sat, leaning a little back in his chair, quite comfortable. His eyes were open, and he had been shot neatly once through the bridge of the nose, so that he appeared to have three eyes in a row. It was a bullet, yet no man about the Square that day, or the old negro who had sat all day long in the chair in the passage, had heard any sound.

....

'PICK-UP ON
NOON STREET'

The man and the girl walked slowly, close together, past a dim stencil sign that said: SURPRISE HOTEL. The man wore a purple suit, a panama hat over his shiny, slicked-down hair. He walked splay-footed, soundlessly.

The girl wore a green hat and a short skirt and sheer stockings, four-and-a-half-inch French heels. She smelled of Midnight Narcissus.

At the corner the man leaned close, said something in the girl's ear. She jerked away from him, giggled.

'You gotta buy liquor if you take *me* home, Smiler.'

'Next time, baby. I'm fresh outa dough.'

The girl's voice got hard. 'Then I tells you goodbye in the next block, handsome.'

'Like hell, baby,' the man answered.

The arc at the intersection threw light on them. They walked across the street far apart. At the other side the man caught the girl's arm. She twisted away from him.

'Listen, you cheap grifter!' she shrilled. 'Keep your paws down, see! Tinhorns are dust to me. Dangle!'

'How much liquor you gotta have, baby?'

'Plenty.'

'Me bein' on the nut, where do I collect it?'

'You got hands, ain't you?' the girl sneered. Her voice dropped the shrillness. She leaned close to him again. 'Maybe you got a gun, big boy. Got a gun?'

'Yeah. And no shells for it.'

'The goldbricks over on Central don't know that.'

'Don't be that way,' the man in the purple suit snarled. Then he snapped his fingers and stiffened. 'Wait a minute. I got me an idea.'

He stopped and looked back along the street towards the dim stencil hotel sign. The girl slapped a glove across his chin caressingly. The glove smelled to him of the perfume, Midnight Narcissus.

The man snapped his fingers again, grinned widely in the dim light. 'If that drunk is still holed up in Doc's place – I collect. Wait for me, huh?'

'Maybe, at home. If you ain't gone too long.'

'Where's home, baby?'

The girl stared at him. A half-smile moved along her full lips, died at the corners of them. The breeze picked a sheet of newspaper out of the gutter and tossed it against the man's leg. He kicked at it savagely.

'Calliope Apartments, 4-B, 246 East 48. How soon you be there?'

The man stepped very close to her, reached back and tapped his hip. His voice was low, chilling.

'You wait for me, baby.'

She caught her breath, nodded. 'OK, handsome. I'll wait.'

The man went back along the cracked sidewalk, across the intersection, along to where the stencil sign hung out over the street. He went through a glass door into a narrow lobby with a row of brown wooden chairs pushed against the plaster wall. There was just space to walk past them to the desk. A bald-headed colored man lounged behind the desk, fingering a large green pin in his tie.

The negro in the purple suit leaned across the counter and his teeth flashed in a quick, hard smile. He was very young, with a thin, sharp jaw, a narrow bony forehead, the flat brilliant eyes of the gangster. He said softly: 'That pug with the husky voice still here? The guy that banked the crap game last night.'

The bald-headed clerk looked at the flies on the ceiling fixture. 'Didn't see him go out, Smiler.'

'Ain't what I asked you, Doc.'

'Yeah. He still here.'

'Still drunk?'

'Guess so. Hasn't been out.'

'Three-forty-nine, ain't it?'

'You been there, ain't you? What you wanta know for?'

'He cleaned me down to my lucky piece. I gotta make a touch.'

The bald-headed man looked nervous. The Smiler stared softly at the green stone in the man's tie pin.

'Get rolling, Smiler. Nobody gets bent around here. We ain't no Central Avenue flop.'

The Smiler said very softly: 'He's my pal, Doc. He'll lend me twenty. You touch half.'

He put his hand out palm up. The clerk stared at the hand for a long moment. Then he nodded sourly, went behind a ground-glass screen, came back slowly, looking towards the street door.

His hand went out and hovered over the palm. The palm closed over a pass-key, dropped inside the cheap purple suit.

The sudden flashing grin on the Smiler's face had an icy edge to it.

'Careful, Doc – while I'm up above.'

The clerk said: 'Step on it. Some of the customers get home early.' He glanced at the green electric clock on the wall. It was seven-fifteen. 'And the walls ain't any too thick,' he added.

The thin youth gave him another flashing grin, nodded, went delicately back along the lobby to the shadowy staircase. There was no elevator in the Surprise Hotel.

At one minute past seven Pete Anglich, narcotic squad under-cover man, rolled over on the hard bed and looked at the cheap strap watch on his left wrist. There were heavy shadows under his eyes, a thick dark stubble on his broad chin. He swung his bare feet to the floor and stood up in cheap cotton pajamas, flexed his muscles, stretched, bent over stiff-kneed and touched the floor in front of his toes with a grunt.

He walked across to a chipped bureau, drank from a quart bottle of cheap rye whiskey, grimaced, pushed the cork into the neck of the bottle, and rammed it down with the heel of his hand.

'Boy, have I got a hangover,' he grumbled huskily.

He stared at his face in the bureau mirror, at the stubble on his chin, the thick white scar on his throat close to the windpipe. His voice was husky because the bullet that had made the scar had done something to his vocal cords. It was a smooth huskiness, like the voice of a blues singer.

He stripped his pajamas off and stood naked in the middle of the room, his toes fumbling the rough edge of a big rip in the carpet. His body was very broad, and that made him look a little shorter than he was. His shoulders sloped, his nose was a little thick, the skin over his cheekbones looked like leather. He had short, curly, black hair, utterly steady eyes, the small set mouth of a quick thinker.

He went into a dim, dirty bathroom, stepped into the tub and turned the shower on. The water was warmish, but not hot. He stood under it and soaped himself, rubbed his whole body over, kneaded his muscles, rinsed off.

He jerked a dirty towel off the rack and started to rub a glow into his skin.

A faint noise behind the loosely closed bathroom door stopped him. He held his breath, listened, heard the noise again, a creak of boarding, a click, a rustle of cloth. Pete Anglich reached for the door and pulled it open slowly.

The negro in the purple suit and panama hat stood beside the bureau, with Pete Anglich's coat in his hand. On the bureau in front of him were two guns. One of them was Pete Anglich's old worn Colt. The room door was shut and a key with a tag lay on the carpet near it, as though it had fallen out of the door, or been pushed out from the other side.

The Smiler let the coat fall to the floor and held a wallet in his left hand. His right hand lifted the Colt. He grinned.

'OK, white boy. Just go on dryin' yourself off after your shower,' he said.

Pete Anglich towelled himself. He rubbed himself dry, stood naked with the wet towel in his left hand.

The Smiler had the bill-fold empty on the bureau, was counting the money with his left hand. His right still clutched the Colt.

'Eighty-seven bucks. Nice money. Some of it's mine from the crap game, but I'm lifting it all, pal. Take it easy. I'm friends with the management here.'

'Gimme a break, Smiler,' Pete Anglich said hoarsely. 'That's every dollar I got in the world. Leave a few bucks, huh?' He made his voice thick, coarse, heavy as though with liquor.

The Smiler gleamed his teeth, shook his narrow head. 'Can't do it, pal. Got me a date and I need the kale.'

Pete Anglich took a loose step forward and stopped, grinning sheepishly. The muzzle of his own gun had jerked at him.

The Smiler sidled over to the bottle of rye and lifted it.

'I can use this, too. My baby's got a throat for liquor. Sure has. What's in your pants is yours, pal. Fair enough?'

Pete Anglich jumped sideways, about four feet. The Smiler's face convulsed. The gun jerked around and the bottle of rye slid out of his left hand, slammed down on his foot. He yelped, kicked out savagely, and his toe caught in the torn place in the carpet.

Pete Anglich flipped the wet end of the bathtowel straight at the Smiler's eyes.

The Smiler reeled and yelled with pain. Then Pete Anglich held the Smiler's gun wrist in his hard left hand. He twisted up, around. His hand started to slide down over the Smiler's hand, over the gun. The gun turned inward and touched the Smiler's side.

A hard knee kicked viciously at Pete Anglich's abdomen. He gagged, and his fingers tightened convulsively on the Smiler's trigger finger.

The shot was dull, muffled against the purple cloth of the

suit. The Smiler's eyes rolled whitely and his narrow jaw fell slack.

Pete Anglich let him down on the floor and stood panting, bent over, his face greenish. He groped for the fallen bottle of rye, got the cork out, got some of the fiery liquid down his throat.

The greenish look went away from his face. His breathing slowed. He wiped sweat off his forehead with the back of his hand.

He felt the Smiler's pulse. The Smiler didn't have any pulse. He was dead. Pete Anglich loosened the gun from his hand, went over to the door and glanced out into the hallway. Empty. There was a pass-key in the outside of the lock. He removed it, locked the door from the inside.

He put his underclothes and socks and shoes on, his worn blue serge suit, knotted a black tie around the crumpled shirt collar, went back to the dead man and took a roll of bills from his pocket. He packed a few odds and ends of clothes and toilet articles in a cheap fibre suitcase, stood it by the door.

He pushed a torn scrap of sheet through his revolver barrel with a pencil, replaced the used cartridge, crushed the empty shell with his heel on the bathroom floor and then flushed it down the toilet.

He locked the door from the outside and walked down the stairs to the lobby.

The bald-headed clerk's eyes jumped at him, then dropped. The skin of his face turned gray. Pete Anglich leaned on the counter and opened his hand to let two keys tinkle on the scarred wood. The clerk stared at the keys, shuddered.

Pete Anglich said in his slow, husky voice: 'Hear any funny noises?'

The clerk shook his head, gulped.

'Creep joint, eh?' Pete Anglich said.

The clerk moved his head painfully, twisted his neck in his collar. His bald head winked darkly under the ceiling light.

'Too bad,' Pete Anglich said. 'What name did I register under last night?'

'You ain't registered,' the clerk whispered.

'Maybe I wasn't here even,' Pete Anglich said softly.

'Never saw you before, mister.'

'You're not seeing me now. You never will see me – to know me – will you, Doc?'

The clerk moved his neck and tried to smile.

Pete Anglich drew his wallet out and shook three dollar bills from it.

'I'm a guy that likes to pay his way,' he said slowly. 'This pays for Room 349 – till 'way in the morning, kind of late. The lad you gave the pass-key to looks like a heavy sleeper.' He paused, steadied his cool eyes on the clerk's face, added thoughtfully: 'Unless, of course, he's got friends who would like to move him out.'

Bubbles showed on the clerk's lips. He stuttered: 'He ain't – ain't—'

'Yeah,' Pete Anglich said. 'What would you expect?'

He went across to the street door, carrying his suitcase, stepped out under the stencil sign, stood a moment looking towards the hard white glare of Central Avenue.

Then he walked the other way. The street was very dark, very quiet. There were four blocks of frame houses before he came to Noon Street. It was all a negro quarter.

He met only one person on the way, a brown girl in a green hat, very sheer stockings, and four-and-a-half-inch heels, who smoked a cigarette under a dusty palm tree and stared back towards the Surprise Hotel.

....

THE KILLING OF
THE SAINTS

Carlos was the first to see José and Ramón enter the store, walking abreast of each other like cheap hoods in a B-movie. He was on the phone trying to reach Beverly Alvarado, a newly hired employee who was already an hour late and had not called in or given any reason for her delay. (Later, during the investigation, police would find that Beverly had gotten into a fender bender coming out of West Adams and was delayed by the other driver.)

The moment he saw the Cubans walk in, Carlos knew there was going to be trouble. He put the phone down, not bothering to let it ring ten times as he routinely did. The two Cubans had shown up three months before, buying pendants, earrings, necklaces, all of gold. They wanted 18 karat but since the store sold only 14k they went along, especially after Carlos convinced them 14k was better because it lasted longer. They'd shown him a card for a discount signed by Mr Schnitzer, so he'd cut the price by half, leaving an outstanding balance of eight hundred dollars, which they financed. While their job references were shaky – they'd only been working at the Meneses Body Shop for six months – Carlos figured he could always repossess if worse came to worst.

When it did, it was a messy affair, one of the messiest he'd ever been in. The men ignored his repeated phone calls to pay up. They claimed the jewelry was supposed to be a present from Schnitzer and they had no intention of paying for gifts. Carlos, refusing to believe Schnitzer would give away his merchandise to these lowlifes, called in the sheriff's department to do its duty by the merchants of Los Angeles and return the goods to their lawful owner. One of the sheriff's deputies who went into the apartment to rescue the jewelry told Carlos the items had been on an altar as an offering to some kind of voodoo god and that the men had sworn they'd get them back.

Carlos turned to Hawkins, nudged him with his elbow.

'Hey, Star, check out those guys.'

Hawkins turned and saw the two black Cubans swagger in. He put down his instant oatmeal and unclipped the safety strap of the holster of his .387 Magnum.

'Be careful,' said Carlos.

It was Hawkins' shuffling gait, the kind of lopy, off-balance walk that made him such a comforting figure even when packing a gun, which sealed his fate. José saw him approaching and before the guard had cleared his throat to ask, 'Could I help you, gentlemen?' he had already tapped Ramón on the arm. They had no prearranged signal but Ramón, seeing the large figure in blue with his hand on his gun, in a split second whipped out his Sten and to the amazement of everyone in the store, including himself, fired two shots at Hawkins' knees, which buckled as the bullets tore through the bone and cartilage, exiting in a perfect oval shape above the upper end of the calf.

Absolute silence descended for an instant, a moment in which all the people that time and circumstance had brought to the store paused to contemplate the bloody disaster before them and to ponder briefly if the same fate awaited them. Then the silence died.

The Asian customer, Nam Do Pang, burst into a stream of obscenities in a high keening pitch while the little girl, her granddaughter, broke out in sobs and cries and quickly wet her pants. Hilda and Schnitzer, who were in the back office examining a shipment of aquas brought by their Romanian friend, Vlad

Lobera, rushed out. Carlos pressed the silent alarm button by the side of his desk to alert police of a robbery in progress and stood up, his hands up, a quivering smile on his lips.

While José pointed the gun at them, Ramón went to Hawkins' side to take his gun. But Hawkins, through some inner reserve of courage that even he was unaware of, refused to be disarmed and swatted at José's hands, as if he were a child grabbing a brownie from the cookie sheet.

'You're not gonna take it, let it be!' hollered Hawkins.

When José finally got hold of the gun, Hawkins struggled briefly. The gun went off and the round slammed into Hawkins' thorax, collapsing his left lung and snipping the main artery to his heart. He gave a quick shudder, then went limp into death, blood dripping from his mouth and nose.

Nam Do Pang attempted to get through and out to the street but Ramón kicked her back into the store.

'Don't move or I'll kill you!' The woman cowered by the emerald earring display case and embraced her granddaughter.

José unraveled two Hefty plastic bags he'd been carrying in his pocket and opened them, puncturing a hole in one in his haste. Then, with the butt of his gun, he smashed the glass cases, shards flying out in showers, setting off another silent alarm. He swept the cases clean, tossing the velvet-lined boxes over his shoulder, moving rapidly from case to case while Ramón kept his gun trained on the group.

Perhaps even then a greater tragedy could have been averted but Carlos chose that moment to show off his *cojones*. He spoke to José and Ramón in the broken, halting Spanish of the barrio: 'You know this will cost you the life.'

José glanced up at Carlos briefly, then at Ramón, who waved the gun, ordering him to go on plundering. Whether out of humiliation or out of some unavowed death wish, or simply because all his life he'd been able to get by through bullying, taunting and hectoring people of color, a foreman with the field hands, Carlos needled the Cubans, not realizing the cultural chasm that divides Castro's children from the sons of Montezuma:

'*Pendejos*, assholes, don't you know the white man is waiting for you? You kill a man, you forget about it. Put down your arms. You don't think that voodoo shit of yours is going to do something, no?'

José looked aghast at Carlos, who did not know he had just uttered the worst insult he could have ever cast at a *santero*. Ramón stood trembling, hesitating whether to shoot Carlos for his impertinence. The little girl's cries broke through the haze of drugs and the singleness of mind with which Ramón had come into the store, her yelping like bells going off in his head, signaling crisis, alarm, imminent death, setting off panicky memories of fire drills when everyone in the Combinado del Este prison would leave their cells running the minute they heard the bells to race down to the yard, and the curses and the taunting and whippings and blows with rifle butts, ax handles, two by fours and chains of the jeering guards rang in Ramón's mind as he turned and stuck his gun in the face of the little girl.

'*Callate, callate,* shut up or I'll kill you, shitty Chink!' Ramón was about to press the trigger to blow her brains out because it didn't matter any more, it was just another life and now he, Oggún, would be able to add her slanty-eyed little head to the mound of skulls his followers laid before him when the old Asian woman covered the girl's mouth with her hand, and pulled the child toward her, telling Ramón in Vietnamese how stupid her little granddaughter was and that she would never bother his lordship again.

Ramón struck Carlos in the jaw with his rifle butt, throwing him to the ground on the carpet of shattered glass.

Carlos got on his knees, rubbing his mouth, his broken upper lip filling his mouth with blood. He spat out a tooth.

'Oh, my God!' whispered Hilda, as though that blow was in some measure harder to explain than what had happened to Hawkins or the threat to the little girl. It was vicious, uncalled-for violence, the whirling cyclone of pain she had seen one time too many growing up in Iran. She moved behind Schnitzer for protection while the old man looked on and pondered if he had enough time to make it to his desk and take out the gun he kept taped to its underside.

'What the fuck's wrong with you niggers,' said Carlos, still defiant. 'What are you, crazy? What are you going to do, kill us all?'

José had stopped plundering and set his bag, half full, by the display counter. Ramón had told him there was an outside chance this might happen, that some fool would put up continued resistance even after the guard was out. He shuddered now as he looked at Ramón, in full embrace of Oggún, as he pranced around in the arrogant posture of the god, belly forward, arms akimbo, legs spread wide. The god had descended from heaven and José feared for what the *orisha* would demand. To refuse him would be worse than death but to obey him was just as tragic.

Meanwhile, in the back, Vlad Lobera, the adipose Romanian who had brought in the aquas for Schnitzer, scanned the old man's office, searching for a way out. It was a windowless cubicle with two doors, one leading to a small bathroom and the other to a hallway which connected the office to the shop in one direction and to the emergency escape in the other. Lobera had heard the gunshots blaring Hawkins' death and now he didn't dare step out. He felt his bowels moving out of fear and ran to the bathroom, locking it behind him. There he would smoke cigarette after cigarette, sitting on the commode, his pants around his ankles, listening but not knowing who spoke, feeling the terror as the bullets rang time and again.

'*Oggún, ña ña nile, Oggún kembo ti le,*' implored José, throwing himself on the ground and kissing Ramón's feet. 'Please return to your house, oh mighty God, do not honor us with your presence for you are a mighty being and these are petty dogs.'

'Dogs are my favorite meal,' replied Ramón, laughing. 'My anger has been aroused. I will not rest until I am appeased.' He stomped his right foot just like the god, shaking his head and moving the rifle in his hand like a spear.

But Carlos, with that same reckless impulse of the matador kissing the rump of the bull as it gallops past him inches away, with the same daring of the Acapulco high diver who plunges down ten storeys off the cliffs at the precise moment when the incoming waves will mattress his fall – which is to say, with stupid thoughtlessness – Carlos rushed to grab Ramón's gun.

Oggún, the proud god who inhabited Ramón, looked on

with contempt at this measly attempt to disarm him. With his free hand, Oggún seized the two-hundred-fifty-pound warrior, lifted him above his head like a squirming iguana and slammed him against the wall.

'No, no, Oggún,' cried José, but Ramón pointed the gun at the unconscious body and riddled Carlos with forty-seven bullets in two seconds of deafening fire. Ramón walked up to the lifeless body, knelt on one knee and scooped up a handful of the warm blood of the victim, smearing the life source on his face.

'*Oggún niká! Oggún kabu kabu, Oggún arere alawo ode mao kokoro yigüe yigüe alobilona, Oggún iya fayo fayo!*' cried Ramón, raising his arms in victory, his feet stomping the ground, a tall black man in white clothes in the guise of a god.

Hilda and Schnitzer had crouched down behind the display counter when Ramón and Carlos had gone into their mano a mano. Now, seeing the gunman in full delirium, the two of them started crawling away, moving to the back door. But before they could turn the door handle that would have opened to salvation, Ramón spotted them. At that instant, his task completed, bowl full of the warm human blood he loves, Oggún departed for his tribal homeland. In his place, left shaking, sweating and confused, stood Ramón, who woefully looked around at the destruction his divine *alter ego* had caused. He felt lifeless, exhausted, his mind a blinding torrent of suds swirling down a drain. He saw, far away, like figures moving down a football field in the slow motion of TV replays, Hilda and Schnitzer clawing at the door. A voice that he recognized as his own but that seemed to emanate from elsewhere shouted out, 'Stop! Stop or I'll shoot you!'

He felt like asking José who was it that had managed to imitate his voice so convincingly and then he saw himself casting down the empty Sten and taking out his pistol from his waistband and he felt like asking if that was the wisest thing to do. He saw the bullet come out of the gun and pierce through Hilda's bobbing brown hair and blast into the base of her skull, which exploded into three pieces. The bullet then entered the old man's right shoulder piercing the layers of padding in the jacket and the shirt fabric and the undershirt and burrowed into the flesh and cartilage and gristle of the shoulder coming out on the opposite side and lodging itself in the acoustic tile by the door. A second bullet spewed out of the gun and traveled with the speed of death toward Schnitzer's jaw.

Ramón stood in the middle of the store, his gun still in his hand, and overcome by the uselessness of it all, collapsed and sat on the ground.

'*Coño, chico*, what the fuck have you done?' shouted José in Spanish, knowing the god was gone. Ramón looked blindly around him, then shrugged his shoulders.

'That's life,' he muttered, remembering the song his wife, Maritza, played time and again at their apartment near El Prado in Havana when their little girl died of typhoid.

(In the back office, on his seat at the commode, Lobera felt another spasm as his bowels moved again.)

Ramón staggered to his feet, bracing himself on the counter, his knees still wobbly from too much divinity, too much anger and blood. He looked down and saw the old Asian woman and the little girl, staring wide-eyed back at him. Then he looked out the door for the first time and saw the police barricading themselves down the street. A bullhorn blared, 'We have you surrounded. Come out with your hands up!'

Ramón had not counted on the police blocking his escape; in his plans he had always given himself enough time to make a clear getaway. He glanced quickly at his gold and diamond Piaget which showed the time and the phases of the moon – 10:35 a.m., rising crescent. He could not understand where the time had gone. By his plans at this moment they should have been on their way out of town, down to the apartment he'd rented in Encinitas to hide in before heading down to Baja. What happened? He noticed the bodies strewn on the glass- and blood-covered floor and smelled the sweetness of the blood on his face, saw the crimson stains on his white suit. His eyes landed on the old woman and the girl, still cowering by the emeralds.

'Grab that old bitch for cover and tell the man we've got hostages.'

As José disentangled the woman from the child, Ramón grabbed the girl by one arm and pulled her away.

'Tell them we've rigged up a bomb and we intend to blow it up if they try to storm their way in.'

The next two hours passed in a confusing welter of voices, threats, telephone calls and whirring of helicopters overhead. Police turned off the ventilation system and the electricity and the sweetish smell of blood mixed with that of the excrement the bodies had voided. Negotiators for the police tried uneventfully to convince José and Ramón to give up the hostages and surrender, but Ramón refused to speak to them after the second phone call asking for an intermediary, Juan 'Cookie' Bongos, a morning DJ at KQOK, the number-one Spanish-language radio station in Los Angeles.

Bongos was a short, slim, terrier-haired man in his late forties. His dark mestizo face was plastered on billboards all over Hollywood and Echo Park, reminding Hispanics that Cookie was the next best thing to a prize-winning Lotto ticket in town. But Bongos found nothing funny when he entered the jewelry store at around eleven that morning. He saw the same carnage he had covered as a reporter back in Central America, in places like Huichinalgo and El Playón, monuments to death, rooms full of slaughter commandeered by madmen.

The smell was so overpowering that Bongos gagged, almost retching into his handkerchief. He carried a tape-recorder with him and turned it on. The sweaty, sour-smelling, blood-streaked captors poured out their message.

'We want a helicopter, with a safe-pass to the airport and a flight to Algeria or we're all going to die here!' hollered José, nervously.

'*Igualdad*, equality, that's what we wanted,' said Ramón in a raspy voice. 'Equality of treatment and consideration. Respect. Nobody had respect for us. They thought they could do what they wanted with us. Well, they were wrong. We demand the respect owed a human being.'

'And tell these sons of bitches they have an hour to give in or we'll blow up the place. We don't mind dying. We're dead already,' insisted José.

'This is the inevitable process of the fight for equality and dignity,' continued Ramón, ignoring the desperation in José's comments. 'If the Anglo won't listen to us and our situation, this is what he'll find. The streets will run crimson with blood and the weeping of the widows and the cries of the children will be heard throughout the land.

'As blacks and as Cubans we have been doubly discriminated against. This is the bitter harvest – raise crows and they will eat out your eyes.

'We are here to recover our honor, our dignity, which had been stolen by these men and their cohorts. What happened here, we are not responsible for, it was beyond our control.'

'OK, you've heard enough,' broke in José. 'Now go tell the sons of bitches they've got an hour or we'll all go up in smoke.'

Cookie left and in the half-hour that followed no words were spoken in the stuffy jewelry store except for the quiet crooning of the old lady calming down her frightened granddaughter. José and Ramón sank into their own reveries, heads low, fingers on the triggers of their weapons. Finally, the whirring of a helicopter broke the stillness, as the aircraft slowly sank through the canyon of concrete and glass and touched down in the street in front of the store.

A bullhorn blared, 'Gentlemen, we have acceded to your demands. This helicopter is ready to take you to the airport if you'll come out now.'

Ramón and José looked at each other jubilantly – their gamble had paid off! They got up, took their arms and walked over to the old woman and the child.

'You take the old lady,' said Ramón, 'I'll take the kid.'

But the moment he laid hands on the little girl, she started to scream and holler, kicking and biting, resistance born of fear. José slapped her but the old lady jumped in to defend the child. He threw the old lady to the ground. As she got up, a sharp pain pierced her left side, then she slapped down to the ground again, striking her head against a display case, dying from the blow. The little girl broke loose from Ramón and hugged the lifeless body. Ramón took the old woman's pulse.

'*Coño*, this shitty old woman just died, would you believe that?'

'What do we do now?'

Ramón thought quickly. Like Pizarro, like the conquistadores, the road went in only one direction – forward. That's it, like El Cid!

'Pick her up and hold her like she's still alive, as a shield till we get to the helicopter.'

José tried the front door to the store.

'*Coño*, it's locked!'

'Look around, there must be another exit.'

With the screaming little girl in his arms, Ramón kicked open the back door leading to the hallway. At the end he saw the emergency door. José followed, carrying the body of the old woman. Ramón put his weapon on the floor.

'What are you doing?' asked José.

'I don't want them to think I'm going to kill her because then they will shoot me. She's too small for protection. You hold the gun, OK?'

'OK.'

Ramón walked out holding the little girl aloft, his arms around her waist. The moment they stepped out of the shop the girl stopped kicking and fighting, staring in surprise all around her.

On rooftops and street corners, from behind dozens of black and whites parked around the store, bristled dozens of guns in the hands of police. The helicopter waited a few dozen yards away, its blades whirring, ready for takeoff.

José came out next, his machine-gun pointed at Ramón and the little girl, as he struggled with the body of the old woman.

They walked cautiously toward the helicopter, dozens of officers observing them quietly, guns pointed at them. From inside the helicopter a man waved.

'Come on, *apúrense*,' shouted the man in Spanish.

Ramón walked on to the chopper as a sharpshooter on a rooftop took a bead on Ramón's head and pulled the trigger. Ramón shifted his head at the last second and the bullet missed; it struck the pavement, then bounced up into the little girl, who gave a muffled scream before going limp. Ramón put her down and looked up at the chopper – three shotgun barrels appeared from inside the cabin, trained on him and José.

Ramón put his hands up, as did José, who let the body of the old woman drop with a thud to the ground.

'I wanna lawyer,' said Ramón. '*No hablo inglés.*'

'Me too,' said José.

....

PART TWO

THE POLICE IN
DIFFERENT VOICES

MICHAEL DIBDIN

···

Nothing more effectively illustrates the isolation of British crime writing than the deferential treatment accorded the police. The prevailing view in most countries where such views may freely be expressed is summed up by one of Chandler's rare decent cops: 'Police business is a hell of a problem. It's a good deal like politics. It asks for the highest type of men, and there's nothing in it to attract the highest type of men.'

After a decade in which scandals about the Royal family have been exceeded only by those revealing persistent and systematic abuse of police power, it is clear that Britain can no longer be considered exempt from the logic of that assessment, yet our crime fiction is still policed by the likes of Inspector Morse, Commander Adam Dalgleish and a host of less memorably idealized figures. A measure of aesthetic escapism may be an intrinsic element of the crime genre, but such a concentrated diet of the moral and political variety comes perilously close to what in different circumstances would be termed propaganda.

It might be argued that G. F. Newman's *Sir, You Bastard* goes to the opposite extreme, but Detective Inspector Terry Sneed would have been perfectly familiar to Victorian readers as the thief-taker, a licensed thug using every weapon at his disposal in a brutal guerrilla war with men who are socially and culturally indistinguishable from him. Newman's London, suffocating under a pall of sleaze and cynicism, is totally convincing, as is the acrid authenticity of his dialogue. Like many promising British crime writers, Newman was subsequently lost to television, but following the success of moves to bring the quality of programming in this country into line with the rest of the world it is to be hoped that he may be tempted back into print.

Exotic locations are usually something to beware of in crime fiction, but James McClure's novels featuring the Afrikaner Lieutenant Kramer and the Zulu Sergeant Zondi are a triumphant exception, exploiting the realities of life in provincial South Africa for structural rather than decorative effect. McClure is an undemonstrative but sly writer – note that 'mostly' at the start of the fourth paragraph – and his sympathetic portrait of the unlovely Kramer is a major achievement.

A similar example of a foreign setting fully justifying its use occurs in *Act of Darkness*. Francis King is not a 'crime writer', but this overwhelmingly powerful study of child murder, sexual repression, and political and social connivance is certainly a crime novel, and one which keeps its terrible secret until the very last pages. The scenes involving the police are a relatively minor aspect of the book, providing some welcome light relief amid its brooding intensity, but the delicacy and freshness with which King handles the well-worn themes of police procedure make them models of their kind.

A different kind of intensity pervades the work of the Swedish Communists Maj Sjöwall and Per Wahlöö, who saw their crime fiction as 'a scalpel cutting open the belly of an ideologically pauperized and morally debatable so-called welfare state of the bourgeois type'. Even in the mid-sixties that sort of rhetoric was calculated to make enemies; thirty years on it is unlikely to make any friends either. Fortunately none of this has any bearing on the quality of the Martin Beck series itself, which is not only unique in presenting a detailed and evolving vision of police work from a definable political perspective but consistently transcends the level of the average police procedural thanks to a prevailing sense of unease which in the end seems as much existential as ideological.

Perhaps socialists are more likely to collective action at a literary as well as political level. G. D. H. Cole and his wife Margaret were leading members of the Fabian movement, distinguished writers on social and economic questions and tireless campaigners for various progressive causes including trades-unionism and women's rights. They also wrote detective stories, which, with a single exception, were formulaic contrivances featuring a cast of the idle rich being genteely bumped off in isolated country houses. The exception is *Murder at the Munition Works*, which is set during a war-time strike at a factory based closely on the Morris Motor Works near Oxford ('Bullbridge'). The Coles' knowledge of the issues involved is evident throughout, but the contradiction inherent in trying to treat the Golden Age realistically was pointed out by a contemporary reviewer: 'The list of *dramatis personae* runs to two pages from which to choose the villain, but as most of the characters are members of the Labour Party, pacifists or readers of the Left Book Club, the field is evidently narrower than might appear at first sight: in fact, proceeding by political elimination, the candidates for the halter are reduced to a mere two.'

Although C. P. Snow's first venture into fiction was a detective story, his mature work is firmly associated in the public mind with academics and mandarins stalking the corridors of power. It therefore comes as quite a shock to find a fully-fledged crime novel among his *œuvre*, and one including a superb example of the police procedural. But Snow was a research physicist as well as a novelist and essayist, and it is the scientific aspects of police work which are highlighted here, with a degree of expertise and attention to detail rare in British crime writing.

Alain Robbe-Grillet's second novel won the prestigious Prix des Critiques, which no doubt afforded the founder of the *nouveau roman* some slight consolation for the failure of his first to win the Crime Writers' Association's coveted Gold Dagger award two years earlier. Its shortlisting caused controversy at the time, but the judges were right: *The Erasers* exploits the conventions of the crime genre, but it does so in ways which are significant and interesting. Traditional fiction assumes that reality is both coherent and knowable; the crime novel makes these assumptions explicit. It thus provided a perfect vehicle for Robbe-Grillet's subversive experiments, as it did for Sjöwall and Wahlöö's political critique. The very fact that crime writing is capable of supporting two such different applications demonstrates the centrality of its basic concerns to key issues in contemporary culture.

The replete bourgeois universe of Inspector Jules Maigret, where every family has its *poule au pot* and its skeleton in the cupboard, might at first sight appear to be the epitome of everything that Robbe-Grillet is seeking to undermine. But the cosy certitudes of the Maigret novels are continually tempered by chill draughts from the bleak existential wasteland of the *romans durs* all around. In *Maigret's Memoirs*, the 'real' Inspector Maigret attempts to correct the misleading impression created by his fictional simulacrum, only to be put in his place by Simenon himself. He has the last word, however, with a deliciously ironical parting shot.

Fear and Loathing in Las Vegas is a masterpiece of the New Journalism, but it is also related to a long tradition of American fiction concerned with paranoia and hallucinatory experiences. As monster drug-users and hippy anarchists, the narrator and his companion ('my attorney') are by definition criminals in the eyes of straight America, whose spiritual capital, Las Vegas, they are visiting. Also in town are 1,500 members of the National District Attorneys' Association attending a convention on Narcotics and Dangerous Drugs, a subject in which our heroes have a lively interest, so they score some name-tags and lay a few trips of their own. Thompson's razor-sharp timing and impeccable ear for dialogue ensure that they easily win the resulting game of dare with the DAs' – and the reader's – incredulity.

Elmore Leonard's timing, dialogue, technical knowledge and sense of the grotesque is second to none; what is unique to 'Dutch' is the laid-back, down-home charm of the narrative voice. Where some American crime writers kick the book open and come out shooting to prove how tough they are, Leonard sidles up like a bar-room buddy with a tale to tell. The story is so good, and the manner so low-key, that it is easy to overlook just how sophisticated the telling actually is. Leonard treats the reader as an equal, supplying all the details but leaving the significance implicit. In the present extract, for example, it is what the policemen *don't* say, even to each other which powers the whole scene and makes a savage punchline of a final paragraph which is completely banal out of context.

....

SIR, YOU BASTARD

As the cab inched along Regent Street with what seemed like not a breath of air coming in through the open windows, Feast said, 'Still doing that spade, Terry?' He didn't shade words with anything resembling tact.

'She's Colombian.'

Feast shrugged without apology. 'Same difference.'

'Tell her that, she'd smack you in the mouth.' For a moment as he glanced sideways at him, Sneed got the impression Lenny was going to ask how Colombian women laid; he had almost certainly asked that before though. 'I've not seen her for about a week,' he said, being purposely vague. He knew it was now eight days precisely.

'D'you have a row?'

'You're a nosy bastard, Lenny. D'you want me to put you in?' he joked, persisting in such callousness despite himself.

'She was round at Bow Street.' Feast smiled. 'As it happens I reckon I could probably have given her a tug.'

'Did you speak to her?'

'She left early.'

Expecting him at court, her presence would have been an obvious chance meeting, Sneed speculated. He knew her thinking; Billie wouldn't return to the flat, but he wasn't sure why. He couldn't remember rowing. Rows were usually loud, demonstrative things and you often forgot the quiet gnawing kind. Perhaps she had despaired at falling asleep while keeping a naked vigil for him. 'Had any mysteries lately?' Sneed asked.

The DS sneered. 'With my missus! You kidding? Did I tell you Vera was pregnant again?'

The DI nodded. 'Put her on the pill.'

'It keeps her out of mischief.'

The fat squashed face next to him grinned.

'Drink more water, Lenny, you'd be less potent.'

'You great gormless cunt!' the cab driver screamed in praise of a wolly who had directed them into a traffic jam around Eros.

Disembarking, the detectives walked through to the Queensberry. The bar was packed with overweight, roll-munching office workers; lean theatrical agents, and yet leaner actors, with a liberal sprinkling of fading actresses. A tall equestrian-looking woman, aspiring through affectation to some artistry, neighed above the clamour every time a pimply youth in a soiled collar stroked her quarters.

At the food counter, Freddy Ryan had by some means managed to reserve a stool for Sneed, and with as much authority as the landlord, acquired another for Feast. He then summoned the barmaid.

'Two Scotches,' Sneed said. 'Freddy?'

'Just 'alf for me, guv.'

'Have you eaten?'

'Eh,' Ryan hesitated as though uncertain, then laughed. 'No.'

'You cunning bastard.' Sneed laughed too, but without mirth.

Informers delighted in having their benefactors laugh with them; it gave them a sense of belonging other than to that cold little world they had chosen. Ryan warmed to Sneed's laughter. There were some people who considered that there was no one more detestable than a grass, yet Sneed knew he was probably more perfidious than any informer. He thought nothing of grassing the grasses to those on whom they had informed – when their usefulness was gone. On such occasions money was usually involved, sometimes a lot of money. Felons were often very vindictive.

Giant hams, barons of beef, turkeys and chickens sweating behind glass made nonsense of Feast's diet. The chef, who was like a bloated, hairless beetroot, with pencil lines drawn above each eye, cut thick slices of red beef until Sneed said, 'That'll do, he's dieting.'

Ryan followed his lead with cheese and green salad. They ate without broaching the business they had come together for. Sneed would indicate when it was time to do so. They touched on the weather – it was unusually hot, and Ryan suffered with his feet; and the traffic – it was getting worse, and the wollies were doing nothing to improve things. Sneed ordered more drinks. A barboy swished. Two actors sniggered. The horse lady neighed as pimply's ink-stained fingers continued stroking her.

Finally pushing his plate away, Sneed said, 'Had it off lately, Freddy?'

Cigarette tar on Ryan's fingers showed in stark relief against the white paper serviette, which he used to wipe his mouth before launching into his own criminal exploits, which in themselves were sufficient to get him a large one had Sneed felt so disposed. Informers were normally compulsive talkers, possessed with an urgent, often desperate need to tell about their own as well as other people's efforts, sometimes without realizing they were doing so – one of the reasons why their period of usefulness was frequently short. Assured of bigger things, it mattered little to Sneed what minor felonies his grass committed. Ryan's grin seemed full of pride. 'A blinding tape-recorder from a car in Long Acre.' He took and lit one of Sneed's cigarettes, even though he hadn't finished eating. 'A German job. A bastard getting it. I almost had m' collar felt.'

Sneed glanced at the DS. 'We heard about that. The car belonged to the Pope's brother-in-law,' he said solemnly. 'We might have to nick you for it, Freddy.'

'Leave off, guv.' Ryan's mouth fell open, but finally he realized it was a joke. 'Any good to you?'

'Haven't got a car, Freddy.'

'A couple of typewriters came out of an office last night. Hear anything about that?' He seemed to imagine that Sneed saw everything passing through his nick. Nothing was further from the truth; he hardly kept pace with the work which did fall his lot. 'There was s'posed to be some dough in the Peter – sevenpence and five poxy postage stamps!' Ryan sounded disgusted – Mayfair should have yielded more!

Unless stopped, Ryan would talk till closing time of things Sneed didn't particularly want to hear about. Ordering the final round of drinks, Sneed asked bluntly, 'What did your friend say, Freddy?' A friend, a third party, or perhaps a whisper, was how grasses always came by their information.

'Nothing much about the dough. But he said Pauly Neal might know.'

The question in Sneed's book was plain enough.

Feast rocked his head, indicating that the name wasn't known to him, then pushed the last of the beef and pickle into his mouth, chewed it twice then swallowed it with some Scotch.

'Where does he hang out, Freddy?'

'This side of the water.' He stopped and sucked on his cigarette in silence, awaiting the barmaid's departure. 'He had some dough to sell, is what I heard.'

Sneed thought about leaving Ryan to pay for the lunch with his anticipated profits from the stolen tape-recorder, but his information was of value. And after a few suggestions about where to look for neal, Sneed put two pound notes on the bar and left the informer to collect the change.

The day outside had got hotter. It was just as hot inside. His office was airless. Sneed eased out of his jacket, revealing the armpits of his shirt and a strip down his back bright wet with sweat.

'Get on to records, Lenny, see what they have on Neal.' The DS needn't need telling as such routine was almost automatic. It simply needed someone to say the words and co-ordinate the actions in order that a semblance of design was maintained. Sneed sat wearily. He regretted the walk back from the pub as he slipped off his ebony Bally shoes. From the desk drawer he removed the thin dossier on the robbery which had relieved the security firm of twelve thousand pounds; it would have been more but for the tenacity of the guards. One ended up in hospital with a fractured skull; the other had identifed James. Sneed considered now the possibility that James might try to intimidate the guard. It was doubtful as he knew; the villain wanted his temporary freedom for another purpose. Further, he reasoned that with an injured colleague and loss of credibility the security guard wouldn't intimidate easily.

Fourteen possible suspects who might have fitted the other two robbers were being checked out. One or two others remained to be found; they would be in due course. Pauly Neal wasn't on the original list.

DC Forrester entered with a list of jewellery far too expensive to have been stolen from a shop such as Horswood owned. A few cheap watches, lighters and a dozen or so lucky charms would have been more his mark. Perhaps with the odd expensive item that he had taken in pawn.

'Bit of a ramp,' Sneed said, scanning the list. 'A diamond pendant, a twoer? I doubt if his entire stock's worth that.' He handed the list back. 'Circulate it. Imply in your report to the insurance loss assessor that something's amiss. Let them investigate it.'

Sneed wondered how much of the missing stock the DC might be responsible for. He had answered the reported break-in with another DC. Horswood himself had taken a long time arriving at the shop, which probably meant he had been disposing of any valuable pieces himself.

CRO showed that Pauly Neal had two previous convictions. One for demanding money with menaces at the age of twenty-one; then two years later for assault, for which he was sentenced to twelve months. That was three years ago. So either he'd been slack or successful since.

Neal's last known address was in a terrace that had been fashionable in an era that had since lapsed from memory. The house looked like it was one step from a condemnation order, which probably made no significant difference to the rents being charged. Sneed wasn't really expecting Neal to still be in residence but he always thought of himself as an optimist. The sagging landlady, who had brown roots growing through her split blonde hair, couldn't even remember the tenant, which wasn't surprising. Even less was the fact of no forwarding address.

The local CID were of little help. Their records had long since gone to Scotland Yard. They made a few suggestions about clubs and snooker halls on their patch, and Sneed and his DS made the rounds. The local spots were full of possible Neals, but none matching the photograph.

Despite having friends able to risk five-thousand pounds surety for his bail, plus proceeds from the robbery, James's home environment was as mean as that in which his confederate had once lived. The house was situated behind Westbourne Grove. The housekeeper, who appeared no less a sloven than the previous, was indignant at having her bell rung. She demanded to know who was calling. Sneed produced his ID, and pushed on past her, ignoring her remarks. James lived at the top of the house; a lift was too much to expect.

'You wanna start training, Lenny,' Sneed said, rounding the first landing and hearing his partner's breath getting short. Like Feast's diet, training was also promised for tomorrow.

A woman in her mid-twenties opened the door. She didn't instantly recognize them as detectives as Sneed walked in past her. Feast followed.

'Oh, do come in,' she said sarcastically.

James appeared from the kitchen, quickly recovering his surprise. 'They're reasonably friendly, Jill.'

A bedroom, lounge and kitchen was all the threadbare flat comprised. Feast made a tour, kitchen first, while James watched, a little anxiously.

'Turning me over again?'

An earlier visit by two detectives after his arrest had revealed nothing.

'Anything here?' Sneed asked.

'Not what you're after.'

'We're looking for your partners.'

James's eyes followed Feast from the kitchen across to the bedroom door, and he hesitated a little too long.

'Leave off, you might embarrass them,' he tried.

Giving him a cold glance, Feast pushed into the bedroom. The large dip in the bed accommodated two – the dying man's last wish was, it seemed, to perpetuate his line. The male occupant wrenched round to protest, but didn't.

'Paul Neal.' Feast wasn't asking.

'Not me,' the man in bed replied, glancing warily at Sneed as he joined the DS.

'You'll do,' Sneed said. 'Up, both of you.'

'What's it all about then?'

'We've some business to discuss.'

'Would you mind leaving the room while we get dressed?'

'Get up!' Sneed ordered. The man, who was certainly Neal, responded, his sexual excitement fading rapidly as he started in to his clothes. 'And you,' Sneed told the woman.

'I'm not getting out of bed to give you a thrill.'

'Thrill?' Feast questioned. 'Haven't I seen you bashing along Old Compton Street?' He tugged at the sheets, which she clutched to herself with a sense of desperation.

'Bastards,' she screamed finally. 'You think you own people,' she added as she hurried pulled on her panties, then finished dressing in silence.

The process of searching Neal didn't pass without protest.

'You got a warrant?'

'You're on his property,' Sneed said, nodding towards James. 'He gave us permission.' Neal had no ID on him. 'Name?'

'Burton. Richard Burton.'

'I'm Elizabeth Taylor. Where were you around eleven yesterday?'

'Working.'

'Working? Where's that, near Guildford?' Neal didn't get the joke. 'Who's your employer?'

'Ibex Brushes. I'm a door-to-door salesman.'

'Bit of a comedown, uncle. We heard you were selling money.' Neal didn't reply. 'A dozen satisfied customers will give you an alibi, no doubt?'

'More than a dozen, cock.'

'I wouldn't have thought you'd be able to go case for one,' Sneed said. 'Got any bracelets for him, Len?'

Suddenly that prospect caused Neal to panic, and thrusting Feast sideways, he tried legging it. Sneed moved fast and caught Neal in the groin with his toe, causing him to double up, screaming. Any inclination to run had suddenly vanished.

The woman went to Neal's assistance as the DS handcuffed him. 'You sadistic bastards,' she said, 'you didn't have to do that.'

'Didn't I? Keep it up, love, you'll get some.' Sneed waited, then said, 'You don't mind if we look round, Danny.' It wasn't a question.

'And if I did?'

James smiled resignedly. Sneed guessed he knew the rules of the game well enough, and that his bung had no bearing on Sneed seeing them enforced.

The money hadn't been at the flat when it had been previously searched in the small hours, but it might possibly have been brought there since, with greater peace of mind for knowing the place had been searched. Peace of mind often made villains careless.

The kitchen revealed nothing, apart from grease and dirt. The bedroom proved fruitless also, the mattress containing only tick, and the carpeting consisting of a piece three feet by six on the worn lino hadn't recently been disturbed – for that oversight Sneed would bollock the detectives who had earlier searched. There were no loose floorboards.

Eleven thousand pounds was found stuffed behind the antiquated gas-fire in the living room, and if so much as eleven pennies were hidden elsewhere, they were in a better place than either Sneed or Feast could think of.

'What did you do with the other grand?' Sneed asked generally. 'Pay your rent?' No one answered. 'The third partner has it, s'a million.'

'I wanna phone my brief,' Neal said from where he was sitting on the floor.

'We've phones at the station.' Feast helped him up.

Finding a hold-all in the bedroom, Sneed packed the money. 'You'll get the bag back,' he told James. 'Ladies?' They both protested their innocence, demanding to know why they had to go too. 'I'm undecided whether to charge you as accessories before or after.' He paused and looked at James, but didn't get the reaction he hoped he would: the third partner in exchange for the girls. He thought about reminding him of their business arrangement, but all he said finally was, 'We'll see how you shape up.'

With Neal in the rear of the car, Feast held the door for Sneed, who climbed in ahead of James's girl-friend. The other woman went in the front.

At the end of its journey the car disappeared down the ramp where it sloped through the arch and into the station's congested compound. The DS took Neal's arm up the iron steps into the building, and motioning the women ahead, Sneed followed with the money.

'Find Sergeant Waugh for me,' Sneed said to the first constable he saw.

The CID room had become busy. The general babble of conversation didn't decrease when Sneed entered with his company but a few heads turned. Handcuffs made rare appearances, and Sneed knew they suggested some sport might be imminent; the women were worth a look alone!

A TDC was sent to find two WDCs to accompany the women.

'Sit down there.' Neal and the two women sat as Sneed indicated. He then left the details for the DS to cope with.

Putting the bag on his desk, Sneed thought about the money. Even without the fifty per cent it would have cost to fence, it amounted to a poor wage for a probable twelve down the road. But then most felons never considered being caught, which was why prison rarely deterred, he supposed. Some blaggers were lucky, or clever enough to avoid capture, though the percentage was low.

Extension 086 clattered out, and rang on the third floor. It was a long time being answered – Sally or Sue was probably combing their hair, getting ready for the off. She finally picked up the phone, and through her gum-chewing or the roll which she hadn't time to eat in her lunch-break, she said, 'Detective Chief Superintendent Wiseman's office.'

'Inspector Sneed. Is he in?'

'One moment, Inspector.' The switching gear brought Wise-man on. 'Yes, Tery?'

'We've just recovered eleven of the missing twelve thousand. We've arrested a second member of the gang.'

The DCS laughed his delight down the phone. 'Well done, Terry. Bloody well done. Who is he?'

Paul Neal. Two previous. Not known here,' Sneed said. 'I'll get the guard down here for an ID.'

'What about James?'

'Be handy to get number three and the balance.'

'Don't lose number one, Terry. I'll leave it to you. Well done. Bloody well done.'

The patronizing bastard just didn't know how easy it was, Sneed thought. Picking up his external phone, he dialled the number of the security guard, to alert him about identifying Neal. As he replaced the phone Sergeant Waugh entered.

'Terry. Busy afternoon.'

'Out there, Steve. Paul Neal. Lenny'll fill you in.'

This sergeant wasn't one who was too concerned with formalities, and Sneed doubted if he would bother to take the prisoner to the front office for charging. Sneed dialled the Station Inspector's extension.

'Willy, Terry Sneed. Can you muster an ID parade. Subjects around six foot, slim build, dark, thirty?'

'A couple of hours Terry,' he said. 'If we're lucky.'

Sneed rang off. He stretched. He was pleased; it had been a good afternoon. Some aftenoons were born ugly; with a ne'er-go-right slant; they were best spent in a drinker, for whatever happened was beyond one's physical control: shoelaces broke, limbs ached, people screamed, tea tasted foul, coffee worse; it rained, or if the sun shone it was too hot. It was hot that afternoon, but bearable now, if not plesant; for on this particular afternoon things had broken just right and the performance had taken little effort.

THE STEAM PIG

A suspect in the next room screamed. Not continuously, but at irregular intervals which made concentration difficult. Then the typewriter unaccountably jammed. The report was not going to be finished on time; Colonel Du Plessis had stipulated four o'clock and it was already 3.55 with at least a page to go.

'So you can bloody well stick it, Colonel sir,' Lieutenant Tromp Kramer declared loudly. He was quite alone in the Murder Squad office.

And finally giving vent to a righteous anger. There was simply no sense in risking a hernia by hammering out the mundane events which had led to the sudden messy death of Bantu female Gertrude Khumalo. No sense at all.

Her killer, one Bantu male Johannes Nkosi, had resisted arrest just before dawn and was mostly in the intensive care unit at Peacevale Hospital. His chances of standing trial were minimal, the doctors said – which was one way of putting it. OK, so there would be an inquest. But an inquest was nothing compared to a court case. Nobody would be interested in more than a brief statement from the witness box. Nor would there be any trouble from the families involved. Gertrude's lot were more than satisfied with the way things had gone. Shanty town folk always relished a bit of rough justice administered in this world and the forensic niceties left for the next. As for Nkosi's relatives, they had never heard of him.

Plainly a lot of totally unnecessary paperwork and fiddle could be avoided by shelving the matter overnight. And the Colonel knew this only too well, the bastard. *He* had not been called out at 4 a.m.

Worse still, he would not even bother to glance through the report when he got it; if you've read one Bantu murder you've read the lot, he inevitably observed. All he wanted was the sordid particulars converted into a docket of nice clean paper which he could delicately press fore and aft with his rubber stamp. That done, he would smugly add the job to his Crimes Solved graph and get back to arse-creeping the Brigadier – yet another triumph for law and order reduced to a colonic toehold. The four o'clock deadline was quite arbitrary, a crude manifestation of incipient megalomania.

Which somehow brought the time up to a minute after the hour and the telephone rang.

Oh Jesus, the Colonel. The voice from the carpeted office above was petulant. Kramer swung the receiver away from his ear and ran a finger down the thigh of his calendar girl. She was delightfully brown.

The shrill squeakings stopped abruptly.

Kramer responded with practised contrition: 'Sorry, sir – I'll have it with you first thing tomorrow. *Hey?*'

Something had upset the Colonel but it was nothing to do with the report, that much was obvious. Kramer grabbed a ballpoint and managed to get down three names before the line went dead. Damn, he should have asked for a recap. He had not the faintest bloody idea what was going on.

Still, he had the names. While he did not know Theresa le Roux from Eve van der Genesis, the old music-hall turn of Abbott and Strydom was all too familiar. It gave more than a fair indication of where a fruitful investigation could start and about time, too.

He buzzed the duty officer, booked himself out, and left the building on foot. Georgie's place was just around the corner, behind the museum.

As Kramer turned into Ladysmith Street, he saw a taxi from the station rank draw up outside the funeral parlour. Almost immediately a great meal sack of a woman topped with ginger frizz launched herself at it from a side entrance, followed by an ageing cook boy dragging two suitcases. Then Georgie emerged cautiously into the street as if expecting sniper fire to do the soap-and-water bit with his hands.

Kramer sidestepped into a bus queue and watched the departure over the top of someone's evening newspaper.

Georgie's mute appeals were to no avail. Without sparing him a glance, Ma Abbott heaved herself aboard the taxi. It shuddered and then took off with a squeal of contempt from its tyres.

Somebody had been a naughty boy again. And this time the old bitch was not going to share in the disgrace. To give her credit where it was due, her loyalty had so far been remarkable, even at the height of the Sister Constance scandal. That was when Georgie had forgotten to finish off the eyes and had displayed the nun in the chapel with a lewd wink for her mourners.

The bus had been and gone and Kramer was standing alone on the kerb. Georgie had vanished. There was no more playing for time to be had – he would have to take a chance on his penchant for patterns.

The front office was empty apart from an elderly customer intent on a catalogue of ornate headstones. From the look of her, she had not a moment to lose.

Kramer went to the farthest end of the high counter and gave the service bell a pat. There was a responding clatter from somewhere offstage behind the curtains. Then nothing. Perhaps Georgie kept a cat – although Christ knew what mice would find to eat in the place.

He rang the bell again, twice.

Come to think of it, a satin-quilted de luxe model would make mice one hell of a boudoir. Maybe they came round at night to sleep and have their friends in. Hmm, premature burial was a risk. No doubt that could account for the frequent preoccupation of pallbearers processing with their ears pressed against the coffin side: they were evaluating the frantic scratching sounds from within.

But it would take some cat to tweak a peephole in the curtains five feet above their hem. And to creak the floorboards so loudly in retreat. Kramer found all this instructive and reassuring. Something was definitely in the air.

An impression which was confirmed almost immediately by the arrival of Sergeant Fanie Prinsloo, who was standing in as official photographer for the week.

'Come to take my little snaps,' he said cheerily, dumping an enormous gadget bag on the counter. Prinsloo could never resist bringing every damn bit of equipment with him; ordinarily he worked in Fingerprints and had to satisfy his artistic drive at weekends with a box camera.

Kramer greeted him guardedly.

'What gives, Lieutenant?' Prinsloo said after a pause.

'You try,' Kramer suggested, pushing across the bell.

Prinsloo was plainly puzzled by all this standing around on ceremony. But he grinned and thumped it with his sirloin of a fist. Still nothing happened.

So Kramer sighed and Prinsloo mistook relief for agitation. Not that the sergeant was stupid, simply new to CID and as yet poorly acquainted with the men in the Murder Squad – something which Kramer intended to exploit. His ploy was to invert the unwritten law No. 178/a which states it is an officer's prerogative to pretend ignorance in order to establish the efficiency of subordinates.

'Right, Sergeant, what were your orders?' Kramer challenged.

Orders was a rather strong word to use in the context of a routine assignment, but Prinsloo recognized the ritual and replied very properly: 'I was told to report to you here and to take what pictures seemed necessary.'

'Of?'

'Some dolly or other.'

'Name?'

'Er – something le Roux, sir.'

'Theresa le Roux?' Kramer snapped, inducing the required degree of discomfiture.

Predictably, in an attempt to appease, it now all came out in a rush: 'Look sir, I was in the darkroom when the chief starts yelling through the door that I'd better get down here quick because you are on your way and Doc Strydom has done a PM on the wrong body because Abbott made a balls and it's murder.'

Kramer remained silent – which took some doing.

'That's all he said, sir. Plus the name. But you—'

'No need to get like that, Sarge,' Kramer said soothingly. 'Got to keep you new boys on your toes.'

So that was it. A murder. And for once it sounded like the real thing.

Prinsloo just had time to grab his gear before Kramer disappeared through the curtains. Beyond them was the chapel, which reeked of stale vase water, and then a passage lined with floral tributes waiting to be distributed to the sick. Stepping carefully, they reached a door marked MORTUARY and pushed it open.

Dr Strydom was alone. He turned sharply at the sound of the door slamming back on its spring and hurriedly waddled over.

'Ah, Lieutenant, I'm delighted to see you.'

'Doctor.'

'Got my little message, did you?'

'Sort of.'

'Ah.'

'What's been going on here, then?'

Dr Strydom overtly looked round Kramer to see if there was anyone standing behind him.

'You've not seen Mr Abbott? Strange, I thought he was out there. This little affair is *rather* delicate.'

'Oh yes?'

A deep breath, then: 'In a nutshell, Lieutenant, I'm afraid there's been a bit of a muddle. Two cadavers, both female, and my official one got cremated this afternoon.'

Prinsloo clucked his tongue like a wog washerwoman finding pee stains.

'Where does that leave us?' Kramer enquired coldly. He had not moved since entering.

Dr Strydom paused to pick his words.

'You could say a lot better off – if not too much fuss is made.'

Now Kramer was certain that the district surgeon had been party to the little affair, as he called it. Georgie had not accomplished it all by himself. However, that side of it could be dealt with later when the old dodderer's co-operation and self-confidence were not so essential. He shrugged negligently.

'Uhuh. Who went in the oven?'

'I took the liberty of checking while you were coming over,' Dr Strydom replied. 'Some poor old dear found under a bush down near Mason's Stream where the sherry tramps hang out. Just a routine. Age? Booze? Both probably. Somebody to sign the certificate. A right tart in her day I hear.'

Kramer turned his gaze to the table.

'And this one? Another tart?'

'I very much doubt it,' Dr Strydom answered, snapping the cuffs of his rubber gloves.

'But you're sure it's murder?'

'Oh, yes! Why not see for yourself?' His tone became curiously gleeful, rather like an amateur magician's opening patter. Friends, I am about to utterly astonish you.

So the two detectives followed him over. On the way Kramer realized why the one place he hated seeing a stiff was a morgue. The trouble was the height of the table which gave you no opportunity to adjust to the sight by degrees on the approach. You had to be on top of it before you knew what it was all about.

Where Mr Abbott had last seen his Ophelia, Kramer now saw a life-size rag doll. Or so it seemed. Large knives, hardly scalpels, are used for opening a body. This one was now held together again by thick black thread in Dr Strydom's erratic herringbone stitch with the surgeon's tow stuffing protruding at intervals. It was also a patchwork of bright colours – the sun having shifted across to act like a giant projector lamp behind the stained glass windows. When Dr Strydom switched on the main light he heightened the illusion by rendering the hues in pastel, which better suited the form, and by making the untouched head and shoulders gleam like fine porcelain. Kramer noticed that a very tiny brush had been used to paint on such long eyelashes.

And he concentrated for a while on the head. One thing was certain: he had never seen it before – that was a face you would never forget. He bent to examine the hair roots.

'Yes, it's dyed,' Dr Strydom said. 'Brown eyes, you see. A common enough failing among nice young women, not only tarts.'

Kramer jerked a thumb crudely.

'Well, on a rough guess, I'd say she lost her virginity about a year ago,' Dr Strydom chuckled. 'But that doesn't amount to much these days either. You should see—'

'Any kids?'

'No, never.'

'Disease?'

'None.'

'Then the chances are she wasn't sleeping around, just having it with a steady.'

'Right.'

'That gives us something to go on. Recently, do you think?'

'Possibly not within twelve hours of death. Although it would depend on precautionary method preferred.'

Kramer smiled wryly at the lapse into clinic jargon. The old bugger was more himself now.

'Well, Doc, what about the MO?'

'Like to take a guess?'

'After you've hacked her around? It looks like a Mau Mau atrocity. What did the death cert. say?'

'Cardiac.'

'And what was it?'

'Bicycle spoke.'

The words stabbed. Christ, this was really something. Bantu murdering Bantu was nothing. White murdering white was seldom any better, they just had counsel who could make a ready reckoner wring your heart. But mix Bantu and white together and you had instant headlines two inches high. It remained to be seen how much larger they could grow when it was known that a bizarre Bantu weapon had been used.

Kramer gestured impatiently for the district surgeon to turn the body on its side.

'Know what the Lieutenant's up to?' Dr Strydom asked Prinsloo.

'He's looking for puncture marks along the spine,' Prinsloo whispered, 'where they put the spoke in to paralyse her – like Shoe Shoe.'

Dr Strydom smiled smugly.

'She's *dead*, not paralysed, man. What's happened here is along the same lines but the intent is quite different. Think for a moment. When the spoke's used by the local boys they sterilize the point first wth a match. Why? So there won't be any infection. So the victim will live to regret his mistakes as long as possible. Like Shoe Shoe, as you said.

'Here, however, it is used the way I saw it done thirty years ago on the Rand, in the Jo'burg townships. Not often, mind you, and it's so clever we probably missed dozens on a Monday with the weekend to clear up. Speciality of the Bantu gangs. Look . . .'

Dr Strydom pulled the left arm away from the body and propped it at right angles on the edge of the slab. He pointed.

'Tell me what you see there,' he said.

Kramer stopped. It was an armpit. A small, hairy armpit. The girl had not used a razor, unusual but without significance.

'Now look again,' Dr Strydom urged, parting the tufts with a retractor.

'Flea bite?'

'All quite simple if you have the stomach for it,' Dr Strydom explained. 'You take your spoke, nicely sharpened up on a brick, and slide it in here between the third and fourth rib. Your target's the aorta where it ascends from the heart.'

'Yirra, you call that simple,' Prinsloo scoffed.

'Oh, but it is. You just aim for the high point on the opposite shoulder. The artery is pretty tough so you know when you've hit it. An expert can do it first time, a novice may take a few shots – like trying to spear spaghetti round on a plate.'

Prinsloo backed off a pace. Big and paunchy, he looked a man who enjoyed his food.

'And then?' Kramer was engrossed.

'Man, the pressure in that aorta's fantastic,' Dr Strydom

continued. 'I've seen blood hit the ceiling with an aneurism that burst during an op. But as you withdraw a thin thing like a bike spoke, it seals off see? All those layers, muscles, lungs, tissue, close up. You just wrap a hankie or rag round the spoke in the armpit and that takes care of any on the way out.'

Kramer straightened up, patted his pockets for cigarettes and took one the district surgeon proffered.

'Not bad, not bad at all, Doctor.'

Dr Strydom attempted modesty: 'Of course I tracked it down from all the blood loose in the cavities. One can't really blame Matthews, I suppose.'

'Who's that?'

'Her doctor, a GP out Morninghill way. The visible signs were identical to certain types of cardiac arrest. She had a history, I'm told.'

That was a slip. In Kramer's experience death certificates never mentioned case histories. This meant that the DS must have already been in touch with Matthews. Pity, now he would have all his excuses off pat, but that was the medical brotherhood for you – more closely knit than the Mafia and often as deadly. Still, he would let that pass, too. He had one or two questions to go.

'How long would it have taken her to die?'

'Ten minutes, fifteen at the outside; although if the shock itself was great enough I'd say almost immediately.'

'Uhuh. Scream?'

'She could've but it'd only take a pillow to muffle it. There's no facial bruising. Anyhow, with her brain starved of blood she'd be out pretty quickly.'

'What about this bruising on her arm?'

'Can't be positive. Easily come by when you've been thrashing round in a convulsion.'

This association of violent action with the violently inactive Miss le Roux had the subtle obscenity of a warm lavatory seat. Kramer decided he had had enough.

'She's all yours, Sergeant. When you've finished the ones for your private album, I'd like a set of six head-and-shoulders not looking too glum.'

Dr Strydom accompanied him from the room.

'Where's Abbott?' Kramer demanded in the passage.

'Here, officer,' came a meek voice from the chapel. And although Ma Abbott had gone, and Farthing was out doing a country removal, he insisted on being interviewed in his show-room, which had a soundproof sliding door.

At this point Dr Strydom took his leave, having suddenly remembered his daily appointment beside the triangle in the central prison. Those sentenced to strokes would already be lining up and waiting for him. He had to certify them fit for punish-ment, see the kidneys were properly protected, and keep an eye on responses. Buttocks are a common vehicle of abuse, but it is not prudent to abuse them overmuch.

FRANCIS KING

ACT OF DARKNESS

'I think it might be a good idea if you were to pop over to take another dekko,' the Governor told his Inspector-General of Police. 'It's a damned nuisance that Hunt should be on leave. I'm not all that happy about the way Singh seems to be handling the case. There have been far too many rumours and innuendoes in the press. He must have been talking. That's always the trouble with Indians, even the most educated. Blab, blab, blab. Can't keep their mouths shut.'

The Inspector-General, Ross, had a high opinion of Singh, whom he thought a far abler officer than his white superior Hunt; but he had no intention of voicing any disagreement with the Governor, who could so easily become pettish and spiteful. 'I'll go over tomorrow,' he said. 'I've been in constant touch on the blower, of course – and Singh's been sending over his reports. But I've been meaning to take another look at things myself.'

The Governor drew in his lips and sucked on his bristly grey moustache. When his subordinates imitated him, it was always doing this. 'It's an important case, an extremely important case. I'd like to see the man – or men – caught as quickly as possible. Not only for the sake of the family but as a deterrent to any madman planning something similar in future.'

When he had left the Governor's office, Ross telephoned to Singh.

'Would you like to meet me up at the house?' Singh suggested.

'Good God, no. The case is yours. I don't want Thompson to think I'm involved in any way. No, I'll call at the station. About ten-thirty. I'll be riding over.'

Putting down the receiver, Singh experienced an all too familiar disgust with his English superiors. Why the hell shouldn't Thompson be allowed to think that the Inspector-General was involved? Presumably because it might make their next game of golf, bridge or billiards embarrassing.

On his arrival, Ross at once began to light his pipe, without asking Singh's permission. Singh loathed the smell of the shag, imported in huge tins from England. He could still detect it in his office days after Ross had gone. 'The Governor would like to see things brought to some conclusion.'

'So should I. But the conclusion has to be the right one. Hasn't it?'

'More than a week has passed.' Ross shifted his massive bulk in a leather armchair too narrow for it. 'What's holding up the inquest?'

'Enquiries,' Singh answered coolly.

'Frankly, I don't get it. You may or may not catch the brute or the brutes. The Governor very much hopes you will. I very much fear you won't. But why can't the inquest go ahead? Murder by person or persons unknown. That's the only verdict possible.'

'Is it?' Singh got up and went to the open window, to escape the pipe smoke billowing towards him. 'It seems to me increasingly likely that what we have here is an inside job.'

'One of the servants?'

'Possibly. Though I doubt it.' The Indian put a delicate hand over his mouth and coughed behind it. 'My almost immediate assumption was that the boy had been killed by the governess and her boyfriend.'

Ross raised his bushy eyebrows, biting on his pipe stem.

'Let's suppose that he was visiting her in secret. And let's suppose that the child woke up and began to scream. They had to silence him. One or other of them stuffed that brassière – the first thing to hand – over his mouth and suffocated him without meaning to do so. Then they had to make it look as if someone from outside – a dacoit, some old enemy of Thompson's paying off a score – had committed the crime. So they mutilated the child, left that window open and dumped him in the privy.' Singh walked back towards his chair. 'Unfortunately, however, that doesn't work. The boyfriend was in his ward at the convalescent home throughout the night. I have eleven witnesses.' He smiled: 'Though I suppose that eleven people could be lying. It's happened before.' He reseated himself and leant forward, elbows on desk and hands clasped before him. He stared at Ross. Then: 'The father?'

'Thompson!' Ross's square face, under close-cropped hair, grew congested with annoyance. 'No man kills his own child.'

'Doesn't he? Men *have* killed their own children. I don't have to tell you that. And perhaps he didn't mean to kill him . . . I should guess that he and the governess are carrying on together.'

'Old women's gossip!'

Singh gave that small, supercilious smile which always irritated his English colleagues. 'Then there must be a lot of old women of both sexes around here at present. You know his reputation. Everyone says that he was carrying on with the present Mrs Thompson while the first Mrs Thompson was dying on him. So he falls for Miss O'Connor, who used to work as a clerk in one of his hotels. He offers her the job of governess. They start an affair – after all, his wife is pregnant. That night he goes to her, slipping out of his dressing room without his wife hearing. Or if she does hear, she thinks nothing of it. He's gone to the lavatory, she decides. Or he's set off on his nightly round of checking all the windows and doors. The child wakes, screams. There's a panic – which results in one of them stuffing the brassière over or into his mouth.'

Ross shook his head: 'I don't buy that one.'

'Isn't there a likelihood of Thompson being appointed to the

Viceroy's Council? Well, there you are! Another reason for panic. If there were to be an open scandal on top of all the hints and rumours . . . We all know what a prude the Viceroy is.'

'I still don't buy it. What *does* seem to me possible is that some Indian, cuckolded by Thompson, may have decided on revenge. Now what about that?'

'Well, yes, of course, that's something I've considered.' Singh's eyes had begun to water from the smoke. He took out a silk handkerchief from his breast pocket and began to dab at them. 'I've considered everything. However unlikely.' The arrogance of the claim annoyed Ross, even though he had to accept that, yes, Singh was the kind of officer, patient and pertinacious, who would examine every possibility before reaching a decision. 'But now . . . there's one suspect I favour above all others.' Singh paused, as though in a deliberate attempt to prolong the suspense of the revelation to follow.

'Well?'

Singh turned his head sideways, to gaze out of the window, as though to avoid Ross's gaze. 'The girl.'

'The governess?'

'No. The other girl.'

'The daughter?' Ross was astounded.

Singh nodded. 'Helen,' he murmured, savouring the name on his tongue as though it were something exotically pungent.

'Why the hell should you pick on her?'

'Well, for one thing – motive.'

'Motive.'

Singh once more leaned across the desk, hands clasped before him. 'It wouldn't be true to say that she and her stepmother had open rows. But it does seem to be generally agreed in the station that they have little use or affection for each other.' Singh twisted the outsize signet ring on his little finger. 'A number of people have told me that Mrs Thompson was, well, not exactly enthusiastic about the prospect of her stepdaughter arriving in the household. And the stepdaughter, when she did get here, seemed to go out of her way to avoid Mrs Thompson.' He picked up a pen from the tray before him. 'Don't forget that the present Mrs Thompson had already entered Thompson's life as so-called housekeeper when the first Mrs Thompson was still living,' he said in a didactic tone, using the pen to emphasize each word. 'Helen would then have been – what? – eight or nine.'

Ross pulled a face, half closing his eyes and drawing down the corners of his mouth, the pipe jutting upwards. Clearly, he was not much impressed.

Singh continued patiently: 'The boy – Peter – was fond of his half-sister. There's no doubt of that. But was she fond of him? The ayah doesn't think so. Visitors to the house don't think so. She's a girl who's fond of children in general – a successful and popular leader of the Bluebells – but with this particular child everyone noticed how cold and even harsh she could be. A neighbour, Mrs Anderson, told me how, when she was playing bridge there one afternoon, the child tried to climb up into Helen's lap but she at once pushed him off. Mrs Anderson told me that some time ago – before the murder – but it stuck in my mind. Mrs Anderson said it was as if the girl could not bear him to be near her. I've heard the same thing from other people . . . The boy made a bead bookmarker for his half-sister – rather touching – but since then no one's seen it, she's not used it, not once. The ayah told me that.'

'Oh, the ayah!'

'There's another Bluebell leader of the same age – Colonel Simpson's daughter. You know her, I'm sure.'

Ross nodded. 'Betty.'

'Well, Betty told me – when I was making what I hope were discreet enquiries – that Helen once spoke of her half-brother as a "beastly little brat".'

Ross shook his head, smiling indulgently. 'I've often referred to my own children as beastly little brats – or worse. But that doesn't mean I'd kill them. Though I may have wanted to do so on a number of occasions.'

'She's an odd girl.' Singh did not add that, from the start, this oddness had had an almost erotic fascination for him. 'A tragedy takes place, all the other members of the family, even the grandmother, are in a state of numb shock. But she goes on with her daily pursuits – her Bluebell meetings, her visits to the bazaar, her morning rides – as though nothing had taken place.'

'I'd have thought that to be a sign of innocence, not of guilt. If a young girl committed a murder as horrible as that, surely she'd go to pieces.'

'Not that young girl. She has an amazing strength.'

Helen reminded Singh of a deodar in his garden. A branch of the slim, graceful tree, with its pendant racemes, as though of pale green lace dripping from it, had begun to rub against his bedroom window. When the wind blew strong, as it often did up here, he would give way first to irritation and then to fury at an insistent scratch, scratch, scratch on the windowpane as he tried to go to sleep. One night he jumped out of bed, fetched a saw, opened the window, and leaning far out, attempted to sever the slender, elegant branch. But, so pliable and delicate in his hand, it resisted with an amazing persistence. He pushed the saw back and forth and then, when he looked to see what he had achieved, in the moonlight he could make out no more than a slight indentation, black on grey, where the bark had been fretted. Sweating and grunting and in constant danger of over-balancing, he had eventually managed to sever the branch. By the time that he had done so, he had conceived for the tree a murderous animosity, as for some living creature bent on thwarting his will.

Ross once again shifted his huge bulk – he had once been a Rugby football player and even now refereed games for the army. Then, massaging his broken nose with the tip of his forefinger as though in a vain attempt to coax it back into shape, he said: 'All right. There's a motive, let's accept that. But a motive is not enough by itself. Is it? We all have motives for committing a variety of crimes but the fact is that most of us do not commit them.' He stared challengingly at Singh. 'What evidence have you got, hard evidence?'

'Some. Admittedly not much.'

Singh began to relate what he had learned from the ayah.

One morning, when he had been climbing, with many pauses for breath, up the steep hillside path to the house – next time, he had decided, he must really come on horseback, much though he hated it – a white-robed figure had suddenly and silently emerged from behind some bushes. It was the ayah. She had bowed to him over hands pressed together, palm against palm, and had then said: 'Sahib, may I talk to you?'

'Here?'

Without replying, she had turned away from him and begun to walk off down a narrow footpath zigzagging into the woods. Singh, exasperated but curious, had followed her.

In a clearing, the folds of her cotton sari white against the pale grey boles of the trees, she had turned.

'Well?' His tone had been peremptory; but the ayah, used to people addressing her in that manner, had not flinched. 'I wish to tell you two things, sahib. But you must not tell anyone that I have told you.'

'You need not worry. What you tell me will be secret.'

The ayah had been satisfied. Calmly, in a low, measured voice, she had first told him about the nightdress. Helen had a nightdress, a pink chiffon nightdress, with embroidery here – the ayah had touched her wrinkled neck with a hand – beautiful embroidery. There was only one such nightdress. She had often folded it up when making Helen's bed, she had often laid it out when turning down the same bed. After the night when the child had been killed, the nightdress had vanished. She had laid it out but the following morning she had found another nightdress, a cream-coloured nightdress with no embroidery, in its place.

Then there was the knife. In the gloom of the trees, with a shrill cacophony of birds all around and above him, clamorously insistent, Singh had felt that quickening of the pulse, constriction of the temples and slight breathlessness familiar to him from all those occasions in the past when he had known, known with total certainty, that he was on to something. A knife? Deliberately he had suppressed any appearance of excitement. What knife did she mean? The girl had had a knife in a sheath, the ayah had answered. For her work with the Bluebells. A big knife, sharp, sharp. The ayah's eyes had widened. She always took it with her, on her belt, when she went down the hill to the Bluebell meetings. The knife was gone. Gone? Singh had again suppressed any appearance of excitement. The ayah had nodded vigorously. Gone! She had searched the room, not once, not twice, but three times. Usually the knife lay in the second drawer down of Helen's dressing-table, under a pile of underclothes. It was no longer there, no longer anywhere. Vanished.

'I see. Yes. Yes.' Singh had nodded, smiled, nodded again. He had not wished the ayah to know how important he had considered this information. 'Well, thank you. That may be useful to me. I don't know.'

Suddenly, under the fold of the sari over her head, there had been a dangerously glittering look in the ayah's eyes. 'I think she killed my *baba*,' she had hissed. 'I think so.'

Singh had stared at her for a moment and she had boldly stared back. Then he had begun to return along the woodland path, expecting her to follow him. But when, after two or three bends, he had glanced over his shoulder, she was nowhere to be seen. Was that the white of her sari between the tree trunks over there? He had peered, halting in his tracks. No, it was only a sheet of newspaper, probably used at some time by someone who had been obliged to come here, off the road, to defecate. He had hurried on, thankful when he had at last left the shrill gloom of the woods for the sunlit calm of the open road.

When he had arrived at the house, he had been amazed to see the ayah shaking a blanket out of an upstairs window. Clearly, she had taken some short cut. She had paused and, very still, had looked down at him, the blanket billowing outwards from the hands that had tethered it. Then she had given it a jerk, drawn back both it and her head, and vanished from sight.

. . . Ross shrugged. 'Well, yes, that's something. If not very much. I suppose you followed it up?'

'Naturally.' Did the fat slob, sucking away at his pipe like a baby at a teat, imagine that he had merely ignored a lead so important?

Once already Singh had interrogated Helen. No, she had heard nothing in the night. Yes, she had been along to the lavatory at about twelve-fifteen before switching off her light. Yes, before that, while she was reading in bed, she had heard her father going round the house, as he always did, to make sure that all the latches and bolts were fastened. Yes, she tended to sleep heavily. No, she had known nothing of Peter's disappearance until her grandmother had knocked on her bedroom door. Her manner had been possessed, her voice clear and steady. 'I wish I could think of something else to tell you that might be of help. But I can't.'

He had then gone over the whole story of the discovery of the body in the pit. Helen had remained composed, even matter-of-fact, as he had elicited one gruesome detail after another. 'I shouted to Clare to fetch the torch . . . We always keep it on a table in the hall – in case of a power failure . . . Unfortunately, the battery was all but worn out, so that it gave only this feeble glow . . . But I was able to make out . . .'

Now, after what the ayah had told him, Singh had asked to see Helen again.

One leg crossed over the other, her hands resting lightly on the arms of her chair, she had sat opposite him in the small downstairs room, used as an extra guest room, which Toby had suggested that the police should make into their office as long as their investigations continued at the house.

'I've one or two more questions,' Singh had begun.

She had inclined her shingled head, smiling. 'No objection.'

'Firstly, I want to ask you about a nightdress.'

'A nightdress? You mean, a nightdress of mine?' He had been watching her reaction closely; she had given no sign of shock or alarm.

'One nightdress had been put out for you by the ayah on the night of the killing. But it seems that that night you wore another one. Or, at least, the ayah found another one on your bed in the morning.'

She had thought for a moment, her chin on her palm. Then she had nodded: 'Yes, that's right.'

'You mean you didn't wear the nightdress laid out for you by the ayah?'

'No. I noticed it was soiled. So I put it in the basket for the dhobi and got myself another.'

'Soiled? How do you mean?' He had had to make an effort to keep the excitement out of his voice, just as he would do when, back in England, he came on a rare Kipling first edition priced at sixpence or a shilling.

'Well . . .' For the first time she had looked disconcerted; she had even begun to blush. Singh had thought: Now we're getting somewhere. His heart seemed to be hammering against his breastbone. 'In the way that women sometimes soil their clothes,' she had murmured. Then she had amplified, almost defiantly: 'I was beginning my period.'

Now it had been his turn to be disconcerted. 'I see. I'm sorry to have to ask these intrusive questions. But there's no way of avoiding them.'

'I understand that.'

'So the nightdress would have gone to the laundry?'

She had nodded. 'On Monday.'

'And when would it have come back?'

She had thought: 'Oh, I should imagine three or four days ago. The dhobi takes anything up to five days – if the weather isn't good. That's about normal, isn't it?'

'And has it come back?'

She had shaken her head. 'No.'

'No?'

'I was hoping that perhaps you were going to tell me what had happened to it. That's my favourite nightdress. Harvey Nichols. A present from my Aunt Sophie in England.'

'Why hasn't it come back?'

She had laughed. 'I only wish I knew. From time to time something gets "lost".' She had put the word into ironic inverted commas. 'I'm sure you must often have the same experience with your dhobi. And the odd thing is that it's always something new or attractive. Old handkerchiefs, for example, never fail to turn up.'

'You mean the dhobi stole your nightdress?'

'I don't know what to think. It appears on the list but the dhobi says that, when he unpacked the basket, it wasn't there. He often says that when something disappears.'

'And who made up the list?'

'I did.'

'You?'

'I often do it for my stepmother. On this occasion, it seemed obvious I must do it. She was – fit for nothing.'

'And you checked the laundry on its return?'

'Yes, I checked it. And told the dhobi that item was missing.'

'I see.'

'My father's terribly hard on the servants for the smallest dishonesty. He got into a rage the other day because a single banana had been taken from the fruit bowl. Booze, cigarettes, small change – it drives him up the wall. But it always amazes me they're as honest as they are. We pay them so little. Do you realize that nightdress probably cost three times the dhobi's earnings for a month? If he pinched it and sold it in the bazaar – as I suspect – well, I can't really be that angry.'

'I'll have a word with him.'

'Will you? But don't be too hard on him. No third degree, I hope.' He had not been able to decide whether she was being ingenuous or disingenuous. How could someone so intelligent have failed to grasp the tenor of his questions?

'There's something else.'

'Yes?'

'Would I be right in thinking you're the possessor of a scout knife?'

'Was.' Again he had been astounded that a question so fraught with dangerous implications should have failed to shake her. 'I lost it. We went to Biwali for a weekend camp not so long ago and I must have left it or dropped it somewhere. I need another but I've had no luck in finding one in a place as small as this. I suppose I'll have to wait until we get back to the plains.'

'Did you tell anyone about losing the knife?'

She had thought for a moment. 'No, I don't think so. Oh, I may have mentioned it to Clare. In fact, I think I did. It wasn't of much importance.'

He had looked closely at her. It was precisely because she had remained so casual and relaxed that his suspicions had been intensified. Any young girl in her position, obliged to answer questions indicating that she was suspected of a hideous crime, would, however innocent, show some shock, agitation, indignation. She had shown none. Her naturalness was, in itself, unnatural.

. . . Now Singh tried to explain all this to Ross; but the Englishman was irritably and irritatingly obtuse in taking his point. Knocking out his pipe on the ashtray before him, with so much vehemence that Singh feared that he would smash it, Ross exclaimed: 'If she were the one, she'd have given herself away! Bound to! At some moment or other. A hardened criminal might succeed in . . . But not someone so young and inexperienced.'

Singh shrugged. 'Anyway – I got nowhere with her.'

'Did you take up the question of the nightdress with the dhobi?'

'Of course.' Once again it exasperated Singh that the Englishman should feel obliged to check on something so obvious. 'As I expected, he said he'd never seen the garment. Told me that the girl had accused him of pinching it but was emphatic that he certainly hadn't done so. Mrs Thompson confirmed that at other times other items of laundry have gone missing – only two or three weeks ago the old lady lost a blouse. That time the dhobi said it must have been stolen off the line.'

'And the knife? Did you ask the governess about it?'

Singh picked up the ashtray between them and fastidiously emptied its charred debris into the waste-paper basket. He straightened, nodded.

He had knocked at Clare's bedroom door and she had called out: 'Yes? Who is it?'

'Inspector Singh.'

'Oh . . . Oh, all right. Come in.'

When he had entered, she was scrambling, barefoot, off her bed, her skirt unzipped and the top of her blouse open. With agitated fingers she had first pulled up the zip and then done up the buttons of the blouse. A hand had gone to her dishevelled hair, patting it into place. 'I was having a little nap. I've been sleeping terribly badly since . . . since . . . It would be even worse in *that* room but it's bad enough in here.' Her lower lip had trembled, distended itself. As she had stood facing him in her stockinged feet, her hands clasped tightly before her, she had looked so terribly thin, small and vulnerable that she had moved him to pity and then to anger with himself for feeling an emotion so alien to his nature. Almost roughly he had told her: 'Oh do sit.'

She had sunk down on to the edge of the bed and from there had looked up at him with a shrinking, beseeching look. Almost as though I were about to rape her, he had thought.

'I wanted to check something with you.'

Her tongue ran over her upper lip, like a child's exploring for traces of chocolate. 'Yes?'

'Did you know Miss Thompson owned a knife?'

'A knife?' The leaden-hued lids had blinked repeatedly over the terrified eyes. Then she had looked up at him and in a whisper had answered: 'Yes. Yes, a scout knife. She used to wear it on her belt when she went to the Bluebells.'

'And have you any idea of what's happened to it?'

She had peered all about her, like some hunted animal looking desperately for a hole or cranny through which to escape from its predator.

'Have you?' He had been disgusted to find that he actually enjoyed the spectacle and the smell (yes, he could smell it) of her terror of him.

At last she had gazed up at him. 'She told me she'd lost it. After that weekend they spent camping at Biwali. She came back and told me she'd lost it. Left it somewhere, dropped it somewhere. That's all I know.'

'You're sure of that?'

She had put her fingers to her lips, as she had done outside the privy when the body of the child had been found. It was a gesture similar to that which she used when she pressed a handkerchief, too ragged for any other purpose, to her lips to take off excessive lipstick. 'Yes, I'm sure.'

. . . 'Well, that confirms the girl's story,' Ross said, with obvious satisfaction. 'You haven't much to go on. Unless, of course, you think that the governess was her accomplice.'

Singh shook his head. 'No. I don't think that. But it's perfectly possible that Helen told Clare she'd lost the knife at Biwali merely in order to have a witness later. She then hid it until she needed it.'

'That argues premeditation over a period of – what? – two, three weeks.'

'Why not? The murder must have been premeditated – if she did it. She can hardly have decided on the spur of the moment to go down to the room, grab the child and kill him.'

'The trouble is – you just haven't got a case. Not one that stands up. There are some suspicious circumstances – nightdress, knife, both of them mislaid – but to a jury . . . No one's going to convict on the strength of just them. *I* wouldn't. *You* wouldn't.' Ross massaged his crotch with a large hand. 'If you'd found the nightdress or the knife . . .'

'We've looked for both, of course – in and around the house, everywhere. But in this sort of countryside – hilly, woody, much of it uninhabited – it's hard enough to find a man, let alone things as small as that. Under a rock, down a well, in another privy. She goes for long rides, usually by herself. I'd need a huge force of men to be sure every possible place had been covered.'

'And even then they'd probably miss out.'

Singh picked up a pencil from the tray before him and stabbed at the blotter. 'And yet . . . and yet I have this hunch.'

Ross shrugged and then flung out an impatient arm. 'Hunches are no good.'

MAJ SJÖWALL
AND PER WAHLÖÖ

....

COP KILLER

It was not a good car. Much too conspicuous for the purpose. A big, light green Chevrolet with three sevens in the license number, a lot of chrome, and a lot of lights.

On top of which it had been seen, and some nosy neighbor had already called the police.

It was early in the morning and rather cold, although it was going to be a warm day for some. The damp rose up from the ground and mixed with the mist drifting lazily in from the sea. The early morning light was grayish-white, hazy, and confusing.

In the back seat of the green car lay a pair of rolled-up oriental rugs, a television receiver, a transistor radio, and five bottles of liquor. The trunk contained several paintings, a figurine of doubtful origin, a pedestal, and some other odds and ends.

In the front seat sat two thieves. They were young and nervous and making a lot of mistakes. They both knew they'd been seen. And their luck was bad. The whole thing had begun badly and was going to get worse.

There were no street lights on at this hour, but the soft glow from the sky reflected in the film of dew that covered the car. The engine hummed gently and, with its lights off, the green car glided along between the hedges surrounding the private gardens on either side of the street. At the end of the block, it slowed and stopped. Then it swung out onto the highway, as cautiously as a circus tiger entering the ring. There had been no rain for some time, but the pavement was streaked with moisture and might have looked to the uninitiated as if it had just been cleaned. The initiated knew, however, that the department of sanitation didn't operate this far from town.

A light green American car with its headlights off. It slid through the mist like a phantom, almost soundless, its contours blurred.

The patrol car, on the other hand, was frighteningly matter-of-fact.

A black and white four-door Valiant with spotlights and two blue flashers on the roof. It was unmistakable. But just to be sure, the actual word POLICE was spelled out in highly visible letters on the doors, hood, and trunk.

Automobile density in Sweden was still high, and patrol car density abnormally so. It was more and more common for these vehicles to stop suddenly and spew out oddly clad men with weapons in their hands, and yet the human element in these occurrences was virtually nonexistent.

Squad cars poked about in unlikely places or stood poisoning the air with idling engines, while the average patrolman inside had a bad back and a steadily decreasing IQ even as he grew more and more alienated from society in general.

A policeman on foot was something of a curiosity these days, and in any case it was a sight that boded unpleasantness.

The patrol in question consisted of three policemen – Elofsson, Borglund, and Hector.

Elofsson and Borglund were an old patrol car team, and they looked like any other middle-aged policemen. Hector was younger and more gung-ho. They didn't really need him, to put it mildly. He was along for the fun of it, and for a little extra overtime. He was very proud of his well-tended sideburns, which seemed to have become standard equipment for younger policemen.

Borglund was lazy and pudgy, and at the moment he was asleep in the back seat with his mouth open. Elofsson was drinking coffee from a plaid Thermos bottle and drowsily smoking a cigarette. Hector disliked tobacco and had pointedly rolled down the side window. He sat with his hands on the wheel and stared silently out through the windshield with a morose and bored expression. All three men were wearing gray-blue uniforms of the jumpsuit variety, with shoulder belts and pistols and night sticks in white leather holsters.

The car was standing by the side of the road with its parking lights on. The engine was indeed idling, and poisonous exhaust fumes laid their shroud of death and suffocation over the languishing vegetation along the edge of the ditch.

None of the policemen had spoken for quite some time.

Hector had turned up the radio a little while ago, but Elofsson had immediately turned it down again, by right of several years' seniority. Hector had sense enough not to make a fuss, and the voice on the radio was now a subdued babble of almost sprightly remarks delivered in a foolish tone of voice. Elofsson wasn't listening at all, Borglund was breathing stertorously in the back seat, and Hector had to strain to hear what was being said.

'Good morning, good morning, good morning, dear friends and colleagues out on the highways and byways. We have a few little tidbits for you. A domestic disturbance on Björkgatan in Sofielund. Complaints about the noise, probably a drunken party. Closest patrol please check it out. What? Yes, music and singing. Björkgatan twenty-three. Suspicious hot rod outside an empty villa in Ljunghusen. Two-tone blue Chrysler, an A plate with three sixes in the number. Closest patrol will investigate. The address is Östersjövägen thirty-six. May be connected with a suspected burglary. A young man and two girls seen in the car. Routine check.'

'That's right nearby,' Hector said.

'What?' said Elofsson.

Borglund's only reaction was a slightly indignant snore.

'You fellows in the area might have a care,' said the voice. 'Usual procedure. Take no chances. Check out the vehicle if it shows up. Direction of travel unknown. Try not to attract attention. Take it a little easy if you spot this item. Ordinary routine checkout. Nothing more at the moment. Good morning, all.'

'That's right nearby,' Hector repeated.

Elofsson slurped some coffee from the mug of his Thermos but didn't say anything. Borglund turned in his sleep.

'Right in this neighborhood,' Hector said.

'Don't bust a gut, boy,' Elofsson said, rooting around in his cookie bag.

He sank his teeth into a cinammon twirl.

'Right close by,' Hector said. 'Let's go.'

'Easy, boy. It's probably nothing at all. And if it is something, we're not the only cops in the world.'

Hector flushed.

'What do you mean?' he said. 'I don't get it.'

Elofsson went on chewing.

Borglund sighed deeply in his sleep and whimpered. Perhaps he was dreaming about the National Commissioner.

They were no more than sixty feet from the intersection when the light green Chevvy swung onto the road ahead of them.

'There's the little bastards now,' Hector said.

'Maybe,' Elofsson said.

The word was muffled by a mouthful of food.

'Let's take 'em,' Hector said.

He put the car in gear and tramped on the gas.

The patrol car leaped forward.

'What?' said Borglund groggily.

'Burglars,' Hector said.

'Maybe,' Elofsson said.

'What?' said Borglund, still half asleep. 'What's going on?'

The youths in the green car didn't discover the patrol car until it was already beside them, and then it was too late.

Hector accelerated, cut in front, and jammed on the brakes. The police car skidded on the damp pavement. The green car was forced to the right and came to a stop with its front wheel three inches from the edge of the ditch. The driver didn't have much choice.

Hector was the first one out on the road. He had already unbuttoned his holster and drawn his 7.65mm Walther.

Elofsson got out on the other side.

Borglund was last, disoriented and breathing hard.

'What's going on here?' he said.

'No headlights,' said Hector in a shrill voice. 'That's a violation. Out of the car, you little sluts.'

He had his pistol in his right hand.

'And when I say "Now" I don't mean tomorrow, by God. Move!'

'Take it easy,' Elofsson said.

'No tricks,' Hector said.

The people in the green car climbed out on opposite sides. Their faces were white patches in the fog.

'Just a little routine chat,' Elofsson said.

He was closer to them than the others but still hadn't touched his revolver.

'Just take it easy,' he said.

Hector was standing behind him to one side, his revolver in his hand and his finger on the trigger.

'We haven't done anything.'

The voice sounded young. It could have come from a girl or from a boy whose voice was breaking.

'That's what they all say,' Hector said. 'Unlawful lighting, for example. What about that? Have a look in their car, Emil.'

From where he was standing, only a few yards away, Elofsson could see that the suspects were two young men. They were both wearing leather jackets, jeans, and tennis shoes, but the similarity ended there. One of them was big and dark, with a crew cut. The other was below normal height and had billowing, shoulder-length blond hair. Neither one of them looked to be more than twenty years old.

Elofsson walked toward the taller of the two youths, fingering his holster but not opening it. Instead, he moved his hand, took out his flashlight, and shone it into the back seat. Then he put it away again.

'Mmm,' he said.

Then he turned abruptly to the tall youth, grabbed for his clothing, and got a grip on the lapels of his jacket.

'All right, you little bastards,' said Hector from behind him.

'What's going on here?' Borglund said.

And that was apparently the remark that set things going.

Elofsson was following normal procedure. He had grabbed the boy's jacket with both hands. The next step was to pull the victim closer and drive his right knee into the man's groin. And that would take care of that. The same way he had done it so many times before. Without firearms.

But Emil Elofsson had kneed his last arrestee. The young man with the crew cut had other ideas. He had his right hand at his belt and his left hand in his pocket. There was a revolver stuck in the waistband of his jeans, and he obviously had no doubts about what it was for. He pulled it and started shooting.

The revolver was a weapon constructed for short range, a nickel-plated Colt Cobra .32 caliber with six shots in the chambered cylinder. The first two shots struck Elofsson in the diaphragm, and the third and fourth passed under his left arm. Both of these bullets hit Hector in the left hip and sent him reeling backwards across the highway where he fell on his back with his head resting on a low wire fence that ran along the edge of the road.

Shots numbers five and six rang out. They were presumably meant for Borglund, but he had a very human fear of guns and at the very first shot had thrown himself headlong into the ditch on the north side of the highway. The ditch was deep and damp, and his large body bounced heavily to the bottom. He wound up on his stomach in the mud, not daring to lift his face, and almost at once he felt a cruel, stinging pain on the right side of his neck.

Elofsson had already pushed off with his foot, and his knee was an inch or so in the air when the bullets struck his body. He clung tightly to the leather jacket and only let go when the man with the gun took several steps back and opened the cylinder to reload.

He fell forward and landed on his side, where he lay with one cheek against the pavement and his right arm trapped helplessly under his body, along with his pistol, still buttoned in its holster.

In spite of the uncertain light, he could see the young man distinctly as he stepped back and loaded new cartridges, which he apparently had loose in his jacket pocket.

Elofsson was in great pain, and the front of his uniform was already soaked and smeared with blood. He could neither talk nor move, only observe. And still he was more dumbfounded than afraid. How could this have happened? For twenty years he'd been driving around shouting and swearing, pushing, kicking, hitting people with his billy club, or slapping them with the flat side of his saber. He had always been the stronger, had always had the advantage of arms and might and justice against people who were weaponless and powerless and had no rights.

And now here he lay on the pavement.

The man with the revolver was twenty steps away. It had grown lighter, and Elofsson saw him turn his head and heard five words.

'Get in the car, Caspar!'

Then the man raised his left elbow, rested the barrel on the crook of his arm, and sighted carefully. At what?

The question was superfluous. A richochet glanced off the pavement less than a foot from Elofsson's face. At the same time, he heard a shot behind him. Was the other bastard shooting at him too? Or was it Borglund? He dismissed that idea. If Borglund wasn't dead already, he was lying somewhere pretending to be.

The man with the revolver was standing still. Legs apart. Aiming.

Elofsson closed his eyes. He felt the blood pulsing out of his body. He didn't see his life pass before his eyes. He merely thought: Now I'm going to die.

Hector hadn't dropped his pistol when he fell. He was lying on his back with his head propped up on the fence, and he too could see the figure with the revolver and the short black hair, though less distinctly and from a greater distance. What's more, Elofsson lay right in his line of fire, but pressed so tightly to the road that there was a free range above him.

145

In contrast to his colleague, Hector was not especially surprised. He was young, and this was roughly what his fervid imagination had always expected of this job. His right arm was still functioning, but there was something wrong with the left, and he had a hard time getting his hand on the housing of his pistol to cock it. And that had to be done, for in accordance with police regulations, he actually did not have a cartridge in the chamber. (Elofsson and Borglund did have, on the other hand, for all the good it did them.) He didn't succeed until the other man had fired the first shot of his second series.

Hector was in agony. The pain in his left arm and his whole left side was excruciating, and his vision was blurred. He fired his first shot carelessly and mechanically, and it went high.

This was not the time for wild shots, he could see that. Hector was generally a decent marksman on the range, but at the moment it would take more than decent marksmanship to save his life. The figure standing in the mist eighty feet away had all the advantages, and his behavior indicated that he wasn't about to go home until every policeman in sight was guaranteed stone dead.

Hector took a deep breath. The pain was so great he nearly lost consciousness. A bullet hit the fence, and the steel wires reverberated. The vibration passed on through the back of his head, and for one instant, his vision became amazingly clear and concentrated. He raised the pistol and forced himself to hold his arm straight and his hand still. The target was indistinct, but he could see it.

Hector squeezed off the shot. Then he lost consciousness, and the automatic fell from his hand.

Elofsson, however, was still conscious. Ten seconds earlier, he had opened his eyes again, and nothing had changed. The man with the revolver hadn't moved. Legs apart, the pistol barrel resting on his elbow, he was carefully and calmly taking aim.

He heard another shot from behind.

And, wonder of wonders, the man with the revolver gave a jerk and threw his arms up over his head. The weapon flew from his hand. And then, in a continuation of the same motion, he collapsed on the pavement and went utterly limp, as if there had been no skeleton in his body. He lay there in a heap. Not a sound crossed his lips.

It would be wrong to call it pure chance, for Hector had aimed carefully and done his very best. But it was an almost incredibly lucky shot. The bullet struck the man's shoulder and followed his collarbone directly to his spinal cord. The youth with the revolver died instantly, probably while he was still on his feet. He didn't even have a chance to lie down and draw his final breath.

Elofsson heard a car peel out and speed away.

And that was followed by total silence, abstract and unnatural.

After what seemed like a very long time, someone moved nearby.

After another long wait, though it could not have been more than minutes or even seconds, Borglund came crawling over on all fours. He was moaning and looking about aimlessly with his flashlight. He stuck his hand in under Elofsson, flinched, and pulled it back. And stared at the blood.

'Jesus Christ, Emil,' he said.

And:

'For God's sake, what did you do?'

Elofsson felt all the strength leave his body, and he could not talk or move.

Borglund got to his feet with gasps and groans.

Elofsson heard him clump over to the patrol car and switch the radio to the emergency frequency.

'Emergency! Come in! Highway 100 at Östersjövägen in Ljunghusen. Two men shot. I'm hurt myself. Gunfire. Shooting. Help!'

From a great distance, Elofsson heard metallic voices responding over the radio. First the nearby districts.

'Trelleborg here. We're coming.'

'Lund district. We're on our way.'

Finally the despatcher in Malmö.

'Good morning. Help on its way. It'll take about fifteen minutes. Twenty at the most.'

After a while, Borglund was back, fumbling with the first aid kit. He turned Elofsson over on his back, cut open his uniform, and started stuffing compresses in at random between his stomach and his blood-drenched underclothes. He kept up a steady, monotonous, thick-tongued babble.

'Jesus Christ, Emil. Jesus Christ.'

Elofsson lay there in the damp. His blood mixed with the dew. He was cold. It hurt even more than it had. He was still dumbfounded.

A little later he heard other voices. The people in the house behind the wire fence had woken up and ventured out.

A young woman knelt down beside Elofsson and took his hand.

'There, there,' she said. 'There, there. They'll be here soon.'

He was more dumbfounded than ever. A person was holding his hand. A member of the general public. After a while she put his head on her lap, and put her hand on his forehead.

They were still in that position when the scream of many sirens began to reach them, first very soft but soon shrill and piercing.

Just then the sun broke through the mist and spread a shallow, pale-yellow light over the absurd scene.

All of this took place on the morning of November 18, 1973, in the farthest corner of the Malmö Police District. For that matter, in the farthest corner of Sweden. Several hundred yards away, long shiny waves surged in against a curving sand beach that seemed to be endless in the fog. The sea.

On the other side was the European continent.

G. D. H. AND M. COLE

....

MURDER AT THE
MUNITION WORKS

Superintendent Wilson, when the chief constable had gone away, promptly rang up a friend of his, by name Tom Bracket, who was in ordinary times a Fellow of one of the Bullbridge colleges, but had taken service, for the duration, in one of the numerous emergency ministries. Tom Bracket, he knew, had taken an active part in Bullbridge local politics; and he would be pretty certain to know all the gossip about Timothy Sullivan and William Pearson, even if his absence from the university city had prevented him from getting all the inside dope about the Bullbridge murder. Tom was out when Wilson rang up; but Mrs Bracket was in, and she enthusiastically invited him round to take pot-luck at their tiny flat in Great Ormond Street.

Thither Wilson duly repaired, after clearing off a mass of small pieces of work that had to be left tidy before he could go off to Bullbridge. By the time he arrived, Tom Bracket had come in; and a savoury smell was exuding from the miniature kitchen of the flat. For Bracket prided himself on his prowess as a cook, and Helen Bracket always left that department of domestic economy in his hands when he was in the mood for it.

Helen had let him in; and Tom had shouted from the kitchen that she was to give the visitor a sherry until the onion soup was ready. Wilson, who liked the smell of onions, followed Mrs

Bracket into the little sitting-room, refused the sherry, and demanded beer, which was promptly provided. He took a deep draught and then asked Mrs Bracket if she knew the Sullivans.

'The woman who was blown up? Are you in on that, Harry?' Wilson nodded.

'What do you want to know about them?' Helen Bracket enquired; and Wilson said, 'Everything.'

'Tom knows them much better than I do, because he and Mr Sullivan were on the Council together.' She raised her voice and shouted into the kitchen. 'Tom, Harry wants to know about the Sullivans.'

'Tell him Sullivan's a revolting worm,' Tom Bracket shouted back.

'Tom hates him,' Helen interpreted. 'He was always up against him when he was on the City Council as one of the University members.' For under the peculiar constitution of the old university city, the University still retains the right to nominate a number of members to the City Council.

'Did Sullivan represent the University?' Wilson asked. 'I thought . . .'

'No, of course not. I meant Tom did. Mr Sullivan was a sort of Tory boss. Tom had a most frightful row with him over the housing of the men at the Anchor Works.'

'I had the chief constable of Bullbridge with me this afternoon. He appears to eat out of Mr Sullivan's hand.'

'Oh, of course. He would. He's one of the old gang Tom has been fighting ever since he got on the Council. Of course, Tom was supposed to be non-party, because he represented the University. But he always worked in with the Labour men, after they first got elected a couple of years ago.'

'Do you know a man called Pearson?' Wilson enquired.

Tom Bracket, overhearing from the kitchen, shouted out that Pearson was a first-rate chap, with plenty of guts. 'I think Willie Pearson is delightful,' said Helen Bracket, simply, 'though he will always look at me as if he wished I wasn't there. He can't abide women; but he and Tom are great friends.'

'Your chief constable seems to think he killed Mrs Sullivan,' said Wilson.

'Absolute rot!' Tom Bracket shouted. 'Those damned Tories'd be only too glad to get Pearson out of the way. It's a damn sight more likely Sullivan bumped her off himself.'

Wilson cocked an interrogative eye at Helen, who said softly, 'You mustn't take any notice of Tom, when he says things like that. He doesn't mean it. He only means Mr Sullivan is not a nice man.'

'He's an infernal little tick,' Tom shouted; and he proceeded, in the same bellow, to give a long account of some of Sullivan's iniquities in opposing the improvement of the drainage system in the part of Bullbridge where the Anchor's employees mostly lived. Wilson listened until he had finished, and then said to Helen, 'What sort of woman was Mrs Sullivan?'

'She was just a poor thing,' Helen answered. 'A good deal older than her husband, and one of those down-trodden, washed-out females it's so difficult to sympathize with, even if you're sorry for them. I'm sure Mr Sullivan bullied her dreadfully. I can't think why they ever married. They seemed to have nothing in common.'

Tom bellowed, 'He married her for her money, of course.'

Helen shouted back, 'I didn't know she had any.'

Tom replied, louder still, 'Must have had, or he wouldn't have married her.'

Helen said, more softly, 'She never looked as if she had, poor creature.'

'What did you say?' Tom roared.

Superintendent Wilson was finding this stentorian conversation rather exhausting. He said, 'For Heaven's sake, Tom, come out of the kitchen, or let's shut up till you do. I hate shouting.'

'I like it,' said Tom, emerging with the soup cups on a tray. 'God meant me to be a mob orator, not a don. Here, sit down and gulp this stuff up, while I make a mushroom omelette.'

'Tom, do sit down and eat your soup like a Christian,' Helen suggested.

'How can I make a mushroom omelette while I'm sitting down? Eat your soup up, woman, and don't either of you dare to say a word more about anything till the omelette's ready.'

'What about your soup?' Wilson enquired.

'I can swallow it in the kitchen.' He bore away his own soup cup, leaving the others. Helen Bracket made a helpless gesture. 'We'd better humour him,' she said. 'It really will be a good omelette, if he isn't upset.'

The two sat down to table. 'At all events, it is the most excellent soup,' Wilson ventured.

'What did you say?' came the voice from the kitchen.

It was Wilson's turn to shout. 'I said the soup was good.'

'Then swallow it, and then keep your mouth shut till I come.'

Wilson and Helen obediently finished their soup in silence. They had just done so, when Tom Bracket entered, bearing the omelette. He banged it down on the table, piping hot. 'How's that for an omelette?' he enquired triumphantly.

'It looks and smells excellent,' Wilson said. 'What about your soup?'

'Blast! I forgot it,' said Tom Bracket. He dashed back into the kitchen, and emerged bearing his soup cup. He sat down and began to consume its contents lustily. 'Damn good soup!' he said a minute later, pushing the cup away from him. 'Here, Helen, don't you eat all that omelette.'

His wife passed him a plateful, and he ate with the same noisy gusto. 'Food!' he said appreciatively. 'Jolly good food, though I say it as shouldn't. Ye gods! I forgot the Chablis.' He dashed off again and returned with a bottle, which he uncorked with a loud plop. He filled his wife's glass, and then Wilson's, and put down the bottle. He returned to his omelette, while Helen filled his glass for him. A minute later he pushed his plate away, took a deep draught exclaimed, 'That's better,' belched slightly, and then observed, 'What's all this about the Sullivans? Have they called Scotland Yard in about our local murder?'

Wilson nodded. 'I'm going down to Bullbridge tomorrow. I came round, because I felt sure you could tell me who did it and save me the trouble of having to find out for myself.'

'What's Helen been saying?' Bracket enquired.

'I haven't been saying anything, Tom, because you kept on shouting so I couldn't get a word in edgeways.'

'I always do,' Bracket said with satisfaction. 'Well, to begin with, you can take my word for it Willie Pearson had nothing to do with it.'

'Chief Constable Murnin's view seems to be that, being a rank Communist, he's certain to have murdered somebody.'

'Communist be blowed! Willie's no more a Communist than I am. We're both solid, moderate Labour men. Transport House loves us.'

'I'm not sure Murnin would know the difference.'

'Murnin's a stupid old goop. He's a fat, easygoing, incompetent old codger, that ought to be pensioned off.'

'I confess he did not impress me greatly,' said Wilson. 'He *would* quote Mr Sullivan at me till I'm afraid I almost lost my temper with him. Mr Sullivan's views are apparently not very advanced.'

'Sullivan's a pest,' said Tom Bracket. 'He's the worst works manager on God's earth. And he's Chairman of the Ratepayers' Association and at the bottom of every bit of iniquity in Bullbridge, besides being a dirty little rip in his off-duty moments.'

'Was he fond of his wife?' Wilson asked.

'Fond of her! He never lost a chance of wiping his feet on her. I never saw a woman so put upon in my whole life.'

'Except me,' said Helen Bracket.

'Shut up, you slut. He insulted her in public, and never let her get a word in when he was there. He shouted her down whenever she opened her mouth. The result was, she ran like a tap without a washer whenever he wasn't there.'

'But . . .' Helen began.

'Be quiet, woman, I'm talking. The chief thing I've got against Sullivan is the way he handled the men at the Anchor Works. They're decent chaps, especially the men who came down from Yorkshire when Bassett and Graham's took the place over; but Sullivan treats them like dirt. He's vindictive too; and when he gets his knife into a chap, Heaven help him.'

'He had his knife into Pearson?'

'I should say so. Willie Pearson is easily the best Labour man we've got at Bullbridge, and he stands up for his chaps. He's been damn good, leading the Labour men since he got elected on the Council. And he's a hundred per cent honest and decent, which makes Sullivan get up against him all the more.'

'Is he a dangerous Red, as the chief constable seems to believe?'

'Dangerous Red be damned! I told you that before. He's an honest-to-God Socialist, the same as I am. He's a left-winger, if that's what you mean, and all for unity, and that sort of thing. But there's no CP nonsense about him.'

'You give him a remarkably good character.'

'Well, if you don't believe me, ask Helen. He's her white-headed boy.'

'She has already told me he is delightful.'

'So he is,' Helen Bracket put in. 'He has the loveliest Yorkshire voice ever, and he's rude to you with a twinkle in his eye till you want to hug him. Only he wouldn't like being hugged. As I told you, he shies at the sight of a woman.'

'Then I take it he's unmarried.'

'You're wrong there. He's got a wife and two children. She was a schoolteacher in Yorkshire, I think. She's nice, probably; but I hardly know her.'

'Nor I,' said Tom Bracket. 'She isn't political, and she doesn't go about much where I should run across her. But people like her, though I understand she's got a tongue.'

'And the children?' Wilson asked. 'You know I'm a whale for irrelevant information.'

Tom Bracket shook his head. 'I can't tell you much there. I've seen the boy: he's about ten, and looks a nice, intelligent lad. The girl's younger. That's all I know.'

Wilson asked Helen if she could add anything further; but she said no.

'Now for the next point,' Wilson went on. 'What's the local gossip about Mrs Sullivan's death?'

'How do I know?' said Bracket, spreading out his arms in a large gesture. 'I'm stuck up in London because of this confounded war, getting right out of touch with the Bullbridge chaps, who are the ones I really care about, and letting those Tory swine on the City Council do what they damn well please because I'm not there to stop them.'

'Have they been doing anything in particular? Couldn't Pearson stop them?' Wilson fired off the two questions in quick succession.

'Trust them to be up to some dirty trick or other,' Tom Bracket answered vaguely. 'Of course, Pearson'd do his best.'

'But he needs your help?'

'Of course he does. I'm a gent, see, and the blighters are frightened of me, because they're all snobs. Besides, I will say this for the University members on the Council. They're mostly reactionaries; but they won't stand for dirty work.'

'But there's no particular piece of dirty work you have in mind?'

'As a matter of fact, there is. Sullivan's been trying to put across the Council a pet plan of his for getting them to sell out their electricity works to one of these blasted combines. I fully expect he's a big shareholder, or stands to get a good rake-off somewhere. Willie Pearson and I have been fighting the scheme like hell; but now I'm out of it I dare say the damned swindler'll pull it through, though Willie will fight them in the last ditch.'

'Then it would be pretty convenient for Sullivan to have Pearson out of the way for the time being, as well as you.'

Tom Bracket swore a great oath. 'By God, I'll swear the little tick wouldn't stop at accusing Willie of murder in order to get him jugged safely till the swindle's through. It'd be quite in character.'

....

A COAT OF VARNISH

A few minutes after Humphrey left the house, Detective Chief
Superintendent Frank Briers entered. He asked a couple of quiet
questions of the policeman on duty outside, gave a couple of
quiet instructions. Any other entrances? There is another policeman outside the garden door? The same instruction was to be
passed on to him. No one was to be allowed inside except his
own officers and the technical people. Then Briers looked at the
lock on the front door, said it must be changed, and went
upstairs. He was followed by a young Detective Inspector
Shingler, who had been sitting beside him in the police car.
Shingler had already been allotted to the chief Scenes of Crime
job.

Briers himself was still under forty. He was restlessly springy
on his feet, exuding force and energy, middle height, built like a
professional footballer, light above the waist, muscular thighs.
His face was neat-featured, not specially distinguished to a
spectator unless and until his eyes were caught. They weren't the
eyes others expected in a detective, not sharp and concentrated.
For that the spectator would have done better to take a look,
under the general air of composure, at Humphrey Leigh. Briers's
eyes were brilliant enough, deep-coloured, a startling blue. They

were the kind of eyes, set under fine brow-ridges, that innocent persons expected to see in artists or musicians, and seldom did.

It was an accident that he had been given this new assignment. After the first survey, the local police station wasted no time. It was clear enough that the murder of Lady Ashbrook was bound to make the news. They tried to summon the Chief Detective of the Division. He was out on another case. Within minutes, the station made an appeal to Scotland Yard. Briers was by chance unoccupied, the appropriate rank, with a reputation already made, tipped to go higher. By 9.20 a good deal was already in train. He had sent off two men with whom he had worked before to get an office organized at the police station. Photographers and laboratory technicians were due to arrive. Briers's favourite pathologist should be at the house before long.

Briers went alone into Lady Ashbrook's drawing-room. 'Give me ten minutes,' he had said softly to Shingler. He stayed still, a yard or so from the body. His senses were alive. He was getting impressions as Humphrey had done not two hours before. Some of Briers's impressions were similar to Humphrey's, but imbibed with more purpose and concentration. It wasn't the first time he had been inside a ransacked room: there were things to look for. Some of his thoughts were different from Humphrey's. A suspicion hadn't crystallized, but was somewhere, as it were in solution, at the back of his mind.

He remained still, except for the direction of his glances, which travelled from the body round the room. He was long-sighted, and the detail of the spilled-out objects thirty feet away he could make out as though it were bold print.

He didn't take a note. Note-taking on the spot didn't suit him. It seemed to shut out impressions which were lurking on the edge of observation. Perhaps that was a minor vanity, for he had faith in his memory. Although he carried a recording machine in his pocket, he rarely used it. He preferred to give reminders to Shingler, who could feed them into his own machine. Then photographs were the best recorders of all.

Soon the first photographs were being taken. After some more solitary moments, he called to Shingler: 'Ready now.'

Shingler came in with a photographic officer. For the first series of shots, Shingler didn't need instructions. The camera clicked, Lady Ashbrook was photographed more often and from more angles than ever in the past, even when as a young society beauty she had been caught by journalists after a supper party with the Prince of Wales. The body finished with, Briers told Shingler what shots he wanted round the room. The visual scouring clicked on.

Shortly after nine-fifty, the constable on duty outside let another man into the room. He was carrying a bag, his face was flushed. His first act was to take off his jacket and throw it back to the constable. 'Too hot for this lark,' he said in a euphonious tenor. 'Sorry I'm late, Frank.'

'You always are.'

In fact, he had come with maximum celerity. This was Owen Morgan, Professor of Forensic Science, who with the curious Anglo-Saxon lack of inventiveness about nicknames was known as Taffy. He was heavily set, fair, round-faced. He and Briers had worked together often. They had respect for each other, and a kind of protective friendship. Each thought the other a master of his trade. They found it necessary to express this by outbursts of sparring, or what used to be called ribbing. This didn't seem particularly appropriate for either of them.

'I suppose everyone's made a mess of things already,' Morgan said, as a thoughtful preliminary. He wasn't referring to the casualty or the litter on the floor.

'Oh, yes, our prints and traces, they're all over the place.' Briers was responding in kind.

'Actually, Professor,' said Shingler, in a placatory manner and a south-of-the-river accent, 'nothing's been touched. It's all yours.'

'That's something, I suppose,' Morgan said, as though displeased. He hadn't met Shingler before, and Briers introduced them. Morgan said: 'Well, let's have a look.'

He put on a pair of near-transparent gloves, trod with elephantine delicacy over particles on the floor, and began to touch the body. Out of proportion to his bulky chest and stomach, his hands were small, delicate, quick-moving, adept. He pulled up an eyelid, glanced at the scalp wounds, sniffed like one who had just opened a good bottle. He twitched an arm, which was limp, all stiffness departed. He turned back the collar of the dress and exposed a bruise on the upper arm. Carefully he passed his fingers round the neck. He grunted, and said: 'Nothing much in it for me.' He was turning back to Briers. 'It's going to be your problem, not mine. Unless you know already.'

Briers shook his head. 'Tell us. What do you get paid for?'

'My God,' Morgan broke out, 'why aren't you coppers given a course in medicine? If you were capable of taking it in. Have you looked at her face, man? Couldn't you see the spots? And on the eyelids? It's too bloody clear. Nothing in it for me.'

'Come off it. You mean she was strangled?'

'What else? Very easy with a woman that age. Almost certainly from in front, coming from her right-hand side. There was a bit of a struggle. One or two bruises. Not much good struggling at that age. I shall want photographs of the bruises, of course. Before I cut her up.'

'So shall we,' said Briers. 'What about her head being bashed in?'

'Done after death.'

'How long after?'

'Difficult to say. Not a great deal of blood. But it might have been done very soon after.'

'Might have been a frenzy. We've seen that before, haven't we?'

'We have.'

They were both used to actions after a killing. More often than not, they would have said, they were not nice for the public to know.

'She passed water, of course,' Morgan commented. The other hadn't seen him make an examination, but his nose was acute. 'No defecation, I think. Her bowels can't have been loose.'

'Any semen?'

'That I can't tell you till I get her to the hospital.' They were used to such consequences, too. They dropped into the formal textbook words. They made it that much more abstract, more hygienic.

Briers asked more questions; Shingler, anxious not to be left out, putting in his own. Had the body been moved after the murder and the blows on the head? Morgan thought not. The blood on the floor and the urine staining didn't look like it. 'You mean,' said Shingler, 'he just killed her, stove her head in afterwards and left her.'

'That seems to be the form.'

'Time of the murder – any idea?' Briers asked.

'That'll have to wait till the hospital as well. Temperature won't tell us anything after this time. Maggots may. The larvae boys are beginning to be useful – you've seen what they can do. There must be plenty of infestation. The maggots have come along damn quickly in this weather. You can see them. My guess is that she's been dead about thirty-six hours, plus or minus three or four. Saturday night, that would take you back to. But we might get a bit nearer than that. Look, have you finished here? It's time we got down to some serious work.'

Briers required some more tests, on the floor and the walls around the body, and called in a laboratory man. Then the body was lifted on to a stretcher, and carried down to the pavement. A few people were watching, for news had filtered round the Square and farther off. A miniature convoy, three vehicles, moved off, ambulance in the lead, Briers's police car, Morgan's private one.

The convoy got through with police speed. Soon they were moving along a wide East End street, low buildings, humble paint-peeling shops, Jewish names, shields of David. Shingler, sitting beside Briers in the back seat, tried to talk. Briers did not respond. He had enough thoughts to occupy him.

The main hospital building was late nineteenth century, solid and dark, but that they were not entering. Morgan's domain was down a side street, small houses run together, a post-war assembly, including a couple of prefabs. There was a large bright-painted notice, as outside a pub or a trend-seeking church, which read: 'Department of Forensic Science and Morbid Anatomy.' Morgan's domain might be ramshackle, but he was proud of it.

When the others had got out of their car, he said to Briers: 'No reason to hang about, is there?'

In fact, none of them gave the appearance of hurrying. That was a beginner's fault. Briers and Morgan kept to a tempo without spurts or stops. One of Morgan's staff met them: he was carrying two notes addressed to DCS Briers. Briers skimmed through them, passed them to Shingler. They were briefs from the Yard, with bits of information about Lady Ashbrook. All formal – age, marriages, names of relatives.

They followed Morgan into the mortuary. Under the strip lighting, there was one large room with stone slab-tables, white, anonymous. Another, smaller with a single table, also shone by the daylight lamp. In the smaller room, the mortuary superintendent, introduced as Agnew, was waiting, already wearing a laboratory coat, olive-coloured, not white. In an alcove, they put on similar coats. There were masks hanging up in that robing-room, but Morgan did not take one or invite them to. He had a reputation for haranguing his pupils: Smell was too important to play tricks with.

When they returned to the mortuary, they could still, from the small room which Morgan kept for dissections, look out to the big classroom. They clustered round the single slab. The party had become Morgan himself, one other medical man, the superintendent and a technical assistant, Briers, Shingler, and the photographer. To begin with, the body had been propped up in a chair standing by the dissecting-table. It was exactly as it had been in the drawing-room, clothed, untouched.

'Right?' Morgan said.

'Right.' Briers nodded.

'From the head down. Hair off later, of course.'

The camera clicked, in front of the head, at the side, from on top.

'Pictures of those wounds,' Briers instructed.

'I want swabs. Get them to the larvae boys straight away,' Morgan said to Agnew. 'Tell them it's priority.' Swabs of the nose and mouth. From both there had been a discharge of both blood and mucus, and maggots had been moving. 'Also for the larvae boys.'

More camera clicks.

'Now get the clothes off. We want to know if anything was put on after she was killed. Go slow.'

That was Morgan speaking. Briers added: 'Photographs at all stages.' Carefully, with clinical caution, the hammer was eased out of the head. Photographs of the crevices. Then Agnew and his assistant stripped off the clothing. It was easy. In the heat, she had been wearing little. The dress came off. Morgan interrupted here, to have an inspection of the bruises on her neck and upper arms. 'Not much force,' he muttered to Briers. Throughout, Shingler was whispering into his recorder.

Under the dress, a silk slip. 'No stains visible,' said Agnew. 'You'll test it,' Morgan replied. A light bra, a very light girdle.

'She didn't need that,' Morgan muttered. 'How old was she?' Briers told him.

Another mutter. 'Christ Almighty, she kept her figure.'

The body would not have seemed so thin as in her clothes, except for the legs below the knees.

'Who was she, by the way?' Morgan, *sotto voce*, to Briers. Again Briers told him.

For the first time, Morgan exclaimed out loud.

'My God,' he said. 'One of the Big People.' He had assumed a Welsh lilt, in which he never spoke. This was some obscure joke, lost to all present but himself.

Stockings off. Silk knickers. 'Test those. You'll find urine. I want to know if there's anything else.'

The instructions were unnecessary. Agnew was as experienced as Morgan himself.

'That's that,' Morgan said. 'Get her ready, will you? Ten minutes do you?'

'Just about.' Agnew was unfussed.

'We'll go outside, then.' Morgan took them into the open. 'You're allowed a cigarette, now,' he said to Briers.

As Morgan knew, Briers was an addictive smoker, deprived for hours that morning. He promptly took out a packet. Both he and Morgan were unusually quiet, and it was Shingler, alert, slick as his own shining black hair, who made conversation. He was alert and observant, and had to be listened to.

'We'll give them a quarter of an hour,' said Morgan, as though he were waiting for unpunctual guests. Then, not delaying for quite as long, they went back to the mortuary.

The body lay stretched out flat on the table. Hair gone from head and body. The head looked much smaller without its hair. The body looked clean, thin but not skeletal, young. Morgan had already said that she was abnormally well preserved. But he, who had dealt with so many bodies, had already noted, what amorists had discovered long ago, that, though faces usually aged, bodies often didn't. To some, that had been an agreeable discovery.

'Right,' Morgan said. He was spreading his nostrils, as he was to do several times during the next half-hour. There was, in the drawing-room, a tinge of the sweet smell of corruption. Nothing else yet, though. Except for another tinge, which he wished wasn't present, the smell of formaldehyde from a previous operation.

Without the policeman realizing, Agnew was already taking off the skull cap. He brought out the brain and handed it, as though it was the most natural of gifts, to Morgan. Morgan studied it for seconds and said: 'Two knocks. The second knock would have killed her. If she hadn't been dead already.'

At that point Morgan took over. There was nothing against the cut from throat to pubis for this dissection, and he made it. He often had a taste for the great V cut, Briers was thinking as he watched. Morgan extracted lungs and heart. 'Not an indication, nothing wrong. She was stronger than most of us,' he said with a touch of envy. Organs deposited in the sink, in a neat row. Liver, kidneys. The stomach bag he held on to longer.

'We'd better have this gone over. We may as well know what she ate at her last meal.' He was fingering one of the passages. 'She may have had some trouble here. Nothing pathological, I think. Wear and tear. It could have been inconvenient.'

The body lay on the table, a cavity, nothing else. The organs were on display. Only the doctors, and perhaps Agnew, could have distinguished them from their own organs if they had been on exhibition, too. Or have distinguished them from the offal in an old-fashioned butcher's shop.

'That's as much as we can do for now.' Morgan left them all

standing, went out, came back with clean white hands. He spoke to Briers: 'Let's go along and have a talk.' He said to Shingler: 'Will you come, too?' He asked the question as though he would have preferred Shingler to decline, but that was unlikely.

'Going along' meant a progress. Across alleyways, up stairs and down corridors, as though in an imperfectly adapted hotel, to Morgan's office. A cluttered room, with photographs of track teams, of medical groups and, apparently somewhat out of place, of sets of teeth. These were actually mementoes of a case reported in *Famous British Trials*, in which Morgan had given decisive evidence. 'Having a talk' in that subdued mortuary language meant, first and foremost, having a drink. As soon as they reached the room, Morgan was feeling for a whisky bottle behind his desk. He poured Briers a stiff drink, took a stiffer one himself. Shingler took a drink, diluted it, sipped at it. The others were downing theirs.

Sometimes they talked, patting references across like so many ping-pong balls, as though they were careless. They certainly talked like professionals, as though they were machines. The fact was, they were relieved to be finished with the post-mortem. Yes, Morgan had done many. Yes, he liked using his skill, and showing it. Yes, Briers loved his job and snatched at the help that the pathologist could give him. But there were parts of the job, and this was one, which were still a submerged strain. He and Morgan were both hearty natural men, and sometimes they showed it. It broke out in their overdone matiness. Most of their time they lived close to death. But they didn't like death. As he had his packet of cigarettes in front of him, Briers was more at ease. No one enjoyed a post-mortem. No one except the indifferent perhaps. Norman Shingler here seemed totally unaffected. He was learning from post-mortems, intent, preoccupied, just pre-occupied with learning his job.

Briers lit another cigarette, and they spoke as colleagues, work in front of them, coping with the case.

'Some of it's straightforward,' he said. 'Cause of death. No doubt in hell what that was. Why her skull was smashed later you'll have to find out. I can't be any good to you there. Time of death? We're getting a bit closer. You'll be lucky if anything more positive crops up. Unless one of your coppers comes up with an eyewitness. But, then, I shouldn't believe him, after all I've been through with you. Anyway, you've heard the score.'

Since they came into the room, there had been two telephone calls. One was from the entomologists. Morgan roared out what he was hearing. First-generation larvae, second-generation larvae, of course. Some argument over the phone. Morgan spoke back into the room. 'Actually it's pretty near what I guessed. Assuming her window was open, temperature not lower than twenty-five Centigrade – I told them what the conditions were, the bloody fools – earliest time for infestation would be 7 p.m. on Saturday night, latest time 11 p.m. That will have to be good enough.'

'Head wounds post-date the murder,' Briers said. 'So time of murder had to be earlier, probably not much.'

'Still, it's Saturday evening-to-night, not late night,' Morgan said.

'Fair enough,' said Briers.

The second report over the telephone was shorter and simple. It just said – no trace of semen. Morgan was surprised. He had found nothing by sight and touch, but nevertheless he was surprised. Briers was robustly teasing him: 'You've seen too many murders, you have, Taffy.'

Morgan took another sizeable whisky, but not Briers. It was now getting on into the afternoon. None of them had eaten. The older men showed no sign of the passing of time. About half-past two Briers said that he had work to do. He and Morgan parted on another robust note, Morgan saying that if the police got into inextricable trouble he would come and sort it out.

....

THE ERASERS

By shifting the dossiers on top of his desk, Laurent covers up the little piece of eraser. Wallas finishes his remarks:

'In short, you haven't found much.'

'You might say nothing,' the chief commissioner answers.

'And what do you intend to do now?'

'Nothing, since it isn't my case any more!'

Commissioner Laurent accompanies these words with an ironically broken-hearted smile. When his interlocutor says nothing, he continues:

'I was wrong, no doubt, to believe myself in charge of public safety in this city. This paper,' he waves a letter between two fingers, 'orders me in specific terms to let the capital take over last night's crime. I couldn't ask for anything better. And now the minister, you say – or in any case a service that is directly attached to him – sends you here to continue the investigation, not "in my place" but "with my co-operation". What am I supposed to make of that? Except that this co-operation is to be limited to handing over to you whatever information I possess – which I have just done – and therefore to having you protected by my men, if necessary.'

With another smile, Laurent adds:

'So now it's up to you to tell me what *you're* going to do, unless of course that's a secret.'

Entrenched behind the papers covering his desk, his elbows propped on the arms of his chair, the commissioner rubs his hands together as he speaks, slowly, almost cautiously, then he sets them down in front of him on the scattered sheets of paper, spreading his short, fat fingers as far apart as possible, and waits for the answer, without taking his eyes from his visitor's face. He is a short, plump man with a pink face and a bald skull. His kindly tone is a little forced.

'You say the witnesses,' Wallas begins . . .

Laurent immediately raises his hands to stop him.

'There are no witnesses, properly speaking,' he says, rubbing his right palm over his left forefinger; 'you can scarcely call the doctor who has not restored the wounded man to life a witness, or the old deaf housekeeper who has seen nothing whatsoever.'

'It was the doctor who informed you?'

'Yes, Dr Juard telephoned the police last night around nine o'clock; the inspector who received the information wrote down what he said – you've just looked at the record – and then he called me at home. I had an immediate examination of the premises made. Upstairs, the inspectors picked up four sets of fresh fingerprints: those of the housekeeper, then three others apparently made by men's hands. If it's true that no outsider has come upstairs for several days, these last could be' – he counts on his fingers – 'first of all, those of the doctor, faint and few, on the stair banister and in Dupont's bedroom; second, those of Dupont himself, which can be found all over the house; third, those of the murderer, quite numerous and very clear, on the banister, on the doorknob of the study, and on certain articles of furniture in his study – mainly the back of the desk chair. The house has two entrances; the doctor's right thumb-print has been found on the front doorbell, and the hypothetical murderer's on the knob of the back door. You see that I'm giving you all the details. Lastly, the housekeeper declares that the doctor came in through the front door and that she found the back door open when she went upstairs to answer the wounded man's call – even though she had closed it a few moments before. If you want me to, I can have Dr Juard's fingerprints taken, just to be sure . . .'

'You can also get the dead man's prints, I suppose?'

'I could, if I had the body at my disposal,' Laurent answers sweetly.

Seeing Wallas's questioning look, he asks:

'Haven't you heard? The body was taken away from me at the same time as the control of the investigation. I thought it was sent to the same organization that sent you here.'

Wallas is obviously amazed. Could other services be concerned with this case? This is a supposition Laurent receives with obvious satisfaction. He waits, his hands lying flat on his desk; his kindly expression is tinged with compassion. Without insisting on this point, Wallas continues:

'You were saying that Dupont, after being wounded, had called to the old housekeeper from upstairs; for the latter to have heard him, deaf as she is, Dupont would have had to shout quite loudly. Yet the doctor describes him as greatly weakened by his wound, almost unconscious.'

'Yes, I know; there seems to be a contradiction here; but he might have had strength enough to go get his revolver and call for help, and then have lost a lot of blood while waiting for the ambulance: there was a relatively large bloodstain on the bedspread. In any case, he wasn't unconscious when the doctor got there, since Dupont told him that he hadn't seen his attacker's face. There's a mistake in the account published by the papers: it was only *after* the operation that the wounded man didn't recover consciousness. Moreover, you'll obviously have to go see this doctor. You should also ask for details from the housekeeper, Mme . . .' he consults a sheet from the dossier – 'Mme Smite; her explanations are somewhat confused: she told us, in particular, some elaborate story about a broken telephone that seems to have nothing to do with the case – at least at first glance. The inspectors haven't made a point of it, preferring to wait until she calms down; they haven't even told her that her employer was dead.'

The two men do not speak for a moment. It is the commissioner who resumes, delicately rubbing his joints with his thumb.

'He may perfectly well have committed suicide, you know. He has shot himself with the revolver once – or several times – without managing to finish himself off; then he has changed his mind, as so often happens, and called for help, trying to disguise his unsuccessful attempt as an attack. Or else – and this would be more in accord with what we know about his character – he has prepared this setting in advance, and managed to give himself a mortal wound that allowed him a few minutes' survival in order to have time to bequeath the myth of his murder to the public. It's very difficult, you'll say, to calculate the consequences of a pistol shot so exactly; he may have fired a second shot while the housekeeper was going for the doctor. He was a strange man, from many points of view.'

'It must be possible to verify these hypotheses from the position of the bullets,' Wallas remarks.

'Yes, sometimes it's possible. And we would have examined the bullets and the revolver of the supposed victim. All I have here is the death certificate the doctor sent this morning; it's the only thing we can be sure of, for the time being. The suspect fingerprints can belong to anyone who came during the day without the housekeeper's knowing it; as for the back door she mentioned to the inspector, the wind might have opened it.'

'You really think Dupont committed suicide?'

'I don't think anything. I find it's not impossible, according to the facts I have. This death certificate, which is drawn up quite correctly, by the way, gives no indication as to the kind of wound that caused death; and the information furnished last night by the doctor and the housekeeper is all too vague in this regard, as you've seen. Before anything else, you'll have to clear up these few details. If necessary, you could even get the additional details that might interest you from the coroner in the capital.'

Wallas says:

'Your help would certainly have made my job easier.'

'But you can count on me, monsieur. As soon as you have someone to arrest I'll send you two or three good men. I'll be eager to get your telephone call; just ask for one-twenty-four – twenty-four, it's a direct line.'

The smile on the chubby face widens. The little hands spread out on the desk, palms smooth, fingers wide. Wallas writes: 'C. Laurent, 124-24.' A direct line to what?

He asks, just to make sure:

'What would you have done, if you had gone on with the investigation yourself?'

'It's not in my line,' the commissioner answers, 'which is why they took it away from me.'

'Then what is the responsibility of the police, in your opinion?'

Laurent rubs his hands a little faster.

'We keep criminals within certain limits more or less fixed by the law.'

'And?'

'This one is beyond us, he doesn't belong to the category of ordinary malefactors. I know every criminal in this city: they're all listed in my files; I arrest them when they forget the conventions society imposes on them. If one of them had killed Dupont to rob him or even to be paid by a political party, do you think we would still be wondering, more than twelve hours after the murder, whether it wasn't a suicide after all? This district isn't very big, and informers are legion here. We don't always manage to prevent crime, sometimes the criminal even manages to escape, but there's never been a case where we haven't found his tracks, whereas this time we're left with a lot of unidentified fingerprints and some draughts that open doors. Our informers are no help here. If we're dealing, as you think, with a terrorist organization, they've been very careful to keep from being contaminated; in this sense, their hands are clean, cleaner than those of a police that maintains such close relations with the men they're watching. Here, between the policeman and the criminal, you find every grade of intermediary. Our whole system is based on them. Unfortunately the shot that killed Daniel Dupont came from another world!'

'But you know there's no such thing as the perfect crime; we must look for the flaw that has to exist somewhere.'

'Where are you going to look? Make no mistake about it, monsieur: this is the work of specialists, they've obviously left few things to chance; but what makes the few clues we have useless is our inability to test them against anything else.'

'This case is already the ninth,' Wallas says.

'Yes, but you'll agree that only the political opinions of the victims and the hour of their deaths have allowed us to connect them. Besides, I'm not so convinced as you that such coincidences correspond to anything real. And even supposing they do, we're not much further: what use would it be to me, for instance, if a second murder just as anonymous were committed in this city tonight? As for the central services, they don't have any more opportunities than I do to get results: they have the same files and the same methods. They've taken the body away from me, and it's all the easier for me to abandon it to them since you tell me they have eight more they don't know what to do with. Before your visit, I already had the impression that the case didn't have anything to do with the police, and your presence here makes me sure of it.'

Despite his interlocutor's evident prejudice, Wallas insists: the victim's relatives and friends could be questioned. But Laurent has no hopes of finding out anything useful from this quarter either:

'It appears that Dupont led an extremely solitary life, shut up with his books and his old housekeeper. He seldom went out and received only rare visits. Did he have any friends? As for relatives, there seem to be none, except for his wife . . .'

Wallas shows his surprise:

'He had a wife? Where was she at the time of the crime?'

'I don't know. Dupont was married only a few years; his wife was much younger than he and probably couldn't endure his hermit's life. They separated right away. But they still saw each other now and then, apparently; by all means ask her what she was doing last night at seven-thirty.'

'You're not saying that seriously?'

'Certainly I am. Why not? She knew the house and her ex-husband's habits well; so she had more opportunities than anyone else to commit this murder discreetly. And since she was entitled to expect a considerable inheritance from him, she's one of the few people I know of who could have any interest in seeing him dead.'

'Then why didn't you mention her to me?'

'You told me that he was the victim of a political assassination!'

'She could have played her part in it anyway.'

'Of course. Why not?'

Commissioner Laurent has resumed his jocular tone. He says with a half-smile:

'Maybe it's the housekeeper who killed him and made up all the rest with the help of Dr Juard, whose reputation – let me tell you in passing – is not so good.'

'That seems rather unlikely,' Wallas observes.

'Even altogether unlikely, but you know that never kept anyone from being a suspect.'

Wallas feels that this irony is in bad taste. Furthermore, he realizes he will not learn much from this official, jealous of his authority but determined to do nothing. Isn't Laurent really trying to wash his hands of the whole affair? Or else would he like to discourage his rivals in order to make his own investigation? Wallas stands up to say goodbye; he will visit this doctor first. Laurent shows him where he is to be found:

'The Juard Clinic, eleven Rue de Corinthe. It's on the other side of the prefecture, not far from here.'

'I thought,' Wallas says, 'that the newspaper said "a nearby clinic"?'

Laurent makes a cynical gesture:

'Oh, you know the papers! Besides, it's not far from the Rue des Arpenteurs.'

Wallas writes down the address in his notebook.

'There is even one paper,' the commissioner adds, 'that mixed up the first names and announced the death of Albert Dupont, one of the biggest wood exporters in the city. He must have been quite surprised to read his obituary this morning!'

Laurent has stood up too. He winks as he says:

'After all, I haven't seen the body; maybe it *is* Albert Dupont's.'

This idea amuses him enormously, his overfed body shakes from fits of laughter. Wallas smiles politely. The chief commissioner catches his breath and holds out his hand amiably.

'If I hear anything new,' he says, 'I'll let you know. What hotel are you staying at?'

'I've taken a room in a café, Rue des Arpenteurs, a few steps away from the house itself.'

'You have! Who told you about that?'

'No one; I found it by chance. It's number ten.'

'Is there a telephone?'

'Yes, I think so.'

'Well, I'll find it in the book if I have anything to tell you.'

Without waiting, Laurent begins leafing quickly through the phone book, licking his index finger.

'Arpenteurs, here we are. Number ten: Café des Alliés?'

'Yes, that's the one.'

'Telephone: two-zero-two–zero-three. But it's not a hotel.'

'No,' Wallas says, 'they only rent a few rooms.'

Laurent goes to a shelf and picks out a ledger. After a moment of fruitless search, he asks:

'That's strange, they're not registered; are there many rooms?'

'No, I don't think so,' Wallas answers. 'You see, your facts aren't so exact after all!'

A broad smile lights up the chief commissioner's face.

'On the contrary, you have to admire our resources,' he says. 'The first person to sleep in this café comes to tell me about it himself, without even giving the landlord a chance!'

'Why the first person? Suppose the murderer had slept there last night, what would you know about it?'

'The landlord would have registered him and reported to me, as he'll do for you – he has until noon.'

'And if he doesn't?' Wallas asks.

'Well, in that case, we would have to admire your perspicacity in having found the only clandestine rooming house in the town so quickly. It would even be bad for you in the long run; you'd be the first serious suspect I've found: recently arrived in town, living twenty yards from the scene of the crime, and completely unknown to the police!'

'But I only arrived last night, at eleven!' Wallas protests.

'If you weren't registered, what proof would there be?'

'At the time the crime was committed, I was a hundred kilometres from here; that can be verified.'

'Of course! Don't good murderers always have an alibi?'

Laurent sits down again behind his desk and considers Wallas with a smiling expression. Then he suddenly asks:

'Do you have a revolver?'

'Yes,' Wallas answers. 'This time I took one, on the advice of my chief.'

'What for?'

'You never know.'

'Right, you never know. Would you show it to me please?'

Wallas hands him his gun, a 7.65mm automatic revolver, a common model. Laurent examines it carefully, after having removed the clip. Finally, without looking at Wallas, he says in the tone of an obvious comment:

'One bullet's missing.'

He hands the weapon back to its owner. Then, very quickly, he clasps his hands, separates the palms though keeping the fingers interlaced, brings his wrists together again and rubs his thumbs against each other. The hands separate and stretch; each doubles over with a faint clapping sound, opens once more and finally comes to rest on the desk, lying flat, the fingers spread apart at regular intervals.

'Yes, I know,' Wallas answers.

In making room for his ledgers, the commissioner has shifted the dossiers that cover his desk, thereby causing the piece of greyish eraser to reappear, an ink eraser probably, whose poor quality is betrayed by several worn, slightly shiny places.

....

MAIGRET'S MEMOIRS

'I'm quite aware that these books are crammed with technical inaccuracies. There's no need to count them up. Let me tell you they're deliberate, and this is why.'

I didn't take note of the whole of his speech, but I remember the essential point in it, which he often repeated to me subsequently with an almost sadistic pleasure:

'Truth never seems true. I don't mean only in literature or in painting. I won't remind you either of those Doric columns whose lines seem to us strictly perpendicular and which only give that impression because they are slightly curved. If they were straight, they'd look as if they were swelling, don't you see?'

In those days he was still fond of displaying his erudition.

'Tell someone a story, any story. If you don't dress it up, it'll seem incredible, artificial. Dress it up, and it'll seem more real than life.'

He trumpeted out those last words as if they implied some sensational discovery.

'The whole problem is to make something more real than life. Well, I've done that! I've made you more real than life.'

I remained speechless. For a moment I could find nothing to say, poor unreal policeman that I was.

And he proceeded to demonstrate, with an abundance of gestures and the hint of a Belgian accent, that my investigations as told by him were more convincing – he may even have said more accurate – than as experienced by myself.

At the time of our first encounters, in the autumn, he had not been lacking in self-confidence. Thanks to success, he was brimming over with it now, he had enough to spare for all the timid folk on earth.

'Follow me carefully, Inspector . . .'

For he had decided to drop the *Monsieur le Commissaire*.

'In a real investigation there are fifty of you, if not more, busy hunting for the criminal. You and your detectives aren't alone on the trail. The police and gendarmerie of the whole country are on the alert. They are busy in railway stations and ports and at frontiers. Not to mention the informers, let alone all the amateurs who take a hand.

'Just try, in the two hundred or two hundred and fifty pages of a novel to give a tolerably faithful picture of that swarming activity! A three-decker novel wouldn't be long enough, and the reader would lose heart after a few chapters, muddling everything, confusing everything.

'Now who is it that in real life prevents this confusion from taking place, who is there every morning putting everyone in his right place and following the guiding thread?'

He looked me up and down triumphantly.

'It's you yourself, as you know very well. It's the man in charge of the investigation. I'm quite aware that a chief inspector from Central Police Headquarters, the head of a special squad, doesn't roam the streets in person to interview concierges and wine merchants.

'I'm quite aware, too, that, apart from exceptional cases, you don't spend your nights tramping about in the rain in empty streets waiting for some window to light up or some door to open.

'None the less things happen exactly as if you were there yourself, isn't that so?'

What could I reply to this? From a certain point of view it was a logical conclusion.

'So then, let's simplify! The first quality, the essential quality of truth is to be simple. And I have simplified. I have reduced to their simplest form the wheels within wheels that surround you, without altering the result in the slightest.

'Where fifty more or less anonymous detectives were swarming in confusion, I have retained only three or four, each with his own personality.'

I tried to object:

'The rest won't like it.'

'I don't write for a few dozen police officials. When you write a book about schoolmasters you're bound to offend tens of thousands of schoolmasters. The same would happen if you wrote about station-masters or typists. What were we talking about?'

'The different sorts of truth.'

'I was trying to prove to you that my sort is the only valid one. Would you like another example? One doesn't need to have spent as long as I have in this building to know that Central Police Headquarters, which belongs to the Prefecture of Police, can only operate within the perimeter of Paris and, by extension, in certain cases, within the Department of the Seine.

'Now in *The Late Monsieur Gallet* I described an investigation which took place in the centre of France.

'Did you go there, yes or no?'

It was yes, of course.

'I went there, it's true, but at a period when . . .'

'At a period when, for a certain length of time, you were working not for the Quai des Orfèvres but for the Rue des Saussaies. Why bother the reader's head with these administrative subtleties?

'Must one begin the account of every case by explaining: This took place in such and such a year. So Maigret was seconded to such and such a department.'

'Let me finish . . .'

He had his idea and knew that he was about to touch a weak point.

'Are you, in your habits, your attitude, your character, a Quai des Orfèvres man or a Rue des Saussaies man?'

I apologize to my colleagues of the Sûreté Nationale, who include many of my good friends, but I am divulging no secret when I admit that there is, to say the least, a certain rivalry between the two establishments.

Let us admit, too, as Simenon had understood from the beginning, that, particularly in those days, there existed two rather different types of policeman.

Those of the Rue des Saussaies, who are directly answerable to the Ministry of the Interior, are led more or less inevitably to deal with political jobs.

I don't blame them for it. I simply confess that for my own part I'd rather not be responsible for these.

Our field of action at the Quai des Orfèvres is perhaps more restricted, more down to earth. Our job, in fact, is to cope with malefactors of every sort and, in general, with everything that comes under the heading 'police' with the specific limitation 'judiciary'.

'You'll grant me that you're a Quai des Orfèvres man. You're proud of it. Well, that's what I've made of you; I've tried to make you the incarnation of a Quai des Orfèvres man. And now, for the sake of minutiae, because of your mania for accuracy, have I got to spoil the clarity of the picture by explaining that in such and such a year, for certain complex reasons, you provisionally changed your department, which enabled you to work in any part of France?'

'But . . .'

'One moment. The first day I met you, I told you I was not a journalist but a novelist, and I remember promising M Guichard that my stories would never involve indiscretions that might prove awkward for the police.'

'I know, but . . .'

'Wait a minute, Maigret, for God's sake!'

It was the first time he had called me that. It was the first time, too, that this youngster had told me to shut up.

'I've changed the names, except for yours and those of two or three of your colleagues. I've been careful to change the place names too. Often, for an extra precaution, I've changed the family relationship between the characters.

'I have simplified things, and sometimes I've described only one cross-examination where there were really four or five, and only two or three trails to be followed where, to begin with, you had ten in front of you.

'I maintain that I am in the right, that my truth is the right one.

'I've brought you a proof of it.'

He pointed to a pile of books which he had laid on my desk when he arrived and to which I had paid no attention.

'These are the books written by specialists on matters concerning the police during the last twenty years, true stories, of that sort of truth that you like.

'Read them. For the most part you're familiar with the investigations which these books describe in detail.

'Well! I'm willing to bet that you won't recognize them, precisely because the quest for objectivity falsifies that truth which always is and which always *must* be simple.

'And now . . .'

Well! I'd rather admit it right away. That was the moment when I realized where the shoe pinched.

He was quite right, dammit, on all the heads he had mentioned. I didn't worry in the least, either, because he'd reduced the number of detectives or made me spend nights in the rain in their stead, or because he had, deliberately or not, confused the Sûreté Nationale with Central Police Headquarters.

What shocked me, actually, although I scarcely liked to admit it to myself, was . . .

Good Lord, how hard this is! Remember what I said about a man and his photograph.

To take merely the detail of the bowler hat. I may appear quite ridiculous, but I must confess that this silly detail hurt me more than all the rest.

When young Sim came to Headquarters for the first time, I still had a bowler hat in my cupboard, but I only wore it on rare occasions, for funerals or official ceremonies.

Now it happened that in my office there hung a photograph taken some years earlier on the occasion of some congress or other, in which I appeared wearing that cursed hat.

The result is that even today, when I am introduced to people who've never seen me before, I hear them say:

'Why, you're wearing a different hat.'

As for the famous overcoat with the velvet collar, it was with my wife that Simenon had to have it out one day, rather than with myself.

I did have such a coat, I admit. I even had several, like all men of my generation. It may even have happened that, round about 1927, on a day of extreme cold or driving rain, I took down one of those old overcoats.

I'm not a dressy man. I care very little about being smart. But perhaps for that very reason I've a horror of looking odd. And my little Jewish tailor in the Rue de Turenne is no more anxious than I am to have me stared at in the street.

'Is it my fault if that's how I see you?' Simenon might have answered, like the painter who gives his model a crooked nose or a squint.

Only in that case the model doesn't have to spend his whole life in front of his portrait, and thousands of people aren't going to believe ever after that he has a crooked nose or a squint.

I didn't tell him all this that morning. I merely averted my eyes and said modestly:

'Was it absolutely necessary to simplify *me*?'

'To begin with, it certainly was. The public has to get used to you, to your figure, your bearing. I've probably hit on the right expression. For the moment you're still only a silhouette, a back, a pipe, a way of talking, of muttering.'

'Thanks!'

'The details will appear gradually, you'll see. I don't know how long it will take. Little by little you'll begin to live with a more subtle, more complex life.'

'That's reassuring.'

'For instance, up till now, you've had no family life, whereas the Boulevard Richard-Lenoir and Mme Maigret actually take up a good half of your existence. You've still only rung up your home, but you're going to be seen there.'

'In my dressing-gown and slippers?'

'And even in bed.'

'I wear nightshirts,' I said ironically.

'I know. That completes the picture. Even if you were used to pyjamas I'd have made you wear a nightshirt.'

I wonder how this conversation would have ended – probably with a regular quarrel – if I hadn't been told that a young informer from the Rue Pigalle wanted to speak to me.

'On the whole,' I said to Simenon, as he held out his hand, 'you're pleased with yourself.'

'Not yet, but it'll come.'

Could I really have announced to him that henceforward I forbade him to use my name? I was legally entitled to do so. And this would have given rise to a typically Parisian lawsuit which would have covered me with ridicule.

The character would have acquired a different name. But he would still have been myself, or rather that simplified myself who, according to the author, was going to grow progressively more complex.

The worst of it was that the rascal was quite right and that every month, for years, I was going to find, in a book with a photograph on its cover, a Maigret who imitated me more and more.

I see that I have spoken only of trivial details, a hat, an overcoat, a stove, probably because those details were what first shocked me.

You don't feel any surprise at growing up first, then at growing old. But let a man so much as cut off the tips of his moustaches and he won't recognize himself.

The truth is that I'd like to have finished with what I consider as trivial defects before confronting the two characters on essential points.

If Simenon is right, which is quite possible, my own character will appear odd and involved by the side of that famous simplified – or dressed-up – truth of his, and I shall look like some peevish fellow trying to touch up his own portrait.

Now that I've made a beginning, with the subject of dress, I shall have to go on, if only for my own peace of mind.

Simenon asked me the other day – actually, he has changed too, from the young fellow I met in Xavier Guichard's office – Simenon asked me, with a touch of mockery:

'Well, what about the new Maigret?'

I tried to answer him in his former words.

'He's taking shape! He's still nothing but a silhouette. A hat, an overcoat. But it's his real hat. His real overcoat! Little by little, perhaps the rest will come, perhaps he'll have arms and legs and even a face, who knows? Perhaps he'll even begin to think by himself, without the aid of a novelist.'

Actually, Simenon is now just about the age I was when we met for the first time. In those days he tended to think of me as a middle-aged man and even, in his heart of hearts, as an elderly one.

I did not ask him what he thought about that today, but I couldn't help remarking:

'D'you know that with the course of time you've begun to walk and smoke your pipe and even to speak like *your* Maigret?'

Which is quite true and which, you'll agree, provided me with a rather piquant revenge.

It was rather as if, after all these years, he had begun to take *himself* for *me*!

....

FEAR AND LOATHING
IN LAS VEGAS

My attorney was downstairs at the bar, talking to a sporty-looking cop about forty whose plastic name-tag said he was the DA from someplace in Georgia. 'I'm a whiskey man, myself,' he was saying. 'We don't have much problem with drugs down where I come from.'

'You will,' said my attorney. 'One of these nights you'll wake up and find a junkie tearing your bedroom apart.'

'Naw!' said the Georgia man. 'Not down in *my* parts.'

I joined them and ordered a tall glass of rum, with ice.

'You're another one of these California boys,' he said. 'Your friend here's been tellin' me about dope fiends.'

'They're everywhere,' I said. 'Nobody's safe. And sure as hell not in the South. They like the warm weather.'

'They work in pairs,' said my attorney. 'Sometimes in gangs. They'll climb right into your bedroom and sit on your chest, with big Bowie knives.' He nodded solemnly. 'They might even sit on your *wife's chest* – put the blade right down on her throat.'

'Jesus God almighty,' said the southerner. 'What's the hell's *goin' on* in this country?'

'You'd never believe it,' said my attorney. 'In LA it's out of control. First it was drugs, now it's witchcraft.'

'Witchcraft? Shit, you can't mean it!'

'Read the newspapers,' I said. 'Man, you don't know trouble until you have to face down a bunch of these addicts gone crazy for human sacrifice!'

'Naw!' he said. 'That's science fiction stuff!'

'Not where *we* operate,' said my attorney. 'Hell, in Malibu alone, these goddamn Satan-worshippers kill six or eight people *every day*.' He paused to sip his drink. 'And all they want is the blood,' he continued. 'They'll take people right off the street if they have to.' He nodded. 'Hell, yes. Just the other day we had a case where they grabbed a girl right out of a McDonald's hamburger stand. She was a waitress. About sixteen years old . . . with a lot of people watching, too!'

'What happened?' said our friend. 'What did they *do* to her?' He seemed very agitated by what he was hearing.

'*Do?*' said my attorney. 'Jesus Christ, man. They chopped her goddamn head off right there in the parking lot! Then they cut all kinds of holes in her and sucked out the blood!'

'God *almighty*!' the Georgia man exclaimed . . . 'And nobody *did* anything?'

'What *could* they do?' I said. 'The guy that took the head was about six-seven and maybe three hundred pounds. He was packing two Lugers, and the others had M-16s. They were all veterans . . .'

'The big guy used to be a major in the Marines,' said my attorney. 'We know where he lives, but we can't get near the house.'

'Naw!' our friend shouted. 'Not a major!'

'He wanted the pineal gland,' I said. 'That's how he got so big. When he quit the Marines he was just a *little guy*.'

'O my God!' said our friend. 'That's horrible!'

'It happens every day,' said my attorney. 'Usually it's whole families. During the night. Most of them don't even wake up until they feel their heads going – and then, of course, it's too late.'

The bartender had stopped to listen. I'd been watching him. His expression was not calm.

'Three more rums,' I said. 'With plenty of ice, and maybe a handful of lime chunks.'

He nodded, but I could see that his mind was not on his work. He was staring at our name-tags. 'Are you guys with that police convention upstairs?' he said finally.

'We sure are, my friend,' said the Georgia man with a big smile.

The bartender shook his head sadly. 'I thought so,' he said. 'I never heard that kind of talk at this bar before. Jesus Christ! How do you guys *stand* that kind of work?'

My attorney smiled at him. 'We *like* it,' he said. 'It's groovy.'

The bartender drew back; his face was a mask of repugnance.

'What's wrong with you?' I said. 'Hell, *somebody* has to do it.'

He stared at me for a moment, then turned away.

'Hurry up with those drinks,' said my attorney. 'We're thirsty.' He laughed and rolled his eyes as the bartender glanced back at him. 'Only *two* rums,' he said. 'Make mine a Bloody Mary.'

The bartender seemed to stiffen, but our Georgia friend didn't notice. His mind was somewhere else. 'Hell, I really hate to hear this,' he said quietly. 'Because everything that happens in California seems to get down our way, sooner or later. Mostly Atlanta, but I guess that was back when the goddamn bastards were *peaceful*. It used to be that all we had to do was keep 'em under surveillance. They didn't roam around much . . .' He shrugged. 'But now, Jesus, *nobody's* safe. They could turn up anywhere.'

'You're right,' said my attorney. 'We learned that in California. You remember where Manson turned up, don't you? Right out in the middle of Death Valley. He had a whole *army* of sex fiends out there. We only got our hands on a few. Most of the crew got away; just ran off across the sand dunes, like big lizards . . . and every one of them stark naked, except for the weapons.'

'They'll turn up somewhere, pretty soon,' I said. 'And let's hope we'll be ready for them.'

The Georgia man whacked his fist on the bar. 'But we can't just lock ourselves in the house and be prisoners!' he exclaimed. 'We don't even know who these people are! How do you *recognize* them?'

'You can't,' my attorney replied. 'The only way to do it is to take the bull by the horns – go to the mat with this scum!'

'What do you mean by that?' he asked.

'You *know* what I mean,' said my attorney. 'We've done it before, and we can damn well do it again.'

'Cut their goddamn heads off,' I said. 'Every one of them. That's what we're doing in California.'

'*What?*'

'Sure,' said my attorney. 'It's all on the QT, but everybody who *matters* is with us all the way down the line.'

'God! I had no idea it was that bad out there!' said our friend.

'We keep it quiet,' I said. 'It's not the kind of thing you'd want to talk about upstairs, for instance. Not with the press around.'

Our man agreed. 'Hell no!' he said. 'We'd never hear the goddamn end of it.'

'Dobermans don't talk,' I said.

'What?'

'Sometimes it's easier to just rip out the backstraps,' said my attorney. 'They'll fight like hell if you try to take the head without dogs.'

'God almighty!'

We left him at the bar, swirling the ice in his drink and not smiling. He was worried about whether or not to tell his wife about it. 'She'd never understand,' he muttered. 'You know how women are.'

....

FREAKY DEAKY

Chris Mankowski's last day on the job, two in the afternoon, two hours to go, he got a call to dispose of a bomb.

What happened, a guy by the name of Booker, a twenty-five-year-old super-dude twice-convicted felon, was in his jacuzzi when the phone rang. He yelled for his bodyguard Juicy Mouth to take it. 'Hey, Juicy?' His bodyguard, his driver and his houseman were around somewhere. 'Will somebody get the phone?' The phone kept ringing. The phone must have rung fifteen times before Booker got out of the jacuzzi, put on his green satin robe that matched the emerald pinned to his left earlobe and picked up the phone. Booker said, 'Who's this?' A woman's voice said, 'You sitting down?' The phone was on a table next to a green leather wingback chair. Booker loved green. He said, 'Baby, is that you?' It sounded like his woman, Moselle. Her voice said, 'Are you sitting down? You have to be sitting down for when I tell you something.' Booker said, 'Baby, you sound different. What's wrong?' He sat down in the green leather chair, frowning, working his butt around to get comfortable. The woman's voice said, 'Are you sitting down?' Booker said, 'I *am*. I have sat the fuck down. Now you gonna talk to me, what?' Moselle's voice said, 'I'm suppose to tell you that when you get up, honey, what's left of your ass is gonna go clear through the ceiling.'

When Chris got there a uniform let him in. There were Thirteen Precinct cars and a Tactical station wagon parked in front of the house. The uniform told Chris that Booker had called 911. They radioed him here and when he saw who it was he called Narcotics and they jumped at it, a chance to go through the man's house wide open with their dog.

A guy from Narcotics who looked like a young vagrant told Chris that Booker was a success story: had come up through the street-dealing organizations, Young Boys Incorporated and Pony Down, and was now on about the third level from the top. Look around, guy twenty-five living in a home on Boston Boulevard, a mansion, originally owned by one of Detroit's automotive pioneers. The guy from Narcotics didn't remember which one. Look how Booker had fucked up the house, painted all that fine old oak paneling puke green. He asked Chris how come he was alone.

Chris said most of the squad was out on a run, picking up illegal fireworks, but there was another guy coming, Jerry Baker. Chris said, 'You know what today is?' And waited for the guy from Narcotics to say no, what? 'It's my last day on the Bomb Squad. Next week I get transferred out.' He waited again.

The guy from Narcotics said, 'Yeah, is that right?'

He didn't get it.

'It's the last time I'll ever have to handle a bomb, if that's what we have, and hope to Christ I don't make a mistake.'

The guy still didn't get it. He said, 'Well, that's what Booker says it is. He gets up, it blows up. What kind of bomb is that?'

'I won't know till I look at it,' Chris said.

'Booker says it's the fucking Italians,' the guy from Narcotics said, 'trying to tell him something. It makes sense, otherwise why not shoot the fucker? Like we know Booker's done guys we find out at Metro in long-term parking. Guy's in the trunk of his car, two in the back of the head. Booker's a bad fucking dude, man.

If there was such a thing as justice in the world we'd leave his ass sitting there, let him work it out.'

Chris said, 'Get your people out of the house. When my partner gets here, don't stop and chat, OK? I'll let you know if we need Fire or EMS, or if we have to evacuate the houses next door. Now where's Booker?'

The guy from Narcotics took Chris down the hall toward the back of the house, saying, 'Wait'll you see what the spook did to the library. Looks like a fucking tent.'

It did. Green-and-white striped parachute cloth was draped on four sides from the center point of the high ceiling to the top of the walls. The jacuzzi bubbled in the middle of the room, a border of green tile around it. Booker sat beyond the sunken bath in his green leather wingback. He was holding on to the round arms, clutching them, fingers spread open. Behind him, French doors opened onto a backyard patio.

'I been waiting,' Booker said. 'You know how long I been waiting on you? I don't know where anybody's at, I been calling – you see Juicy Mouth?'

'Who's Juicy Mouth?'

'Suppose to be guarding my body. Man, I got to go the toilet.'

Chris walked up to him, looking at the base of the chair. 'Tell me what the woman said on the phone.'

'Was the bitch suppose to be in love with me.'

'What'd she tell you?'

'Say I get up I'm *blown* up.'

'That's all?'

'Is that *all*? Man, that's final, that's all there is all, nothing else.'

Chris said, 'Yeah, but do you believe it?'

'Asshole, you expect me to stand up and find out?'

Chris was wearing a beige tweed sportcoat, an old one with sagging pockets. He brought a Mini-Mag flashlight out of the left side pocket, went down flat on the floor and played the light beam into the four-inch clearance beneath the chair. The space was empty. He came to his knees, placed the Mini-Mag on the floor, brought a stainless Spyder-Co lockback pocketknife from the right side pocket and flicked open the short blade with one hand in a quick, practiced motion.

Booker said, 'Hey,' pushing back in the chair.

'Cover yourself,' Chris said. 'I don't want to cut anything off by mistake.'

'Man, be careful there,' Booker said, bringing his hands off the chair arms to bunch the skirts of the robe between his bare legs, up tight against his crotch.

'You feel anything under you?'

'When I sat down it felt . . . like, different.'

Chris slit open the facing of the seat cushion, held the edges apart and looked in. He said, 'Hmmmmm.'

Booker said, 'What you mean, hmmmmm? Don't give me no hmmmmm shit. What's in there?'

Chris looked up at Booker and said, 'Ten sticks of dynamite.'

Booker was clutching the chair arms again, his body upright, stiff, telling Chris, 'Get that shit out from under me, man. Get it out, get it out of there!'

Chris said, 'Somebody doesn't like you, Booker. Two sticks would've been plenty.'

Booker said, 'Will you pull that shit *out*? Do it.'

Chris sat back on his heels, looking up at Booker. 'I'm afraid we have a problem.'

'What problem? What you talking about?'

'See, most of the foam padding's been taken out. There's something in there that looks like an inflatable rubber cushion, fairly flat, laying on top of the dynamite.'

'So pull the shit out, man. You see it, pull it out.'

'Yeah, but what I don't see is what makes it go bang. It must be in the back part, where the cushion zips open.'

'Then open the motherfucker.'

'I can't, you're sitting on it. It's probably a two-way pressure switch of some kind. I can't tell for sure, but that'd be my guess.'

Booker said, 'Your *guess*? You telling me you don't know what you doing?'

'We get all kinds,' Chris said. 'I have to see it before I know what it is . . . or whether or not I can disarm it. You understand?'

'Wait a minute now. You saying *if* you can take it apart?'

'And the only way to get to it,' Chris said, 'is to cut through the back of the chair.'

'Then cut it, cut it, I don't give a shit about the chair.'

'You run into the frame, all that heavy wood and springs . . .' Chris paused. He said, 'I don't know,' shaking his head.

Booker said, 'Look, motherfucker. You get this shit out from under me. You cut, you do what you have to do, you get it out.'

'On the other hand,' Chris said, 'it might not be a bomb at all. Just the dynamite in there. You know, to scare you, keep you in line. I mean, is there a reason anybody'd want to take you out?'

Booker said, 'You mean like just the shit, but no way to blow it?'

'Yeah.'

'Like they telling me look what could happen?'

'Maybe.'

'Say I could just get up, was all bullshit what they made her say to me? On the phone?'

'That's possible,' Chris said, 'but I don't think I'd take the chance.'

'You wouldn't, huh?'

'Let's see what my partner says, when he gets here.'

Booker said, 'Man, I got to go the toilet, bad.'

Chris watched Jerry Baker taking in the size of the house as he came up the walk, away from the uniforms and the blue Detroit Police radio cars blocking both sides of the boulevard. It was Jerry's day off. He wore a black poplin jacket and a Detroit Tigers baseball cap: a tall man, bigger and older than Chris, twenty-five years on the force, fifteen as a bomb tech. He remembered what day this was and said to Chris, 'You shouldn't be here.'

Standing inside the doorway, Chris told him about the green leather chair Booker was sitting in.

And Jerry said it again, looking at his watch. 'No, you shouldn't be here. Forty minutes, you'll be through.'

He looked outside at the guy from Narcotics waiting on the

porch, waved him over and told him to call for Fire and EMS and get everybody away from the house. The guy from Narcotics said, 'Can't you guys handle this one?'

Jerry said, 'You'll hear it if we can't.' Walking down the hall to the jacuzzi room he said to Chris, 'If we save this asshole's life, you think he'll appreciate it?'

Chris said, 'You mean will he say thank you? Wait'll you meet him.'

They entered the room, Jerry gazing up at the green-and-white tenting, and Booker said, 'Finally, you motherfuckers decide you gonna do something?'

Chris and Jerry took time to look at each other. They didn't say anything. Jerry got down to inspect the sliced-open seat cushion between Booker's muscular legs and said, 'Hmmmmm.'

Booker said, 'Another one goes hmmmmm. I'm sitting here on high explosives the motherfucker goes hmmmmm.'

Jerry stood up, looking at Chris again. 'Well, he's cool. That's a good thing.'

Chris said, 'Yeah, he's cool.'

As Jerry walked around to the back of the green leather chair, Booker, sitting upright, raised his head.

'Hey, I got to go the toilet, man, bad.'

Jerry reached over the backrest to put his hand on Booker's shoulder. 'You better wait. I don't think you can make it.'

'I'll tell you what I have to make. I mean it.'

Jerry said, over Booker to Chris, 'The boy looks fast.'

'Used to run from the Narcs in his Pony joggers, one of those Pony Down delivery boys,' Chris said. 'Yeah, I imagine he's fast.'

Booker was still upright with his head raised. 'Wait now. What're we saying here if I'm fast? Bet to it, man, I'm fast.'

Chris said, 'We don't want you to get the idea you can dive out of your chair into your little swimming pool and make it.'

Booker said, 'In the jacuze? I get in there I be safe?'

'I doubt it,' Chris said. 'If what you're sitting on there, if it's wired and it's not one of your friends being funny . . .'

Jerry said, 'Or if it's not a dud.'

Booker said, 'Yeah, what?'

Chris said, 'If it's a practical joke – you know, or some kind of warning – then there's nothing to worry about. But if it's wired, you raise up and it goes . . .'

'I couldn't get in the jacuze quick enough, huh?'

'I doubt it.'

'His feet might stay on the floor,' Jerry said, 'remain in the house.'

Chris agreed, nodding. 'Yeah, but his ass'd be sailing over Ohio.'

Jerry moved from behind the chair to the French doors. 'We better talk about it some more.'

Booker's head turned to follow Chris. 'Where you going? Hey, motherfucker, I'm talking to you!'

Chris stepped out and closed the door. He moved with Jerry to the far edge of the slate patio before looking back at the French doors in the afternoon sunlight. They could hear Booker in there, faintly. They crossed the yard, Jerry offering Chris a cigarette. He took one and Jerry gave him a light once they reached the driveway and were standing by the three-car garage, alone in the backyard. Jerry looked up at the elm trees. He said, 'Well, they're finally starting to bud. I thought winter was gonna run through May.'

Chris said, 'That's my favourite kind of house. Sort of an English Tudor, before Booker got hold of it.'

Jerry said, 'Why don't you and Phyllis buy one?'

'She likes apartments. Goes with her career image.'

'She must be jumping up and down, finally got her way.'

Chris didn't say anything.

'I'm talking about your leaving the squad.'

'I know what you meant. I haven't told her yet. I'm waiting till I get reassigned.'

'Maybe Homicide, huh?'

'I wouldn't mind it.'

'Yeah, but would Phyllis?'

Chris didn't answer. They smoked their cigarettes and could hear fire equipment arriving. Jerry said, 'Hey, I was kidding. Don't be so serious.'

'I know what you're saying,' Chris said. 'Phyllis is the kind of person that speaks out. Something bothers her, she tells you about it.'

'I know,' Jerry said.

'There's nothing wrong with that, is there?'

'I'm not saying anything against her.'

'What it is, Phyllis says things even some guys would like to but don't have the nerve.'

'Yeah, 'cause she's a woman,' Jerry said, 'she doesn't have to worry about getting hit in the mouth.'

Chris shook his head. 'I don't mean putting anybody down or being insulting. Like we're at a restaurant, one of those trendy places the waiter introduces himself? This twinkie comes up to the table, he goes, "Hi, I'm Wally, I'm gonna be your waitperson this evening. Can I get you a cocktail?" Phyllis goes, "Wally, when we've finished dinner, you gonna take us out and introduce us to the dishwasher?" She goes, "We really don't care what your name is as long as you're here when we want something."'

Jerry grinned, adjusting his Tiger baseball cap. 'That's good, I can appreciate that. Those guys kill me.'

They drew on their cigarettes. Chris looked at his, about to say something, working the butt between his thumb and second finger to flick it away, and the French doors and some of the windows on this side of the house exploded out in a billow of gray smoke tinged yellow. They stood looking at the shattered doorway, at the smoke and dust thinning, settling over glass and wood fragments, shreds of blackened green-and-white debris on the patio, silence ringing in their ears now. After a few moments they started down the drive, let the people waiting in front know they were OK.

Chris said, 'Yeah, the twink comes up to the table, says he's gonna be our waitperson. But you have to understand, Phyllis wasn't trying to be funny, she was serious. That's the way she is.'

....

PART THREE

SENTENCE FIRST, VERDICT AFTERWARDS

A CRITICAL INTERLUDE

EDGAR ALLAN POE

These tales of ratiocination owe most of their popularity to being something in a new key. I do not mean to say that they are not ingenious – but people think them more ingenious than they are – on account of their method and *air* of method. In 'The Murders in the Rue Morgue', for instance, where is the ingenuity of unravelling a web which you yourself (the author) have woven for the express purpose of unravelling? The reader is made to confound the ingenuity of the supposititious Dupin with that of the writer of the story.

ROBERT LOUIS STEVENSON AND LLOYD OSBOURNE

We had long been at once attracted and repelled by that very modern form of the police novel or mystery story, which consists in beginning your yarn anywhere but at the beginning, and finishing it anywhere but at the end; attracted by its peculiar interest when done, and the peculiar difficulties that attend its execution; repelled by that appearance of insincerity and shallowness of tone, which seems its inevitable drawback. For the mind of the reader, always bent to pick up clues, receives no impression of reality or life, rather of an airless, elaborate mechanism; and the book remains enthralling, but insignificant, like a game of chess, not a work of human art.

EDMUND WILSON

I began to nurse a rankling conviction that detective stories in general are able to profit by an unfair advantage in the code which forbids the reviewer to give away the secret to the public – a custom which results in the concealment of the pointlessness of a good deal of this fiction and affords a protection to the authors which no other department of writing enjoys. It is not difficult to create suspense by making people await a revelation, but it does demand a certain talent to come through with a criminal device which is ingenious or picturesque or amusing enough to make the reader feel that the waiting has been worthwhile.

RAYMOND CHANDLER

Since a concealment of the truth is implied, there must be some means of effecting that concealment. It is all a question of degree. Some tricks are offensive because they are blatant and because, once they are shown up, there is nothing left. Some are pleasing because they are insidious and subtle, like a caught glance the meaning of which one does not quite know although one is suspicious that it is not flattering. There is no possibility of perfection. Complete frankness would destroy the mystery. The better the writer, the farther he will go with the truth, the more subtly he will disguise that which cannot be told. It often seems to this particular writer that the only reasonably honest and effective method of fooling the reader that remains is to make the reader exercise his mind about the wrong problem, to make him, as it were, solve a mystery (since he is almost sure to solve something) which will land him in a bypath because it is only tangential to the central problem. And even this takes a bit of cheating here and there.

G . K . CHESTERTON

For the detective story is only a game; and in that game the reader is not really wrestling with the criminal but with the author. What the writer has to remember, in this sort of game, is that the reader will not say, as he sometimes might of a serious or realistic study: 'Why *did* the surveyor in green spectacles climb the tree to look into the lady doctor's back garden?' He will insensibly and inevitably say, 'Why did the author *make* the surveyor climb a tree, or introduce any surveyor at all?' The reader may admit that the town would in any case need a surveyor, without admitting that the tale would in any case need one. It is necessary to explain his presence in the tale (and the tree) not only by suggesting why the town council put him there, but why the author put him there. Over and above any little crimes he may intend to indulge in, in the inner chamber of the story, he must have already some other justification as a character in a story and not only as a mere miserable material person in real life. The instinct of the reader, playing hide-and-seek with the writer, who is his real enemy, is always to say with suspicion, 'Yes, I know a surveyor might climb a tree; I am quite aware that there are trees and that there are surveyors, but what are you doing with them?'

PHILIP VAN DOREN STERN

The great need of the mystery story today is not novelty of apparatus but novelty of approach. The whole genre needs overhauling, a return to first principles, a realization that murder has to do with human emotion and demands serious treatment. Mystery story writers need to know more about life and less about death – more about the way people think and feel and act, and less about how they die.

T. S. ELIOT

Without dispraise of any individual writer we may be allowed to complain that modern detective fiction in general is weak in that it fails between two possible tasks. It has neither the austerity, the pure intellectual pleasure of Poe's *Marie Rogêt*, nor has it the fullness and abundance of life of Wilkie Collins. We often wish that the majority of our detective writers would either concentrate on the detective interest, or take more trouble and space over the characters as human beings and the atmosphere in which they live.

EDMUND WILSON

My contention is that Sherlock Holmes is literature on a humble but not ignoble level, whereas the mystery writers most in vogue now are not. The old stories are literature, not because of the conjuring tricks and the puzzles, not because of the lively melodrama, which they have in common with many other detective stories, but by virtue of imagination and style.

JAMES JOYCE

Finnegans Wake

I should like to ask that Shedlock Homes person who is out for removing the roofs of our criminal classics by what *deductio ad domunum* he hopes *de tacto* to detect anything unless he happens of himself, *movibile tectu*, to have a slade off.

JOHN HEATH-STUBBS

'Send for Lord Timothy'

The Squire is in his library. He is rather worried.
Lady Constance has been found stabbed in the locked
Blue Room, clutching in her hand
A fragment of an Egyptian papyrus. His degenerate half-brother
Is on his way back from New South Wales,
And what was the butler, Glubb,
Doing in the neolithic stone-circle
Up there on the hill, known to the local rustics
From time immemorial as the Nine Lilywhite Boys?
The Vicar is curiously learned
In Renaissance toxicology. A greenish Hottentot,
Armed with a knobkerry, is concealed in the laurel bushes.

Mother Mary Tiresias is in her parlour.
She is rather worried. Sister Mary Josephus
Has been found suffocated in the scriptorium,
Clutching in her hand a somewhat unspeakable
Central American fetish. Why was the little novice,
Sister Agnes, suddenly struck speechless
Walking in the herbarium? The chaplain, Fr. O'Goose,
Is almost too profoundly read
In the darker aspects of fourth-century Neoplatonism.
An Eskimo, armed with a harpoon
Is lurking in the organ loft.

The Warden of St Phenol's is in his study.
He is rather worried. Professor Ostracoderm
Has been found strangled on one of the Gothic turrets,
Clutching in his hand a patchouli-scented
Lady's chiffon handkerchief.
The brilliant undergraduate they unjustly sent down
Has transmitted an obscure message in Greek elegiacs

All the way from Tashkent. Whom was the Domestic Bursar
Planning to meet in that evil-smelling
Riverside tavern? Why was the Senior Fellow,
Old Doctor Mousebracket, locked in among the incunabula?
An aboriginal Philipino pygmy,
Armed with a blowpipe and poisoned darts, is hiding behind
The statue of Pallas Athene.

A dark cloud of suspicion broods over all. But even now
Lord Timothy Pratincole (the chinless wonder
With a brain like Leonardo's) or Chief Inspector Palefox
(Although a policeman, patently a gentleman,
And with a First in Greats) or that eccentric scholar,
Monsignor Monstrance, alights from the chuffing train,
Has booked a room at the local hostelry
(*The Dragon of Wantley*) and is chatting up Mine Host,
Entirely democractically, noting down
Local rumours and folklore.

Now read on. The murderer will be unmasked,
The cloud of guilt dispersed, the church clock stuck at three,
And the year always
Nineteen twenty or thirty something,
Honey for tea, and nothing
Will ever really happen again.

....

ANTONIO GRAMSCI

Two things haven't been given to me yet – *Bibliografia fascista*
and Chesterton's short stories. I'm looking forward to reading
the latter for two reasons – firstly, because I'm sure that they will
be as interesting as the earlier series, and secondly, because I will
try to imagine what kind of impression they must have made on
you. The second will undoubtedly give the most pleasure. I
distinctly remember your reaction to the first series. You were

completely open to what you were reading and did not notice the residual cultural elements. You were not even aware that Chesterton had written an extremely subtle caricature of detective stories rather than straight detective stories. Father Brown is a Catholic who mocks the mechanical habits of thought of Protestants, and the book is basically a defence of the Roman Church against the Anglican Church. Sherlock Holmes is the Protestant detective who unravels the tangled skein of a crime starting from the outside, using scientific and experimental methods and induction. Father Brown is the Catholic priest who uses the subtle psychological experience gained from the confessional and from the vigorous moral casuistry of the Fathers, depending particularly on deduction and introspection while not totally ignoring science and experiment. In this way he completely outshines Sherlock Holmes and makes him look like a pretentious schoolboy with a mean and narrow view of things. Moreover, Chesterton is a great artist, whereas Conan Doyle was a second-rate writer, even though he was made a baronet for his supposed literary merits. In Chesterton the stylistic divergence between the content, the plot of the detective story, and the form results in a subtly ironical treatment of the material that makes the stories more amusing. Do you agree? I remember that you read these stories as though they were a chronicle of real events and became so involved in them that you openly declared your admiration for Father Brown's marvellous acumen, with an ingenuousness that amused me enormously. You mustn't be offended though, because this amusement was tinged with envy for your fresh, unabashed impressionability. To tell you the truth, I've no great desire to write: my brain is tired.

HARRISON R. STEEVES

The mystery tale can be good art, at least in those respects which are elemental for any work of fiction. We should be allowed to breathe the real air of real places, feel the charm or the pressure of a distinct local life, hear the stir and play of agreeable conversation, and savour the everyday emotions. Above all, we can ask that the story be inhabited by convincing human beings, doing things that human beings do. So far as the detective story is deficient in these clear requirements of good art it is deficient in fundamentals. And that deficiency in organic or 'functional' art is intensified for the good reader's consciousness by an increasingly disturbing use of every sort of irrelevant and trivial appliqué art – glitter, gratuitous flippancy, meaningless wit, and conventional beautification. This is no depreciation of decorative purpose, but merely a reminder that art must be *in* a work, and not *on* it.

NORMAN SHRAPNEL

Never has man, English-speaking man in particular, been at once so threatened and so secure. The writer is baffled by the paradox, just as the citizen is haunted by it. Violence is the core and perhaps the clue to our time, but we cannot come to terms with it. For the curtained citizen it is a background, a rumour sustained by reports and statistics, a menace always just over the horizon or just round the next street corner. For the writer, whether or not it breaks surface in his work, it is a state of mind.

Yet all the time, unseen by the citizen and the writer, it acts. Crime, though no more than a shuffling folk dance to the grand opera in rehearsal, is the patterned, articulated, vernacular form of violence we ought to be able to get to grips with. In a sense that it takes a writer like Simenon to comprehend, crime is normal. If it is true to say that a fiction which managed to ignore the violence of our day would be a total lie, there must surely be something suspect about a fiction which has its crime department hived away on special shelves.

Though there are signs at last of the beginnings of a shift away from the attitude, it is still usual to regard crime fiction as the black sheep of the novel family – shady if not downright delinquent, prone to brutality and unrestrained sex, dubiously affluent on easy money, scarcely to be mentioned in decent company. The view has a good deal of justification, of course, and we are in one of those vicious circles in which the accusation is partly the cause of its truth. It is still the general view, both among readers of ordinary fiction (who may also read thrillers on the side) and among literary editors and critics, who separate the two schools of writing by a wall as high as any that might exist between a ladies' college and a borstal institution. Both may properly be visited, but there is no door through the wall.

The removal of the barrier would be a formidable demolition job. Nothing would be harder than to get the necessary licence from the literary planning authorities, for the whole subject is deeply filed away in custom and taboo.

Whether or not there are any direct lessons that the conventional novel can learn from thrillers and crime fiction, it is at least possible to point to certain plain advantages enjoyed by writers in this field. First, it has a natural dynamic, in contrast with the entranced state of the novel in its latest stage of development, moving at the pace of a minute-hand or a creeping shadow-edge. The next logical stage in this progression must surely be the ending of any impulse to turn a page at all. Yet readability in the old sense is not to be despised, and there must be a future for it if books are themselves going to survive. It is always easier to stop reading than to turn a switch, and it is easier still never to start.

ALLEN PRYCE-JONES

When Dickens sat down to write *Bleak House* we must not suppose that he was greatly troubled by the exact definition of the book he was writing. Was it to be a psychological novel built round the dilemma of Lady Dedlock? Was it to be a novel of social realism, turning on such pivots as Mr Tulkinghorn and Jo? Was it to be just the orchestration of idiosyncrasy, with Mrs Jellby and Mr Skimpole and the intolerable Esther Summerson rising to their solo notes from time to time, answered by Messrs Turveydrop, Bucket and Guppy, and all scored above a ground bass of threat and apprehension? Such questions mattered very little to Dickens. From the stores of his profusion he was content to spill out an immense novel which embraces a multitude of attitudes. Romance, satire, pure fantasy, the detailed transcription of life: there they all are, improvidently flung together upon the bones of a detective story. It is the underlying detective story which keeps the tale moving, however, and the generations which have delighted in *Bleak House* have been able to do so only because Dickens himself felt free to mix his ingredients as he chose in order to extend his thriller through half the domain of fiction.

Later novelists have never felt so free again. Either they have been obsessed by the novel as a work of art or they have been content to make it the vehicle for an exciting anecdote. And as it has become more and more subtle in its effects under such influences as those of Virginia Woolf and Miss Elizabeth Bowen, so the novel has come, at its opposite extreme, to demand an ever-greater crudity of intention. The novelist vaporizes or he bludgeons. It is rare indeed for him to blend the two approaches.

....

BERTOLT BRECHT

If someone cries 'The same old thing again!' when he realizes that a tenth of all murders take place in a churchyard, then he has not understood the crime novel. He might just as well cry 'The same old thing again!' in the theatre when the curtain rises. The originality resides elsewhere. Indeed, the fact that one character-istic feature of the crime novel is the variation of more or less fixed elements is precisely what gives the whole genre its aesthetic quality. It is one of the properties of a cultivated branch of literature. Besides, the ignorant man's cry of 'The same old thing again!' is based on the same fallacy as the white man's idea that all blacks look the same.

....

JOSEPH WOOD KRUTCH

No inconsiderable part of the great literature of the world has been written within the limitations of an established tradition, and so written not because the authors lacked originality but because the acceptance of a tradition and with it of certain fixed themes and methods seems to release rather than stifle the effective working of the imagination.

....

T. S. ELIOT

Those who have lived before such terms as 'highbrow fiction', 'thrillers' and 'detective fiction' were invented realize that melo-drama is perennial and that the craving for it is perennial and must be satisfied. If we cannot get this satisfaction out of what the publishers present as 'literature', then we will read – with less and less pretence of concealment – what we call 'thrillers'. But in the golden age of melodramatic fiction there was no such distinction. The best novels *were* thrilling. Perhaps Henry James – who in his own practice could be not only 'interesting', but had a very cunning mastery of the finer melodrama – may have had as a critic a bad influence. We cannot afford to forget that the first – and not one of the least difficult – requirements of either prose or verse is that it should be interesting.

....

BERTOLT BRECHT

The characters in crime novels do not just leave their imprint in the souls of their fellow men but also in their bodies, as well as in the earth beneath the library window. In real life a man rarely finds that he leaves any traces behind, at least unless he is a criminal with the police on his trail. The lives of the atomized masses and of the collectivized individuals of our times vanish without trace. An adventure novel can hardly be written except in the form of a crime novel: in our society, adventures are criminal.

....

FRIEDRICH DÜRRENMATT

The Pledge

To be honest I have never thought very highly of mystery stories, and I regret to hear that you too have to do with them. Sheer waste of time. What you had to say in your lecture yesterday was worth hearing, no doubt; since the politicians fail us in so reprehensible a fashion – and I ought to know, since I'm one myself, Federal Deputy, as you probably know – well, since the politicians are such failures, people hope that at least the police will know how to keep order in the world. I must admit that I myself can conceive of no rottener hope than that. The trouble is that in all these mystery stories an altogether different kind of fraud is perpetrated. I am not even referring to the fact that the criminal has his punishment meted out to him. Such pretty fairy-tales are morally necessary too, I suppose. They are in the same class with the other lies that help preserve the State, like that pious phrase that crime does not pay, whereas anyone has only to look at human society to find out just how much truth there is in that. But I would let all that ride, if only out of strict commercial principles – for every audience and every taxpayer has a right to his heroes and his happy ending, and we of the police and you of the writing profession are equally obliged to supply these. No, what really annoys me is the plot in your novels. Here the fraud becomes too raw and shameless. You build your plots up logically, like a chess game; here the criminal, here the victim, here the accomplice, here the master mind. The detective need only know the rules and play the game over, and he has the criminal trapped, has won a victory for justice. This fiction infuriates me. Reality can be only partially attacked by logic. Granted, we police officials are forced to proceed logically, scientifically, but the factors that muck up the works for us are so common that all too frequently only pure professional luck and chance decide the issue for us. Or against us. But in your novels chance plays no part, and if something looks like chance it's represented as some kind of destiny or divine dispensation. You writers have always sacrificed truth for the sake of your dramatic rules. It's time you threw those rules out of the window. These things can never be equated because we never know all the necessary unknowns. We know only a few, and usually unimportant ones. Chance, the incalculable, the incommensurable, plays too great a part. Our rules are based only on probabilities, on statistics, not causality; they apply only in general and not in particular. The individual stands outside our calculations. Our criminological tools are inadequate, and the more we try to sharpen them the more inadequate they become. But you fellows in the writing game don't worry about that. You don't try to get mixed up with the kind of reality that is always slipping through our fingers. Instead you set up a world that you can manage. That world may be perfect – who knows? – but it's also a lie. Drop the perfection if you want to get anywhere, if you want to get at things, at reality, which is what a man ought to be doing. Otherwise you'll be left behind, fooling around with useless stylistic exercises.

....

PAUL AUSTER

City of Glass

Like most people, Quinn knew almost nothing about crime. He had never murdered anyone, had never stolen anything, and he did not know anyone who had. He had never been inside a police station, had never met a private detective, had never spoken to a criminal. Whatever he knew about these things, he had learned from books, films, and newspapers. He did not, however, consider this to be a handicap. What interested him about the stories he wrote was not their relation to the world but their relation to other stories. Even before he became William Wilson, Quinn had been a devoted reader of mystery novels. He knew that most of them were poorly written, that most could not stand up to even the vaguest sort of examination, but still, it was the form that appealed to him, and it was the rare, unspeakably bad mystery that he would refuse to read. Whereas his taste in other books was rigorous, demanding to the point of narrow-mindedness, with these works he showed almost no discrimination whatsoever. When he was in the right mood, he had little trouble reading ten or twelve of them in a row. It was a kind of hunger that took hold of him, a craving for a special food, and he would not stop until he had eaten his fill.

What he liked about these books was their sense of plenitude and economy. In the good mystery there is nothing wasted, no sentence, no word that is not significant. And even if it is not significant, it has the potential to be so – which amounts to the same thing. The world of the book comes to life, seething with possibilities, with secrets and contradictions. Since everything seen or said, even the slightest, most trivial thing, can bear a connection to the outcome of the story, nothing must be overlooked. Everything becomes essence; the center of the book shifts with each event that propels it forward. The centre, then, is everywhere, and no circumference can be drawn until the book has come to its end.

The detective is the one who looks, who listens, who moves through this morass of objects and events in search of the thought, the idea that will pull all these things together and make sense of them. In effect, the writer and the detective are interchangeable. The reader sees the world through the detective's eye, experiencing the proliferation of its details as if for the first time. He has become awake to the things around him, as if they might speak to him, as if, because of the attentiveness he now brings to them, they might begin to carry a meaning other than the simple fact of their existence. Private eye. The term held a triple meaning for Quinn. Not only was it the letter 'i,' standing for 'investigator,' it was 'I' in the upper case, the tiny life-bud buried in the body of the breathing self. At the same time, it was also the physical eye of the writer, the eye of the man who looks out from himself into the world and demands that the world reveal itself to him. For five years now, Quinn had been living in the grip of this pun.

....

CHARLES RYCROFT

Of the various psychoanalysts who have discussed the psychology of the detective story only one, Geraldine Pedersen-Krag, has put forward a specific hypothesis to account for their popularity. In her article 'Detective Stories and the Primal Scene' (1949) she suggests that it arises from their ability to reawaken the interest and curiosity originally aroused by observation of the primal scene. According to her the murder is a symbolic representation of parental intercourse and

> the victim is the parent for whom the reader (the child) had negative oedipal feelings. The clues in the story, disconnected, inexplicable and trifling, represent the child's growing awareness of details it had never understood, such as the family sleeping arrangements, nocturnal sounds, stains, incomprehensible adult jokes and remarks . . . The reader addicted to mystery stories tries actively to relive and master traumatic infantile experiences he once had to endure passively. Becoming the detective, he gratifies his infantile curiosity with impunity, redressing completely the helpless inadequacy and anxious guilt unconsciously remembered from childhood.

It is possible to draw a deduction from this hypothesis which Pedersen-Krag does not herself explicitly make. If the victim is the parent for whom the reader (the child) had negative oedipal feelings, then the criminal must be a personification of the reader's own unavowed hostility towards that parent. The reader is not only the detective; he is also the criminal. One reason, I suspect, why the detective story so rarely achieves the status of a work of art is that this identification of the reader with the criminal remains denied. The detective story writer connives with the reader's need to deny his guilt by providing him with ready-made fantasies in which the compulsive question 'whodunnit?' is always answered by a self-exonerating 'not I'. In the ideal detective story the detective or hero would discover that he himself is the criminal for whom he has been seeking.

UMBERTO ECO

In essence, the basic question of philosophy (as of psychoanalysis) is the same as that of the detective novel: who is guilty? To know the answer (to think you know) you have to conjecture that the facts possess a logic – the logic that the guilty party has imposed on them.

BERTOLT BRECHT

We gain experience in life in the form of disasters. We must infer the manner in which social interaction functions from various catastrophes. We have to establish the 'inside story' of crises, depressions, revolutions and wars by thinking them through. Behind the events reported to us we suspect other unreported happenings. These are the *real* happenings. Only if we know them can we understand. This basic situation in which intellectuals find themselves – as the objects rather than subjects of history – shapes the type of reasoning which they enjoy putting into effect in reading crime novels. Existence depends upon unknown factors. Clarification comes, if at all, only after the catastrophe. The murder has taken place. What was afoot beforehand? What happened then? What sort of situation arose? Now, perhaps, we can work it all out.

MICHEL BUTOR

Passing Time

Any detective story is constructed on two murders of which the first, committed by the criminal, is only the occasion of the second, in which he is the victim of the pure, unpunishable murderer, the detective, who kills him not by one of those despicable means he was himself reduced to using, poison, the knife, a silent shot or the twist of a silk stocking, but by the explosion of truth.

The aim of his whole existence is that tremendous moment in which the power of his explanations, of his disclosure, of the words by which he tears off veils and masks, uttered generally in a tone of grave melancholy as if to soften the terrible, dazzling light they shed, so welcome to those whom it sets free but so cruel, so appalling, so blinding too, the power of his speech actually destroys the criminal, achieves that death that confirms and crowns his work – that moment when reality is transformed and purified by the sole power of his keen and accurate vision.

A major part of the relations existing between the participants in the drama were maintained only through the errors, ignorances and lies which he abolishes; the actors group themselves in a new pattern from which one member of the former grouping is automatically excluded.

He cleanses this small fraction of the world from its offence, which was not so much the mere fact that one man has killed another (for there might be such a thing as a pure murder, a kind of rejuvenation sacrifice) but rather the defilement that murder brings with it, the bloodstained shadows that it casts about it, and at the same time that deep-seated, age-old discord which becomes incarnate in the criminal from the moment when, by his act, he revealed its presence, and aroused those vast buried forces which now disturb the hitherto accepted order of things and betray its fragility.

The detective is a true son of the murderer Oedipus, not only because he solves a riddle, but also because he kills the man to whom he owes his title, without whom he would not exist in that capacity (without crimes, without mysterious crimes, what would he be?) because this murder was foretold for him from the day of his birth or, if you prefer, because it is inherent in his nature, through it alone he fulfils himself and attains the highest power.

....

W. H. AUDEN

'Detective Story'

Who is ever quite without his landscape,
The straggling village street, the house in trees,
All near the church? Or else, the gloomy town-house,
The one with the Corinthian pillars, or
The tiny workmanlike flat, in any case
A home, a centre where the three or four things
That happen to a man do happen?
Who cannot draw the map of his life, shade in
The country station where he meets his loves
And says goodbye continually, mark the spot
Where the body of his happiness was first discovered?

An unknown tramp? A magnate? An enigma always,
With a well-buried past: and when the truth,
The truth about our happiness comes out,
How much it owed to blackmail and philandering.

What follows is habitual. All goes to plan:
The feud between the local common sense
And intuition, that exasperating amateur
Who's always on the spot by chance before us;
All goes to plan, both lying and confession,
Down to the thrilling final chase, the kill.

Yet, on the last page, a lingering doubt:
The verdict, was it just? The judge's nerves,
That clue, that protestation from the gallows,
And our own smile . . . why, yes . . .

But time is always guilty. Someone must pay for
Our loss of happiness, our happiness itself.

....

PIERRE WEISZ

A Maigret novel often starts with the good news that Mme Maigret is preparing a great *cassoulet* for the commissaire's enjoyment, only to see him frustrated from his meal by some fulsome crime. For two hundred pages, Maigret carries in his head, nostrils and tastebuds the false memory of a summit of *cuisine bourgeoise* while gobbling stale sandwiches or greasy fries. Even the sacred monthly dinner at Dr Pardon's house will occasionally be interrupted by some unwitting criminal who, having disturbed one of the chief elements of order in this universe (beef bourguignon, that is), will thus have sealed his own fate. Every investigation is placed under the sign of a certain dish, a particular liquor or both. There are ham sandwich investigations, *rouelle-de-veau* investigations, sauerkraut investigations, some washed down with cheap beer, others laced with dry white wine, or digested with the help of a sturdy burgundy. Every shot of Calvados, every gulp of brandy, every glass of vermouth adds to the commissaire's and our intimate, intuitive knowledge of some corner of Paris, some village in Normandy, some man with a knife in his chest or in his hand. Maigret eats it all, drinks it all and, in the end, knows it all.

....

HAROLD NICHOLSON

It is not the impossible I object to in detective novels: it is the improbable that destroys all suspension of disbelief. It is for this reason that the works of Georges Simenon delight me above all others. He is frequently impossible: but never does he allow himself to descend to the improbable.

....

JAMES THURBER

'The Wings of Henry James'

One night nearly thirty years ago, in a legendary New York *boîte de nuit et des arts* called Tony's, I was taking part in a running literary gun fight that had begun with a derogatory or complimentary remark somebody made about something, when one of the participants, former Pinkerton man Dashiell Hammett, whose *The Maltese Falcon* had come out a couple of years before, suddenly startled us all by announcing that his writing had been influenced by Henry James's novel *The Wings of the Dove*. Nothing surprises me any more, but I couldn't have been more surprised than if Humphrey Bogart, another frequenter of that old salon of wassail and debate, had proclaimed that his acting bore the deep impress of the histrionic art of Maude Adams.

I was unable, in a recent reinvestigation, to find many feathers of 'The Dove' in the claws of 'The Falcon', but there are a few 'faint, far' (as James used to say) resemblances. In both novels, a fabulous fortune – jewels in 'The Falcon', inherited millions in 'The Dove' – shapes the destinies of the disenchanted central characters; James's designing woman Kate Croy, like Hammett's pistol-packing babe, Brigid O'Shaughnessy, loses her lover, although James's Renunciation Scene is managed, as who should say, rather more exquisitely than Hammett's, in which Sam Spade speaks these sweetly sorrowful parting words: 'You angel! Well, if you get a good break you'll be out of San Quentin in twenty years and you can come back to me then.' Whereupon he turns her over to the cops for the murder of his partner, Miles Archer (a good old Henry James name, that). Some strong young literary excavator may one day dig up other parallels, but I suggest that he avoid trying to relate the character in *The Falcon* called Cairo to James's early intention to use Cairo, instead of Venice, as the major setting of his novel. That is simply, as who should not say, one of those rococo coincidences.

RAYMOND QUENEAU

In some twenty years, the American crime novel has changed out of all recognition. Writers and readers are no longer concerned with the puzzle as much as with the characters who embody it; the detective has ceased to be a godlike reasoning machine and assumed the guise of a tough cop given to the third-degree and drinking heavily; in short, the detective story has ceased to be cerebral and become, so to speak, existentialist (in the journalistic sense). Brutality and eroticism have replaced clever deduction. The detective no longer gathers cigarette ash but breaks witnesses' noses with his fist. The criminals are foul-mouthed, sadistic cowards; the women all have great legs, and are deceitful and treacherous, and no less cruel than the men. A lovely bunch, in short, and there's no need to make the slightest intellectual effort to follow the more or less bloodstained trail of the detective left to his own devices in this inferno. Not that these books present a realistic portrait of American gangster life: they are works of pure imagination which have their conventions and arbitrary rules just like the old-fashioned detective story.

....

JEAN-PAUL SARTRE

I dragged my mother down to the banks of the Seine, and we set out to search the stalls one by one from the Gare d'Orsay to the Gare d'Austerlitz: we sometimes brought back fifteen instalments at a time; I soon had five hundred. All I had to do to go wild with delight was to look at the coloured illustrations on the covers. I preferred the illustrations of Nick Carter. They might be thought monotonous: in nearly all of them the great detective is felling someone or is himself being bludgeoned. But these brawls were taking place in the streets of Manhattan, waste land, enclosed by brown wooden fences or frail cubic buildings the colour of dried blood: that fascinated me. I imagined a puritan and bloody city devoured by space and barely concealing the savannah which lay beneath it: crime and virtue were both outside the law there; the assassin and the representative of justice, each of them free and sovereign, had it out in the evenings, with knives. In that city, as in Africa, under the same blazing sun, heroism again became an endless improvisation: hence my passion for New York.

....

S. J. PERELMAN

'Somewhere a Roscoe . . .'

'Arms and the man I sing,' sang Vergil some twenty centuries ago, preparing to celebrate the wanderings of Aeneas. If ever a motto was tailor-made for the masthead of Culture Publications, Inc., it is 'Arms and the Woman,' for in *Spicy Detective* they have achieved the sauciest blend of libido and murder this side of Gilles de Rais. They have juxtaposed the steely automatic and the frilly panty and found that it pays off. Above all, they have given the world Dan Turner, the apotheosis of all private detectives.

Out of Ma Barker by Dashiell Hammett's Sam Spade, let him characterize himself in the opening paragraph of 'Corpse in the Closet,' from the July 1937 issue:

> I opened my bedroom closet. A half-dressed feminine corpse sagged into my arms ... It's a damned screwy feeling to reach for pajamas and find a cadaver instead.

Mr Turner, you will perceive, is a man of sentiment, and it occasionally gets him into a tight corner. For example, in 'Killer's Harvest' (July 1938) he is retained to escort a young matron home from the Cocoanut Grove in Los Angeles:

> Zarah Trenwick was a wow in a gown of silver lamé that stuck to her lush curves like a coating of varnish. Her make-up was perfect; her strapless dress displayed plenty of evidence that she still owned a cargo of lure. Her bare shoulders were snowy, dimpled. The upper slopes of her breast were squeezed upward and partly overflowed the tight bodice, like whipped cream.

To put it mildly, Dan cannot resist the appeal of a pretty foot, and disposing of Zarah's drunken husband ('I clipped him on the button. His hip pockets bounced on the floor'), he takes this charlotte russe to her apartment. Alone with her, the policeman in him succumbs to the man, and 'she fed me a kiss that throbbed all the way down my fallen arches,' when suddenly:

> From the doorway a roscoe said 'Kachow!' and a slug creased the side of my noggin. Neon lights exploded inside my think-tank ... She was as dead as a stuffed mongoose ... I wasn't badly hurt. But I don't like to be shot at. I don't like dames to be rubbed out when I'm flinging woo at them.

With an irritable shrug, Dan phones the homicide detail and reports Zarah's passing in this tender obituary: 'Zarah Trenwick just got blasted to hellangone in her tepee at the Gayboy. Drag your underwear over here – and bring a meat-wagon.' Then he goes in search of the offender:

> I drove over to Argyle; parked in front of Fane Trenwick's modest stash ... I thumbed the bell. The door opened. A

Chink house-boy gave me the slant-eyed focus. 'Missa Tlen-
wick, him sleep. You go way, come tomollow. Too late fo'
vlisito'.' I said 'Nerts to you, Confucius,' and gave him a shove
on the beezer.

Zarah's husband, wrenched out of bed without the silly
formality of a search warrant, establishes an alibi depending upon
one Nadine Wendell. In a trice Dan crosses the city and makes
his gentle way into the lady's boudoir, only to discover again
what a frail vessel he is *au fond*:

> The fragrant scent of her red hair tickled my smeller; the
> warmth of her slim young form set fire to my arterial system.
> After all, I'm as human as the next gazabo.

The next gazabo must be all too human, because Dan betrays
first Nadine and then her secret; namely, that she pistoled Zarah
Trenwick for reasons too numerous to mention. If you feel you
must know them, they appear on page 110, cheek by jowl with
some fascinating advertisements for loaded dice and wealthy
sweethearts, either of which will be sent you in plain wrapper if
you'll forward a dollar to the Majestic Novelty Company of
Janesville, Wisconsin.

The deeper one goes into the Dan Turner saga, the more one
is struck by the similarity between the case confronting Dan in
the current issue and those in the past. The murders follow an
exact, rigid pattern almost like the ritual of a bullfight or a classic
Chinese play. Take 'Veiled Lady,' in the October 1937 number
of *Spicy Detective*. Dan is flinging some woo at a Mrs Brantham
in her apartment at the exclusive Gayboy Arms, which apparently
excludes everybody but assassins:

> From behind me a roscoe belched 'Chow-chow!' A pair of
> slugs buzzed past my left ear, almost nicked my cranium. Mrs
> Brantham sagged back against the pillow of the lounge . . . She
> was as dead as an iced catfish.

Or this vignette from 'Falling Star,' out of the September
1936 issue.

The roscoe said 'Chow!' and spat a streak of flame past my shoulder . . . The Filipino cutie was lying where I'd last seen her. She was as dead as a smoked herring.

And again, from 'Dark Star of Death,' January 1938:

From a bedroom a roscoe said 'Whr-r-rang!' and a lead pill split the ozone past my noggin . . . Kane Fewster was on the floor. There was a bullet hole through his think-tank. He was as dead as a fried oyster.

And still again, from 'Brunette Bump-off,' May 1938:

And then, from an open window beyond the bed, a roscoe coughed 'Ka-chow!' . . . I said, 'What the hell—!' and hit the floor with my smeller . . . A brunette jane was lying there, half out of the mussed covers . . . She was as dead as vaudeville.

The next phase in each of these dramas follows with all the cold beauty and inevitability of a legal brief. The roscoe has hardly spoken, coughed, or belched before Dan is off through the canebrake, his nostrils filled with the heavy scent of Nuit de Noël. Somewhere, in some dimly lit boudoir, waits a voluptuous parcel of womanhood who knows all about the horrid deed. Even if she doesn't, Dan makes a routine check anyway. The premises are invariably guarded by an Oriental whom Dan is obliged to expunge. Compare the scene at Fane Trenwick's modest stash with this one from 'Find That Corpse' (November 1937):

A sleepy Chink maid in pajamas answered my ring. She was a cute little slant-eyed number. I said 'Is Mr Polznak home?' She shook her head. 'Him up on location in Flesno. Been gone two week.' I said 'Thanks. I'll have a gander for myself.' I pushed past her. She started to yip . . . 'Shut up!' I growled. She kept on trying to make a noise. So I popped her on the button. She dropped.

It is a fairly safe bet that Mr Polznak has forgotten the adage that a watched pot never boils and has left behind a dewy-eyed coryphée clad in the minimum of chiffon demanded by the postal authorities. The poet in Dan ineluctably vanquishes the flatfoot ('Dark Star of Death'): 'I glued my glims on her blond loveliness; couldn't help myself. The covers had skidded down from her gorgeous, dimpled shoulders; I could see plenty of delishful, she-male epidermis.' The trumpets blare again; some expert capework by our *torero*, and ('Brunette Bump-off'): 'Then she fed me a kiss that sent a charge of steam past my gozzle . . . Well, I'm as human as the next gink.'

From then on, the author's typewriter keys infallibly fuse in a lump of hot metal and it's all over but the shouting of the culprit and '*Look, Men: One Hundred Breezy Fotos!*' Back in his stash, his roscoe safely within reach, Dan Turner lays his weary noggin on a pillow, resting up for the November issue.

....

PAUL CAIN

Fast One

Kells lifted one point of his vest, stuck the automatic inside the waistband of his trousers. He let his belt out a notch or so until the gun nestled as comfortably and as securely as possible beneath his ribs. Then he pulled the point of his vest down over the butt. It made only a slight bulge against the narrowness of his waist. He said: 'Jakie, have you any idea how fast I can get this tool out and how well I can use it?'

....

NORTHROP FRYE

In the melodrama of the brutal thriller we come as close as it is normally possible for art to come to the pure self-righteousness of the lynching mob.

PART FOUR

UNCOMMON
MURDERERS

MICHAEL DIBDIN

....

In the classic detective story, the murderer was a mere question mark, a ghostly cipher whose personality could never be more than schematic since it had to be compatible with each of half a dozen suspects. By the time his or her identity was finally revealed, the reader was already disengaging himself from a book which had only a few pages of ritualistic coda left to run. But there is another kind of whodunnit, where the pronoun denotes not 'Which suspect?' but 'What manner of man?'

The artificiality of any attempt to segregate these two aspects of the genre is demonstrated by the fact that both were forged in the mind of one man: Edgar Allan Poe. If 'The Murders in the Rue Morgue' is a compendium of just about every trick and trope of the detective story, 'The Tell-Tale Heart' has never been surpassed as a self-portrait of a mind snared in the web of its own delusions. Even the punctuation – a frantic glissade of dashes – contributes to the effect of manic instability. Robert Browning's poem, written at about the same time, was originally titled 'Madhouse Cell'.

In one sense, it is but a short step from here to the private hell of Kees Popinga, the clerk turned murderer in *The Man Who Watched the Trains Go By*. But where Poe and Browning sought to replicate the lush conventions of the Gothic novel in a domestic context, Simenon forces us to confront the unglamorous banality of evil. Popinga's murders rate no more than a few passing words, but the hours he spends in cafés are documented with hallucinatory precision. As banal details succeed one another like drops of drizzle, our sense of significance seeps away and normality stands revealed as a mere convention.

One of Simenon's many eminent admirers was André Gide, who commented: 'Simenon's subjects often have a profound psychological and ethical interest, but insufficiently indicated, as if he were not aware of their importance himself, or as if he expected the reader to catch the hint. This is what attracts and holds me in him.' Gide's own description of a motiveless, impulsive crime dates from 1914, but its effects continue to be felt in crime fiction – notably the killings of Freddie Miles and Dickie Greenleaf in Patricia Highsmith's *The Mysterious Mr Ripley*, which also shares the homoerotic undercurrents of Gide's novel. As does *The Picture of Dorian Gray*. The scene in which Wilde's Dorian Gray persuades a former friend to dispose of a corpse, presumably by threatening him with the fate to which Wilde himself eventually succumbed, is particularly powerful. The languid affectation of the final paragraph, a commonplace of Wilde's work, takes on a new edge in this context.

Japanese crime writing is a fascinating but largely inaccessible subject: English translations are rare and of uneven quality. In *A Kiss of Fire* Masako Togawa manages to combine a virtuoso display of plotting and misleading revelations in the Golden Age manner with profound and authentic insights into the psychopathology of family life.

Suppressed domestic tensions lurking behind a respectable façade also underpin Edward Grierson's *Reputation for a Song*. Grierson was a distinguished barrister, and the book concludes with a courtroom scene which is not only superbly accomplished but avoids any reassuring pretence that law and justice are in any sense to be equated.

Courtroom scenes also dominate Raymond Postgate's *Verdict of Twelve*, which precedes an account of a murder trial with biographies of the jurors, one of whom proves to be a murderer herself. Postgate was a committed socialist – the book carries an epigraph from Karl Marx – and his sensitivity to his characters' differing backgrounds, mentalities, aspirations and assumptions give his work a humanity very rare in British crime fiction at this period (1940).

The exception, *A Pin to See the Peepshow*, by the splendidly named Fryniwyd Tennyson Jesse, is an extended exploration of the facts and implications of a real-life *cause célèbre* in which a woman was executed for the murder of her husband by her lover, although she herself was not involved. The Thompson–Bywaters case of 1922 elicited much controversy – T. S. Eliot publicly supported calls for Edith Thompson to hang, prompting one critic to remark that 'if only indirectly, Eliot got the wish of his protagonist Sweeney to "do a girl in"' – and Jesse's novel draws much of its considerable power and pathos from the contrast between the sordid realities of Julia's situation and the hypocritical, self-righteous attitudes which led to her 'judicial lynching'.

Different from all these – different, indeed, from anything which has appeared in English before or since – was a book published in 1937 under the memorable title *The Face on the Cutting-Room Floor*. The author, who is also the narrator and (probably) the murderer, is named as Cameron McCabe, although the extract printed here is from a long 'Epilogue' by one A. B. C. Müller. ('I want to say how sorry I am for the alphabet of my initials. They stand for Adolf Benito Comrade. Originally Comrade was Conrad, but I felt obliged to introduce some left-wing appeal.') The true identity of the man who perpetrated this astounding hoax remained secret for another thirty years, when he was revealed as Ernst Bornemann, a German socialist, collaborator of Brecht and later Orson Welles, who emigrated to England when Hitler came to power and wrote the novel because 'writing was the only activity *not* forbidden by the British authorities'. The book's aggressive, hectoring tone and highly idiosyncratic English can become wearisome, but it remains an astonishing deconstruction of the conventions of detective fiction. The extract from Carol Ann Duffy's poem makes a similar point in a more straightforward way.

The earlier of Julian Symons' treatments of the uxoricide theme is both a subtle psychosocial analysis of a stifling marriage and a sombre, hallucinatory study of induced paranoia. While Symons is quite capable of resorting to the tactics of the detective story – an apparently damning admission in the second paragraph, for instance, can be read in more than one way – he exploits them not for meretricious effect but to articulate the overall themes of the book.

The introductory stanzas from James Fenton's poem 'A Staffordshire Murderer' consider the relationship between murderer and victim as a collaboration. This may seem just a conceit, but it is in fact the generating concept behind the technique of 'psychological profiling' which is an important aspect of police work. Nor is it a recent idea. As long ago as 1916, D. H. Lawrence wrote: 'It takes two people to make a murder: a murderer and a murderee.'

The shock provoked by the publication of *Malice Aforethought* has been discussed earlier, but this 'story of a commonplace crime' would be of no more than historical interest if the writing itself did not continue to enthrall readers for whom the Golden Age format is itself ancient history. The extract printed here draws together all the elements which impel Dr Bickleigh to murder, as well as the fatal slip which ultimately leads to his downfall, but Iles's major achievement is the portrait of Bickleigh himself: meek yet masterful, cunning but credulous, both prim and passionate.

EDGAR ALLAN POE

'THE TELL-TALE HEART'

Upon the eighth night I was more than usually cautious in opening the door. A watch's minute hand moves more slowly than did mine. Never before that night had I *felt* the extent of my own powers – of my sagacity. I could scarcely contain my feelings of triumph. To think that there I was, opening the door, little by little, and he not even to dream of my secret deeds or thoughts. I fairly chuckled at the idea; and perhaps he heard me; for he moved on the bed suddenly, as if startled. Now you may think that I drew back – but no. His room was as black as pitch with the thick darkness (for the shutters were close fastened, through fear of robbers), and so I knew that he could not see the opening of the door, and I kept pushing it on steadily, steadily.

I had my head in, and was about to open the lantern, when my thumb slipped upon the tin fastening, and the old man sprang up in the bed, crying out – 'Who's there?'

I kept quite still and said nothing. For a whole hour I did not move a muscle, and in the mean time I did not hear him lie down. He was still sitting up in the bed listening; – just as I have done, night after night, hearkening to the death watches in the wall.

Presently I heard a slight groan, and I knew it was the groan of mortal terror. It was not a groan of pain or of grief – oh, no!

– it was the low stifled sound that arises from the bottom of the soul when overcharged with awe. I knew the sound well. Many a night, just at midnight, when all the world slept, it has welled up from my own bosom, deepening, with its dreadful echo, the terrors that distracted me. I say I knew it well. I knew what the old man felt, and pitied him, although I chuckled at heart. I knew that he had been lying awake ever since the first slight noise, when he had turned in the bed. His fears had been ever since growing upon him. He had been trying to fancy them causeless, but could not. He had been saying to himself – 'It is nothing but the wind in the chimney – it is only a mouse crossing the floor,' or 'it is merely a cricket which has made a single chirp.' Yes, he had been trying to comfort himself with these suppositions; but he had found all in vain. *All in vain*; because Death, in approaching him, had stalked with his black shadow before him, and enveloped the victim. And it was the mournful influence of the unperceived shadow that caused him to feel – although he neither saw nor heard – to *feel* the presence of my head within the room.

When I had waited a long time, very patiently, without hearing him lie down, I resolved to open a little – a very, very little crevice in the lantern. So I opened it – you cannot imagine how stealthily, stealthily – until, at length, a single dim ray, like the thread of the spider, shot from out the crevice and full upon the vulture eye.

It was open – wide, wide open – and I grew furious as I gazed upon it. I saw it with perfect distinctness – all a dull blue, with a hideous veil over it that chilled the very marrow in my bones; but I could see nothing else of the old man's face or person: for I had directed the ray as if by instinct, precisely upon the damned spot.

And now have I not told you that what you mistake for madness is but over-acuteness of the senses? – now, I say, there came to my ears a low, dull, quick sound, such as a watch makes when enveloped in cotton. I knew *that* sound well too. It was the beating of the old man's heart. It increased my fury, as the beating of a drum stimulates the soldier into courage.

But even yet I refrained and kept still. I scarcely breathed. I held the lantern motionless. I tried how steadily I could maintain the ray upon the eye. Meantime the hellish tattoo of the heart increased. It grew quicker and quicker, and louder and louder every instant. The old man's terror *must* have been extreme! It grew louder, I say, louder every moment! – do you mark me well? I have told you that I am nervous: so I am. And now at the dead hour of the night, amid the dreadful silence of that old house, so strange a noise as this excited me to uncontrollable terror. Yet, for some minutes longer I refrained and stood still. But the beating grew louder, louder! I thought the heart must burst. And now a new anxiety seized me – the sound would be heard by a neighbor! The old man's hour had come! With a loud yell, I threw open the lantern and leaped into the room. He shrieked once – once only. In an instant I dragged him to the floor, and pulled the heavy bed over him. I then smiled gaily, to find the deed so far done. But, for many minutes, the heart beat on with a muffled sound. This, however, did not vex me; it would not be heard through the wall. At length it ceased. The old man was dead. I removed the bed and examined the corpse. Yes, he was stone, stone dead. I placed my hand upon the heart and held it there many minutes. There was no pulsation. He was stone dead. His eye would trouble me no more.

If still you think me mad, you will think so no longer when I describe the wise precautions I took for the concealment of the body. The night waned, and I worked hastily, but in silence. First of all I dismembered the corpse. I cut off the head and the arms and the legs.

I then took up three planks from the flooring of the chamber, and deposited all between the scantlings. I then replaced the boards so cleverly, so cunningly, that no human eye – not even *his* – could have detected any thing wrong. There was nothing to wash out – no stain of any kind – no blood-spot whatever. I had been too wary for that. A tub had caught all – ha! ha!

When I had made an end to these labors, it was four o'clock – still dark as midnight. As the bell sounded the hour, there came a knocking at the street door. I went down to open it with a light heart, – for what had I *now* to fear? There entered three men, who introduced themselves, with perfect suavity, as officers of the police. A shriek had been heard by a neighbor during the night; suspicion of foul play had been aroused; information had been lodged at the police office, and they (the officers) had been deputed to search the premises.

I smiled, – for *what* had I to fear? I bade the gentlemen welcome. The shriek, I said, was my own in a dream. The old man, I mentioned, was absent in the country. I took my visitors all over the house. I bade them search – search *well*. I led them, at length, to *his* chamber. I showed them his treasures, secure, undisturbed. In the enthusiasm of my confidence, I brought chairs into the room, and desired them *here* to rest from their fatigues, while I myself, in the wild audacity of my perfect triumph, placed my own seat upon the very spot beneath which reposed the corpse of the victim.

The officers were satisfied. My *manner* had convinced them. I was singularly at ease. They sat, and while I answered cheerily, they chatted familiar things. But, ere long, I felt myself getting pale and wished them gone. My head ached, and I fancied a ringing in my ears: but still they sat and still chatted. The ringing became more distinct: – it continued and became more distinct: I talked more freely to get rid of the feeling: but it continued and gained definitiveness – until, at length, I found that the noise was *not* within my ears.

No doubt I now grew *very* pale; – but I talked more fluently, and with a heightened voice. Yet the sound increased – and what could I do? It was a *low, dull, quick sound – much such a sound as a watch makes when enveloped in cotton*. I gasped for breath – and yet the officers heard it not. I talked more quickly – more vehemently; but the noise steadily increased. I arose and argued about trifles, in a high key and with violent gesticulations, but the noise steadily increased. Why *would* they not be gone? I paced the floor to and fro with heavy strides, as if excited to fury by the observation of the men – but the noise steadily increased. Oh God! what *could* I do? I foamed – I raved – I swore! I swung the chair upon which I had been sitting, and grated it upon the boards, but the noise arose over all and continually increased. It grew louder – louder – *louder*! And still the men chatted pleasantly, and smiled. Was it possible they heard not? Almighty God! – no, no! They heard! – they suspected! – they *knew*! –

they were making a mockery of my horror! – this I thought, and this I think. But any thing was better than this agony! Any thing was more tolerable than this derision! I could bear those hypocritical smiles no longer! I felt that I must scream or die! – and now – again! – hark! louder! louder! louder! *louder!* –

'Villains!' I shrieked, 'dissemble no more! I admit the deed! – tear up the planks! – here, here! – it is the beating of his hideous heart!'

ROBERT BROWNING

'PORPHYRIA'S LOVER'

The rain set early in tonight,
   The sullen wind was soon awake,
It tore the elm-tops down for spite,
   And did its worse to vex the lake:
   I listened with heart fit to break.
When glided in Porphyria; straight
   She shut the cold out and the storm,
And kneeled and made the cheerless grate
   Blaze up, and all the cottage warm;
   Which done, she rose, and from her form
Withdrew the dripping cloak and shawl,
   And laid her soiled gloves by, untied
Her hat and let the damp hair fall,
   And, last, she sat down by my side
   And called me. When no voice replied,
She put my arm about her waist,
   And made her smooth white shoulder bare,
And all her yellow hair displaced,
   And, stooping, made my cheek lie there,
   And spread, o'er all, her yellow hair,
Murmuring how she loved me – she
   Too weak, for all her heart's endeavour,
To set its struggling passion free

From pride, and vainer ties dissever,
  And give herself to me for ever.
But passion sometimes would prevail,
  Nor could tonight's gay feast restrain
A sudden thought of one so pale
  For love of her, and all in vain:
  So, she was come through wind and rain.
Be sure I looked up at her eyes
  Happy and proud; at last I knew
Porphyria worshipped me; surprise
  Made my heart swell, and still it grew
  While I debated what to do.
That moment she was mine, mine, fair,
  Perfectly pure and good: I found
A thing to do, and all her hair
  In one long yellow string I wound
  Three times her little throat around,
And strangled her. No pain felt she;
  I am quite sure she felt no pain.
As a shut bud that holds a bee,
  I warily oped her lids: again
  Laughed the blue eyes without a stain.
And I untightened next the tress
  About her neck; her cheek once more
Blushed bright beneath my burning kiss:
  I propped her head up as before,
  Only, this time my shoulder bore
Her head, which droops upon it still:
  The smiling rosy little head,
So glad it has its utmost will,
  That all it scorned at once is fled,
  And I, its love, am gained instead!
Porphyria's love: she guessed not how
  Her darling one wish would be heard.
And thus we sit together now,
  And all night long we have not stirred,
  And yet God has not said a word!

....

THE MAN WHO WATCHED

THE TRAINS GO BY

It was only three. He had ample time in hand and he gazed thoughtfully across the café, in which the atmosphere was steadily thickening as the afternoon advanced.

I see from your paper that Basinger, my cashier at de Coster's, stated as follows:

"'Popinga was so devoted to the Firm that he may be said to have identified himself with it; the discovery that it was insolvent must have been a terrible shock and may well have affected his brain."

I assure you, sir, that statements of this sort make very painful reading. Suppose that someone were to tell you that you were doomed to eat nothing but black bread and Bologna sausage for the rest of your days. Would you not, as a sensible man, try to convince yourself that these were the ideal diet? Well, for sixteen years I convinced myself that de Coster and Son was the most substantial and honourable firm in Holland.

Then one evening at the Saint George tavern (you will not follow the allusion, but that has no importance) I discovered, amongst other things of the same nature, that Julius de Coster was a crook.

"'Crook" is perhaps too strong a word. In reality, de Coster had always done, though without proclaiming it on the housetops, every-

thing that I had wished to do. For instance, he had had a mistress, that young woman Pamela whom I . . .

I am coming to the point. I will only ask you to note this fact: that for the first time in my life, looking at my face in the glass, I asked myself:

"What reason is there for you to go on living as you do?"

What reason indeed! And perhaps you will now put the same question to yourself, and so will many of your readers. What reason? None at all. That is the discovery I made when, for the first time, calmly and logically, I applied my mind to certain problems which invariably one tackles from the wrong angle. I saw that I had settled into a groove. The groove of a trusted employee, of a conventional married man and father, and I had settled into it simply because others had decided it should be thus and not otherwise. And suppose I decided for myself, for a change, and decided it should be otherwise?

You cannot imagine how simple everything became, once I had come to this decision. No more reason to worry what So-and-so might think, what was forbidden or permitted, proper or improper.

For instance, in the past, even if I was merely going to a neighbouring town for the night, there was all the business of packing up and phoning to book a room at an hotel. But all I had to do the other day was to walk to the station and buy a ticket to Amsterdam, a ticket that was not 'return'.

There I looked up Pamela; I had heard so much about her from de Coster and for two years had regarded her as the most attractive woman on earth. Wasn't it only natural I should look her up? She asked me what I wanted, and I explained in quite simple language, the sort I am using in this letter. But, instead of taking it seriously, she went into peals of idiotic, insulting laughter.

I ask you, what could it matter to her, since it was her profession? One man more or less . . . Anyhow, I was determined to see it through. Only next day I learned that I had tied the towel a trifle too tight. Indeed, it took so little to cause her death that one cannot help suspecting she suffered from heart disease.

So here, too, your reporter is mistaken all along the line. You have only to read what he says. That I was acting like a madman when I left Groningen. That people in the train noticed the state I was in, and the steward on the ferry-boat saw something "abnormal" in my behaviour.

'Nobody seems to realize that it was before this happened I was not in my normal state. In those days, when I was thirsty, I didn't dare to say so, or to drop into a café. And often, at friends' houses, I felt called on, out of politeness, to decline what was offered me to eat, however hungry I might be feeling.

'On railway journeys I had to pretend to read a book or look out of the window, instead of showing any interest in those around me, and to wear gloves, uncomfortable as they might be – because it's the right thing to do when travelling.

'And here is something else your reporter says:

'"At this stage the man made one of those slips which are the beginning of the end for criminals; in his excitement he left his attaché case behind him, in the bedroom of the murdered girl."

'That is sheer nonsense. I made no slip, and I was not excited. I had taken my attaché case with me by force of habit, and as I did not need it, had to leave it somewhere. Pamela's bedroom did as well as anywhere else. In any case, on learning of her death I should have written to the police to let them know I was responsible for it.

'If you doubt this, I need only remind you that it was I myself who yesterday sent Superintendent Lucas an express letter informing him that I had committed another "crime".

'The heading in your paper is flattering, I admit, with its intimation that I was out to "quiz" the police. But that, too, is a misstatement. I am not out to "quiz" anybody. Nor am I a lunatic, and if I used some violence to Mlle Rozier this was not due to a "mad frenzy".

'Certainly it is difficult explaining to you why I used force, though in several ways it was a repetition of the Pamela episode. For two whole days I had had Mlle Rozier at my disposal, but for some reason she left me cold. Not till I was alone and started thinking about her did I realize she interested me. I paid her a visit to tell her so. And then, most unreasonably, it was she who turned me down!

'What possessed her to do this? And why, under the circumstances, should I have refrained from using a little violence? Not too much, for she is a charming young person, and I should have hated to hurt her *badly. Any more than Pamela. What happened to Pamela was pure bad luck. I was a beginner!*

'So you see I am not crazy, nor the "homicidal maniac" some people think. I am merely a man who at the age of forty has determined to live as he thinks fit, without bothering about convention or the laws; for I have discovered, if somewhat late in life, that I was the dupe of appearances and the truth is that nobody obeys the law if he can help it.

'I have no plans for the moment and cannot say if there will be other "crimes" for the police to investigate. That will depend on how I feel.

'Actually, appearances notwithstanding, I am of a peaceful disposition. If one of these days I come across a girl who seems worth while I shall very likely marry her, and nothing more will be heard of me. If, however, I am harassed by the powers that be and feel like engaging in a life-and-death conflict with them, there are no lengths to which I shall not go.

'I have put up with forty years of boredom. For forty years I lived like the hungry urchin who flattens his nose against a teashop window and watches other people eating cake. Now I have learnt that cakes are always to be had by those who have the guts to take them.

'By all means, if it amuses you, go on publishing statements that I am mad. But it will only prove that you, Mr Editor, are suffering from delusions, the same delusions as I had before that evening at the Saint George tavern.

'In asking you to publish this letter I do not claim the right of reply due to an injured person; I suspect that such a claim would make you smile. Yet why should you regard it as absurd? Surely if anyone has a right to insist on publication of his answer to allegations made against him in the Press, it is a man who is fighting for his life!

'In the hope of seeing these lines in print tomorrow, I beg to remain, – Your most obedient servant (untrue of course, but it looks well), Kees Popinga.'

....

THE VATICAN CELLARS

Lafcadio, though his eyes were shut, was not asleep; he could not sleep.

The old boy over there believes I am asleep, thought he; if I were to take a peep at him through my eyelids, I should see him looking at me. Protos used to make out that it was particularly difficult to pretend to be asleep while one was really watching; he claimed that he could always spot pretended sleep by just that slight quiver of the eyelids . . . which I'm repressing now. Protos himself would be taken in . . .

The sun meanwhile had set, and Fleurissoire, in sentimental mood, was gazing at the last gleams of its splendour as they gradually faded from the sky. Suddenly the electric light that was set in the rounded ceiling of the railway carriage, blazed out with a vividness that contrasted brutally with the twilight's gentle melancholy. Fleurissoire was afraid, too, that it might disturb his neighbour's slumbers, and turned the switch; the result was not total darkness but merely a shifting of the current from the centre lamp to a dark blue night-light. To Fleurissoire's thinking, this was still too bright; he turned the switch again; the night-light went out, but two side brackets were immediately turned on, whose glare was even more disagreeable than the centre light's; another turn, and the night-light came on again; at this he gave up.

Will he never have done fiddling with the light? thought Lafcadio impatiently. What's he up to now? (No! I'll *not* raise my eyelids.) He is standing up. Can he have taken a fancy to my portmanteau? Bravo! He has noticed that it isn't locked. It was a bright idea of mine to have a complicated lock fitted to it at Milan and then lose the key, so that I had to have it picked at Bologna! A padlock, at any rate, is easy to replace . . . God damn it! Is he taking off his coat? Oh! all the same, let's have a look!

Fleurissoire, with no eyes for Lafcadio's portmanteau, was struggling with his new collar and had taken his coat off, so as to be able to put the stud in more easily; but the starched linen was as hard as cardboard and he struggled in vain.

He doesn't look happy, went on Lafcadio to himself. He must be suffering from a fistula or some unpleasant complaint of that kind. Shall I go to his help? He'll never manage it by himself . . .

Yes, though! At last the collar yielded to the stud. Fleurissoire then took up his tie, which he had placed on the seat beside his hat, his coat and his cuffs, and going up to the door of the carriage, looked at himself in the window-pane, endeavouring, like Narcissus in the water, to distinguish his reflection from the surrounding landscape.

He can't see.

Lafcadio turned on the light. The train at that moment was running alongside a bank, which could be seen through the window, illuminated by the light cast upon it from one after another of the compartments of the train; a procession of brilliant squares was thus formed which danced along beside the railroad and suffered, each one in its turn, the same distortions, according to the irregularities of the ground. In the middle of one of these squares danced Fleurissoire's grotesque shadow; the others were empty.

Who would see? thought Lafcadio. There – just to my hand – under my hand, this double fastening, which I can easily undo; the door would suddenly give way and he would topple out; the slightest push would do it; he would fall into the darkness like a stone; one wouldn't even hear a scream . . . And off tomorrow to the East! . . . Who would know?

The tie – a little ready-made sailor knot – was put on by now and Fleurissoire had taken up one of the cuffs and was arranging it upon his right wrist, examining, as he did so, the photograph above his seat, which represented some palace by the sea, and was one of four that adorned the compartment.

A crime without a motive, went on Lafcadio, what a puzzle for the police! As to that, however, going along beside this blessed bank, anybody in the next door compartment might notice the door open and the old blighter's shadow pitch out. The corridor curtains, at any rate, are drawn . . . It's not so much about events that I'm curious, as about myself. There's many a man thinks he's capable of anything, who draws back when it comes to the point . . . What a gulf between the imagination and the deed! . . . And no more right to take back one's move than at chess. Pooh! If one could foresee all the risks, there'd be no interest in the game! . . . Between the imagination of a deed and . . . Hullo! the bank's come to an end. Here we are on a bridge, I think; a river . . .

The window-pane had now turned black and the reflections in it became more distinct. Fleurissoire leant forward to straighten his tie.

Here, just under my hand the double fastening – now that he's looking away and not paying attention – upon my soul, it's easier to undo than I thought. If I can count up to twelve, without hurrying, before I see a light in the countryside, the dromedary is saved. Here goes! One, two, three, four (slowly! slowly!), five, six, seven, eight, nine . . . a light! . . .

Fleurissoire did not utter a single cry. When he felt Lafcadio's push and found himself facing the gulf which suddenly opened in front of him, he made a great sweep with his arm to save himself; his left hand clutched at the smooth framework of the door, while, as he half turned round, he flung his right well behind him and over Lafcadio's head, sending his second cuff, which he had been in the act of putting on, spinning to the other end of the carriage, where it rolled underneath the seat.

Lafcadio felt a horrible claw descend upon the back of his neck, lowered his head and gave another push, more impatient than the first; this was followed by the sensation of nails scraping

ANDRÉ GIDE

through his flesh; and after that, nothing was left for Fleurissoire to catch hold of but the beaver hat, which he snatched at despairingly and carried away with him in his fall.

Now then, let's keep cool, said Lafcadio to himself. I mustn't slam the door to; they might hear it in the next carriage.

He drew the door towards him, in the teeth of the wind, and then shut it quietly.

He has left me his frightful sailor hat; in another minute I should have kicked it after him, but he has taken mine along with him and that's enough. That was an excellent precaution of mine – cutting out my initials . . . But there's the hatter's name in the crown, and people don't order a beaver hat of that kind every day of the week . . . It can't be helped, I've played now . . . Perhaps they'll think it an accident . . . No, not now that I've shut the door . . . Stop the train? . . . Come, come, Cadio! no touching up! You've only yourself to thank.

To prove now that I'm perfectly self-possessed, I shall begin by quite quietly seeing what that photograph is the old chap was examining just now . . . *Miramar!* No desire at all to go and visit *that* . . . It's stifling in here.

He opened the window.

The old brute has scratched me . . . I'm bleeding . . . It hurts like anything! I must bathe it a little; the lavatory is at the end of the corridor, on the left. Let's take another hankerchief.

He reached down his portmanteau from the rack above him and opened it on the seat, in the place where he had been sitting.

If I meet anyone in the corridor I must be calm . . . No! my heart's quiet again. Now for it! . . . Ah! his coat! I can easily hide it under mine. Papers in the pocket! Something to while away the time for the rest of the journey.

The coat was a poor threadbare affair of a dingy liquorice colour, made of a harsh-textured and obviously cheap material; Lafcadio thought it slightly repulsive; he hung it up on a peg in the small lavatory into which he locked himself; then, bending over the basin, he began to examine himself in the glass.

There were two ugly furrows on his neck; one, a thin red streak, starting from the back of his neck, turned leftwards and

245

came to an end just below the ear; the other and shorter one, was a deep scratch just above the first; it went straight up towards the ear, the lobe of which it had reached and slightly torn. It was bleeding, but less than might have been expected; on the other hand, the pain, which he had hardly felt at first, began to be pretty sharp. He dipped his handkerchief into the basin, staunched the blood and then washed the handkerchief. Not enough to stain my collar, thought he, as he put himself to rights; all is well.

....

THE PICTURE OF
DORIAN GRAY

Campbell took a chair by the table, and Dorian sat opposite to him. The two men's eyes met. In Dorian's there was infinite pity. He knew that what he was going to do was dreadful.

After a strained moment of silence, he leaned across and said, very quietly, but watching the effect of each word upon the face of him he had sent for, 'Alan, in a locked room at the top of this house, a room to which nobody but myself has access, a dead man is seated at a table. He has been dead ten hours now. Don't stir, and don't look at me like that. Who the man is, why he died, how he died, are matters that do not concern you. What you have to do is this—'

'Stop, Gray. I don't want to know anything further. Whether what you have told me is true or not true doesn't concern me. I entirely decline to be mixed up in your life. Keep your horrible secrets to yourself. They don't interest me any more.'

'Alan, they will have to interest you. This one will have to interest you. I am awfully sorry for you, Alan. But I can't help myself. You are the one man who is able to save me. I am forced to bring you into the matter. I have no option. Alan, you are scientific. You know about chemistry and things of that kind. You have made experiments. What you have got to do is to destroy the thing that is upstairs – to destroy it so that not a vestige of it will be left. Nobody saw this person come into the house. Indeed, at the present moment he is supposed to be in Paris. He will not be missed for months. When he is missed, there must be no trace of him found here. You, Alan, you must change him, and everything that belongs to him, into a handful of ashes that I may scatter in the air.'

'You are mad, Dorian.'

'Ah! I was waiting for you to call me Dorian.'

'You are mad, I tell you – mad to imagine that I would raise a finger to help you, mad to make this monstrous confession. I will have nothing to do with this matter, whatever it is. Do you think I am going to peril my reputation for you? What is it to me what devil's work you are up to?'

'It was suicide, Alan.'

'I am glad of that. But who drove him to it? You, I should fancy.'

'Do you still refuse to do this for me?'

'Of course I refuse. I will have absolutely nothing to do with it. I don't care what shame comes on you. You deserve it all. I should not be sorry to see you disgraced, publicly disgraced. How dare you ask me, of all men in the world, to mix myself up in this horror? I should have thought you knew more about people's characters. Your friend Lord Henry Wotton can't have taught you much about psychology, whatever else he has taught you. Nothing will induce me to stir a step to help you. You have come to the wrong man. Go to some of your friends. Don't come to me.'

'Alan, it was murder. I killed him. You don't know what he had made me suffer. Whatever my life is, he had more to do with the making or the marring of it than poor Harry has had. He may not have intended it, the result was the same.'

'Murder! Good God, Dorian, is that what you have come to? I shall not inform upon you. It is not my business. Besides, without my stirring in the matter, you are certain to be arrested. Nobody ever commits a crime without doing something stupid. But I will have nothing to do with it.'

'You must have something to do with it. Wait, wait a moment; listen to me. Only listen. Alan. All I ask of you is to perform a certain scientific experiment. You go to hospitals and dead-houses, and the horrors that you do there don't affect you. If in some hideous dissecting-room or fetid laboratory you found this man lying on a leaden table with red gutters scooped out in it for the blood to flow through, you would simply look upon him as an admirable subject. You would not turn a hair. You would not believe that you were doing anything wrong. On the contrary, you would probably feel that you were benefiting the human race, or increasing the sum of knowledge in the world, or gratifying intellectual curiosity, or something of that kind. What I want you to do is merely what you have often done before. Indeed, to destroy a body must be far less horrible than what you are accustomed to work at. And, remember, it is the only piece of evidence against me. If it is discovered, I am lost; and it is sure to be discovered unless you help me.'

'I have no desire to help you. You forget that. I am simply indifferent to the whole thing. It has nothing to do with me.'

'Alan, I entreat you. Think of the position I am in. Just before you came I almost fainted with terror. You may know terror yourself some day. No! don't think of that. Look at the matter purely from the scientific point of view. You don't enquire where the dead things on which you experiment come from. Don't enquire now. I have told you too much as it is. But I beg of you to do this. We were friends once, Alan.'

'Don't speak about those days, Dorian – they are dead.'

'The dead linger sometimes. The man upstairs will not go away. He is sitting at the table with bowed head and outstretched arms. Alan! Alan! If you don't come to my assistance, I am ruined. Why, they will hang me, Alan! Don't you understand? They will hang me for what I have done.'

'There is no good in prolonging this scene. I absolutely refuse to do anything in the matter. It is insane of you to ask me.'

'You refuse?'

'Yes.'

'I entreat you, Alan.'

'It is useless.'

The same look of pity came into Dorian Gray's eyes. Then he stretched out his hand, took a piece of paper, and wrote something on it. He read it over twice, folded it carefully, and pushed it across the table. Having done this, he got up and went over to the window.

Campbell looked at him in surprise, and then took up the paper, and opened it. As he read it, his face became ghastly pale and he fell back in his chair. A horrible sense of sickness came over him. He felt as if his heart was beating itself to death in some empty hollow.

After two or three minutes of terrible silence, Dorian turned round and came and stood behind him, putting his hand upon his shoulder.

'I am so sorry for you, Alan,' he murmured, 'but you leave me no alternative. I have a letter written already. Here it is. You see the address. If you don't help me, I must send it. If you don't help me, I will send it. You know what the result will be. But you are going to help me. It is impossible for you to refuse now. I tried to spare you. You will do me the justice to admit that. You were stern, harsh, offensive. You treated me as no man has ever dared to treat me – no living man, at any rate. I bore it all. Now it is for me to dictate terms.'

Campbell buried his face in his hands, and a shudder passed through him.

'Yes, it is my turn to dictate terms, Alan. You know what they are. The thing is quite simple. Come, don't work yourself into this fever. The thing has to be done. Face it, and do it.'

A groan broke from Campbell's lips and he shivered all over. The ticking of the clock on the mantelpiece seemed to him to be dividing time into separate atoms of agony, each of which was too terrible to be borne. He felt as if an iron ring was being slowly tightened round his forehead, as if the disgrace with which he was threatened had already come upon him. The hand upon his shoulder weighed like a hand of lead. It was intolerable. It seemed to crush him.

'Come, Alan, you must decide at once.'

'I cannot do it,' he said, mechanically, as though words could alter things.

'You must. You have no choice. Don't delay.'

He hesitated a moment. 'Is there a fire in the room upstairs?'

'Yes, there is a gas fire with asbestos.'

'I shall have to go home and get some things from the laboratory.'

'No, Alan, you must not leave the house. Write out on a sheet of notepaper what you want and my servant will take a cab and bring the things back to you.'

Campbell scrawled a few lines, blotted them, and addressed an envelope to his assistant. Dorian took the note up and read it carefully. Then he rang the bell and gave it to his valet, with orders to return as soon as possible and to bring the things with him.

As the hall door shut, Campbell started nervously, and having got up from the chair, went over to the chimneypiece. He was shivering with a kind of ague. For nearly twenty minutes, neither of the men spoke. A fly buzzed noisily about the room, and the ticking of the clock was like the beat of a hammer.

As the chime struck one, Campbell turned round, and looking at Dorian Gray, saw that his eyes were filled with tears. There was something in the purity and refinement of that sad face that seemed to enrage him. 'You are infamous, absolutely infamous!' he muttered.

'Hush, Alan. You have saved my life,' said Dorian.

'Your life? Good heavens! what a life that is! You have gone from corruption to corruption, and now you have culminated in crime. In doing what I am going to do – what you force me to do – it is not of your life that I am thinking.'

'Ah, Alan,' murmured Dorian with a sigh, 'I wish you had a thousandth part of the pity for me that I have for you.' He turned away as he spoke and stood looking out at the garden. Campbell made no answer.

After about ten minutes a knock came to the door, and the servant entered, carrying a large mahogany chest of chemicals, with a long coil of steel and platinum wire and two rather curiously shaped iron clamps.

'Shall I leave the things here, sir?' he asked Campbell.

'Yes,' said Dorian. 'And I am afraid, Francis, that I have another errand for you. What is the name of the man at Richmond who supplies Selby with orchids?'

'Harden, sir.'

'Yes – Harden. You must go down to Richmond at once, see Harden personally, and tell him to send twice as many orchids as I ordered, and to have as few white ones as possible. In fact, I don't want any white ones. It is a lovely day, Francis, and Richmond is a very pretty place – otherwise I wouldn't bother you about it.'

MASAKO TOGAWA

....

A KISS OF FIRE

Michitaro's mother put on the glasses that she would never allow herself to be seen wearing in public as she studied the report of Ikuo's death. With Ikuo gone, it meant that two of the three children were now dead. Never for a moment had she ever imagined that they would go before her.

She thought about Ikuo. He had been a strange child, and twenty-six years ago he had said something that almost made people suspect her of killing her husband. She had been doing so well until he started saying those things, but she thought she had managed to put off everyone's suspicions. It had cost her dearly, though. She had had to change the whole course of her life, but now as she looked back on it, it seemed worthwhile.

She walked over to the window and watched the plane trees blowing wildly in the wind.

It said in the papers that he had gone to his girl's apartment, and, after strangling her, he had poured gasoline around the room and set fire to it. It sounded very out of character for him to do something like that, but if he was to be accused of being the arsonist, it meant that she would be quite safe. When he had come around to see her that last time, he had said all kinds of nasty things to threaten her, and it served him right if he was accused of being the arsonist.

Nobody was left who would be able to accuse her of having started that fire twenty-six years ago. There was no proof, but she realized she had been lucky. If she was to do the same thing now, she would probably be caught.

She had held the pillow over his face for five minutes before she poured the gasoline around his bed. She had been sure that she had suffocated him, but there had been evidence of smoke in his lungs, and that was why it was put down as death by fire. Had it really been a crime of passion? No, she had decided some time before that she did not want to remain tied down to a sick man forever, and, even if he had not started that sordid little affair with the nurse, she was no longer faithful to him anyway. She stood at the window shaking her head as she thought over what she had done so long ago.

She had first thought of killing him when the children began to play with matches in the house. She had warned them about it repeatedly, but then one day the idea had come to her. It was as if the devil were tempting her, and no matter how many times she put the idea out of her mind, it kept coming back.

If she put the blame on the children, she could kill her husband and set fire to the house without being caught. She wondered now how things could have seemed so simple to her in those days. Now she would be too scared to act; it was because she was young that she had managed it. The future had seemed so bleak that she had felt it was worth any risk to escape, to punch a hole in the darkness that tried to envelop her.

She knew that her husband had taken out a huge insurance policy in Michitaro's name. He had been a careful man and had worried about what would happen to his son if he were to die. Even though he was a sick man, he used his influence at his father's company to take out a policy. The executives at the company had done him proud, but it was not just the money that drove her to kill him. More than anything, she was worried about what he would do if he found out that Michitaro was not his real son.

When Michitaro had injured himself at nursery school, she had been shocked to learn that his blood type was different from her husband's. When she thought about her lifestyle in Paris before she met her husband, she realized that he could have been anybody's child, but why was it that when he was born, the hospital had said his blood type was the same as her husband's?

She learned later from the police that blood tests could not be one hundred per cent accurate. All the same, it had been a cruel trick of fate, and it had led her to commit murder.

She had tied a fuse to his dog's tail and let it run up the stairs, but when she thought of it now, she realized she must have been mad to think that such a harebrained scheme would work. Maybe she had not really wanted to kill her husband, and she only treated his pet like that because she was jealous of the attention it received.

It was all that person's fault. They had tried to break up their marriage from the beginning, and it was they who had first sent that nurse over to look after him. When she had first realized that he was having an affair, she had feigned indifference and spurned him, but really she had been mad with jealousy. She had still been young.

But it had all been for nothing in the end. Michitaro had been her one reason for living, but he was dead now and Ikuo had also died. She no longer felt the energy to compete with that person. Everything seemed pointless, and nothing remained to afford her any pleasure. She guessed that this must be one of the effects of menopause.

But why had Ikuo behaved like he had, and why had he made it appear that he had been the arsonist? It didn't seem like him. He had been such a bright child and had never taken any chances.

Her thoughts were interrupted by the buzzing of the front door, and, looking down, she saw that it was the detective. Of the three children, he was the only one left now.

He had always been different from the other two. He had never been afraid of her. All three had sensed what she had done, but he hadn't been worried by the thought of her crime. All he had worried about had been the punishment he might receive from an adult.

She led him into the living-room.

'As I'm sure you must have read in the papers, Ikuo betrayed our trust in him. He was the arsonist all along, and now that he's dead the investigation has been brought to a close, and I have come to report to you.'

He spoke in a vigorous tone, which she found very pleasant, but it made her feel even more strongly the deaths of Ikuo and her son.

'That nurse was lucky to escape,' she commented.

'Yes, she fell unconscious when he strangled her, and she came to when she smelled the gasoline. She got out without much injury, just a burn on the leg, but as you say, she was lucky to escape. Without her testimony we would never have known that Ikuo was the arsonist. We would still be wasting our time looking for someone else. I won't have to visit Kaenji Temple anymore. I felt strangely drawn there while he was still alive.'

He smiled brightly.

The minute she heard the nurse's story, she recognized a kindred spirit. She had been lucky. It was because she was young and she had only tried it once that she had got away with it so easily. If she tried it again, she would be caught.

'But why do you think Ikuo decided to go back to the scene of the crime like that? Especially when the fire was burning so fiercely?'

'There are any number of theories. Maybe he remembered some vital piece of evidence that he had left on the scene, or perhaps he wanted to carry out the body of his victim to make it look as if he was a hero. We have no way of knowing for sure, though. Dead men don't tell tales.'

That is true, she thought. *Twenty-six years ago the papers had claimed all kinds of things, but it was only speculation. As long as the person involved did not say anything, the truth would never come out.*

'You are right,' she said aloud, 'it's only speculation. Let me show you something. I didn't intend to let anyone else see it, but I'll make an exception for you.'

She took out the copy of the sutra the priest had given her and showed it to him.

'What do you make of this?'

'"That the perpetrator die by fire,"' he said, reading it out loud. 'I wonder what it means and who could have written it?'

'I don't know, but I suppose it must be someone who hated the arsonist very much. I wonder what they think now that Ikuo is dead.'

'Well, they have no right to feel happy. As far as that fire twenty-six years ago is concerned, Ikuo was blameless. Even when we were children, Ikuo used to walk around with a water pistol and put out the matches as we lit them. I now know exactly what happened that day. After he died, I couldn't sleep. I stayed up all night thinking about that day, and then suddenly it all came back to me. I started that fire. We had been playing hide-and-seek, and I hid in a cupboard on the first floor. It was filled with cotton that was to be used to make new bed quilts. It was white and fluffy, and it felt like being in a cave in the snow.'

'What, like the match girl in the story?'

'No, I wasn't interested in that kind of game. That was Michitaro and Ikuo. I just enjoyed watching things burn. I had a box of matches with me, and I struck them all and watched as the cotton started to smolder. Then I went out and forgot all about it.'

'Why didn't you tell anyone afterward?'

'Because even though I was still a child, I realized what a terrible thing I'd done and I was scared. I knew I would have to tell someone eventually, but there was nobody for me to talk to. I didn't have a mother to confide in, and as time passed it became even harder to say anything. Now it is different. Michitaro and Ikuo became arsonists because of a fire they had nothing to do with. But not me. I have my own life.'

Michitaro's mother had recovered her composure and spoke in her usual tone. 'Yes, children don't have any responsibility for what they do. It is the people who made them think they were at fault that should be blamed. It is their education that was at fault.'

That's right, I am the one who is to blame for their death, she thought. *If I hadn't tried to protect myself by insisting for all these years that they were responsible for the fire, those two young men would still be alive today.* After she had seen the detective out, she sat by herself at the dining table and started to laugh hysterically.

When she thought about it, she remembered that she had

come back to the house that day and had noticed the smell of smoke, but she never for a minute suspected that the children had really started a fire. She had scolded them repeatedly about playing with matches and had even thought of setting the house on fire and putting the blame on them, but she had not thought that it could actually happen.

To think that when she had held the pillow over her husband's face, sprinkled benzene around his bed, and tied a fuse to the dog's tail, he had already been dead. It had not been Ikuo or Michitaro. It had been the third boy. He had lit a fire in the cupboard directly under the room where her husband had been sleeping, causing him to die of carbon monoxide poisoning. There was no need for her to have spent the last twenty-six years feeling threatened by her crime. She could have lived a fuller life.

She could not believe the pointlessness of it all and sat with her head buried in her hands, laughing and crying for what seemed like an eternity.

EDWARD GRIERSON

....

REPUTATION FOR
A SONG

The solicitor ponderously mounted the stairs and unlocked his office door. The fire was still burning in the grate, and having switched on the table lamp and drawn the curtains he went and stood in front of it, warming his hands, for the autumn night was bleak. With the instinct of the householder he tended it, prodding out the embers with the heavy poker, adding more coal and a log of wood till the result satisfied even his exacting taste. Hemmings was a good fellow, an invaluable assistant, he reflected, but a poor hand at a fire, willing but unteachable.

Now that this had been attended to the next task was to select a pipe. A rack containing a dozen of them was hanging beside the mantelpiece, for smoking was his one acknowledged vice, as it had been his father's. There was an old meerschaum there, relic of his student days, a fanciful affair carved in the German style so fashionable in his youth, another was his father's gift in the last year of his life, a briar, solid and severely practical, old and foul now beyond redemption, the mouthpiece stained from constant use. How many happy smokes he had had from them!

He took his most recent acquisition from the rack and leaning one elbow on the mantelpiece began to fill it, seriously, intently, as one who performs a ritual, then lit it, blowing out regular jets of smoke towards the prints and diplomas on the wall above the fire. It was a performance that never failed to comfort him, a sequence of countless repetitions, a pledge of order and normality. Once his whole life had been like that, for no one could have taken more pleasure in the average, but now late in life when his adaptability had deserted him he found himself faced with hateful, bewildering situations. The round of actions had become corrupt: he had fought with his wife for the happiness of Margaret, had been driven from his home in consequence – he who hated scandal more than anything except injustice – and now saw that by that action of deserting, so natural, so necessary, he had completed the destruction of the very thing he had tried his best to save. John had succeeded to the betrayer Laura, a young man also of a conventional turn of mind – conventional in a disgraceful, cowardly way, thought Mr Anderson, seeing with a human weakness his own virtues as vices in another. It was certainly ironical that this man, the pattern of respectability, grieving over his daughter's unhappiness and the break-up of his home, should have been seen at Turlminster bridge tables in the role of an adulterer; it was a tribute to that sense of drama innate in human beings, who can see the light of adventure in the most unlikely places. But even the good ladies of the town, with all their fertility of imagination, had not imagined their story's end – the shadow waiting in the fading light, the footfall on the stairs.

Mr Anderson caught the sound – there was a loose board near the middle of the second flight – and wondered who his visitor could be. Perhaps Hemmings had returned as he sometimes did, around quarter days when the work was heaviest. He would know soon enough, for the methodical clerk, in arrival, in departure, in all his daily round, repeated his actions and his very steps with the regularity of a machine. No sounds of any kind succeeded; it seemed as though the visitor had halted half-way up the stairs, uncertain perhaps whether the offices were open at that hour. The idea of burglary no more entered his head than it had entered Mr Hemmings', for the office was in the centre of the town, a town, moreover, where crime was almost too great a rarity – looking at the matter from the professional point of view.

But there had been someone on the stairs, Mr Anderson was

sure of that. When a minute had gone by without a repetition of the sound, he crossed the heavily carpeted room to the private door that gave access to the stairhead and opened it.

He expected to see a figure on the landing just below him; instead, there was Rupert on the threshold not a yard away, his body bent so that he appeared even smaller than he was, his white oval face thrust forward, eerie in the dim light shining out into the landing from the lamp on the office desk.

Mr Anderson took a quick step backwards into the room; he was not a nervous man but the effect of that sudden snap of vision had been profoundly disconcerting. How silent, how secretive, that passage up the stairs had been; how unnecessary, his common sense reminded him the moment the flash of fear had passed and he was himself again. But a trace of uneasiness remained, and his voice was far from friendly as he demanded: 'What are you doing here?' With any other visitor he would no doubt have added: 'You quite scared me, creeping up like that,' but such an admission in this case somehow seemed unwise – well, undesirable, perhaps. It was a strange time for a call, a very strange time. He looked at the boy again; a puny chap nearly a head shorter than himself; he did not consciously reassure himself by these comparisons. 'Never mind, come in,' he said.

He led the way into the room, pointed out a chair for the visitor by the fire, then seated himself at his desk and swivelled round to face him. His pipe had gone out and he relit it, rather clumsily, being liberal with matches in a way that would have surprised Mr Hemmings very much.

'Well, what is it?' he said at last.

Rupert held out his hands to the fire. It had been cold waiting in the street and he too had been disconcerted by that sudden opening of the door. But he was certainly not afraid. The obvious signs of disquiet in this gross, hateful man delighted him; they lent him the advantage of the hunter, that disparity that gives the fat rabbit to the stoat.

'It's about Mother, of course,' he said.

Mr Anderson set down his pipe and his face took on its most stubborn look, 'Old Anderson's pug jaw', as it was known to brother attorneys in the county courts. The chances were that she had put him up to this. It was an impertinence and he was not prepared to suffer it.

'About your mother? May I ask whether she has sent you here?'

Rupert shook his head.

'It would have been most improper if she had. You are not qualified by age or anything else to interfere.' In this Mr Anderson was being a little hard. But the memory of his last experience of this boy had deeply impressed itself on his mind and left him with a feeling of aversion so that he added: 'You and I have nothing whatsoever to discuss.'

Rupert from his chair beside the fire replied very coolly: 'Oh, but haven't we!'

'We have not,' said Mr Anderson, looking at his visitor with distaste. Now that he could see him in the light of Laura's words he marvelled that he had ever been deceived and seen traces of his blood in this effeminate – for even to this extent did he misjudge the boy. Yet his sense of justice did not desert him and prompted him to add: 'I'm sorry things have happened the way they have. You didn't deserve it. But one thing's certain: I won't discuss my wife with you.'

'We'll discuss my mother, if you please.'

'*You* can discuss it,' said Mr Anderson pointedly.

Rupert turned his attention from the fire and looked his enemy directly in the face. 'Are you coming back to her?' he asked.

'I certainly am not.'

'Why?'

There was no answer.

'I said, why? What has she done? Tell me one thing that she's done.'

How much he could have said! But as with her, so with her son: it had always been his fate to be put into the wrong. He did not reply but fumbled with his tobacco pouch.

This silence had all the quality of guilt, and Rupert, observing him, felt the revival of those feelings that had come to him as he had sat beside his mother's bed. This was the author of their misfortunes, this large, smug man who dared to play the role of the respectable solicitor. His anger boiled up and he demanded almost threateningly: 'I'll ask again. Are you coming back?'

'I think you'd better go,' said Mr Anderson.

A dull flush of colour had spread in Rupert's cheeks. 'So that's it! You think you've finished with us. You're very wrong. You think you can write letters to my mother and hurt her and we can't hit back. And then, best of all, you think you can play around with other women too.' His voice rose. 'I know,' he said. 'I know why it is you're always hanging round that bar. And I know how it is between you and Mrs Grey.'

Mr Anderson laughed. He felt that Providence in thus pursuing him was showing a rather low sense of the absurd. It never entered his head to think how close he was to tragedy; indeed, so absent was all sense of danger that he swivelled round towards his desk, reaching for the ashtray near the telephone.

It was the unwisest action of his life. That laugh, which had been his answer to the most ridiculous of charges, had quite another meaning for the boy; to him it could only mean a confession, the blatant confirmation of his mother's words. Almost by chance his eyes lighted on the heavy poker lying against the fender; it was close to him as he sat in the fireside chair, and moved by a sudden diabolic impulse, he leaned forward and put his hand caressingly against the handle. In that instant, as he felt the polished iron, smooth and clinging to his touch, he knew what he would do. His grip tightened and as he drew the implement from the fender, weighing its balance like a man with a new tennis racquet, he rose noiselessly to his feet. From where he stood Mr Anderson's back was presented to him at a range of a few yards; above it the pale waxy tonsure of the skull in its circlet of greying hair. And as he struck there were many conflicting images in his mind: memories of jealousies and small passions, his mother's face and body on the bed, the seductive warmth of Joy, images of a nightmare, sensual, violent, all blotted out in the red tide of hatred sweeping over him as the blow went home.

Something of these movements seemed to have been divined: the victim had half turned and was rising from the chair; the glancing stroke caught him on the right side of the scalp above the ear. Almost stunned, he still had the strength to stagger towards his enemy and still had the wit to raise his arm as a protection against the blows, till one, more accurately delivered, dropped his guard and three more rained upon him, so that consciousness left him and he dropped on his knees, then rolled on to his left side by the fire. He had not spoken or cried out; his fall made little sound; he seemed dead as he lay there, yet took some time to die. When they found him, late that night, his body was sprawled out on the carpet, his head close against the grate. The fourth in line from the temple had been the lethal blow, the doctors said.

Just before eleven o'clock on that same evening Laura awoke from the sleep of exhaustion that had followed the departure of her son; she had heard a step outside in the corridor – Rupert on his way to bed. Always avid for sympathy and assured of his tender care for her, she sat up against the pillows and patted her hair into place, composing a picture for his entry. But no hand was set on the latch and she could hear the steps grow fainter down the passage in the direction of his room. It was not till she was fully awake that she realized how slight the noise had been, the sound of someone moving cautiously in stockinged feet. Then perhaps it was not Rupert after all. But Laura dismissed the thought, telling herself that it must be he: this silence was just another illustration of his love for her and his anxiety that she should sleep. It was not long before another possible explanation had occurred. This was not the first time he had come in quietly, late at night, returning, as she correctly guessed, from some adventure with a woman. She had even taxed him with it once, tolerantly, with an appearance of good humour that disguised her jealousy, for it was a curiously attractive, curiously wounding thought to imagine a woman in his arms. She would go to him now and speak of it again.

But first she must make up; she must not expose herself to unfavourable comparisons. How hideous she looked! Her eyes were red with weeping, the skin above the cheekbones was puffy and discoloured, the whole face had relapsed into that state from which it was daily rescued at so great a cost of cosmetics and art. She applied herself diligently till the reflection of her skill gazed back at her from the glass, the mouth and eyes corrected, all possible lines erased – a touch of black pencil smeared in below the eyes, a little reminder of the tragic experience she had undergone, and the picture was complete. Her friends, even her hairdresser, would have applauded the effect.

Thus armed, she went down the corridor to Rupert's room and tapped gently on the door. She heard a scuffling noise beyond, and when, without waiting for his answer, she went in she found him between the washstand and the bed, half dressed and with his shirt – a rather dirty shirt, it seemed – carried in his hand. Unsuspicious as she was, she found his manner odd and furtive, as though he had a secret he did not want to share. And perhaps he had, for she knew something of the habits of young men and the follies of young women; there might be some trophy in the room, or even – amazing thought – the girl herself.

'What's the matter, dear?' she said. She had by now reached the centre of the room and there was no possible mistaking the terrified expression in his eyes. Whatever the cause, the fear was surely overdone: she loved him, she was forgiving, he must know, and even if the girl were there in hiding quite undressed . . .

'Why, what is it, Rupert? Why do you look at me like that?' He murmured, 'Nothing,' but in so low a voice she scarcely heard. And now he was sitting on the bed, the shirt still clutched tightly in his hand, absurdly, as though precious to him in some way and not just destined for the laundry basket. How very soiled it looked!

Perhaps at that moment she first had some dim understanding of the truth. Of course her mind rejected it, clinging to the only other explanation that could fit the facts, so that she asked appealingly: 'Is it a girl, Rupert? Is it that?'

He did not reply but remained staring at her from the bed. How ill he looked and how dishevelled! That was no new, surprising thing, for in spite of all her efforts to make him in her image the soul of tidiness, he had always been careless in his dress and in the keeping of his room. But surely even he was not in the habit of throwing his tie and pullover on the floor and bundling his coat up like a sack. There they were, lying in a heap on the patch of linoleum near the washing basin, and with that instinct of fussiness that will reveal itself in mothers at the most unexpected times she went over to pick them up.

Then it was that she saw against the white porcelain surface of the basin the stains of blood.

She bent down towards the coat. And there the blood lay, too, though it was not so immediately apparent against the dark texture of the cloth. Then he must be injured.

She came over to him by the bed. There was blood on the shirt that he was carrying, blood diluted in the washing so that it looked as innocuous as ink; there was blood on his trousers and on his hands. Silently she searched his face, his arms, his body under its thin cotton singlet, hopeful that she would find some explanation there. But there was no wound on him. It sent a shudder through her to see him sitting there so whole, so unblemished, and then to think what he had done. Intuitively she had reached the truth. Yet she remained calm. Her earlier breakdown was an advantage to her now, for it had so drained her of emotion that she had none to spare and could face the new crisis without scruples of conscience and in reliance on her wits. She said very quietly: 'Is he dead?'

And somehow the admission came easily to him, almost as a relief after the intolerable memories of the night. Once the words were spoken they stood between him and his actions, a protective skin, so that what was done seemed almost bearable in the calm light of what was said.

In the same spirit she listened. It was surprising, really, how words could be detached from the ideas dictating them, how one could hear of the weapon without seeing the wound, of death without knowledge of that body writhing in its last agony on the floor.

So though he tried to say what he had done he did not say it, and she, after the first moment of revulsion, was not greatly shocked, for whatever truth may be, it is ephemeral, existing only for the instant and submerged the moment that it enters memory.

She asked him what had made him strike the blow. 'Because you wanted it,' he said.

And had she wanted it? The result, most probably, for she had hated the dead man with all her heart and would have struck him down herself if she had dared. Now she did not hate him any more. With a flash of generous emotion she remembered earlier, happier times, small kindnesses long buried under the accumulation of her bitter thoughts.

But whatever tender feelings for her husband were reviving at this hour were stilled by the sound of a car drawing up outside in Colbert Row. She ran to the window and lifting a corner of the curtain stared down into the street. She saw the compact blue limousine, saw the uniform of the driver as he got out to open the rear door, and turned back into the room, her terror only held in check by her determination to save her son.

'It's the police,' she said.

It was enough to deflate all his new-found confidence; whereas she was vibrant with energy, he sat indecisively on the bed, white of face and very near collapse.

'Rupert, did you hear? They've come to question us.'

Still he could say nothing, while from outside there came the noise of the closing of a door and steps on the pavement of the Row.

'Rupert, listen to me. Did anyone see you there?'

'Hemmings,' he said.

'When?'

'About an hour before.'

'And later no one? Are you sure?'

He hung his head, quite unable to match this tremendous vitality of hers, at its peak now that he was in danger and dependent on her.

'Did you meet anyone on your way back home?'

'I don't remember.'

'You must remember,' she cried. 'There's so little time.'

And as though to prove it there came a loud ringing of the front-door bell. He jumped up from the bed, panic close upon him, till she gripped him fiercely by the arm.

'It's all right. You're safe. Just answer me.'

'I don't think I saw anyone,' he said.

'Good, good! And it happened about eight. You were here

then, do you understand?' He looked blankly at her, so that she repeated in a louder voice: 'You were here. Here at home. I saw you. You spoke with Hemmings and then you came back home.'

The bell rang again, insistently, pealing through the house, a terrible stimulus to her wits and to the plan rapidly forming in her mind.

'They've come for me,' he said.

It was not a very helpful contribution to her problem and she shook his arm angrily, contemptuously, as one might shake a stupid, naughty child.

'Listen,' she commanded. 'Listen and you're safe. They'll ask you questions. You know nothing. You called at the office but your father was out, so you came home. Have you got it? You came home.'

His answer was to glance across the room towards the washing-stand. It was another call on her for action.

'Wash your hands,' she said.

His movements were still dazed, lethargic, and she pushed him across the room and turned the tap. And while he slowly began to rinse his hands she seized the bloodstained clothing and ran with it down the passage to her room, thrusting it in a bundle among her underclothes. Her return journey was pursued by the third pealing of the bell, mingled this time with the noise of voices and the heavy clash of the brass knocker on the door.

At last he had been stirred to action of a kind. His hands were washed, but so carelessly that thin rivulets of blood lay in the soap dish and around the waste pipe of the basin. She rinsed them out, then took a quick glance round the room. There was blood on the linoleum at her feet. She used the towel on this, and all the while her active mind was racing on ahead, planning, ordering, encouraging.

'Get your clothes off. Get into bed. You know nothing. You were home. Get into bed and leave the rest to me.'

Gradually under the spell of her energy and courage he was beginning to respond. He slipped off his shoes and socks, his singlet; the trousers too were stained and he handed them to her. She came over to the bed, and though bell and knocker were sounding madly through the house, kissed him gently on the cheek. He was helpless, he relied on her, and the knowledge of these things, the memory of his childhood, brought out all the strength and passion of her nature. She would save him as she had saved him from thrashings in those earlier days, making a virtue of deceit.

And now delay was no longer possible. They were already suspicious and might break down the door. Picking up the towel and trousers she fled down to her room, roughed out her hair, and running down the stairs unlocked the door.

She was not afraid when she saw the police inspector and his subordinates standing there. She had retrieved disaster, she had made a plan. In her elation she had not for one moment stopped to think whether that plan was really wise.

RAYMOND POSTGATE

....

VERDICT OF TWELVE

'Oxford and Cambridge are two delightful towns, dominated by the Universities and retaining much of their medieval character.' This is a lie, as you would know if you had lived in Coronation Street, Cambridge, as Victoria Mary Atkins did. The life of the university has, and had when she was born, nothing, nothing whatever, to do with the life of the town – not of such streets as Coronation Street, anyway. And there was nothing medieval about that unbroken line of yellow-brick little houses, flush on the street, and each identical with the other. Except in so far as wretchedness, darkness and dirt are medieval.

Victoria was the fifth of nine children; her father died when she was eleven. He was an unskilled labourer, and no loss to anyone. His wages, when at work, had averaged 21s. a week, and he drank. He beat his children, and his wife, with a strap, but Victoria did not hold that against him. Being beaten was, after all, a natural thing to happen to any child. With a bit of sneaking and slyness you could often enough get bigger children into trouble and see your grudges avenged; an occasional sore behind yourself was a small price to pay. No, it was not the beatings which Victoria held against her father. It was the continual hunger which made her grow pinched and rickety, the shame of existing for months on relief, the worse shame of dressing in rags, and an earlier violence that she could not remember, which had resulted in one of her legs being slightly shorter than the other.

Even so, father was a less dangerous enemy than mother. Father was at least away at work sometimes, and sometimes harmlessly drunk or even jolly. Mother was never away for more than a few minutes from the two rooms which were home, and was never anything but sour. Father was not 'noticing'; Mother was, and what's more, would twist your arm till you screamed if you sulked and wouldn't answer.

Two years after her father's death Victoria slapped her mother's face, scratched her cheek, and tripped her over the coal scuttle. She had realized that at thirteen she was probably as strong as her mother, and certainly quicker witted. While her mother was picking herself up from the scuttle, she didn't run away; fists clenched, breathing very fast and a little frightened she stood her ground. When her mother, instead of attacking her began to scream, 'You wicked, wicked girl!' she knew that she had won. Henceforward she was free. One of her two elder brothers might perhaps belt her now and again, but that would be all. She could run about the streets like a dog if she chose.

But beyond petty thieving, from which she had never been discouraged, there was not much harm that an ugly little girl could come to in Cambridge in 1911. She was dirty, dressed in patches, with twisted front teeth, a limp, and a hideous slum accent. She was known to have a nasty temper. Naturally she found few companions. The freedom of the streets after a year had become a bore, and she was not really distressed (though she complained on principle) when it was suddenly ended.

Mother collapsed on the stairs one Monday morning. The ambulance fetched her away, and her family was told she would never come back; in fact, she died in the infirmary.

The Guardians had resented their statutory obligation to feed and care for this shiftless and over-large family; they had evaded doing it properly as long as they could; now they could not avoid it any more. But, at least, they made every effort they could to put the burden elsewhere. They cajoled and bullied Aunt Ethel, a square-shaped woman of nearly forty who kept a shop in Cherry Hinton, to come down to the house with their representative, a bright and experienced woman of middle age. The two found the family, or what was left of it, under the reluctant care of a neighbour, Mrs Elizabeth Saunders.

'And glad I am to see you,' said Mrs Saunders. 'Not one minute longer will I stay with such a dirty and disagreeable lot of children. There are very few would be so Christian as to look after them as I have done, with no obligations whatever. And now you *have* come, I'll leave you with them and nothing more will I do.'

Surprised at this vehemence, the Guardians' lady began to say she was sure everyone was very grateful, and much appreciated all that Mrs Saunders – but she realized she was speaking to a departing back and gave it up.

'Now, my dears,' she said briskly, 'your Aunt Ethel has very kindly come in from Cherry Hinton, and we must all get together and have a nice comfy talk and settle what to do while your poor Mummy is ill. I thought there would be some *older* children here,' she added enquiringly. 'Are you Violet?' she said to the one who appeared to be the eldest.

The girl addressed dribbled and made a kind of mooing noise.

'That's Lily,' said Aunt Ethel. 'Lacking. Always was. Ought to be in a 'sylum. Violet's in service in Cottenham and it's not her day off. She gets 5s. 6d. a week and lucky to get it. You won't get any help from *her*.'

'Oh, I see. Dear me. Well, there's Edward – no, of course, he went away three years ago. But where's Robert?'

Victoria piped up, delighted to offer bad news. 'You won't find 'im. 'E went to ve stition vis morning; saw 'im. Soon as 'e 'eard Ma was gorn 'e said 'e was off. Not going to be responsible for us lot, 'e said, not —— likely.' There was a participle before the last word which is even now not widely used by young women, and the Guardians' lady and Aunt Ethel glared.

Victoria stared back: it took more than a glare to discompose her. In that moment Aunt Ethel took a resolution: she would not let that foul-mouthed child into her house. The Guardians' lady was talking to her, but she did not listen. She broke into her suggestions without ceremony.

'You'll have to take poor Lily where she belongs. You know quite well what your obligations are, miss. As for these poor orphans, I'll take these three into my house and look after them and be glad.' She pointed to the three younger children – two boys and the baby, May. 'Victoria can't come. There's no room for her, and she's too old. She's a bad girl and a bad influence already.'

Nothing would shift her from this decision, and in the end the Guardians' lady took Victoria with her, to be put in a Home.

Now a Home for Girls, even before the war, even in the provinces, was not always one of the hell-holes which realistic writers will describe for you. The West Fen Home did the best that could be done for Victoria, and if it did no better it was because she came to it too late. It fed her properly for the first time in her life, gave her glasses which were approximately what her eyes needed, and provided a built-up boot for her left leg. It clothed her drably, but sufficiently and warmly. It taught her to speak correctly and modified her abominable accent. Since she had benefited scarcely at all from her interrupted attendances at the Board school it taught her properly reading, writing and arithmetic, and to read the Bible.

More than that, she was taught thoroughly the art of being a domestic servant. She could wash, clean rooms, make beds, blacklead grates, sew and do plain cooking with unsurpassed thoroughness. If drilling could make one, she was the perfect maid; moreover, she was respectful. The staff would have been kind to her as well as strict if she had responded to kindness; as she did not, it was satisfied by her covering up with an impassive and silent manner her undiminished bad temper and spite. It would have been very surprised to know her real opinion both of itself and of the rare adults from outside whom she met.

In 1915 it sent her out from the Home into a good position with the wife of a don. She kept her place for six months and left, with an excellent reference, to go into munitions. She moved to London and saved all that she could; by the end of the war, when the factory closed down, she had just over £200. She was parsimonious, had few friends, and dressed always in black: she was not attractive, but after the war mistresses could not be too particular. Servants were too rare. A girl with such excellent references and so universally competent about the house was a treasure; and, at least, there would be no trouble with 'followers'. All the same, Victoria did not keep her situations long. One she left under a strong suspicion of stealing, though when her mistress threatened not to give her a reference she enforced one with well-informed and vitriolic threats. One she left after a fierce quarrel with the cook, and in another she poured boiling water over the arm and hand of the parlourmaid. In 1926 she lost all her money, which she had invested in cotton shares; she visited the office of the defaulting company and opened the face of the unhappy reception clerk from mouth to eye with a blow from the ferrule of her umbrella. The magistrate reprimanded her severely but did not sentence her as it was her first offence and she had undoubtedly a real grievance. She was out of work for several weeks afterwards.

The sight of her Aunt Ethel made things worse for her: Ethel had sold her Cherry Hinton shop and gone into munitions, too (she had been just young enough), but she had kept her money. She had bought houses with it in the Bloomsbury district, and had had sense enough to choose the west side of Gray's Inn Road. Values had gone up, and now Ethel was comfortably off. She rigidly refused to lend Victoria a penny, but promised to remember her in her will, together with her younger sister, May Ena, and a waif named Irene Olga Hutchins, sole reminder of the two younger male Atkinses . . . 'two' because there was a regrettable doubt which of them was the father, and both were beyond reach of questioners in a Flanders cemetery. Their last letters to the mother had been brief and unfriendly, consisting only of a refusal to pay, couched in identical terms. Irene now did practically all the housework for Great-Auntie, sustained by promises that in due course she would be a rich woman. The figures varied: sometimes it would be three thousand, sometimes five, and once even ten, that Irene was told she could expect as her third share when Great-Auntie passed on. Great-Auntie never spoke so detailedly to Victoria, of course, but Irene naturally told her disagreeable aunt whatever she chose to ask, and there were few things about which she asked more frequently.

So, in 1927, there were only four members of the once numerous Atkins family left, as far as was known, anyway. There were Aunt Ethel, Victoria herself, her sister May, and the small niece, whose unfortunate lack of the surname Atkins was forgotten, as she was invariably called nothing but Young Ireen. Of these four, the last three were in indigent circumstances, and the first had plenty of money. This circumstance formed the first and most essential of the facts in a dossier assembled by the police in the winter of that year.

The next significant fact was an event that the police never noted in their records at all. On a Thursday afternoon in late November, May, who spelt her name Mae even before Miss West wiped out any memory of Princess May, was taking tea with Victoria in Mrs Mulholland's boarding-house in Lewisham. It was Victoria's custom to entertain her sister once a week, more to insist on her rights than from family affection, and also to provide for herself by fair exchange a place to go to on her own afternoon off.

Mae laid down her cup. 'Tea's not up to much,' she said, rather diffidently.

'And that's a fact,' replied Victoria equably. 'The old girl's mean. I don't know where she gets the tea; she brings it in herself. Mouse-dirt I found in it last time; *inside* the packet, mind you. I— Don't you feel well, Mae?'

'I do seem to have come over queer,' said Mae faintly.

'Are you going to be *sick*?' said Victoria, with the anxious rising tone in which those words are always said.

'I'm afraid so . . .'

'Well, for goodness' sake run *quick*; you know where the W is,' snapped her elder sister, shooing her out.

Mae was very sick indeed; her sister even relented and came to hold her head, so deplorable were the noises. Actually no harm resulted whatever; Mae's health was, if anything, improved by the upset, and you might have thought she had merely taken unintentionally a dose of ipecacuanha. But at the moment she felt she was going to die and miserably said so. Her sister was sympathetic, most unusually.

'I don't like it at all, Mae; I don't. You look as white as anything. Suppose there is something really wrong. You go straight home this moment and lie down. I'll come round and see you in the morning, first thing I can. It's no good my asking the old cat for permission to go out tonight; but I'll get up early and the moment I've laid breakfast I'll pop across.'

She fussed over her sister and bundled her out, very surprised and a little unwilling. But Mae was a little scared, too; Victoria had never shown anything like this sisterly anxiety. Perhaps she was really ill? Personally she'd have said it was nothing but Victoria's nasty tea, and the mention of mouse-dirt in it had been enough to turn anyone up. Anyway, she'd better go and if Victoria came round in the morning it couldn't do any harm.

Victoria watched her sister from the basement window with a curiously pleased expression. She said nothing to Mrs Mulholland about the incident.

About five o'clock next morning the figure of a middle-sized woman in black with a veil could have been, but was not, seen moving at a sedate pace down a poorish street in Camberwell. Her feet made no sound; she presumably was wearing rubber-soled shoes. She went straight up to the corner house, which was Aunt Ethel's, and let herself in with a key, absolutely silently. There was a bolt on the inner side of the door, but the wood had warped years ago, and it could not be shot into its socket. The woman stood a full half-minute inside the door, listening. There was no sound at all except the ticking of a large hall-clock.

With a firm silent step, as of someone who knew her way, she moved across to Aunt Ethel's bedroom, turned the handle softly and listened. Steady breathing. The door closed behind her.

In the room there is darkness, except for the faint glimmer of the pillow case and turned-down sheet: on the pillow a dim round marks the place where the old lady's head lies. A dark figure is standing beside the bed: you could not, if you were there, make out precisely what its hands are doing. They seem to be reaching underneath the old lady's head to her second pillow.

To steal something? No, it is the second pillow itself the hands want. And, sudden speed contrasting with previous caution, the pillow is swept away and down on to the old lady's face; and there pressed down with fanatical energy. The sleeper breaks into violent and blind activity; her legs thrash madly about in the bed, her helpless, rather clawlike hands grab into the empty air but never find her attacker. The pillow drowns any sounds she may try to make.

These few minutes seem to last an hour. Down and down the hands press. The struggle grows weaker, but the hands cannot wait for them to end. The strong fingers separate the feathers in the pillow till they feel beneath them the skin of the throat. Then both thumbs with a sort of fierce delight thrust downwards and hold.

A little while later there is a slight sigh and the black figure straightens up. A spark of light appears, as from a small, nearly run-out electric torch. By its light the pillow is removed and above the old lady's mouth appears, held in the air, a little mirror such as is carried in a vanity bag. No clouding on it, no moisture. The mirror is held there until its owner is satisfied it would remain clear for ever, and then the light is snapped out. In the dark, hands put back the pillow and roughly re-arrange the bed; the black figure slips silently out again.

Back into the street. Two turnings, past silent homes and unwinking electric lights. Round into the main road and straight to a telephone box. The woman in black put in her twopence and dialled, not 999, but the local police station. When the answer came she said in an oddly high-pitched but not loud voice: 'Oh, come at once, come at once! Me great-auntie's dead. Ow, it's too frightful . . . She's dead, I tell you, and I'm all alone. Are you going to leave me to be murdered? . . . It's 68 Duke Street . . . Oh, get *here* and don't ask silly questions.' The station sergeant, who tried to stem and answer this rush of frightened words, automatically noted the time of the call before he turned to take action. It was 5.52 a.m.

The woman rang off, and then after a moment's hesitation rang Ethel's number. Ethel was rich and did have a telephone. She heard the ringing tone for quite a time, and then Irene's voice answered. 'What do you want at this time of night?' it asked querulously. The woman in black made no reply: she pressed button B, took her twopence and went away. Irene would be up and awake now; she could let the police officers in and maybe do a little explaining to them. The woman in black walked away from the telephone box and in a minute or two took her place on an early workman's tram which was already in sight. Everyone, including the conductor, was sleepy, and she was inconspicuous. She might be any rather superior charlady going to work. Nobody was likely to notice and remember her, and nobody did.

At exactly six o'clock, trained by years of experience, Mrs Mulholland awoke temporarily, looked at her watch and listened to hear if the servant was getting up. Victoria had been late once or twice recently. She heard distantly the tinkle of the girl's alarm, which was stopped almost immediately. Soon after there came the unmistakable bump of a chair being knocked over. 'How clumsy that girl is getting,' she thought, and turned over for another half-hour's sleep. Her cup of tea would come at 6.30.

6.40. No cup of tea. Mrs Mulholland rose, wrapped a dressing-gown round herself, and called downstairs. 'Victoria!' There was no answer. Cross and cold, she pattered down to the kitchen. Breakfast was laid, trays put out, curtains drawn, and everything tidy. But no kettle was on, and in the middle of the table was a folded note:

> *Madam, — Having heard my sister Mae was very ill yesterday I have just slipped out to see how she is. Am sorry if this causes any inconvenience but I am very anxious and think I should know. Will be back as quick as possible.*
>
> V. M. Atkins.

Mrs Mulholland was very angry, and when Victoria returned well after seven, threatened her with dismissal. Victoria was unmoved – said it was just as Mrs Mulholland pleased, that she had no father nor mother and it was her duty to look after her younger sister, and that she was glad to say, though not asked, that her sister was much better. Mrs Mulholland considered the matter, remembered the rarity of good maids, and agreed to overlook it. Victoria went upstairs, tidied her bedroom, brought down and threw in the fire two scraps of string and a candle end, and nothing further happened of note until the police arrived later in the morning.

The police had had some difficulty in getting into 68, Duke Street. Irene had gone back to bed, and when induced to answer the door told them the message was nonsense. At last she consented to summon her great-aunt, and went into her room. A few seconds later she began to scream shrilly, and intermittently, rather like a steam engine. The two policemen – one in mufti – hurriedly shut the front door and ran into the bedroom. In a minute one of them came back again, went to the telephone and summoned the police doctor. There was no doubt the old lady was dead, and two very indistinct marks on the throat made it look like strangulation. The body was warm: it seemed only just dead. The time, the Inspector noted, was 6.15.

For a short while it looked like an 'open and shut' case. The young girl, Irene, was obviously prostrated by grief and shock. She was hardly strong enough to strangle the old lady, anyway, and if she was the murderer the mysterious telephone call was very difficult to explain. She insisted that she had never made it; that she had indeed been called up a quarter of an hour or so earlier to answer the telephone, but there was no one there by the time she got to it. Inspector Hodson acquitted her mentally: adding that apart from anything else no girl of her age could be so consummate an actress. Also she had told him that her Aunt Victoria was co-heir to the old lady's money and had a key to the door. He verified for himself that the bolt would not fit.

Inspector Hodson himself was convinced that Victoria was guilty, but her defence seemed impregnable. Both her mistress and Miss Meakin remembered clearly hearing her get up, and though they were not certain as to when she left, there was no reasonable doubt that it was after six, when two policemen were standing by Ethel's newly dead body, a good half-hour away.

In the end Victoria inherited £2,327 11s. 0d. from her aunt and purchased with it a tobacconist's and newsagent's business. In three years' time she had made enough to buy her house: and this new prosperity was responsible for her receiving a juror's summons. She spent 7s. 6d. with a lawyer, to receive the information that she could not escape her duties; and in consequence, half displeased, half interested, she made her way to court on the day.

She thought to herself, in a manner as near to humour as any thought of hers could be, that it wouldn't half be queer if she had to be juror in a murder case. Somebody who did know how, judging somebody that didn't. For she never attempted to forget that she had killed her aunt, and she never had the least regret. She was rather proud of it, though she remembered having several bad scares and was certain she'd never do such a thing again.

It had been pretty simple. The alarm clock was easy. Even the coppers had suspected that. It was only a matter of testing the winding, and she'd done that several times, holding the bell in her handkerchief. She had found exactly the number of turns of the alarm key necessary to make it ring twenty seconds and no more. Then she had set it and left it. She had been intentionally irregular in her getting up for some days before, to make sure Mrs Mulholland would listen for her alarm. Anyway, Miss Meakin was safe. There is sometimes a very slight difference between an alarm that has run down and one that is cut short, but it is not the sort of thing a sleepy woman notices, let alone remembers to tell a rozzer.

The bumping of the furniture had been a little more difficult. But only a little patience was needed, and sleeping with your window shut to avoid a draught. Candles burn exactly to time: didn't the Romans use them as clocks or something? Victoria had spent many nights testing and retesting their speed, marking out the hours, halves, and quarters on them. She didn't use her knowledge until she was absolutely certain to a few minutes either way. Then on the night she pulled her blind down and arranged what looked like a sort of booby trap.

To a nail driven into the window-sill she attached a long piece of string; the other end she tied to the wooden chair which was almost her complete bedroom furniture. She leant the chair against her bed, tipped to one side. If the string were to break, it would fall down to the floor on its side, with a reasonable but not excessive noise.

Then she made a triangular cut in the candle on the table by her bed, at a particular place which she had marked. She moved the table underneath the string, so that the string pressed into the triangular cut, right against the wick, and then, taking the time from her watch, lit the candle. Unless her calculations were wrong, the candle flame would reach the place at six exactly, and in a minute or so the string would snap.

Her calculations were not wrong; on top of that she had a bit of luck on which she had not reckoned. People hear what they expect to hear. Miss Meakin and Mrs Mulholland had for day after day heard Victoria's alarm go off, then heard her bump about a bit while dressing, and after that if they strained their ears heard her move faintly and distantly doing the kitchen out downstairs. When, half asleep, they heard the beginning of this process they assumed that they had heard the rest. If Inspector Hodson had cross-questioned both of them closely and immediately that very morning he might perhaps have raised a doubt in their minds whether Victoria's getting up was actually followed by the usual sounds of work downstairs. Even if he had, as the Inspector knew very well, doubt about almost any evidence can be induced by sufficiently long cross-examination: results obtained that way don't generally stand up too well in court. Anyway, when he did examine the two ladies in detail, they showed none of the phenomenal feats of detailed memory that occur in detective stories. They merely remembered that things had gone as usual that morning, and said so.

It had taken a bit of nerve (Victoria remembered) to go on to Mae's after It, instead of hurrying back. But as soon as she got home she had gone back upstairs, pulled up the blind, made the bed, set the chair straight, wound up the alarm, and twisted the nail out. She'd put in a new candle and let it burn a minute. She'd taken the two ends of string and the candle stump and thrown them on the kitchen fire. So even if the coppers had gone over her room they must have found nothing.

F. TENNYSON JESSE

....

A PIN TO SEE
THE PEEPSHOW

Two things were hanging Julia Starling – her birth certificate, and her place in the social scale. If only she had not been seven years older than Carr, and if only she had been higher or lower in the world! In the class above hers the idea of divorce would not have shocked, and a private income would even have allowed her and Carr to live together without divorce, and no one would have been unduly outraged. Had their walk in life been the lowest, had they been tramps or part of the floating population of the docks down London River, they could have set up in one room together, and no one thought twice about it, as long as the husband wasn't a big strong man who made a row and tried to do them in.

Starling's two gifts had undoubtedly been her business capacity and the finely attuned orchestra of her body – if only she had combined the two, the most sensible thing to do! But he supposed that was immoral. Why, many people would have thought the worse of her if they knew even that her body was a source of pleasure to her. If she actually marketed that talent, she would be lost indeed. What had there been for her but escape? And such was the compulsion of circumstances, it was only into a world that she had dreamed for herself that she could escape.

And a dangerous world it had of necessity proved, but surely not the vulgar world that a vulgar-minded judge had called it?

It was bad luck, all of it. Bad luck for her, bad luck for the stupid husband – who had as good a right to live, poor devil, as anybody else, and bad luck for that other poor devil, who also had to toe the line that morning. And bad luck for himself, and the rest of the poor devils who had to assist at the beastly business in both places. In both prisons the prisoners would be unmanageable and gloomy, and officers would feel like criminals. Here he would have the job of testing the heart that had been stilled for ever, of noting at which cervical the fracture had occurred, even of noting the haemorrhage that might burst forth.

And why, in spite of all logic and reason, did the idea persist, even in his well-balanced mind, that it was somehow worse to hang a woman than a man? The dark consciousness of the womb was present with every man who had to do with the business, of the womb that was the holder of life, from which every living soul had issued in squalor and pain. Some deep awareness of the mother, the source of life, worked in the mind of every man. Perhaps, too, they felt that such a job should be left to another woman to carry through; but then women wouldn't carry it through. Women, as this poor creature had been, were rather the instigators of deeds than the performers.

They were borrowing a couple of warders from the men's prison for tomorrow's performance, the female officers wouldn't go to the scaffold, except the unfortunate Lady Superintendent, whose duty obliged her to do so.

This Julia Starling had evaded the womb's responsibilities, while partaking of its pleasures; but, nevertheless, that dark consciousness of it as the medium by which each one of them had come into the world, would be present to every man at the execution. Ogilvie agreed that if a guilty man were hanged, a guilty woman should meet the same fate, but even with him persisted that dark awareness of the womb.

At that other prison nature would take her last ironic revenge in the body of the man who had killed for what he had called love, making a final gesture, lewd as a sneer. The very officers, the doctor who examined his body afterwards, would feel an almost superstitious dread of that impudent and useless jibe of nature's. And, God knew, hanging a man was a bad enough business, even without that wretched commentary on love which the hanged man presented despite himself.

Davidson made no attempt to sleep. He prayed, and when he could pray no more he tried to read. Then he would make himself some black coffee, lest sleep should come over him. For he had a curious idea that little as he had been able to do for her, he would be doing still less if he let his mind slip into unconsciousness; that perhaps the intensity of his thoughts and his prayers would be permitted to be of some slight help to her in her extremity. Irresistible as temptation's self, sleep came over him at about three in the morning, but he forced it back, drank more coffee, and went on wrestling with the dark angel. A phrase began to repeat itself again and again in his head. *Whom God hath joined together let no man put asunder* . . . That was out of the marriage service . . . he'd repeated it hundreds of times. What was it that Ogilvie had been theorizing about . . . something about everyone alive being a marriage, generally an ill-assorted one, between body and mind? If that were so, he was going to assist next morning at the forcible sundering of a marriage.

He was tortured by the knowledge that he had been of very little help to Julia Starling. The thing that he had tried to appeal to was not there – that sense of spiritual awareness which had made his own life; this was lacking in Starling. Armed as he was with the authority of voluntary celibacy, with the fervour of intense conviction: burning as he was with the love of souls, he had not succeeded in finding hers – much less in awakening it.

During the last few weeks he had been reading, not for the first time, the reminiscences of the Abbé Pirot, who had attended that most notorious and cold-blooded of poisoners, Marie-Madeleine de Brinvilliers. He had been turning over and over the pages of these portentous tomes, which somehow gained instead of losing by their naïve repetitions. The classic beauty of style might have been lost, but the passion survived just because the Abbé Pirot hadn't troubled over-much over the niceties of fine writing, because he had simply poured out on paper, day by day, every little thing that this penitent had said or done. That last day, that terrible last day, he had recorded moment by moment. Pirot had succeeded in obtaining remorse, not a mere regret, from his penitent, but he, Davidson, had failed. He was not, he admitted humbly, a Pirot. But then, on the other hand, poor Julia Starling, whatever the measure of her guilt, had not attained to those horrible peaks of depravity of the Brinvilliers. Perhaps the times were out of joint. Starling could not care enough about her immortal soul, she was too occupied with the thought of her mortal body. Who was not nowadays? And, not for the first time in his life, Davidson found himself regretting bitterly that he hadn't been able, as he expressed it to himself, to 'go the whole way'. If he had had the authority of Rome behind him; if instead of trying to impress upon Starling his belief of the necessity of the Sacraments he had had behind that belief the whole authority of his Church, instead of, as he knew only too well, a mere mass of conflicting opinions!

But then, even so, and even admitting that he could have obtained an emotional response from Starling, how much would she really have known, or cared or understood? She was thinking of nothing but the injustice that was to be meted out to her; of nothing but the terrifying death of her body. Of her soul she knew nothing, and cared less. In the days of the Brinvilliers there had been more crime, and more cruelty; but nevertheless everybody believed. There had been no initial difficulty of a complete lack of interest to be overcome; and so the Marquise de Brinvilliers, with murder thick upon her conscience, had made the most edifying end, and the Abbé Pirot, having wrestled with the dark angels for her soul until he was almost as exhausted as his penitent, was convinced of her ultimate salvation.

None of these words would convey anything to Julia Starling, or to those of her generation brought up as she had been. The Brinvilliers had been able to say: 'But are there any sins that by their gravity, or their number, cannot be forgiven, even by the Church?' and Pirot, conscious that the voice of centuries spoke through his mouth, to one who listened with ears which the centuries had not yet dulled, was able to reply: 'Madame, there are no sins which cannot be expiated.' And with his ardour, his faith, he had succeeded in assuring the cold-blooded woman, who had poisoned for profit from her youth, that there was a gate, straight and narrow indeed, through which she could pass to a remission of her sins.

Why, the very word 'sin' meant nothing to Julia Starling. The Brinvilliers had hours when she lapsed from grace, when the tigress in her had shown itself, when her anger at humanity had been too strong for her new-found grace – hours such as that dread one after her torture when once again she was the jungle animal who hated all humanity – and yet Pirot, endlessly patient, had once again brought her to the foot of the cross. What could Davidson offer? Only a belief as passionate, an ardour as intense, a pity as deep as Pirot's, but without Pirot's conviction and authority. More important still, what could Julia receive? Nothing. What she must be suffering now, unless God were good and sent her sleep. And even so there would be the awakening . . .

He told himself that the actual business would be over very quickly, everyone assured him of that. But what did 'quickly' mean? Who could say how long that moment of dropping seemed? Time was relative, an hour of happiness could whip through a man's mind like the flaunt of a blown banner. In misery, five minutes could seem hours. In sleep a lifetime could be lived through in the space of time taken to lift the latch of a door. Who could say how long those few moments seemed to the prisoner, those moments that the authorities flattered themselves were over so swiftly? There was a theory that a man's whole life flashed before him in the moment of drowning. What was time, as the clock knew it, in the face of such tricks as these? One didn't even know to what one was condemning the victim, that was what it worked out at . . . 'A thousand years in Thy sight are but as yesterday'. . . easy for Him if that was how He was able to look at it, seeing Time all in one piece. Not easy for man, to whom the next moment is the horizon which, like the sea's horizon, always advances with his own advance, so that never is he able to peer over the rim.

*

At the other prison men turned uneasily, or paced their cells, or broke up the furniture in the cell, head in hands, wishing the hours would go more quickly. All excepting Leo, who wished they would go more slowly. He still had so much to do – another letter to his mother, one to his shipmates. He was getting sleepy by the time he'd finished them. Might as well take a rest. Christ Almighty! what a fool he'd been. Well, it was no good crying over spilt milk. Anyway, he'd show them he wasn't afraid. When his shipmates heard of him, they'd know he'd met it all right. No brandy for him, he'd leave that for the others – they'd want it. He slept – so peacefully, that the officers looked at him and then at each other. Poor devil . . . let him sleep. What a pity he couldn't go off in his sleep, like you did to sick dogs and cats. He'd never know anything about it then.

One of the officers wished, rather uneasily, that the hangman hadn't altered the drop that evening. It wasn't a good thing to experiment with drops at the last moment. It was bad enough, of course, if the man's head were torn off. You had to go down below and clean up the mess; but at least the man himself knew nothing of it. But suppose the drop were wrong the other way about . . .? Then the poor devil just thrashed about, kicking with his pinioned legs against the brick sides of the pit, so that you had to rush down and hang on to his feet, as in the days of hanging by strangulation. Nothing like that, he hoped, would happen to this nice young chap. A damned shame that a woman should have brought him to this. A decent young chap, who didn't make the warders' job any harder for them than needs be. You'd have thought something better could have been found to put out the light of a fine young chap with such guts, and such a lot of good in him.

Julia tried to lie quietly, even tried to keep her eyes shut. But what was the good? She opened her eyes and saw the shadows of the watching women like great birds against the green and white wall. She shut her eyes again, so as to be able to try and pretend she was alone.

She was very tired, and it seemed to her for a while that she suffered very little. Her nerves, aided by the bromide, were more relaxed than they had been for days past. She had been a fool to be so frightened, of course they didn't mean to do that dreadful nightmare thing to her. Things like that couldn't happen. Her imagination had always been her curse, everyone on both sides had said so at the trial . . . it had actually led her into believing the Governor when he had told her that the appeal was turned down. She had screamed and fought then, and tried to climb up the bare wall, and they had given her all that bromide and it hadn't done her any good, because she was so frightened. But now she saw that she had been a fool to believe it. They were only doing it to frighten her, that was it. Perhaps she did deserve a little punishment, and this was how it was being given to her. They were letting her own imagination give it to her on this night that they pretended was to be her last. But it couldn't really be so, because this sort of thing didn't happen to people who were in perfect health. Only dying people knew for a certainty that their last night had come. When healthy people died suddenly it was by an accident, not by a set and certain catastrophe. That would be too arbitrary and silly, it just couldn't happen. She relaxed still more in that blessed certainty.

She was in a big shop, it was important she should finish buying what she wanted before the shop closed, and it was going to close any moment now. The stocking department was on the top floor, she must hurry or it would be too late, and she would not be allowed to go up to it. Already the shop assistants were leaving. There was the lift, one of those terrifying lifts one worked oneself; she got in, pulled the iron gates across, and pressed the button.

She had made an awful mistake, it was a lift that went down, not up, she'd been on the top floor and not known it. And the lift was out of order, she couldn't stop it, it was falling . . . falling. With a thin scream she awoke and sat up, wet with sweat. For a moment it was a relief to be awake, to realize that that falling lift had been a dream . . . but the next moment full realization of everything had flooded in upon her. All relaxation of the nerves had gone, she knew what the Governor had told her was the truth, that it wasn't impossible that they should do that dreadful thing to her next morning. These were her last hours of life; never after tonight would she see shadows on a wall, feel the prickle of a blanket against her cheek, draw her finger down the flesh of her inner arm. Not much to want – to see shadows, to touch your own flesh, rub your skin against a blanket, yet they were going to take it from her. Everything was to be taken from her, and yet she'd never asked or wanted much. Was it her fault that she'd married Herbert when she was too young to know what she was doing? Had it been her fault that she'd thought she'd loved Leo? Who wouldn't have thought they loved almost anybody who came along and was nice, leading the dreary sort of life she'd had to lead? Leo ... a faint thought of him, perhaps also lying awake in that other dread place not far away, brushed across the surface of her mind like a moth's wing, and was gone. She'd always worked hard and worked well. Mr Coppinger and Gipsy had always said so. She'd never had the chance to do all she could have with her gifts; life had always been against her. Naturally she'd tried to make a dream world where she had all she wanted, where she was admired and beloved; naturally she'd snatched at any love and admiration that came her way in actuality. Who wouldn't have, who didn't? Everyone tried to get what they wanted, and it didn't go wrong for all of them. Just because in spite of the dreariness of her life, she had been able to create a sort of fairy story that ran alongside the drab reality, was she to be punished in this dreadful fashion? As though she'd intended the fairy story to be real! Leo ought to have known she hadn't meant it to be real; it was all his fault. Just because she was seven years older than he – that seven years which, she had once heard, saw the changing of the whole fabric of the body – people seemed to think that she was responsible for what Leo had done.

She had always been aware of time, and afraid of it. Leo's fewer years had set his whole life at a different place in time from hers, and she had endeavoured, by setting a term for things – such as three years till she got her freedom – to make them match. Life was only time slipping past you; you tried to grab at it, but it went on from between your fingers. Leo had never been aware of any time but the present; he'd never seen that the present was always becoming the past, just as the future was always becoming the present.

There he was again, right in her mind now, but not as himself; it was not for what he also might be feeling that she agonized. She thought of him with a deep and bitter resentment. It was his stupidity that had lost her; she saw him as her executioner . . . As the awful word struck into her mind, her heart seemed to leap and almost stop, then went on thudding slowly, angrily.

After all, she had not had so very much to do with Leo in reality; he was more terribly real to her now in this aspect than he had often been in real life. It wasn't fair. Why, even the love that she and he had had – how rare it had been, what with the difficulties of meeting, and his voyages. Only those few days in Essex, and once at the shop. More often than not she had only possessed him through her husband's flesh, or in the fastnesses of her own mind and body, lying on her bed alone.

Now that imaginary Leo and the actual Leo of such physical contacts as had been theirs, had fused into the agent of her destruction. It was as though Leo's hands were going to close about her throat. What did that remind her of? Some song . . . long ago, at school; she'd thought it beautiful then . . . something about sooner feeling your lover's hands closing about your throat, choking out life, than bidding you farewe-hell . . . Rotten nonsense. Nothing mattered but life. Not to have life choked out . . . that was all that mattered.

Leo ought to have known that, would have known it if he hadn't been drunk. He ought to have known she hadn't meant it . . . not to that point. Nobody could. Life was what mattered, life. Not to be going to suffer such a horror. Oh, to be alone, unmarried, old, ugly, poor, sleeping in some doorway, dirty, cold, starving, for no one to be interested in one . . . but to be alive . . . just to be alive. How could people take that away from one? Stop all that that meant? They were killing everything: the trams down Chiswick High Road, the young trees in leaf, the bright winking faces of the shops, the clanging of the bells, all the sparkle and the glitter and the music.

The papers said that Mrs Starling was to be hanged on Tuesday, but that wasn't really what was happening. Mrs Starling was a romantic figure, who wrote passionate love-letters, a figure in an Italian officer's blue cape and a helmet hat; a figure that had never really existed except as a pretence. They weren't hanging that Mrs Starling, they were hanging Julia, who cleaned her teeth night and morning, who went to the lavatory – who would have to even on this Tuesday morning – who ate and drank, and smoked, and dressed, and sent clothes to the wash; whose hair grew greasy and lost its wave, whose nails needed cleaning and filing, whose head sometimes ached, and whose feet always ached at the end of a long day; who kept count of her money in a shabby little leather purse, whose back hurt her every month so that she could hardly go to business, who stopped outside the cinema when the programme was changed twice weekly to look at the new posters . . . That was what they were killing . . . What had a person like that, a person just like the rest of them, done to be killed? You couldn't kill a person who cleaned her teeth and went to the lavatory; you only killed romantic people. And no one was really a romantic person, no one. It was not worth this stark reality.

True, Herbert had been killed, but that had really been an accident. He hadn't had to know about it beforehand, hadn't dreaded it. They hadn't waked him at the chill hour of morning and told him that now – now – he had to dress, make use of the conduits of his body for the last time, go through the farce of putting something into his stomach that he and everyone else knew would never nourish him. People hadn't looked at him with a dread apology in their sick eyes. . .

What was it the chaplain had told her? That we are all under sentence of death . . . The sort of thing that sounds clever and isn't a bit true. If you didn't know when or how it was going to overtake you, what did it matter? It was this relentless knowledge that was so cruel; she wouldn't have inflicted that upon her worst enemy. 'Her own worst enemy' . . . wasn't that an expression she had heard? Probably it was true, but it hadn't been her fault. Everyone spoke of her, especially Herbert's relations, as though she'd been a sort of spoiled darling, but that wasn't true. She'd never had a chance of anything she really wanted. That was why she'd always pretended. She'd only pretended Herbert's death, and it had suddenly come alive in spite of her. Now her own death was here, and she couldn't pretend any more. If, when morning came, she were to stay lying on her bed, pretending something quite different, they'd pull her up; they'd make her stand on her feet, they wouldn't let her go on pretending. She had come to that place where dreams fail.

She struggled to her feet and the two women moved towards her anxiously. She needed their support, her legs failed her; it was as though they were made of straw. She began to moan and cry as they laid her back on the bed. She caught the hard, firm hand of one of them, held on to it desperately. *Don't let them do it, don't let them do it . . . promise you won't let them do it . . .* They soothed her, gave her more bromide, but she was not deceived. She lay biting her pillow, beating her hands beside her head.

Oh, to sleep, to sleep . . . But if she slept It would be upon her all the sooner, she mustn't sleep. She must grab back the minutes and the hours. She sat up and held her hands to that unwinking light; she stared at those hands she knew by heart as though she had never seen them before. They were real and alive, there was the shiny oval nail of her left thumb, that had never given her any trouble, and there was the squat nail of the right thumb, with its unchanging ribbed band . . . She spread out her fingers, held them higher towards the light, while the women watched her anxiously. The blood informed those fingers, she could see the rosy web of skin between them against the light.

Tomorrow people would use their hands for all sorts of things; for dressing, and opening train doors, and writing and eating, and doing accounts, and for snatched love too, if they were lucky. They would use their hands for hanging her . . . hanging her . . . hanging her. Because of their hands her own, with their long capable fingers, her thumbs with the smooth nail and the ribbed, would be lying inert; the processes of decay already invisibly begun. No, no, it wasn't possible that people would deliberately cause those hands, so alive and well and strong for years to come, to be dead and useless tomorrow. No one could do a thing like that. They would come and tell her of a last-minute reprieve in the morning, that was what always happened.

Back she was at it again, hope – nay more, almost certainty, giving her the relief of relaxation for a brief minute. Hands, she thought childishly, were very dangerous; people oughtn't to have them. If Leo hadn't had hands he couldn't have killed Herbert, she couldn't have written those letters. But without hands she wouldn't be able to hold on right up in this big plane tree where she was, so high that it made her giddy to look down, and the tree shook so, too . . . Even with hands she couldn't hold on, she was going to fall . . .

She fell, screaming, and again the cell rushed up to meet her, the unwinking light and the unwinking pitiful eyes. Oh, it was true, it was true, they were going to hang her; she was going to fall just like that, with that awful sickening empty feeling, she was going to fall.

It was true, it was true. She saw one of the women – Mrs Horner, with the pale rigid face that looked paler than ever – look surreptitiously at her watch. That watch would go on ticking after she, Julia, had ceased to exist; after her pulses were still. There was more life in that watch than there was in her, because of the certainty that it would go on ticking. She was dead already, because she had to die at nine next morning. Or was it this morning by now? Was that why Mrs Horner had looked at her watch? The doctor was here now, and again she felt the needle thrust into her arm, and again she fell into a heavy sleep.

The time, slowly for some, fast for others, continued to exist, and nine o'clock struck.

Morning was fine for those who went to work and for those preparing for Ascot. The trees stood up into the sunlight, their full foliage still a deep untarnished green. Everywhere was the life of sunshine – flickering shadows and bright reflections. Soon the tinted wind-blown posters of the evening papers burgeoned along the streets. For it was ten o'clock, and the 'noon' edition, playing its strange trick of forcing Time ahead, was on sale. The posters bore the legend: 'Carr and Starling Hanged', or 'Double Hanging. Special', but only the stop-press gave a bare statement, the papers themselves gave the latest betting and racing advice. The Lunch edition, on sale long before lunch, reported on its front page that: 'Leonard Carr and Julia Starling were executed this morning for the murder of the latter's husband, Herbert Starling. Death was instantaneous in each case. The usual notices were posted on the prison gates, where small crowds had collected.' But already the posters had dropped the stale news and replaced it by 'Noon Wire and Double'. When, after lunch, the 6.30 edition was on sale, the first Ascot winners held pride of place. And when working London had finished brewing its tea in thousands of offices, and the Late Extra was pored over by office-boys and heads of departments alike, it was the racing news that was read. Two lines in a column headed 'News from Everywhere' and tucked away on an inconspicuous page, recorded the fact of a successful double execution. This item was sandwiched between two others; one saying that sixty police summonses for road traffic offences had been granted at Lambeth that day, the other recording that a Mr and Mrs Merritt, of Croydon, had celebrated their Golden Wedding. Mr Merritt, though now retired, had been for thirty years in the service of the Metropolitan Water Board.

The gleaming cars rolled back from Ascot, the workers of London went homewards in the towering scarlet buses, or the swaying trains. And, after supper, in the extra hour of sunlight man had re-parcelled from his older system, young people played tennis in leafy Greater London, and the older men worked in their gardens.

CAMERON McCABE

....

THE FACE ON THE
CUTTING-ROOM FLOOR

In *The Times* book column of 27th October we find the following sentences: 'In the fever of city life infatuations are apt to grow like mushrooms. The noise, the hurry and the sensation of being one alone among millions of unknown and therefore exciting people, make for a curious instability in those who live on what may be called the fringe of the artistic world. What they conceive to be love becomes with them an obsession and the whole of experience.'

Here is the key to McCabe's whole story, to his crime, to his curious love story, to McCabe himself, to Maria, to their interrelation and to McCabe's account of it.

I tried to show Mr McCabe's dependence on the age, class and environment from which he came: twentieth-century, middle-class and big-city, a product of the pressing need 'to earn increasingly more money so as not to sink into a relative pauperization'. This pressure produced a void, which is normally filled – and filled it must be – with the primitive essentials of human requirements: food and the other sex. Parts of the void are filled with various kinds of dope: with the last fragments of nineteenth-century religion, with nineteenth- and twentieth-century bogus politics, with pseudo-science, pseudo-art and other substitutional products of modern civilization. The result: 'a growing disregard for those human qualities which have not yet become purchasable and marketable merchandise'.

'*The fever of city life* – noise – hurry – the sensation of being one alone among millions of unknown and therefore exciting people': all of it breaks through McCabe's account in almost every line. McCabe in Soho, McCabe in the docks, McCabe in a traffic block on the way home from Whitechapel, McCabe in a Negro night-club – there is no getting away from it.

Here *infatuations are apt to grow like mushrooms*. 'Sentimental attachments breed like rabbits': what the inhabitants of this world 'conceive to be love becomes with them an obsession and the whole of experience': it fills the great void.

But once an infatuation becomes 'an obsession and the whole of experience', what else is it then but love? A peculiar kind of love, it is true, a post-war, big-city kind of love, but *love* nevertheless, love so strong and complete that it 'fills the whole of experience'.

And if it fills the whole of experience then there is simply nothing else left. Nothing else matters, neither the rules of society nor the code of morals, neither the law external nor the law internal. Even murder is no longer a crime – it is simply a means to an end, a natural and necessary means to an all-justifying end: 'There's no way out for you . . . No way out for a man once a woman has got hold of him.'

Maria becomes an obsession, the whole of experience. But Jensen is about to take her away. The whole of existence is in danger. Therefore Jensen must be got out of the way. First by cunning and trickery, then, both having failed, by force.

But the crime does not come off. Not because McCabe is detected as the murderer, but because Maria leaves him in spite of the murder. To be exact: just because of the murder. Which is only natural.

So we find McCabe in the end bemoaning the ultimate futility of all things: 'Oh Lord! what had I killed Jensen for, if Maria wouldn't reply afterwards.'

Reason begins to work again after a long time of utter confusion of all senses.

This can be clearly followed in McCabe's own words.

In the beginning his brain works very well. He realizes the social futility of his work: '. . . a worker working on a work that does not help to make the world better . . .'

He comes to realize even the dilemma of society and its influence on his own crime.

At the beginning of chapter nineteen he meditates on this: 'It makes you think and once you start thinking you see it's all messed up. And if you try to clear up the mess you get a kick in the pants. They like to keep it muddled up as it is. It's better for them. They get more out of it.'

Now if I understand this correctly, I must assume that 'they' is meant to stand for the rulers of present-day society, in short, to use the Marxist term, the *ruling class*.

Then we must accept Mr McCabe as a rather extremist social critic, in fact that type of social critic which is liable to coin slogans like 'Exploit the Exploiters' or 'Don't produce any surplus value by working. Only Mugs work. The Wide people enjoy the fruits of the Mugs' labour.'

This type of social-parasite-turned-social-critic is bound to develop convictions like this uttered by Mr McCabe in a later paragraph of the same chapter nineteen:

'If a guy allows you to make a sap of him you'd better take your hat and go away. It's better to be welshed on and know it than to welsh on another guy and get away with it': *fascist heroism*: there is honour between gangsters.

And again a few lines later:

'Get your food before the other one gets it: he is also hungry. Hit him on the jaw when he tries to be quicker': *fascist economics*.

This gangster-cum-fascist philosophy shows its plainly hysterical character as it reaches its final stage which can be found in sentences like: 'Never let a bad man down: the good ones will follow you. But there are few good ones left. The penitence is long but the deed was short enough.'

Here one can clearly discover the way of a diseased mind, working from a sound analysis of society into a complete intellectual and moral muddle, a muddle that is a direct product and an exact image of the muddle of society itself.

The muddle of society, reflected in McCabe's brain, is naturally re-reflected in his actions and views. These are reflected in the third power by his book, both in plot and pattern. The *plot* is merely an account of the actual events which were, however, nothing else but McCabe's actions and reactions towards the other 'characters'.

The *pattern* of construction of Mr McCabe's book is the *circulus vitiosus*. Like the degenerating society which he represents McCabe tries to prove one proposition from another that depends on the first for proof.

McCabe gained his acquittal by pointing out the irregularities in Smith's conduct of the investigations. Smith, therefore, was directly responsible for McCabe's acquittal. McCabe's acquittal, however, caused Smith to kill McCabe. And so Smith was hanged because he helped – against his own will – to get McCabe acquitted.

A plain vicious circle of events for which McCabe is responsible and which forms, at the same time, the plot of his book.

The pattern follows the plot: McCabe tells and retells the same story over and over again – not because he aims consciously at a literary pattern but because he is incapable of writing the story in any other way: the pattern of the story, with its constant repetitions which lead always back to the start, reflects the same vicious circle which we find in the plot and which we will later find for the third time in the style of writing which McCabe adopts to transmit plot and pattern of his book to his readers.

In the first nineteen chapters we get the story told in the first form by McCabe. Then in the twentieth chapter we get it all retold by Smith. In the twenty-first chapter we get it for the third time in the special version which McCabe makes up for my benefit. In the twenty-second chapter we get it served up for the fourth time – this time again told by Smith. In the twenty-third chapter you have that conversation between Smith and McCabe which begins like 'the famous solution dinner that should occur at the end of every good detective story'. It begins like that, but it ends in disaster and repetition: you get the story warmed up for the fifth time. Then, in the twenty-fourth chapter you get the counsel for the prosecution innocently telling you the same thing for the sixth time. When the prosecutor has finished McCabe gets up and starts his defence, in the course of which all good things become seven. McCabe is acquitted, spends the night in Highgate Village, comes back the next morning and finds Smith on his doorstep. So you get the conversation between the two which brings the number of repetitions up to eight. And it is not the end yet. Not even McCabe's death ends it. He writes a last will and makes me tell you the story now again for the ninth time.

It is true that every time the story is retold you learn more about it, new clues are discovered, new facts are disclosed, you see the thing from a new angle.

A dialectic method; things are built up only in order to be broken down again: evidence is discovered in one version of the story only to be discovered as worthless in the next one. First the mere facts are described, but no explanation is given. Then you get the explanation, but a few lines later you learn that the explanation was all wrong. And Mr McCabe proceeds to give you some new information which changes everything completely. In the next chapter, however, the same thing starts all over again. The old explanations are recanted and new information is given. This is again recanted in the next chapter and so it goes on and on: uncertainty and instability govern. Nothing is firmly fixed, nothing steadfast, nothing solidly established. Everything is in the process of change, demolition, destruction, decay: an exact picture of the man and his age.

....

'MODEL VILLAGE'

See the cows placed just so on the green hill.
Cows say *Moo*. The sheep look like little clouds,
don't they? Sheep say *Baa*. Grass is green
and the pillar-box is red. Wouldn't it be strange
if grass were red? This is the graveyard
where the villagers bury their dead. Miss Maiden
lives opposite in her cottage. She has a cat.
The cat says *Miaow*. What does Miss Maiden say?

I poisoned her, but no one knows. Mother, I said,
drink your tea. Arsenic. Four sugars. He waited
years for me, but she had more patience. One day,
he didn't come back. I looked in the mirror,
saw her grey hair, her lips of reproach. I found
the idea in a paperback. I loved him, you see,
who never so much as laid a finger. Perhaps now
you've learnt your lesson, she said, pouring
another cup. Yes, Mother, yes. Drink it all up.

Quack, say the ducks on the village pond. Did you
see the frog? Frogs say *Croak*. The village-folk shop
at the butcher's, the baker's, the candlestick maker's.
The Grocer has a parrot. Parrots say *Pretty Polly*
and *Who's a pretty boy then*? The Vicar is nervous
of parrots, isn't he? Miss Maiden is nervous
of Vicar and the Farmer is nervous of everything.
The library clock says *Tick-tock*. What does the Librarian say?

Ssssh. I've seen them come and go over the years,
my ears tuned for every whisper. This place
is a refuge, the volumes breathing calmly
on their still shelves. I glide between them
like a doctor on his rounds, know their cases. Tomes
do no harm, here I'm safe. Outside is chaos,
lives with no sense of plot. Behind each front door
lurks truth, danger. I peddle fiction. Believe
you me, the books in everyone's head are stranger . . .

....

THE THIRTY-FIRST
OF FEBRUARY

Now it is all over. The funeral is over, the inquest is over, the verdict has been given. Two people who had very little in common have ceased to live together. One has fallen down a flight of stairs and broken her neck; the other continues an existence in which he regards his own ridiculous occupation with extraordinary gravity. Is there anything more to be said?

Yes, there is a great deal more to be said. Why should Valerie and I have lived together for years? What possible meaning can one attach to our life together, how can one understand it? And if such a ridiculous end to a shared life is possible, doesn't this illuminate the absolute absurdity of existence itself? Now that Valerie is dead, I see quite certainly that I didn't love her. I am absolutely unable to understand why I married her. I can't see why I didn't push her down the stairs long ago. Wyvern, at the office, has a phrase which he uses every now and again when things are going wrong: 'Why don't we all get in one great bed and — one another?'

Well, why don't we?

But of course that kind of thing won't do – that pure abandonment to the idea that life is nonsense. There must be somewhere an explanation of human activity which isn't purely biological, which interprets life in terms of some kind of meaning.

It's to try to get some idea of what it all means that I'm putting down this individual case history of my life with Val.

I met Val first at a party given by Elaine Fletchley. At least it was given by *Woman Beautiful*, the high-class fashion magazine she works for, and Elaine was a hostess. They asked somebody from all the bright advertising agencies, and I went from Vincent's. It was a very dull party. I had a bit of chat with other advertising figures and was just working my way over to say goodbye to Elaine when I bumped into a girl and upset her drink. 'Oh dear,' she said. 'Oh dear, my poor frock.' She stared at me with wide-apart eyes of a curious hazel colour. Then she said: 'But I want another drinky.' There was just the faintest suggestion of a lisp in the way she rolled her r's. So I got her a drink and we talked, and it turned out that she worked for *Woman Beautiful*, too, as an assistant fashion editress. I told her that I was a copywriter and she said: 'Oh, but you must be awfully clever.' She was so short that she had to look up at me, and she did so with a kind of starry gaze. I can remember wondering what I was doing talking to her. She was just the kind of girl, I can remember thinking, for whom I had no use at all. How is it possible, then, to account for my next action? I leaned over (I can see myself doing it quite clearly) and said: 'Let's get out of this din and go somewhere else?' And what did she say? She giggled and answered with quite a definite lisp: 'I say, you are a quick worker.' We left the party, had some drinks – she soaked up drink like a sponge – and she stayed at the flat I lived in then, in Kensington. When she left in the morning we arranged to meet that evening. We did. And the next and the next. In six months we were married.

So there it is, or there's the beginning of it. During the whole of that six months if I'd ever asked myself whether I liked Val, the answer would have been an unhesitating 'No.' I dislike girls who lisp, girls who are kittenish, girls who drink too much. Valerie did all of those things. Why did I marry her, then? Partly I'd got into the habit of seeing her – but what made me start the habit? Partly no doubt I was the victim of that feeling war and bombing gave you, that no relationship you formed mattered much or was likely to be permanent – and how damned mistaken that feeling was. Partly she was good in bed, and although I was over thirty when I met her I hadn't much experience of that sort of thing. Although Val was nearly ten years younger than I was, I gathered she'd had plenty. But although I enjoyed our times in bed, I wasn't all that interested. That certainly won't do for a main motive.

And why did Val marry me? If I can't explain my own motives, I certainly can't understand hers. I think she found me attractive – although few women have done so. I believe she liked men older than herself. And – although I may be quite wrong – I believe she regarded me as a very different person from the man I am. Subconsciously I assumed that we should stop drinking and going to parties after we got married. But Val assumed that we should go on drinking, and go to more parties than ever.

So we started off wrong. And then there was trouble about this house. Val was essentially what I think of as an Earl's Court girl – nice gay parties with people in the rag trade as she called it, a few commercial artists, some bad actors. Well, you can get all that in our bit of Pimlico if you want it, but in rather too sordid a way for Val. She liked a bit of glamour spread over it – not too much, just a thin layer. She was horrified when she first saw the house and even more so when I told her I liked it. 'But how *can* you like it? It's so vulgar. That woman Flossie Williams – she's just a tart.' And what are your friends, do you think? I asked her. And what are you? Didn't you sleep with me the first time you met me? The only difference was that you got marriage instead of a spot cash settlement. At that she burst into tears, and it's true I was unfair, because Val was a one-man woman. I say I think she found me attractive, but I'm doing myself an injustice. The fact is that she never looked at anybody else at all. She told Elaine Fletchley so, and Elaine told me. And how can one explain that? That's as nonsensical as the rest of it.

So Val burst into tears. She was always bursting into tears; it was one of the most irritating things about her. Then she asked me again why I liked living here, but I couldn't answer that, because I didn't know. There was just something about the streets and the people and the atmosphere, that's all.

But if Valerie couldn't get her own way about the house, at

least she made it look the way she wanted. It's all round me now, as it's been round me for years – the glaring colours, the fumed oak paradise in the bedroom. 'It's so bright and gay and new,' she'd say – but with the lisp, of course. 'I hate old stuff. I'd like life to start again every morning. New people, new job, new places, new everything. Wouldn't you like that?' And when I said truthfully that I'd like nothing less, she'd be upset. And she not only had her way about the look of the place; she got Elaine to live in it as well. First she said the house was too big for just the two of us. Maybe there'll be three one day, I said, but she didn't want children. Then she wanted Elaine to come and live here with us. I didn't want it; I wanted to be alone. But she had it her way. We turned the place into two self-contained flats and we had the ground floor and the Fletchleys had the first. We shared the cellar, where we both kept a small stock of drink. Elaine is a neat, tarty little piece, slick and smart and hard. What did she see in Fletchley to marry him? That's another problem, but I can't go into it now.

Val had kept her job on *Woman Beautiful*, so when Elaine came the girls could talk office gossip all evening long. Fletchley never seemed to mind, just as he never seemed to mind Elaine going out with other men. 'She always comes back,' he used to say to me. 'She always comes back to old Fletch.' But at that time, when they first came here, Elaine didn't go out much. She would talk office gossip with Val in the evening until I was nearly crazy. Occasionally I thought she was intending to make a pass at me, but Fletchley never seemed to notice, so perhaps I was wrong. I got so crazy with their talk that I suggested in desperation to Val that we should go out and drink. Six months ago she'd have leapt at the suggestion, but now she didn't much want to do anything but drink a glass or two of black-market whisky by her own comfortable electric fireside while she chattered to Elaine. And when we did go out it wasn't any good, because I didn't really care for drinking and I could hardly even be polite to Val. 'You're never nice to me, Andy, the way you used to be,' she'd say tearfully, and look at me with her head slightly on one side. Was it true? Had I ever been nice to her? I can't believe that I ever was. She'd invented my niceness in the past to contrast with my horridness in the present. We can't recreate the past, but we can always soothe sorrow and vanity by inventing it.

So drinking was no good, and after a couple of years there was another thing that was no good, too. I couldn't work up the least flicker of interest in Val while I was with her. When I was away from her – in the office writing copy, interviewing a client, sitting round a conference table – then very often I would positively shiver with desire for her. The most powerful and violent sexual images came to my mind, and they were not merely vague images – they had a positive association with Val. As soon as I saw her, though – as soon, even, as I knew I should see her within half an hour – they vanished altogether. It would all have been comic if it had not been deeply humiliating.

All this sounds like a good case for divorce, or at any rate separation. But strangely enough, Val never wanted a separation – throughout the whole of our life together she was absolutely devoted to me. And why did I stay with Val? I find the question absolutely unanswerable. It would have been difficult, I suppose, to arrange a separation. She would have wanted to go on living with Elaine. I should have had to get out of Joseph Street, and I didn't want to get out. Then again I should have been lonely. She had become a habit, and we live by our habits. But there was something outside all that, something that held me to her. It was, it seems to me, precisely *because* I disliked her, because she filled our home with hideous furniture and empty chatter, that I wanted to live with her. The things that I most detested were the things I most desired! Shall I put down the image that came to me most often when I saw Val, tearstained and reproachful, or limply acquiescent in my unkindness? It was of my mother, and the ghastly house we lived in so many years ago – and of holding my mother's hand as she lay, a pitiful and repulsive skeleton, upon her deathbed.

But now I come to the real reason for writing in this book – the effect Val's death has had on me. We lived together for several detestable years. For the whole of that time I had seen with irritation the grease on her face at night, and her intolerable cheerfulness in the morning. I'd listened all that time to her inanities about clothes and film stars. Unconsciously, I must dozens of times have wished her dead. But now that she *is* dead, and the bathroom is free when I want to use it and I no longer find hairpins in the bed, I am oppressed by an extraordinary sense of loss. Not loss of Val exactly – that seems not to enter into it. Rather, part of myself seems to have disappeared. I feel like one of those insects that goes on living even after being cut in half.

On Monday, February 4th, we went to work as usual. Val sang 'Berkeley Square', from her repertory of out-of-date songs, in her bath. I had a worrying day at the office.

JAMES FENTON

'A STAFFORDSHIRE MURDERER'

Every fear is a desire. Every desire is fear.
The cigarettes are burning under the trees
Where the Staffordshire murderers wait for their accomplices
And victims. Every victim is an accomplice.

It takes a lifetime to stroll to the car park
Stopping at the footbridge for reassurance,
Looking down at the stream, observing
(With one eye) the mallard's diagonal progress backwards.

You could cut and run, now. It is not too late.
But your fear is like a long-case clock
In the last whirring second before the hour,
The hammer drawn back, the heart ready to chime.

Fear turns the ignition. The van is unlocked.
You may learn now what you ought to know:
That every journey begins with a death,
That the suicide travels alone, that the murderer needs company.

And the Staffordshire murderers, nervous though they are,
Are masters of the conciliatory smile.
A cigarette? A tablet in a tin?
Would you care for a boiled sweet from the famous poisoner

Of Rugeley? These are his own brand.
He has never had any complaints.
He speaks of his victims as a sexual braggart
With a tradesman's emphasis on the word 'satisfaction'.

You are flattered as never before. He appreciates
So much, the little things – your willingness for instance
To bequeath your body at once to his experiments.
He sees the point of you as no one else does.

....

MALICE AFORETHOUGHT

Before he killed her Dr Bickleigh did give Julia a last chance.

Now that it had come to the point, he intensely disliked the idea of killing her. He had, in fact, thoroughly hated the whole thing. It had been almost as much of a strain to him as to Julia. He was not callous, and the daily sight of so much suffering inflicted by himself had got completely on his nerves: it was awful that Julia should have to suffer so. He certainly did not love her; he had not much fondness for her; as an individual he did not like her at all: but he could hardly bear to go on torturing her, as a mere human being, to this extent. It was necessary to drive himself to the administration of the headache-producing medium. He would almost weep as he scattered it into her food.

Three weeks after the Crewstantons' visit he decided that he could stand it no longer. His growing nerviness had made him almost quarrel with Madeleine the day before – well, quite quarrel with her. And over Denny Bourne, of all absurd causes. Five days after the beginning of the summer term, his last term, Denny had been sent down for three weeks for depriving an unpopular don of his trousers and painting his hinder parts scarlet. If the don had not been so unpopular Denny would have been sent down for good, but the rest of the senior common-room, who also did not love their colleague, had felt that a certain justification, and more, was to be found in the existence of the fellow at all. Still, the man was a don, and one cannot have dons going about forcibly disguised as mandrills; so Denny had been sent down for three weeks.

To Dr Bickleigh's disgust Madeleine seemed delighted with this exploit: that the idea of a trouserless don with a scarlet posterior is about as far removed from the spiritual as one can well get, Dr Bickleigh pointed out; but Madeleine, though agreeing, and looking for a moment as a nun might on being confronted with such a spectacle, continued to give the impression that she thought Denny really had done something rather clever.

That Denny thought so himself was obvious. Dr Bickleigh had been forced to be quite rude to him over The Hall tea-table. Then he and Madeleine had nearly quarrelled. Well, quite quarrelled. He had been unable to control himself, and said things to her in front of Denny. And Denny, flushed with impertinent rage, had had the impudence to tell him that if he didn't clear out that minute he'd take him to the stableyard and do the same to him, then and there, with whatever substitute for red paint presented itself. And Madeleine had sat there with her big eyes and not interfered. Dr Bickleigh had cleared out.

That was the last straw. An end had got to be made.

He made it the next day.

On purpose he lay in wait for Julia's arrival in the surgery, having made a pretence of leaving the house and returning secretly on foot. She came surreptitiously, and jumped violently when he surprised her. The movement added to the aching of her head, and she swayed for a moment.

Dr Bickleigh put his arm round her waist. He was wearing his hat and gloves. 'Hush,' he warned. 'Don't want Florence to hear. You were after the morphia, Julia.'

Julia nodded defiantly, holding her head. 'It's very bad today,' she muttered. 'I must have an injection, please, Edmund.'

'Well, it's a long time since I gave you one,' he said in a low voice. 'Perhaps you might have one.'

He filled the syringe, keeping his body between her and his hands, so that she could not see how much he was putting in.

Now that the moment had come he felt quite calm. His course lay like a map in his mind, every action noted down. He was surprised at the coolness with which he made his preparations; he had expected to be flustered and anxious.

Pretending to be busy with something else for a second, he gave her the syringe to hold so as to secure her fingerprints on it, just in case.

Julia pushed up her sleeve and held her arm out to him.

'Just half a minute,' he said. 'Before this takes effect, I want to ask you something, Julia. Will you reconsider your decision about divorcing me? Madeleine and I still love each other, and we want to marry.'

'No, Edmund,' she replied decisively. 'I will not.'

'It's been going on for nearly a year now,' he pointed out patiently. 'I'm not a child. I know my own mind. I ask you, Julia, not as a wife, but as a friend. I'm very much in earnest.'

'Edmund, nothing on earth would persuade me to divorce you for that girl. She's no good. No good at all.'

'That's absolutely final?'

'Absolutely.'

Julia had had her chance.

Dr Bickleigh took the syringe from her. With perfectly steady hands he injected into her veins fifteen grains of morphia. His brain seemed to have gone curiously blank. He felt no emotion at all, no pity, remorse, fear, nor even responsibility. It was as if the conduct of affairs had somehow been taken out of his control and he was following a course from which he had neither physical nor moral powers of deviation. The only thought in his mind was: In twenty minutes Julia will be dead. *Julia . . .*

'Thank you, Edmund,' Julia said gratefully, as he automatically dropped the syringe back in the drawer.

'Go straight upstairs and lie down,' Dr Bickleigh said tonelessly, not looking at her.

'Very well. Oh, yes, there's something I wanted to ask you. Will you—'

'Not now. Some other time.' He could not bear to be with her a moment longer. He must get away from her. It was terrible. He had really done it. In twenty minutes Julia would be dead.

Dead . . . *Julia!* In spite of its familiarity to his imagination, the thing in practice was inconceivable. And yet he had done it: he had killed her.

He escaped from her in something like panic. The power of thought had returned, terrifyingly.

But he did not regret it. Even now he could have saved her, but there was not the slightest impulse to do so. Nor did he lose his head. He got out of the house just as secretly as he had got in; for all that anyone but Julia could know, he had been out on his rounds for the last half-hour. The car even had been left in a road some distance away, carefully chosen in advance; a handy spot, quite a long way round by road, but to be gained in three or four minutes by crossing a couple of fields at the bottom of the garden; and the whole way was sheltered by shrubs and hedges from the windows of the house if one crept in a few places. He had been over the route several times.

He gained the car without the slightest mishap.

In twenty minutes – no, in seventeen minutes now, Julia would be dead. Incredible!

Freedom . . .

He simply couldn't realize it.

For some reason the engine was sticky and wouldn't start. Not that it mattered now, but it was annoying. The self-starter gave out too, as it usually did on such occasions, and he had to get out and swing her. The engine started at last, and he got back into the car. As he did so, he saw someone topping a crest in the road just ahead. It was Ivy. Excellent. Ivy should help to prove his alibi for him. He was in admirable spirits once more as he waited for her. Really, when one came to consider it, he *had* done something rather notable, put it how you liked.

'Hullo, Teddy,' gloomed Ivy. They had met several times since the incident in the wood. It had never been referred to between them.

'Hullo, Ivy. This wretched car. Really, I shall have to think about getting a new one. Suddenly stopped, ten minutes ago. Did you see me swinging her?'

'Yes. I say, Teddy . . .'

'Yes? Oh, by the way, lucky I met you. My watch has

stopped. Most awkward. Haven't got the time on you, Ivy, have you?'

'Yes, I have.' She pulled down the sleeve of her glove and looked at her wrist-watch. 'Just twenty to three.'

'Twenty to three, eh? Thanks. Sure that's right?'

'It was right this morning. Teddy . . .'

'Yes?'

'You know I'm engaged now?'

'To Chatford? Yes, somebody told me months ago. Quarnian, I think. Congratulations. Capital fellow, Chatford.'

'I don't seem to have seen you for years,' Ivy mourned. 'Are you glad, Teddy?'

'What, that you haven't seen me? Of course I'm not. I've missed you, Ivy.'

'No, that I'm engaged, I mean.'

'Oh! Yes, very glad. You'll be happy, my dear. I'm sure you will. And Chatford's a coming man. Well, can I give you a lift anywhere?'

'No, thanks. I'm taking Juno for a walk. Where is she? Juno! Juno!'

'Then I must be getting along. *Au revoir*, Ivy.'

'*Au revoir*, Teddy.' Her eyes tried to detain him, as usual.

Ivy was the kind whose love thrives on blows.

Most useful, thought Dr Bickleigh with satisfaction as he drove on. But how normal. Ivy just the same as ever, everything just the same as ever. He did not believe he had killed Julia at all. Julia dead. No, it was unbelievable. Julia could never be dead. And yet in twelve minutes now Julia would be dead.

He couldn't believe it.

As nearly as he could compute, Julia died while he was sounding old Mr Tracey's chest just four miles away.

During the afternoon his repugnance from returning home grew and grew. There was a horrible time ahead of him, beginning from the moment he set foot in the house again. Horrible. But it had got to be gone through. Yet minute after minute he kept putting off the beginning of it. No need to hurry things.

As he drove from patient to patient (he had purposely left most of his visits for the afternoon, in order to have plenty to do) his thoughts roved endlessly round Julia – his marriage with Julia, life with Julia, Julia's way of treating him like a small dog, Julia's masterfulness, peremptoriness, rudeness, Julia's quite unconscious habit of humiliating him before other people. He had been afraid of Julia. That he had always acknowledged to himself. Now he saw, for the first time quite clearly, that he had killed Julia simply because of this fear of her. He had been afraid to run away from her.

That was very curious, and interesting. Dr Bickleigh, not as a rule given to introspection more than any other person of some imagination, found himself turning over pages of his mind never before perused. Yes, that was quite true. He might have solved his problem so much more simply. He had asked Madeleine, and she had said she would go with him. It was only by way of a test, and he had never intended for a moment to do it, but Madeleine did not know that; she would have gone with him. And they could have lived on her money till he could establish himself somewhere else; their love was above petty considerations of convention like that; no economic difficulties had held him back. Why had he not gone, then? Simply because he could not have found the courage to run away from Julia. He had plucked up enough of it to ask for a divorce by consent; but when that had been refused he had accepted her ruling as always. No divorce: so another way had had to be found.

Dr Bickleigh smiled to himself. Was this the first time that murder was directly traceable to an inferiority complex? He did not think so.

But really, what a little worm he had been then; there was no getting away from it. And how far from a little worm he was now. Put it any way you like, a successful murder (yes, it was murder: no need to shirk the word), brilliantly planned and flawlessly carried out, lifted one out of the category of worms for good and all.

Would Florence have found Julia yet?. . .

He would go to The Hall for tea. Why not? It was a Wednesday, and he always went to tea at The Hall on Wednesdays. The great thing was to carry on just as usual. And they could always get him on the telephone there. It would not look to suspicious eyes as if he had been trying to keep out of touch.

Not, of course, that there would be any suspicious eyes, but still . . .

That infernal Denny, lounging in the garden as if the place belonged to him. He'd laugh the other side of his face if he did know who it belonged to now – well, practically. Dr Bickleigh felt quite angry for a moment. Really, it was too bad of Madeleine, on a Wednesday. And infernally awkward, after the *contretemps* of yesterday.

Then his anger disappeared. Things fell into their right proportions. Denny was now utterly insignificant: did not count at all. Only one person counted, and that was himself. He and Madeleine . . .

What *was* Madeleine worth? He had never liked to ask; nor really bothered; considerations of that sort were beside the main issue. But nevertheless it was a marvellous feeling, that one was going to be actually rich – all the little economies and scrapings finished with for ever; able to afford any whim that took the fancy of the moment; soft living and luxury, owning this magnificent place. He and Madeleine . . .

Where was Madeleine?

Dr Bickleigh got out of his car and walked towards the front door. A shout from the lawn arrested him. Denny had got up and was strolling towards him. Damn the fellow! Oh, well, he probably wanted to apologize for yesterday. Dr Bickleigh would accept that. But a hint must be dropped pretty soon, and more than a hint, if you like. Dr Bickleigh felt quite equal to telling him in so many words. It was amusing to think that only last summer he had been quite ill-at-ease in the presence of Denny – forced, awkward, bad form, out of it. Lord, what a little worm . . .

'Come and sit on the lawn,' said Denny, rather abruptly.

'I'm sorry,' Dr Bickleigh returned coldly. 'I have come to see Miss Cranmere about—'

'Well, she's out. Come and sit on the lawn. I want to say something to you.'

What a parade the boy's making, thought Dr Bickleigh as he walked with Denny to the chairs under the cedar. Clumsiness of youth, no doubt. Why can't people realize that an apology is even more embarrassing to receive than to offer, and cut it short? A form of egotism.

Funny there had been no telephone message. Florence couldn't have found her yet, obviously.

But would Florence try The Hall? Probably. If he knew anything of Wyvern's Cross, his visits here would be common talk in the kitchen. Well, let them talk.

Poor Julia. It was a relief to think she was out of all that pain at last.

They sat down in two deck-chairs.

Denny stared straight in front of him. 'Look here, Bickleigh . . .'

'Yes?'

'About Madeleine.'

All thought of Julia disappeared from Dr Bickleigh's mind. 'Well?'

'She's – a very unusual girl, you know. Extraordinarily sensitive, and all that.'

'Yes?'

'I've seen a good deal of her lately.'

'Have you?'

'Yes.'

The conversation seemed to be languishing.

Denny, for some reason, was remarkably embarrassed – more so than Dr Bickleigh would ever have expected from such a normally self-possessed young man. And it was an odd way of beginning an apology.

Denny suddenly turned a somewhat flushed face towards his companion. 'She doesn't really care for you, Bickleigh, you know,' he mumbled.

'What the devil are you talking about?'

'She told me about – you,' said Denny, looking supremely uncomfortable; but his eyes did not shift from the other's face.

'She did, did she?' Dr Bickleigh had recovered his equilibrium. This young cub must have been pumping Madeleine, annoying her. Imagined himself in love with her, no doubt, and had the impudence to be jealous.

'Yes. She – she *doesn't* care for you, you know.'

'Indeed?' Dr Bickleigh was more amused than anything now. This really was rather humorous, in the circumstances. 'Who does she care for, then?'

'Me,' returned Denny simply, and blushed a deeper tint.

It was all Dr Bickleigh could do not to laugh in his face. 'Really, Denny?'

'Damn it, you needn't smile. I mean what I say. I love Madeleine, and I'm dam' well going to marry her. So now you've got it.'

'Well, well,' said Dr Bickleigh. Poor Denny; it really was rather touching. 'And what has Madeleine got to say about all this?' he asked tolerantly.

'She hasn't tried to hide from me that she cares too, if that's what you mean,' Denny replied in a gruff voice. 'She's too straight. She'd have let me kiss her when I went up this term, and you can imagine what that means with a girl like her.'

'But you didn't, eh?'

'No, I didn't. Well, I'm glad we've got that straight. Of course, she was carried away by your being so much older,' Denny grumbled. 'Flattered her inexperience, or something. You sort of swept her off her feet. When she wasn't with you she knew she wasn't in love with you, but when she was you seem to have exercised some extraordinary kind of fascination over her. That's what happened.'

'I see,' said Dr Bickleigh, with a small smile. He might have recognized the voice of Madeleine speaking; but he didn't.

There was a little silence.

'Well, I must say,' observed Denny, if rather grudgingly, 'that you take it dam' well.'

'Take what?'

'Why, our engagement.'

'Your – what?'

'Our engagement. I told you, I'm going to marry her. We got engaged this morning.'

'Nonsense!' Dr Bickleigh spoke perhaps rather sharply, but

otherwise betrayed nothing of the turmoil that had suddenly invaded him.

'Fact. I tried to break it as easily as I could. Afraid it's a bit rotten for you.' Denny was no longer embarrassed; he was the proudly possessive male, only held back by good form from being flauntingly possessive. 'Here – Madeleine asked me to give you this after I'd told you.'

Dr Bickleigh took the note and broke open the envelope. He had to read the contents through half a dozen times before their meaning was clear to him.

> EDMUND DEAR,—I have asked Denny to tell you our news. I
> know you will be terribly upset, but it is the best way out for
> both of us. You know things could not go on, could they?
> For the last time, Edmund, my love from
>
> MADELEINE.

He crammed the note into his pocket at last and began to walk rapidly towards the house. 'It's no good,' Denny said, 'if you want to see Madeleine, she's out.'

That, thought Dr Bickleigh, is a lie, a damned lie, a filthy lie, another filthy lie. He walked on.

Denny, who had started after him, stood for a moment in indecision, then shrugged his shoulders and dropped back into his chair. Perhaps better let them have it out and get it over.

Dr Bickleigh did not trouble to ring the bell. Madeleine would be upstairs, in her bedroom, waiting, hiding. He got there just as she was locking the door, and forced it open.

'Edmund,' she said, looking at him with big, sorrowful eyes, 'you shouldn't have tried to see me.'

'Look here, Madeleine – this is all nonsense, of course?' Dr Bickleigh appeared perfectly normal. His face was rather white, and there was a curious spot of red on each of his cheekbones, but he articulated quite distinctly; almost over-distinctly.

Madeleine, who had looked a little frightened as well as sorrowful, seemed to be reassured. 'No, Edmund, it isn't non-sense. I've thought it all out. We couldn't go on. This is the easiest way.'

'You don't love Denny?'

Madeleine looked at him reproachfully. 'Edmund, need you have asked me that?' She sat down on the edge of the bed.

Dr Bickleigh went up to her and took her by the shoulders. 'I'll tell you what you're going to do, Madeleine.'

'Edmund, you're hurting me.'

His fingers sunk deeper into her flesh. The spots of colour on his cheekbones burned a little brighter. 'You're going downstairs this minute to break off this preposterous engagement. Tomorrow I'm going to London, to buy a special licence. You'll come with me. We'll be married in three days from now.'

'But, Edmund – Julia! Oh, please let me go. You're hurting me terribly.'

'Julia,' said Dr Bickleigh, through his teeth, 'is dead.'

Madeleine looked up into the white face glaring down at hers and began to shriek. 'Denny! Denny! Help – help! Denny – he'll . . .' She tore herself free and ran, shrieking, to the window.

But it was not Denny who got into the room first. It was the friendly parlourmaid. She looked from one to the other in anxious bewilderment.

'Your mistress is hysterical,' said Dr Bickleigh coldly. 'Get me some cold water, please.'

'Yes, sir, but – you're wanted on the telephone, sir. Your housemaid. I – I'm afraid there's bad news, sir.'

With Madeleine's hysterical screams ringing through his head, Dr Bickleigh went downstairs to the telephone.

PART FIVE

THE DANGEROUS
EDGE OF THINGS

....

Bloody murder, cops and killers – these are the very stuff of crime fiction, yet they are also the easiest to 'do'. Even mediocre writers can hold our attention if the subject matter is sufficiently gory or dramatic; only the best can do so without such help. A man comes to a boarding house, two men enter a diner, a woman follows a man home, a man goes for a walk in the fog or takes his child to the park, two strangers share a drink on a train. Nothing much happens, but the banality of the actual events merely heightens the oppressive sense that anything *could* – anything at all, at any moment. This is crime writing at its finest: not a series of 'big scenes' cobbled together with stretches of lacklustre prose or facetious dialogue but a sustained imaginative creation whose smallest details are significant and telling.

'If you don't want to read what is bad, and want to read something that will hold your interest and is marvellous in its own way, you should read Marie Belloc Lowndes.' Thus Gertrude Stein, in the rather stilted late-Hemingway diction ascribed to her in *A Moveable Feast*. He took her advice, and comments: 'They were splendid after-work books, the people credible and the action and the terror never false . . . I never found anything as good for that empty time of day or night until the first fine Simenon books came out.' This is high praise indeed, but there is no question that Marie Lowndes – she was Hilaire Belloc's sister – deserves it. Her depiction of the symbiotic relationship between Mrs Bunting and her sinister lodger is a masterpiece of psychological and social insight, conveyed in prose which keeps the tension screwed tight without ever drawing attention to itself.

Ernest Hemingway typically found inspiration among soldiers or hunters rather than criminals or the police, but 'The Killers' is one of his very finest accomplishments. The vaudeville team hit men are an inspired creation, grotesque yet perfectly credible, while the dialogue has the disjunctive quality we now associate with Harold Pinter (whose play *The Dumb Waiter* is an intriguing variation on the same theme). Above all, Hemingway scores a stunning technical triumph in writing a gripping crime story whose most significant event is the one that doesn't happen.

It comes as something of a shock to realize that Dashiell Hammett did not die until 1961, for his reputation depends almost entirely on the four novels he wrote between 1929 and 1931. The last of these was *The Glass Key*, which Julian Symons considers 'the peak of the crime writer's art in the twentieth century'. It is certainly the most concentrated, tightly plotted and subtle of Hammett's books, and one which demands – and rewards – careful and attentive reading, but it also displays growing stylistic mannerisms (how many times does 'Ned Beaumont' occur in the first two pages?) which in retrospect look like symptoms of Hammett's impending block.

The novels that make up Paul Auster's *New York Trilogy* (see the extract on p.210) are to the rules of the crime genre what an Escher print is to the laws of perspective, but before embarking on this project Auster tested his draughtsmanship by writing a straight crime novel under the pseudonym Paul Benjamin. The result is a taut, sassy homage to the private-eye tradition written in the limpid and evocative prose for which Auster is famous.

The difference between British and American crime writing in the handling of speech says a lot about both schools. The British regard dialogue essentially as a medium for conveying information. Occasionally a minor or comic character will be allowed some generalized 'regional' turn of phrase, but everyone of any consequence talks like the cast of an afternoon radio play. By contrast, American crime writers listen to the way the kind of people they are writing about actually speak and then try – with a greater or lesser degree of stylization – to transcribe it. No one is a greater virtuoso in this respect than George V. Higgins. The passage extracted here is an absolutely basic bread-and-butter scene – man goes into shop to ask directions – but Higgins has the gift of transforming a banal encounter into a memorable scene which also exemplifies the central theme of the book.

With its wartime detail and backwoods setting, *The Lady in the Lake* is something of a misfit among Chandler's novels, but scenes such as this one show him at his best: quirky, observant, the tone fluctuating between humour and hysteria without ever settling down or going over the top. And while our attention is delightedly distracted, Chandler smuggles the solution to the whole mystery past our noses with a panache worthy of Agatha Christie.

Marlowe clones are two a dime, but to invent a 1950s Los Angeles private-eye series which isn't always looking over its shoulder is a more difficult exercise. If Walter Mosley succeeds, it is not simply because his LA is a city which Chandler barely knew but because he puts his knowledge of life in the black community to good *fictional* – as opposed to merely tokenistic – use. The scene included here is merely an incidental episode from a long and complex novel, but every line crackles with an authentic tension.

The name C. S. Forester is now synonymous with the Hornblower series, but on the evidence of his first two novels he could well have become a major crime writer if circumstances had been more propitious. As it was, authors were required to submit to voluntary emasculation in order to maintain the profitable and reassuring sterility of the Golden Age product, so Forester not unnaturally preferred to run away to sea. The loss was theirs, and is ours. *Plain Murder* – the adjective is used as in 'a good plain cook' – is a socially and psychologically penetrating study of an ordinary man who discovers that he has a talent for murder, as it might be for darts or seduction.

Ernest Raymond's *We, the Accused* suffers to some extent from the elephantiasis which is such a feature of some would-be 'literary' crime writing today. The difference is that Raymond is much better equipped technically to sustain the feat, as this exhumation scene proves with a superbly judged combination of realistic detail and epic resonance.

The lingering effects of the pressures which silenced or marginalized so many promising British crime writers of the 30s and 40s can be seen even today in the tardy and defensive transformation of Ruth Rendell into 'Ruth Rendell writing as Barbara Vine'. While the pseudonym also served to market Rendell's staggering output, there is no reason to doubt her statement that caution was also involved. However that may be, the resounding success of *A Dark-Adapted Eye* proved that it was at last safe for British crime writers to come out of the closet.

Dorothy B. Hughes might justifiably be tagged the Barbara Vine of an earlier generation. The mixture of precise observation and a pitiless and disturbed subjectivity make this one of the most gripping opening scenes in American crime fiction. But that accolade must surely go to Patricia Highsmith for the first chapters of *Strangers on a Train*, a dumbshow which perfectly prefigures the themes and tensions of the entire book. It is interesting to speculate that the scenario would be impossible today, when Guy and Bruno would travel by plane or car. Even a darkened hotel, as in Shizuko Natsuki's version *The Third Lady*, is a poor second to the impersonal privacy of Bruno's stateroom in a train wending its way across a flat, featureless, darkened landscape. As David Hare observes: 'In Patricia Highsmith's books there is no obvious mystery except the mystery of why we are alive. She works against the expectations of the genre to make violent actions seem neither colourful nor dramatic but commonplace, fitting all too easily into ordinary lives.'

This is also an excellent description of the work of William Irish, a.k.a. Cornell Woolrich. Even more than Poe, to whom he has been compared, Irish is the paranoid's paranoid, a writer who

clearly terrified himself as much as he did his readers. In the scene excerpted here, a woman sets out to break a witness whose perjury is sending her lover to his death. There is no violence, no memorable dialog, and hardly any action, yet the result is insidiously gripping and completely unforgettable—crime writing at its finest indeed.

....

THE LODGER

Opening the door which separated the sitting-room from the bedroom behind, and – shutting out the aggravating vision of Bunting sitting comfortably by the now brightly burning fire, with the *Evening Standard* spread out before him – she sat down in the cold darkness and pressed her hands against her temples.

Never, never had she felt so hopeless, so – so broken as now. Where was the good of having been an upright, conscientious, self-respecting woman all her life long, if it only led to this utter, degrading poverty and wretchedness? She and Bunting were just past the age which gentlefolk think proper in a married couple seeking to enter service together, unless, that is, the wife happens to be a professed cook. A cook and a butler can always get a nice situation. But Mrs Bunting was no cook. She could do all right the simple things any lodger she might get would require, but that was all.

Lodgers? How foolish she had been to think of taking lodgers! For it had been her doing. Bunting had been like butter in her hands.

Yet they had begun well, with a lodging-house in a seaside place. There they had prospered, not as they had hoped to do, but still pretty well; and then had come an epidemic of scarlet fever, and that had meant ruin for them, and for dozens, nay, hundreds, of other luckless people. Then had followed a business experiment which had proved even more disastrous, and which had left them in debt – in debt to an extent they could never hope to repay, to a good-natured former employer.

After that, instead of going back to service, as they might have done, perhaps, either together or separately, they had made up their minds to make one last effort, and they had taken over, with the trifle of money that remained to them, the lease of this house in the Marylebone Road.

In former days, when they had each been leading the sheltered, impersonal, and, above all, financially easy existence which is the compensation life offers to those men and women who deliberately take upon themselves the yoke of domestic service, they had both lived in houses overlooking Regent's Park. It had seemed a wise plan to settle in the same neighbourhood, the more so that Bunting, who had a good appearance, had retained the kind of connection which enables a man to get a job now and again as waiter at private parties.

But life moves quickly, jaggedly, for people like the Buntings. Two of his former masters had moved to another part of London, and a caterer in Baker Street whom he had known went bankrupt.

And now? Well, just now Bunting could not have taken a job had one been offered him, for he had pawned his dress-clothes. He had not asked his wife's permission to do this, as so good a husband ought to have done. He had just gone out and done it. And she had not had the heart to say anything; nay, it was with part of the money that he had handed her silently the evening he did it that she had bought that last packet of tobacco.

And then, as Mrs Bunting sat there thinking these painful thoughts, there suddenly came to the front door the sound of a loud, tremulous, uncertain double knock.

Mrs Bunting jumped nervously to her feet. She stood for a moment listening in the darkness, a darkness made the blacker by the line of light under the door behind which sat Bunting reading his paper.

And then it came again, that loud, tremulous, uncertain double knock; not a knock, so the listener told herself, that boded any good. Would-be lodgers gave sharp, quick, bold, confident raps. No; this must be some kind of beggar. The queerest people came at all hours, and asked – whining or threatening – for money.

Mrs Bunting had had some sinister experiences with men and women – especially women – drawn from that nameless, mysterious class made up of the human flotsam and jetsam which drifts about every great city. But since she had taken to leaving the gas in the passage unlit at night she had been very little troubled with that kind of visitors, those human bats which are attracted by any kind of light, but leave alone those who live in darkness.

She opened the door of the sitting-room. It was Bunting's place to go to the front door, but she knew far better than he did how to deal with difficult or obtrusive callers. Still, somehow, she would have liked him to go tonight. But Bunting sat on, absorbed in his newspaper; all he did at the sound of the bedroom door opening was to look up and say, 'Didn't you hear a knock?'

Without answering his question she went out into the hall.

Slowly she opened the front door.

On the top of the three steps which led up to the door, there stood the long, lanky figure of a man, clad in an Inverness cape and an old-fashioned top hat. He waited for a few seconds blinking at her, perhaps dazzled by the light of the gas in the passage. Mrs Bunting's trained perception told her at once that this man, odd as he looked, was a gentleman, belonging by birth to the class with whom her former employment had brought her in contact.

'Is it not a fact that you let lodgings?' he asked, and there was something shrill, unbalanced, hesitating in his voice.

'Yes, sir,' she said uncertainly – it was a long, long time since anyone had come after their lodgings, anyone, that is, that they could think of taking into their respectable house.

Instinctively she stepped a little to one side, and the stranger walked past her, and so into the hall.

And then, for the first time, Mrs Bunting noticed that he held a narrow bag in his left hand. It was quite a new bag, made of strong brown leather.

'I am looking for some quiet rooms,' he said; then he

repeated the words, 'quiet rooms', in a dreamy, absent way, and as he uttered them he looked nervously round him.

Then his sallow face brightened, for the hall had been carefully furnished, and was very clean.

There was a neat hat-and-umbrella stand, and the stranger's weary feet fell soft on a good, serviceable dark-red drugget, which matched in colour the flock-paper on the walls.

A very superior lodging-house this, and evidently a superior lodging-house keeper.

'You'd find my rooms quite quiet, sir,' she said gently. 'And just now I have four to let. The house is empty, save for my husband and me, sir.'

Mrs Bunting spoke in a civil, passionless voice. It seemed too good to be true, this sudden coming of a possible lodger, and of a lodger who spoke in the pleasant, courteous way and voice which recalled to the poor woman her happy, far-off days of youth and of security.

'That sounds very suitable,' he said. 'Four rooms? Well, perhaps I ought only to take two rooms, but, still, I should like to see all four before I make my choice.'

How fortunate, how very fortunate it was that Bunting had lit the gas! But for that circumstance this gentleman would have passed them by.

She turned towards the staircase, quite forgetting in her agitation that the front door was still open; and it was the stranger whom she already in her mind described as 'the lodger', who turned and rather quickly walked down the passage and shut it.

'Oh, thank you, sir!' she exclaimed. 'I'm sorry you should have had the trouble.'

For a moment their eyes met. 'It's not safe to leave a front door open in London,' he said, rather sharply. 'I hope you do not often do that. It would be so easy for anyone to slip in.'

Mrs Bunting felt rather upset. The stranger had still spoken courteously, but he was evidently very much put out.

'I assure you, sir, I never leave my front door open,' she answered hastily. 'You needn't be at all afraid of that!'

And then, through the closed door of the sitting-room, came

the sound of Bunting coughing – it was just a little, hard cough, but Mrs Bunting's future lodger started violently.

'Who's that?' he said, putting out a hand and clutching her arm. 'Whatever was that?'

'Only my husband, sir. He went out to buy a paper a few minutes ago, and the cold just caught him, I suppose.'

'Your husband—?' he looked at her intently, suspiciously. 'What – what, may I ask, is your husband's occupation?'

Mrs Bunting drew herself up. The question as to Bunting's occupation was no one's business but theirs. Still, it wouldn't do for her to show offence. 'He goes out waiting,' she said stiffly. 'He was a gentleman's servant, sir. He could, of course, valet you should you require him to do so.'

And then she turned and led the way up the steep, narrow staircase.

At the top of the first flight of stairs was what Mrs Bunting, to herself, called the drawing-room floor. It consisted of a sitting-room in front, and a bedroom behind.

She opened the door of the sitting-room and quickly lit the chandelier.

This front room was pleasant enough, though perhaps a little over-encumbered with furniture. Covering the floor was a green carpet simulating moss; four chairs were placed round the table which occupied the exact middle of the apartment, and in the corner, opposite the door giving on to the landing, was a roomy, old-fashioned chiffonier.

On the dark-green walls hung a series of eight engravings, portraits of early Victorian belles, clad in lace and tarletan ball-dresses, clipped from an old Book of Beauty. Mrs Bunting was very fond of these pictures; she thought they gave the drawing-room a note of elegance and refinement.

As she hurriedly turned up the gas she was glad, glad indeed, that she had summoned up sufficient energy, two days ago, to give the room a thorough turn-out.

It had remained for a long time in the state in which it had been left by its last dishonest, dirty occupants when they had been scared into going away by Bunting's rough threats of the police. But now it was in apple-pie order, with one paramount exception, of which Mrs Bunting was painfully aware. There were no white curtains to the windows, but that omission could soon be remedied if this gentleman really took the lodgings.

But what was this—? The stranger was looking round him rather dubiously. 'This is rather – rather too grand for me,' he said at last. 'I should like to see your other rooms, Mrs—er—'

'—Bunting,' she said softly. 'Bunting, sir.'

And as she spoke the dark, heavy load of care again came down and settled on her sad, burdened heart. Perhaps she had been mistaken, after all – or rather, she had not been mistaken in one sense, but perhaps this gentleman was a poor gentleman – too poor, that is, to afford the rent of more than one room, say eight or ten shillings a week; eight or ten shillings a week would be very little use to her and Bunting, though better than nothing at all.

'Will you just look at the bedroom, sir?'

'No,' he said, 'no. I think I should like to see what you have farther up the house, Mrs—', and then, as if making a prodigious mental effort, he brought out her name, 'Bunting,' with a kind of gasp.

The two top rooms were, of course, immediately above the drawing-room floor. But they looked poor and mean, owing to the fact that they were bare of any kind of ornament. Very little trouble had been taken over their arrangement; in fact, they had been left in much the same condition as that in which the Buntings had found them.

For the matter of that, it is difficult to make a nice, genteel sitting-room out of an apartment of which the principal features are a sink and a big gas-stove. The gas-stove, of an obsolete pattern, was fed by a tiresome, shilling-in-the-slot arrangement. It had been the property of the people from whom the Buntings had taken over the lease of the house, who, knowing it to be of no monetary value, had thrown it in among the humble fittings they had left behind.

What furniture there was in the room was substantial and clean, as everything belonging to Mrs Bunting was bound to be, but it was a bare, uncomfortable-looking place, and the landlady now felt sorry that she had done nothing to make it appear more attractive.

To her surprise, however, her companion's dark, sensitive, hatchet-shaped face became irradiated with satisfaction. 'Capital! Capital!' he exclaimed, for the first time putting down the bag he held at his feet, and rubbing his long, thin hands together with a quick, nervous movement.

'This is just what I have been looking for.' He walked with long, eager strides towards the gas-stove. 'First-rate – quite first-rate! Exactly what I wanted to find! You must understand, Mrs – er – Bunting, that I am a man of science. I make, that is, all sorts of experiments, and I often require the – ah, well, the presence of great heat.'

He shot out a hand, which she noticed shook a little, towards the stove. 'This, too, will be useful – exceedingly useful, to me,' and he touched the edge of the stone sink with a lingering, caressing touch.

He threw his head back and passed his hand over his high, bare forehead; then, moving towards a chair, he sat down – wearily. 'I'm tired,' he muttered in a low voice, 'tired – tired! I've been walking about all day, Mrs Bunting, and I could find nothing to sit down upon. They do not put benches for tired men in the London streets. They do so on the Continent. In some ways they are far more humane on the Continent than they are in England, Mrs Bunting.'

'Indeed, sir,' she said civilly; and then, after a nervous glance, she asked the question of which the answer would mean so much to her, 'Then you mean to take my rooms, sir?'

'This room, certainly,' he said, looking round. 'This room is exactly what I have been looking for, and longing for, the last few days;' and then hastily he added, 'I mean this kind of place is what I have always wanted to possess, Mrs Bunting. You would be surprised if you knew how difficult it is to get anything of the sort. But now my weary search has ended, and that is a relief – a very, very great relief to me!'

He stood up and looked round him with a dreamy, abstracted air. And then, 'Where's my bag?' he asked suddenly, and there came a note of sharp, angry fear in his voice. He glared at the quiet woman standing before him, and for a moment Mrs Bunting felt a tremor of fright shoot through her. It seemed a pity that Bunting was so far away, right down the house.

But Mrs Bunting was aware that eccentricity has always been a perquisite, as it were the special luxury, of the well born and of the well educated. Scholars, as she well knew, are never quite like other people, and her new lodger was undoubtedly a scholar. 'Surely I had a bag when I came in?' he said in a scared, troubled voice.

'Here it is, sir,' she said soothingly, and, stooping, picked it up and handed it to him. And as she did so she noticed that the bag was not at all heavy; it was evidently by no means full.

He took it eagerly from her. 'I beg your pardon,' he muttered. 'But there is something in that bag which is very precious to me – something I procured with infinite difficulty, and which I could never get again without running into great danger, Mrs Bunting. That must be the excuse for my late agitation.'

'About terms, sir,' she said a little timidly, returning to the subject which meant so much, so very much to her.

'About terms?' he echoed. And then there came a pause. 'My name is Sleuth,' he said suddenly, 'S-l-e-u-t-h. Think of a hound, Mrs Bunting, and you'll never forget my name. I could provide you with a reference – ' (he gave her what she described to herself as a funny, sideways look) 'but I should prefer you to dispense with that, if you don't mind. I am quite willing to pay you – well, shall we say a month in advance?'

A spot of red shot into Mrs Bunting's cheeks. She felt sick with relief – nay, with a joy which was almost pain. She had not known till that moment how hungry she was – how eager for a good meal. 'That would be all right, sir,' she murmured.

'And what are you going to charge me?' There had come a kindly, almost a friendly note into his voice. 'With attendance, mind! I shall expect you to give me attendance, and I need hardly ask if you can cook, Mrs Bunting?'

'Oh, yes, sir,' she said. 'I am a plain cook. What would you say to twenty-five shillings a week, sir?' She looked at him deprecatingly, and as he did not answer she went on falteringly, 'You see, sir, it may seem a good deal, but you would have the best of attendance and careful cooking – and my husband, sir – he would be pleased to valet you.'

'I shouldn't want anything of that sort done for me,' said Mr Sleuth hastily. 'I prefer looking after my own clothes. I am used to waiting on myself. But, Mrs Bunting, I have a great dislike to sharing lodgings—'

She interrupted eagerly, 'I could let you have the use of the two floors for the same price – that is, until we get another lodger. I shouldn't like you to sleep in the back room up here, sir. It's such a poor little room. You could do as you say, sir – do your work and your experiments up here, and then have your meals in the drawing-room.'

'Yes,' he said hesitatingly, 'that sounds a good plan. And if I offered you two pounds or two guineas? Might I then rely on your not taking another lodger?'

'Yes,' she said quietly. 'I'd be very glad only to have you to wait on, sir.'

'I suppose you have a key to the door of this room, Mrs Bunting? I don't like to be disturbed while I'm working.'

He waited a moment, and then said again, rather urgently, 'I suppose you have a key to this door, Mrs Bunting?'

'Oh, yes, sir, there's a key – a very nice little key. The people who lived here before had a new kind of lock put on to the door.' She went over, and throwing the door open, showed him that a round disc had been fitted above the old keyhole.

He nodded his head, and then, after standing silent a little, as if absorbed in thought, 'Forty-two shillings a week? Yes, that will suit me perfectly. And I'll begin now by paying my first month's rent in advance. Now, four times forty-two shillings is' – he jerked his head back and stared at his new landlady; for the first time he smiled, a queer, wry smile – 'why, just eight pounds eight shillings, Mrs Bunting!'

He thrust his hand through into an inner pocket of his long cape-like coat and took out a handful of sovereigns. Then he began putting these down in a row on the bare wooden table which stood in the centre of the room. 'Here's five – six – seven

– eight – nine – ten pounds. You'd better keep the odd change, Mrs Bunting, for I shall want you to do some shopping for me tomorrow morning. I met with a misfortune today.' But the new lodger did not speak as if his misfortune, whatever it was, weighed on his spirits.

'Indeed, sir. I'm sorry to hear that.' Mrs Bunting's heart was going thump – thump – thump. She felt extraordinarily moved, dizzy with relief and joy.

'Yes, a very great misfortune! I lost my luggage, the few things I managed to bring away with me.' His voice dropped suddenly. 'I shouldn't have said that,' he muttered. 'I was a fool to say that!' Then, more loudly, 'Someone said to me, "You can't go into a lodging-house without any luggage. They wouldn't take you in." But *you* have taken me in, Mrs Bunting, and I'm grateful for – for the kind way you have met me—' He looked at her feelingly, appealingly, and Mrs Bunting was touched. She was beginning to feel very kindly towards her new lodger.

'I hope I know a gentleman when I see one,' she said, with a break in her staid voice.

ERNEST HEMINGWAY

....

'THE KILLERS'

The door of Henry's lunch-room opened and two men came in. They sat down at the counter.

'What's yours?' George asked them.

'I don't know,' one of the men said. 'What do you want to eat, Al?'

'I don't know,' said Al. 'I don't know what I want to eat.'

Outside it was getting dark. The street-light came on outside the window. The two men at the counter read the menu. From the other end of the counter Nick Adams watched them. He had been talking to George when they came in.

'I'll have a roast pork tenderloin with apple sauce and mashed potatoes,' the first man said.

'It isn't ready yet.'

'What the hell do you put it on the card for?'

'That's the dinner,' George explained. 'You can get that at six o'clock.'

George looked at the clock on the wall behind the counter.

'It's five o'clock.'

'The clock says twenty minutes past five,' the second man said.

'It's twenty minutes fast.'

'Oh, to hell with the clock,' the first man said. 'What have you got to eat?'

'I can give you any kind of sandwiches,' George said. 'You can have ham and eggs, bacon and eggs, liver and bacon, or a steak.'

'Give me chicken croquettes with green peas and cream sauce and mashed potatoes.'

'That's the dinner.'

'Everything we want's the dinner, eh? That's the way you work it.'

'I can give you ham and eggs, bacon and eggs, liver—'

'I'll take ham and eggs,' the man called Al said. He wore a derby hat and a black overcoat buttoned across the chest. His face was small and white and he had tight lips. He wore a silk muffler and gloves.

'Give me bacon and eggs,' said the other man. He was about the same size as Al. Their faces were different, but they were dressed like twins. Both wore overcoats too tight for them. They sat leaning forward, their elbows on the counter.

'Got anything to drink?' Al asked.

'Silver beer, bevo, ginger ale,' George said.

'I mean you got anything to *drink*?'

'Just those I said.'

'This is a hot town,' said the other. 'What do they call it?'

'Summit.'

'Ever hear of it?' Al asked his friend.

'No,' said the friend.

'What do you do here nights?' Al asked.

'They eat the dinner,' his friend said. 'They all come here and eat the big dinner.'

'That's right,' George said.

'So you think that's right?' Al asked George.

'Sure.'

'You're a pretty bright boy, aren't you?'

'Sure,' said George.

'Well, you're not,' said the other little man. 'Is he, Al?'

'He's dumb,' said Al. He turned to Nick. 'What's your name?'

'Adams.'

'Another bright boy,' Al said. 'Ain't he a bright boy, Max?'

'The town's full of bright boys,' Max said.

George put the two platters, one of ham and eggs, the other of bacon and eggs, on the counter. He set down two side-dishes of fried potatoes and closed the wicket into the kitchen.

'Which is yours?' he asked Al.

'Don't you remember?'

'Ham and eggs.'

'Just a bright boy,' Max said. He leaned forward and took the ham and eggs. Both men ate with their gloves on. George watched them eat.

'What are *you* looking at?' Max looked at George.

'Nothing.'

'The hell you were. You were looking at me.'

'Maybe the boy meant it for a joke, Max,' Al said.

George laughed.

'*You* don't have to laugh,' Max said to him. '*You* don't have to laugh at all, see?'

'All right,' said George.

'So he thinks it's all right.' Max turned to Al. 'He thinks it's all right. That's a good one.'

'Oh, he's a thinker,' Al said. They went on eating.

'What's the bright boy's name down the counter?' Al asked Max.

'Hey, bright boy,' Max said to Nick. 'You go around on the other side of the counter with your boy friend.'

'What's the idea?' Nick asked.

'There isn't any idea.'

'You better go around, bright boy,' Al said. Nick went around behind the counter.

'What's the idea?' George asked.

'None of your damn business,' Al said. 'Who's out in the kitchen?'

'The nigger.'

'What do you mean the nigger?'

'The nigger that cooks.'

'Tell him to come in.'

'What's the idea?'

'Tell him to come in.'

'Where do you think you are?'

'We know damn well where we are,' the man called Max said. 'Do we look silly?'

'You talk silly,' Al said to him. 'What the hell do you argue with this kid for? Listen,' he said to George, 'tell the nigger to come out here.'

'What are you going to do to him?'

'Nothing. Use your head, bright boy. What would we do to a nigger?'

George opened the slit that opened back into the kitchen. 'Sam,' he called. 'Come in here a minute.'

The door to the kitchen opened and the nigger came in. 'What was it?' he asked. The two men at the counter took a look at him.

'All right, nigger. You stand right there,' Al said.

Sam, the nigger, standing in his apron, looked at the two men sitting at the counter. 'Yes, sir,' he said. Al got down from his stool.

'I'm going back to the kitchen with the nigger and bright boy,' he said. 'Go on back to the kitchen, nigger. You go with him, bright boy.' The little man walked after Nick and Sam, the cook, back into the kitchen. The door shut after them. The man called Max sat at the counter opposite George. He didn't look at George but looked in the mirror that ran along back of the counter. Henry's had been made over from a saloon into a lunch-counter.

'Well, bright boy,' Max said, looking into the mirror, 'why don't you say something?'

'What's it all about?'

'Hey, Al,' Max called, 'bright boy wants to know what it's all about.'

'Why don't you tell him?' Al's voice came from the kitchen.

'What do you think it's all about?'

'I don't know.'

'What do you think?'

Max looked into the mirror all the time he was talking.

'I wouldn't say.'

'Hey, Al, bright boy says he wouldn't say what he thinks it's all about.'

'I can hear you, all right,' Al said from the kitchen. He had propped open the slit that dishes passed through into the kitchen with a catsup bottle. 'Listen, bright boy,' he said from the kitchen to George. 'Stand a little farther along the bar. You move a little to the left, Max.' He was like a photographer arranging for a group picture.

'Talk to me, bright boy,' Max said. 'What do you think's going to happen?'

George did not say anything.

'I'll tell you,' Max said. 'We're going to kill a Swede. Do you know a big Swede named Ole Andreson?'

'Yes.'

'He comes here to eat every night, don't he?'

'Sometimes he comes here.'

'He comes here at six o'clock, don't he?'

'If he comes.'

'We know all that, bright boy,' Max said. 'Talk about something else. Ever go to the movies?'

'Once in a while.'

'You ought to go to the movies more. The movies are fine for a bright boy like you.'

'What are you going to kill Ole Andreson for? What did he ever do to you?'

'He never had a chance to do anything to us. He never even seen us.'

'And he's only going to see us once,' Al said from the kitchen.

'What are you going to kill him for, then?' George asked.

'We're killing him for a friend. Just to oblige a friend, bright boy.'

'Shut up,' said Al from the kitchen. 'You talk too goddam much.'

'Well, I got to keep bright boy amused. Don't I, bright boy?'

'You talk too damn much,' Al said. 'The nigger and my bright boy are amused by themselves. I got them tied up like a couple of girl friends in the convent.'

'I suppose you were in a convent?'

'You never know.'

'You were in a kosher convent. That's where you were.'

George looked up at the clock.

'If anybody comes in you tell them the cook is off, and if they keep after it, you tell them you'll go back and cook yourself. Do you get that, bright boy?'

'All right,' George said. 'What you going to do with us afterward?'

'That'll depend,' Max said. 'That's one of those things you never know at the time.'

George looked up at the clock. It was a quarter past six. The door from the street opened. A street-car motorman came in.

'Hello, George,' he said. 'Can I get supper?'

'Sam's gone out,' George said. 'He'll be back in about half an hour.'

'I'd better go up the street,' the motorman said. George looked at the clock. It was twenty minutes past six.

'That was nice, bright boy,' Max said. 'You're a regular little gentleman.'

'He knew I'd blow his head off,' Al said from the kitchen.

'No,' said Max. 'It ain't that. Bright boy is nice. He's a nice boy. I like him.'

At six-fifty-five George said, 'He's not coming.'

Two other people had been in the lunch-room. Once George had gone out to the kitchen and made a ham-and-egg sandwich 'to go' that a man wanted to take with him. Inside the kitchen he saw Al, his derby hat tipped back, sitting on a stool beside the wicket with the muzzle of a sawed-off shotgun resting on the ledge. Nick and the cook were back to back in the corner, a towel tied in each of their mouths. George had cooked the sandwich, wrapped it up in oiled paper, put it in a bag, brought it in, and the man had paid for it and gone out.

'Bright boy can do everything,' Max said. 'He can cook and everything. You'd make some girl a nice wife, bright boy.'

'Yes?' George said. 'Your friend, Ole Andreson, isn't going to come.'

'We'll give him ten minutes,' Max said.

Max watched the mirror and the clock. The hands of the clock marked seven o'clock, and then five minutes past seven.

'Come on, Al,' said Max. 'We better go. He's not coming.'

'Better give him five minutes,' Al said from the kitchen.

In the five minutes a man came in, and George explained that the cook was sick.

'Why the hell don't you get another cook?' the man asked. 'Aren't you running a lunch-counter?' He went out.

'Come on, Al,' Max said.

'What about the two bright boys and the nigger?'

'They're all right.'

'You think so?'

'Sure. We're through with it.'

'I don't like it,' said Al. 'It's sloppy. You talk too much.'

'Oh, what the hell,' said Max. 'We got to keep amused, haven't we?'

'You talk too much, all the same,' Al said. He came out from the kitchen. The cut-off barrels of the shotgun made a slight bulge under the waist of his too tight-fitting overcoat. He straightened his coat with his gloved hands.

'So long, bright boy,' he said to George. 'You got a lot of luck.'

'That's the truth,' Max said. 'You ought to play the races, bright boy.'

The two of them went out the door. George watched them, through the window, pass under the arc-light and cross the street. In their tight overcoats and derby hats they looked like a vaudeville team. George went back through the swinging-door into the kitchen and untied Nick and the cook.

....

THE GLASS KEY

The Buckman was a square-built yellow apartment-building that filled most of the block it stood in. Inside, Ned Beaumont said he wanted to see Mr Dewey. When asked for his name he said: 'Ned Beaumont.'

Five minutes later he was walking away from an elevator down a long corridor towards an open door where Bernie Despain stood.

Despain was a small man, short and stringy, with a head too large for his body. The size of his head was exaggerated until it seemed a deformity by long thick fluffy waved hair. His face was swarthy, large-featured except for the eyes, and strongly lined across the forehead and down from nostrils past the mouth. He had a faintly reddish scar on one cheek. His blue suit was carefully pressed and he wore no jewelry.

He stood in the doorway, smiling sardonically, and said: 'Good morning, Ned.'

Ned Beaumont said: 'I want to talk to you, Bernie.'

'I guessed you did. As soon as they phoned your name up I said to myself: "I bet you he wants to talk to me."'

Ned Beaumont said nothing. His yellow face was tight-lipped.

Despain's smile became looser. He said: 'Well, my boy, you don't have to stand here. Come on in.' He stepped aside.

The door opened into a small vestibule. Through an opposite door that stood open Lee Wilshire and the man who had struck Ned Beaumont could be seen. They had stopped packing two travelling-bags to look at Ned Beaumont.

He went into the vestibule.

Despain followed him in, shut the corridor-door, and said: 'The Kid's kind of hasty and when you come up to me like that he thought maybe you were looking for trouble, see? I give him hell about it and maybe if you ask him he'll apologize.'

The Kid said something in an undertone to Lee Wilshire, who was glaring at Ned Beaumont. She laughed a vicious little laugh and replied: 'Yes, a sportsman to the last.'

Bernie Despain said: 'Go right in, Mr Beaumont. You've already met the folks, haven't you?'

Ned Beaumont advanced into the room where Lee and the Kid were.

The Kid asked: 'How's the belly?'

Ned Beaumont did not say anything.

Bernie Despain exclaimed: 'Jesus! For a guy that says he came up here to talk you've done less of it than anybody I ever heard of.'

'I want to talk to you,' Ned Beaumont said. 'Do we have to have all these people around?'

'I do,' Despain replied. 'You don't. You can get away from them just by walking out and going about your own business.'

'I've got business here.'

'That's right, there was something about money,' Despain grinned at the Kid. 'Wasn't there something about money, Kid?'

The Kid had moved to stand in the doorway through which Ned Beaumont had come into the room. 'Something,' he said in a rasping voice, 'but I forget what.'

Ned Beaumont took off his overcoat and hung it on the back of a brown easy-chair. He sat down in the chair and put his hat behind him. He said: 'That's not my business this time. I'm – let's see.' He took a paper from his inner coat-pocket, unfolded it, glanced at it, and said: 'I'm here as special investigator for the District Attorney's office.'

For a small fraction of a second the twinkle in Despain's eyes was blurred, but he said immediately: 'Ain't you getting up in the world! The last time I saw you you were just punking around for Paul.'

Ned Beaumont refolded the paper and returned it to his pocket.

Despain said: 'Well, go ahead, investigate something for us – anything – just to show us how it's done.' He sat down facing Ned Beaumont, wagging his too-large head. 'You ain't going to tell me you came all the way to New York to ask me about killing Taylor Henry?'

'Yes.'

'That's too bad. I could've saved you the trip.' He flourished a hand at the travelling-bags on the floor. 'As soon as Lee told me what it was all about I started packing up to go back and laugh at your frame-up.'

Ned Beaumont lounged back comfortably in his chair. One of his hands was behind him. He said: 'If it's a frame-up it's Lee's. The police got their dope from her.'

'Yes,' she said angrily, 'when I had to because you sent them there, you bastard.'

Despain said: 'Uh-huh, Lee's a dumb cluck, all right, but those markers don't mean anything. They—'

'I'm a dumb cluck, am I?' Lee cried indignantly. 'Didn't I come all the way here to warn you after you'd run off with every stinking piece of—'

'Yes,' Despain agreed pleasantly, 'and coming here shows just what a dumb cluck you are, because you led this guy right to me.'

'If that's the way you feel about it I'm damned glad I did give the police those IOUs, and what do you think of that?'

Despain said: 'I'll tell you just exactly what I think of it after our company's gone.' He turned to Ned Beaumont. 'So honest Paul Madvig's letting you drop the shuck on me, huh?'

Ned Beaumont smiled. 'You're not being framed, Bernie, and you know it. Lee gave us the lead-in and the rest that we got clicked with it.'

'There's some more besides what she gave you?'

'Plenty.'

'What?'

Ned Beaumont smiled again. 'There are lots of things I could say to you, Bernie, that I wouldn't want to say in front of a crowd.'

Despain said: 'Nuts!'

The Kid spoke from the doorway to Despain in his rasping voice: 'Let's chuck this sap out on his can and get going.'

'Wait,' Despain said. Then he frowned and put a question to Ned Beaumont: 'Is there a warrant out for me?'

'Well, I don't—'

'Yes or no?' Despain's bantering humor was gone.

Ned Beaumont said slowly: 'Not that I know of.'

Despain stood up and pushed his chair back. 'Then get the hell out of here and make it quick, or I'll let the Kid take another poke at you.'

Ned Beaumont stood up. He picked up his overcoat. He took his cap out of his overcoat pocket and, holding it in one hand, his overcoat over the other arm, said seriously: 'You'll be sorry.' Then he walked out in a dignified manner. The Kid's rasping laughter and Lee's shriller hooting followed him out.

Outside the Buckman Ned Beaumont started briskly down the street. His eyes were glowing in his tired face and his dark moustache twitched above a flickering smile.

At the first corner he came face to face with Jack. He asked: 'What are you doing here?'

Jack said: 'I'm still working for you, far as I know, so I came along to see if I could find anything to do.'

'Swell. Find us a taxi quick. They're sliding out.'

Jack said, 'Ay, ay,' and went down the street.

Ned Beaumont remained on the corner. The front and side entrances of the Buckman could be seen from there.

In a little while Jack returned in a taxicab. Ned Beaumont got into it and they told the driver where to park it.

'What did you do to them?' Jack asked when they were sitting still.

'Things.'

'Oh.'

Ten minutes passed and Jack, saying, 'Look,' was pointing a forefinger at a taxicab drawing up to the Buckman's side door.

The Kid, carrying two travelling-bags, left the building first, then, when he was in the taxicab, Despain and the girl ran out to join him. The taxicab ran away.

Jack leaned forward and told his driver what to do. They ran along in the other cab's wake. They wound through streets that were bright with morning sunlight, going by a devious route finally to a battered brownstone house in West Forty-ninth Street.

Despain's cab stopped in front of the house and, once more, the Kid was the first of the trio out on the sidewalk. He looked up and down the street. He went up to the front door of the house and unlocked it. Then he returned to the taxicab. Despain and the girl jumped out and went indoors hurriedly. The Kid followed with the bags.

'Stick here with the cab,' Ned Beaumont told Jack.

'What are you going to do?'

'Try my luck.'

Jack shook his head. 'This is another wrong neighborhood to look for trouble in,' he said.

Ned Beaumont said: 'If I come out with Despain, you beat it. Get another taxi and go back to watch the Buckman. If I don't come out, use your own judgement.'

He opened the cab door and stepped out. He was shivering. His eyes were shiny. He ignored something that Jack leaned out to say and hurried across the street to the house into which the two men and the girl had gone.

He went straight up the front steps and put a hand on the door-knob. The knob turned in his hand. The door was not locked. He pushed it open and, after peering into the dim hallway, went in.

The door slammed shut behind him and one of the Kid's fists struck his head a glancing blow that carried his cap away and sent him crashing into the wall. He sank down a little, giddily, almost to one knee, and the Kid's other fist struck the wall over his head.

He pulled his lips back over his teeth and drove a fist into the Kid's groin, a short sharp blow that brought a snarl from the Kid and made him fall back so that Ned Beaumont could pull himself up straight before the Kid was upon him again.

Up the hallway a little, Bernie Despain was leaning against the wall, his mouth stretched wide and thin, his eyes narrowed to dark points, saying over and over in a low voice: 'Sock him, Kid, sock him . . .' Lee Wilshire was not in sight.

The Kid's next two blows landed on Ned Beaumont's chest, mashing him against the wall, making him cough. The third, aimed at his face, he avoided. Then he pushed the Kid away from him with a forearm against his throat and kicked the Kid in the belly. The Kid roared angrily and came in with both fists going, but forearm and foot had carried him away from Ned Beaumont and had given Ned Beaumont time to get his right hand to his hip-pocket and to get Jack's revolver out of his pocket. He had not time to level the revolver, but, holding it at a downward angle, he pulled the trigger and managed to shoot the Kid in the right thigh. The Kid yelped and fell down on the hallway floor. He lay there looking up at Ned Beaumont with frightened bloodshot eyes.

Ned Beaumont stepped back from him, put his left hand in his trousers pocket, and addressed Bernie Despain: 'Come on out with me. I want to talk to you.' His face was sullenly determined.

Footsteps ran overhead, somewhere back in the building a door opened, and down the hallway excited voices were audible, but nobody came into sight.

Despain stared for a long moment at Ned Beaumont as if horribly fascinated. Then, without a word, he stepped over the man on the floor and went out of the building ahead of Ned Beaumont. Ned Beaumont put the revolver in his jacket-pocket before he went down the street-steps, but he kept his hand on it.

'Up to that taxi,' he told Despain, indicating the car out of which Jack was getting. When they reached the taxicab he told the chauffeur to drive them anywhere, 'just around till I tell you where to go.'

They were in motion when Despain found his voice. He said: 'This is a hold-up. I'll give you anything you want because I don't want to be killed, but it's just a hold-up.'

Ned Beaumont laughed disagreeably and shook his head. 'Don't forget I've risen in the world to be something or other in the District Attorney's office.'

'But there's no charge against me. I'm not wanted. You said—'

'I was spoofing you, Bernie, for reasons. You're wanted.'

'For what?'

'Killing Taylor Henry.'

'That? Hell, I'll go back and face that. What've you got against me? I had some of his markers, sure. And I left the night he was killed, sure. And I gave him hell because he wouldn't make them good, sure. What kind of case is that for a first-class lawyer to beat? Jesus, if I left the markers behind in my safe at some time before nine-thirty – to go by Lee's story – don't that show I wasn't trying to collect that night?'

'No, and that isn't all the stuff we've got on you.'

'That's all there could be,' Despain said earnestly.

Ned Beaumont sneered. 'Wrong, Bernie. Remember I had a hat on when I came to see you this morning?'

'Maybe. I think you did.'

'Remember I took a cap out of my overcoat pocket and put it on when I left?'

Bewilderment, fear, began to come into the swarthy man's small eyes. 'By Jesus! Well? What are you getting at?'

'I'm getting at the evidence. Do you remember the hat didn't fit me very well?'

Bernie Despain's voice was hoarse: 'I don't know, Ned. For Christ's sake, what do you mean?'

'I mean it didn't fit me because it wasn't my hat. Do you remember that the hat Taylor was wearing when he was murdered wasn't found?'

'I don't know. I don't know anything about him.'

'Well, I'm trying to tell you the hat I had this morning was Taylor's hat and it's now planted down between the cushion-seat and the back of that brown easy-chair in the apartment you had at the Buckman. Do you think that, with the rest, would be enough to set you on the hot seat?'

Despain would have screamed in terror if Ned Beaumont had not clapped a hand over his mouth and growled, 'Shut up,' in his ear.

Sweat ran down the swarthy face. Despain fell over on Ned Beaumont, seizing the lapels of his coat with both hands, babbling: 'Listen, don't you do that to me, Ned. You can have every cent I owe you, every cent with interest, if you won't do that. I never meant to rob you, Ned, honest to God. It was just that I was caught short and thought I'd treat it like a loan. Honest to God, Ned. I ain't got much now, but I'm fixed to get the money for Lee's rocks that I'm selling today and I'll give you your dough, every nickel of it, out of that. How much was it, Ned? I'll give you all of it right away, this morning.'

Ned Beaumont pushed the swarthy man over to his own side of the taxicab and said: 'It was thirty-two hundred and fifty dollars.'

'Thirty-two hundred and fifty dollars. You'll get it, every cent of it, this morning, right away.' Despain looked at his watch. 'Yes, sir, right this minute as soon as we can get there. Old Stein will be at his place before this. Only say you'll let me go, Ned, for old times' sake.'

Ned Beaumont rubbed his hands together thoughtfully. 'I can't exactly let you go. Not right now, I mean. I've got to remember the District Attorney connexion and that you're wanted for questioning. So all we can dicker about is the hat. Here's the proposition: give me my money and I'll see that I'm alone when I turn up the hat and nobody else will ever know about it. Otherwise I'll see that half the New York police are with me and— There you are. Take it or leave it.'

'Oh, God!' Bernie Despain groaned. 'Tell him to drive us to old Stein's place. It's on . . .'

....

SQUEEZE PLAY

Under normal conditions it's a thirty-five- or forty-minute drive to Irvingville. I had grown up in New Jersey and was familiar with the terrain. After you get out of the tunnel you take one of those highways that's given New Jersey its reputation as armpit of the Western world. Although there are no more pigs in Secaucus, there is enough industrial stench along the way to make you think you've travelled through a time warp back into nineteenth-century England. Thick white smoke charges out of giant factory chimneys, polluting the grotesque landscape of swamps and abandoned brick warehouses. You see hundreds of seagulls circling hills of garbage and the rusted hulks of a thousand burned-out cars. In a low mood it's enough to make you want to live as a hermit in the Maine woods, feeding off wild berries and the roots of trees. But people are wrong to say this is a preview of the end of civilization. It is the essence of civilization, the exact price we pay for being what we are and wanting what we want.

The traffic was heavy when I reached the Garden State Parkway, but it moved steadily. It wasn't hot enough yet to be the season of overheated radiators and bald tire blow-outs, and the beautiful weather seemed to urge the drivers on. They probably were hurrying home to spend the rest of the spring afternoon in their backyards planting tomatoes or drinking beer, rushing to flee the scene of their monotonous days and make a stab at pretending to be alive. It was twenty to six when I reached the ramp for the Irvingville exit.

Like most of the towns and small cities around Newark, Irvingville was a down-at-the-heels working-class community. Its better days were behind it, and even those had been nothing to rave about. Unlike the neighboring cities, however, all of which had become predominantly black in the past twenty years, Irvingville was still almost completely white. It was a little alcove of reactionary fervor in the midst of a changing world. Back in the thirties there had been a Nazi Bund in Irvingville, and its cops were well known to be the most brutal in the county. The town was inhabited by Poles and Italians, and most of them had never had anything better than gruelling factory jobs and desperate, exhausted lives. These were the people who stood just a half-step away from the welfare office, a half-step away from the black man's poverty, and because of this threat many of them found release in a particularly vicious kind of racism. It was a rough place, a depressing place. You didn't want to be there unless you had to.

Seventeenth Street was a neighborhood of two-family houses bravely trying to keep a smile on its face as it went under. Most of the houses were covered with gravelly maroon or green tar shingles, and many of them had flower boxes in the windows filled with bright red geraniums. Old people sat on the porches and gazed out at the kids swarming over the sidewalks below, shouting and screaming at their games.

The Pignato house was no better or worse than any of the other houses on the street. I walked up the rickety steps, saw their name on the black tin mailbox beside the left-hand door, and knocked. Nothing happened for thirty seconds. I knocked again, this time much harder. From inside the house a woman's voice called out wearily, 'I'm coming, I'm coming.' It sounded as though she expected it to be one of the neighborhood kids coming to beg for a cookie.

I heard the sound of slippered feet padding towards me, and

then the door jerked open. Marie Pignato was a dark, sallow-faced woman in her early forties. She stood at about five three, her stomach and voluminous hips bulging in tight black stretch pants. There were fluffy pink mules on her feet, and she wore a yellow smock-like blouse with a small silver cross hanging from a chain around her neck. She had that washed-out expression that told you she had stopped waiting for her ship to come in a long time ago. From the dark bags under her eyes it looked as if she hadn't had a decent night's sleep in years.

'Mrs Pignato?'

'Yes?' Her voice was tentative, unsure of itself. She seemed a little taken aback to find a stranger standing at her door.

'My name is Max Klein. I'm an attorney representing the Graymoor Insurance Company.' I took out one of my old attorney-at-law cards and handed it to her. 'Do you think it would be possible for me to see Mr Pignato?'

'We don't want no insurance,' she said.

'I'm not selling insurance, Mrs Pignato. I represent the insurance company. It seems that your husband has come into some luck and I'd like to tell him about it.'

She looked at my face, then down at the card in her hand, and then back at my face. 'What are you, some kind of lawyer?'

'That's right,' I said with a smile, 'I'm a lawyer. And if I could just see your husband for a few minutes, I'm sure you wouldn't regret it.'

'Well, Bruno isn't in,' she said, still sceptical, but softening.

'Do you know when he'll be back?'

She shrugged. 'How do I know? Bruno comes and goes, you can't keep no tabs on him. He's on disability, you know, so he don't have to work.' She made it sound as though a job was the only thing that kept a man coming home every night.

'Was he around today?'

'Yeah. He was here before. But then he went out.' She paused, shook her head, and sighed, as if trying to cope with the behavior of a difficult child. 'Sometimes he don't come back for days at a time.'

'I hear your husband hasn't been well.'

'No, he ain't been well. Not for four or five years, ever since his accident. They have to take him away every once in a while for a rest.'

'What kind of accident was that?'

'With his truck. There wasn't nothing wrong with him. But mentally he ain't been the same since.'

'Do you know where I might find him, Mrs Pignato? This is rather important, and I'd hate to leave without trying to find him.'

'Well, you could go over to Angie's on Fifteenth and Grand. He sometimes goes there for a beer.'

'I think I will,' I said. 'Thank you for your help.'

I turned around to leave.

'Hey, mister,' she said, 'you forgot your card.' She held it out to me, now knowing what to do with it. It was a foreign object to her, and she almost seemed afraid of it.

'That's all right, you can keep it.'

She looked down at the card once again. 'Is there going to be money in this for us?' she asked timidly, not wanting to expect too much.

'There's money,' I said. 'I don't think it's a lot, but I'm sure there will be something.'

I smiled at her and again she looked down at the card. It seemed to exert a magical force over her, as if it were somehow more real than I was.

Fifteenth and Grand was only a few blocks away, but I decided to take my car. I didn't want to leave it there with its New York license plates as a temptation for the kids on Seventeenth Street. Driving along with the window down I passed more rows of two-family houses, a vacant lot filled with weeds and stray dogs, and a school yard in which a pick-up softball game was going on. The pitcher had just released the ball and the batter was drawing back his arms to swing as I went by, but before I could see what happened I was gone, my view blocked by the brick wall of the school. It was a moment frozen in time, and the image of the white ball hanging in the air stayed with me, like a vision of eternal expectation.

The neighborhood became more commercial on Grand

Avenue, and I found Angie's Palace sitting between a liquor store and a corner Gulf station. I parked my car a few doors down in front of a beauty parlour. A red and blue hand-painted sign in the window announced: 'Dolores is Back'. I hoped she wouldn't regret her decision.

In spite of its name, Angie's Palace was just a local bar, like a thousand others on a thousand streets like this one. Neon beer signs in the window, peeling green paint on the façade, and a battered red door that had been pushed open by a million thirsty hands. Over the door there was a sign displaying two tilted martini glasses with bubbles coming out of them. The lettering for the word 'Lounge' had been reduced to a dismal L U G .

It was dark inside, like the inside of a fish's brain, and it took a few moments for my eyes to adjust. The only moving things in the bar were the undulating purple lights of the juke-box, and they danced with incongruous gaiety as a mournful song of rejection and despair poured from the machine. There were only five or six customers in the place. Two of them, dressed in the gray uniforms of telephone repairmen, sat hunched over their beers at the bar talking about the relative merits of BMWs and Audis. A few others were sitting alone at wooden tables in the room reading copies of the *Newark Star Ledger*. The bartender, dressed in a short-sleeved white shirt and a white apron, looked like a former defensive tackle who had gone to fat reminiscing over too many beers with his customers.

I went up to the bar and ordered a Bud. When the bartender returned with the beer and a glass, I put down a dollar and said, 'I'm looking for Bruno Pignato. His wife said I might find him here.'

'You're not a cop, are you?' It was a matter-of-fact question, and he wasn't trying to make an issue of it. But he had his customers to protect, and he didn't know my face.

'No, I'm a lawyer. I just want to talk to him.'

The bartender looked me over, testing me with his eyes, and then gestured to the back corner of the room. A man was sitting there at a table with a full glass of beer in front of him and staring off into space.

'Thanks,' I said. I picked up my drink and walked over.

GEORGE V. HIGGINS

··

TRUST

The center of Lafayette is eight miles east of the Connecticut border, six miles east of 95 on RI 189. On the eastern side of the road, the water of Rhode Island Sound shines blue and choppy white on sunny days; sailboats shimmer in the wind, and the waves roll in on small patches of tawny sand between big, black rocks. The westerly side of the road, bulldozed during the late fifties into a flat about two hundred yards deep and three-quarters of a mile long, is crowded by small shopping plazas and a small supermarket, all surrounded by asphalt parking lots and made of cinder block with brick fronts and flat, tarred roofs decorated with ventilator shafts and massive, faded green air-conditioning condensers.

Earl turned in at the third parking entrance and parked very close to a pair of white posts supporting a white sign made of hollow glass, very far from the yellow line marking the limit of his space and the vacant one next to it. The sign had been damaged by a thrown rock that had broken a jagged hole in the glass, exposing three fluorescent tubes inside and breaking a fourth in its trajectory. The remaining glass was block-lettered in red paint: CHUCKIE'S DIS   NT LIQUORS. Earl put up the windows of the Dodge, got out of the car, and locked it. He surveyed it from the rear and satisfied himself that he had left as much space as possible on the right side. He made his way through three double rows of angle-parked cars to the liquor store, its windows plastered with posters – red paint on white butcher paper – advertising UNBELIEVABLE savings on wines, PRICEBUSTER SPECIALS ON BEERS FOR YOUR BUSTS, and EVERY-DAY PRICE-SLASHING BONANZAS.

There were three aisles of shelved stock inside and a wall-to-wall glass-doored refrigerator across the back. Three middle-aged men in faded plaid shirts peered myopically at the labels of imported wines and stocked their shopping carriages with half-gallons of Ballantine's scotch, Gilbey's gin, Jim Beam bourbon, and cases of Löwenbräu. An elderly woman with flying white hair and puffiness around the eyes made quick movements, selecting openly a bottle of domestic sherry, using it and a bag of unsalted potato chips to conceal partially the bottle of blackberry brandy she had furtively picked up first and placed at the bottom of her plastic basket. Her lips moved rapidly in silent speech as she went to the registers at the front.

Three large young men – gray sweatshirts, the sleeves ripped off at the armholes, Hawaiian-print surfing jams, and sneakers with no socks – carried three cases of Budweiser each from the cold room behind the refrigerator. The one in the lead stopped next to the gin. 'I'm telling you, shithead, it's true,' the first said over his shoulder to the one last in line. 'You can ask Joanie, don't believe me, that's exactly what Patti did. Right after you left, we went down to the cove, and Patti is so fuckin' drunk she's got no *idea* where she is. And Tony says: "It's too cold to go swimming. Too cold for that. Patti, show us your tits." And she says: "All right, I will." And she did. Took off her sweater and did it. And then Philip says: "I don't believe it. Too dark to see if they're real." And she says: "Oh yeah?" and goes over to him, and says: "Give 'em a squeeze, and you'll see." So he does, and says: "Fuck, what do I know? They sure feel like real tits to me." And she says: "For punishment, suck 'em," and sticks them way out. And, he's lying down. He says: "How?" And she kneels down, you know, and then sits on his crotch, and sticks them right in his face, and he's sucking away, and she's grinding, and then she stands up, rips down his pants there, and of course he's as hard as a rock. And she jerked him off. He's lying there, moaning, "Blow me, blow me," and she's pulling away at his dick, and then he comes, all over his stomach, and she puts her hand in it and rubs it into his mouth.'

'What'd he do?' the second one said.

'Tried to spit it out,' the first one said. 'Making all of these kinds of faces, and Patti puts her top back on and says: "Well, I don't like sluck either. Not in my mouth, at least." And she went home.' He shifted the cargo of beer in his hands and resumed the march towards the front. The last one in line said, 'Shee-it, those Texans're tough. She prolly blows horses at home. Should send *her* to Vietnam. Few broads like her got over there, war'd end tomorrow. Chinks'd drop their guns.'

Earl went up the aisle between the second and third rows of shelves and found a quart bottle of Cossack vodka on sale for $4.99. He retraced his steps toward the back and went up the last aisle between the fourth row of shelving and the cases of beer and soft drinks stacked high against the wall. He took two six-packs of canned Coca-Cola and headed toward the registers at the front. A tall woman – five nine or so, around thirty-five – in a dark leopard-pattern leotard top, very tight faded jeans, and camel-colored shoes with stubby high heels was in the act of bending over the lower basket of a two-tiered display of liqueurs. She had platinum hair, and she was deeply tanned. The neckline of the leotard plunged to the middle of her cleavage; she had a large costume jewelry brooch of fake diamonds pinned to it there. She had very long legs. Earl stopped and pretended to be interested in various brands of rum. She straightened up without taking anything from the basket when a blocky man in a blue windbreaker, sleeves pushed up, yellowed white polo shirt, and shorts came up behind her with two cases of Miller beer. He was running to paunch, and losing his blondish hair. 'You want any, that shit for diabetics?' he said. She shook her head, and preceded him into the checkout lane. Earl followed them toward the register. When he reached the place where she had stood, he could smell a lingering aroma of perfume. It grew stronger as he came up behind the man, who was presenting a twenty-dollar bill. 'Don't worry,' the man said. 'It's not one of those.'

The cashier was a woman just shy of forty. She wore a short black wig with ringlets that framed her face, and a pink smock with 'Chuckie's Discount' embroidered in red over her left breast. She accepted the money and snorted, ringing up the sale. 'It's fifties now,' she said, tapping a notice taped to the glass partition on the other side of the register. 'I guess they're movin' up inna world.' She glanced sidelong at the woman in the leotard. 'Like lots of us'd like, and some already did.' The woman did not say anything. She stared into the middle distance, and licked her bottom lip once.

The man chuckled and accepted his change. 'Good thing for you, I guess,' he said, 'they didn't start two months ago.' He picked up his beer, and the woman went ahead of him toward the exit, her buttocks swaying smoothly under the denim. She used her right hand to brush the hair from her right temple, tossing her head back as she did so. She gave the blocky man half a smile, her eyelids lowered, as he followed her out through the door.

'You, ah,' the cashier said to Earl, 'you want me to ring that stuff up, sir?'

Earl took a deep breath and put the bottle and the two six-packs on the counter. He shook his head as he pulled out his wallet. 'Fine lookin' woman,' he said.

'Best advertisement Revlon ever had,' the cashier said, running her forefinger down a flip-card list of prices. She rang up the price of the vodka, and added $3.29 for the Coke. 'Eight twenny-eight,' she said.

'Revlon?' he said.

She nodded. 'The perfume,' she said. 'She douses herself. Must pour it on over her head.'

'I kind of liked it,' he said. 'I thought it smelled nice. Sort of spicy.' He separated one bill from a respectable wad in his wallet and handed it to the cashier.

'Hell,' she said, 'I used to like it myself. Wore the stuff all of the time. But that was before she started coming in here every week, absolutely reeking of it. Now I wouldn't wear the damned poison. I dumped all of mine down the toilet. Right after the rest of my life.' She rested the bill on edge on the buttons of the top row of the register. 'Course the fact that the guy she comes *in* here with now, happens to be my ex-husband – well, that might have something to do with it.' She peered at the bill. 'Hey,' she said.

'Your ex-husband?' he said.

'You deaf or something, mister?' she said, offering the bill back to him. 'I can't take this.'

'You used to be married, that guy?'

She sighed. 'I swear,' she said, 'you got wax in your ears. You oughta go to the doctor. Yeah, I used to be married, that guy. We got what they call "divorce" in this state. "Providence, and these Plantations." You come from some other planet or something, you never heard of divorce? You should live in Italy. But what I'm talking about now, though, is this.' She waved the fifty under his nose. 'This's what I'm talking about, all right? I can't take this, for your stuff. You got something smaller, that's fine. Or something bigger, a hundred – also fine. But no fifties no way now, in Chuckie's – we eighty-sixed them 'fore Memorial Day. Hell, we didn't even take twennies, till almost the Fourth of July. Counterfeit, you know? Like "No good"? Like "Dunno where you got this, ma'am" – you take it to the bank – "but the Treasury didn't print it and we sure don't want it here." And you say: "Do I do?" And they look at you, and they just sort of shrug, and they tell you that that's your decision. Paper your spare room, if you got enough, or use them for toilet paper.

'Well, now it's fifties they're passing,' she said. 'So it's fifties now, we're not taking. And bad's I got burned, the first part of May, at least I'm glad it was twennies. Cost me, I hadda give Chuckie a hundred and eighty, taken right out of my pay. And Al and Lucy, and Chuckie himself, they all got nailed pretty bad too. Those bastards got into us a good thousand bucks, before the bank tipped us off. So, you got something smaller, if you wanna buy this stuff?'

'Oh,' he said, fumbling for his wallet again. 'I didn't know. Lemme see here. My boss always pays me, he pays me in cash. He just paid me that one last night. But maybe I got here . . .' He pulled out a number of one-dollar bills that had been wadded up and then smoothed out. He began to count them out. 'Nine,' he finished. He pushed them towards her. 'That oughta do it,' he said.

She picked up the soiled bills and raised her eyebrows. 'How long you had these items?' she said. 'Your mother at your confirmation?'

He grinned and tried to look sheepish. 'I'm not very good about money,' he said. 'I buy something, I always use the biggest bill I got, 'cause it's easier'n counting out singles. Then I get the change, and I stick it in my pocket till I get home and change my pants and I just put it in my wallet.'

She rang the drawer open and gave him his change. 'You, ah,' he said. 'I'm looking, the Beachmont Motel?'

'It's downah road,' she said, jerking her head to indicate the direction. 'You should've followed those three lugs with the beer – that's where they were going. Goddamned kids. Hiding out in college so they maybe miss the draft. Which they seem to think gives them the right, just roll right over everybody. Call a cop on those kids, they start whining right away: "I'm gonna be in 'Nam next year." Bull*shit* is what I say. They'll figure out another wrinkle. Wish my kid was like that.' She paused. 'Or,' she said, 'four-five years ago, you could've followed your showgirl. She used to spend *lots* of time there. Most of it on her back. But now that she's married, the owner, lady of leisure and all, she never goes near the damned place.'

'That guy with her, he's the owner?' Earl said.

'Yup,' the cashier said, extending her left hand to receive the purchases of one of the middle-aged men who had finished his deliberations. 'Good old Jimmy Battles. Looks as soft as a bowl fulla custard, but meaner'n snakes when he's pissed. And the closest thing to a jackhammer I ever saw in bed.' She glanced back at Earl. 'You're thinking of staying, staying at Jimmy's, I'd change my mind, I was you. I know that joint on the inside and out. There's not a bed in it, 'll fit you.' She snickered. "Less he cuts you down to size, like he does everybody else. Or has his beef-boys do it.'

'I can take care of myself all right,' Earl said, picking up his goods.

'*Oh*,' she said. 'Well, that's too bad. Jimmy don't like guys like you. Takes care of them himself.'

THE LADY IN THE LAKE

I drove past the intersection of Altair Street to where the cross street continued to the edge of the canyon and ended in a semicircular parking place with a sidewalk and a white wooden guard fence around it. I sat there in the car a little while, thinking, looking out to sea and admiring the blue-gray fall of the foothills towards the ocean. I was trying to make up my mind whether to try handling Lavery with a feather or go on using the back of my hand and the edge of my tongue. I decided I could lose nothing by the soft approach. If that didn't produce for me – and I didn't think it would – nature could take its course and we could bust up the furniture.

The paved alley that ran along half-way down the hill below the houses on the outer edge was empty. Below that, on the next hillside street, a couple of kids were throwing a boomerang up the slope and chasing it with the usual amount of elbowing and mutual insult. Farther down still a house was enclosed in trees and a red brick wall. There was a glimpse of washing on the line in the backyard and two pigeons strutted along the slope of the roof bobbing their heads. A blue and tan bus trundled along the street in front of the brick house and stopped and a very old man got off with slow care and settled himself firmly on the ground and tapped with a heavy cane before he started to crawl back up the slope.

The air was clearer than yesterday. The morning was full of peace. I left the car where it was and walked along Altair Street to No. 623.

The venetian blinds were down across the front windows and the place had a sleepy look. I stepped down over the Korean moss and punched the bell and saw that the door was not quite shut. It had dropped in its frame, as most of our doors do, and the spring bolt hung a little on the lower edge of the lock plate. I remembered that it had wanted to stick the day before, when I was leaving.

I gave the door a little push and it moved inward with a light click. The room beyond was dim, but there was some light from west windows. Nobody answered my ring. I didn't ring again. I pushed the door a little wider and stepped inside.

The room had a hushed warm smell, the smell of late morning in a house not yet opened up. The bottle of Vat 69 on the round table by the davenport was almost empty and another full bottle waited beside it. The copper ice-bucket had a little water in the bottom. Two glasses had been used, and half a siphon of carbonated water.

I fixed the door about as I had found it and stood there and listened. If Lavery was away I thought I would take a chance and frisk the joint. I didn't have anything much on him, but it was probably enough to keep him from calling the cops.

In the silence time passed. It passed in the dry whirr of the electric clock on the mantel, in the far-off toot of an auto horn on Aster Drive, in the hornet drone of a plane over the foothills across the canyon, in the sudden lurch and growl of the electric refrigerator in the kitchen.

I went farther into the room and stood peering around and listening and hearing nothing except those fixed sounds belonging to the house and having nothing to do with the humans in it. I started along the rug towards the archway at the back.

A hand in a glove appeared on the slope of the white metal railing, at the edge of the archway, where the stairs went down. It appeared and stopped.

It moved and a woman's hat showed, then her head. The woman came quietly up the stairs. She came all the way up, turned through the arch and still didn't seem to see me. She was a slender woman of uncertain age, with untidy brown hair, a scarlet mess of a mouth, too much rouge on her cheekbones, shadowed eyes. She wore a blue tweed suit that looked like the dickens with a purple hat that was doing its best to hang on to the side of her head.

She saw me and didn't stop or change expression in the slightest degree. She came slowly on into the room, holding her right hand away from her body. Her left hand wore the brown glove I had seen on the railing. The right-hand glove that matched it was wrapped around the butt of a small automatic.

She stopped then and her body arched back and a quick distressful sound came out of her mouth. Then she giggled, a high nervous giggle. She pointed the gun at me, and came steadily on.

I kept on looking at the gun and not screaming.

The woman came close. When she was close enough to be confidential she pointed the gun at my stomach and said:

'All I wanted was my rent. The place seems well taken care of. Nothing broken. He has always been a good tidy careful tenant. I just didn't want him to get too far behind in the rent.'

A fellow with a kind of strained and unhappy voice said politely: 'How far behind is he?'

'Three months,' she said. 'Two hundred and forty dollars. Eighty dollars is very reasonable for a place as well furnished as this. I've had a little trouble collecting before, but it always came out very well. He promised me a check this morning. Over the telephone. I mean he promised to give it to me this morning.'

'Over the telephone,' I said. 'This morning.'

I shuffled around a bit in an inconspicuous sort of way. The idea was to get close enough to make a side swipe at the gun, knock it outwards and then jump in fast before she could bring it back in line. I've never had a lot of luck with the technique, but you have to try it once in a while. This looked like the time to try it.

I made about six inches, but not nearly enough for a first down. I said: 'And you're the owner?' I didn't look at the gun directly. I had a faint, a very faint hope that she didn't know she was pointing it at me.

'Why, certainly. I'm Mrs Fallbrook. Who did you think I was?'

'Well, I thought you might be the owner,' I said. 'You talking about the rent and all. But I didn't know your name.' Another eight inches. Nice smooth work. It would be a shame to have it wasted.

'And who are you, if I may inquire?'

'I just came about the car payment,' I said. 'The door was open just a teeny weensy bit and I kind of shoved in. I don't know why.'

I made a face like a man from the finance company coming about the car payment. Kind of tough, but ready to break into a sunny smile.

'You mean Mr Lavery is behind in his car payments?' she asked, looking worried.

'A little. Not a great deal,' I said soothingly.

I was all set now. I had the reach and I ought to have the speed. All it needed was a clean sharp sweep inside the gun and outward. I started to take my left foot out of the rug.

'You know,' she said, 'it's funny about this gun. I found it on the stairs. Nasty oily things, aren't they? And the stair carpet is a very nice grey chenille. Quite expensive.'

And she handed me the gun.

My hand went out for it, as stiff as an eggshell, almost as brittle. I took the gun. She sniffed with distaste at the glove which had been wrapped around the butt. She went on talking in exactly the same tone of cockeyed reasonableness. My knees cracked, relaxing.

'Well, of course, it's much easier for you,' she said. 'About the car, I mean. You can just take it away, if you have to. But taking a house with nice furniture in it isn't so easy. It takes time and money to evict a tenant. There is apt to be bitterness and things get damaged, sometimes on purpose. The rug on this floor cost over two hundred dollars, second-hand. It's only a jute rug, but it has a lovely colouring, don't you think? You'd never know it was only jute, second-hand. But that's silly too because they're always second-hand after you've used them. And I walked over here too, to save my tires for the government. I could have taken a bus part way, but the darn things never come along except going in the wrong direction.'

I hardly heard what she said. It was like surf breaking beyond a point, out of sight. The gun had my interest.

I broke the magazine out. It was empty. I turned the gun and looked into the breech. That was empty too. I sniffed the muzzle. It reeked.

I dropped the gun into my pocket. A six-shot .25-calibre automatic. Emptied out. Shot empty, and not too long ago. But not in the last half-hour either.

'Has it been fired?' Mrs Fallbrook inquired pleasantly. 'I certainly hope not.'

'Any reason why it should have been fired?' I asked her. The voice was steady, but the brain was still bouncing.

'Well, it was lying on the stairs,' she said. 'After all, people do fire them.'

'How true that is,' I said. 'But Mr Lavery probably had a hole in his pocket. He isn't home, is he?'

'Oh no.' She shook her head and looked disappointed. 'And I don't think it's very nice of him. He promised me the check and I walked over—'

'When was it you phoned him?' I asked.

'Why, yesterday evening.' She frowned, not liking so many questions.

'He must have been called away,' I said.

She stared at a spot between my big brown eyes.

'Look, Mrs Fallbrook,' I said. 'Let's not kid around any more, Mrs Fallbrook. Not that I don't love it. And not that I like to say this. But you didn't shoot him, did you – on account of he owed you three months' rent?'

She sat down very slowly on the edge of a chair and worked the tip of her tongue along the scarlet slash of her mouth.

'Why, what a perfectly horrid suggestion,' she said angrily. 'I don't think you are nice at all. Didn't you say the gun had not been fired?'

'All guns have been fired sometime. All guns have been loaded sometime. This one is not loaded now.'

'Well, then—' she made an impatient gesture and sniffed at her oily glove.

'OK, my idea was wrong. Just a gag anyway. Mr Lavery was out and you went through the house. Being the owner, you have a key. Is that correct?'

'I didn't mean to be interfering,' she said, biting a finger. 'Perhaps I ought not to have done it. But I have a right to see how things are kept.'

'Well, you looked. And you're sure he's not here?'

'I didn't look under the beds or in the icebox,' she said coldly. 'I called out from the top of the stairs when he didn't answer my ring. Then I went down to the lower hall and called out again. I even peeped into the bedroom.' She lowered her eyes as if bashfully and twisted a hand on her knee.

'Well, that's that,' I said.

She nodded brightly. 'Yes, that's that. And what did you say your name was?'

'Vance,' I said. 'Philo Vance.'

'And what company are you employed with, Mr Vance?'

'I'm out of work right now,' I said. 'Until the police commissioner gets in a jam again.'

She looked startled. 'But you said you came about a car payment.'

'That's just part-time work,' I said. 'A fill-in job.'

She rose to her feet and looked at me steadily. Her voice was cold saying: 'Then in that case I think you had better leave now.'

I said: 'I thought I might take a look around first, if you don't mind. There might be something you missed.'

'I don't think that is necessary,' she said. 'This is my house. I'll thank you to leave now, Mr Vance.'

I said: 'And if I don't leave, you'll get somebody who will. Take a chair again, Mrs Fallbrook. I'll just glance through. This gun, you know, is kind of queer.'

'But I told you I found it lying on the stairs,' she said angrily. 'I don't know anything else about it. I don't know anything about guns at all. I — I never shot one in my life.' She opened a large blue bag and pulled a handkerchief out of it and sniffled.

'That's your story,' I said. 'I don't have to get stuck with it.'

She put her left hand to me with a pathetic gesture, like the erring wife in *East Lynne*.

'Oh, I shouldn't have done!' she cried. 'It was horrid of me. I know it was. Mr Lavery will be furious.'

'What you shouldn't have done,' I said, 'was let me find out the gun was empty. Up to then you were holding everything in the deck.'

She stamped her foot. That was all the scene lacked. That made it perfect.

'Why, you perfectly loathsome man,' she squawked. 'Don't you dare touch me! Don't you take a single step towards me! I won't stay in this house another minute with you. How *dare* you be so insulting—'

She caught her voice and snapped it in mid-air like a rubber band. Then she put her head down, purple hat and all, and ran for the door. As she passed me she put a hand out as if to stiff-arm me, but she wasn't near enough and I didn't move. She jerked the door wide and charged out through it and up the walk to the street. The door came slowly shut and I heard her rapid steps above the sound of its closing.

I ran a fingernail along my teeth and punched the point of my jaw with a knuckle, listening. I didn't hear anything anywhere to listen to. A six-shot automatic, fired empty.

'Something,' I said out loud, 'is all wrong with this scene.'

The house seemed now to be abnormally still. I went along the apricot rug and through the archway to the head of the stairs. I stood there for another moment and listened again.

I shrugged and went quietly down the stairs.

....

A RED DEATH

That night I went to the Cozy Room on Slauson. It was a small shack with plaster walls that were held together by tar paper, chicken wire, and nails. It stood in the middle of a big vacant lot, lopsided and ungainly. The only indication you got that it was inhabited was the raw pine plank over the door. It had the word 'Entrance' painted on it in dripping black letters.

It was a small room and very dark. The bar was a simple dictionary podium with a row of metal shelves behind it. The bartender was a stout woman named Ula Hines. She served gin or whiskey, with or without water, and unshelled peanuts by the bag. There were twelve small tables hardly big enough for two. The Cozy Room wasn't a place for large parties, it was there for men who wanted to get drunk.

Because it wasn't a social atmosphere Ula didn't invest in a jukebox or live music. She had a radio that played cowboy music and a TV, set on a chair, that only went on for boxing.

Winthrop was at a far table drinking, smoking, and looking mean.

'Evenin', Shaker,' I said. Shaker Jones was the name he went by when we were children in Houston. It was only when he became an insurance man that he decided he needed a fancy name like Winthrop Hughes.

Shaker didn't feel very fancy that night.

'What you want, Easy?'

I was surprised that he even recognized me, drunk as he was.

'Mofass sent me.'

'Wha' fo'?'

'He need some coverage down on the Magnolia Street apartments.'

Shaker laughed like a dying man who gets in the last joke.

'He got them naked gas heaters, he could go to hell,' Shaker said.

'He got sumpin' you want though, man.'

'He ain't got nuthin' fo' me. Nuthin'.'

'How 'bout Linda an' Andre?'

My Aunt Vel hated drunks. She did because she claimed that they didn't have to act all sloppy and stupid the way they did. 'It's all in they minds,' she'd say.

Shaker proved her point by straightening up and asking, in a very clear voice, 'Where are they, Easy?'

'Mofass told me t'get them papers from you, Shaker. He told me t'drive you out almost to 'em an' then you give me the papers an' I take you the whole way.'

'I pay you three hundred dollars right now and we cut Mofass out of it.'

I laughed and shook my head.

'I'll see ya tomorrow, Shaker.' I knew he was sober because he bridled when I called him that. 'Front'a Vigilance Insurance at eight-fifteen.'

I turned back to look at him before I went out of the door. He was sitting up and breathing deeply. I knew when I saw him that I was all that stood between Andre and an early grave.

I was in front of his office at the time I said. He was right out there waiting for me. He wore a double-breasted pearl-gray suit with a white shirt and a maroon tie that had dozens of little yellow diamonds printed on it. His left pinky glittered with gold and diamonds and his fedora hat had a bright red feather in its band. The only shabby thing about Shaker was his briefcase, it was frayed and cracked across the middle. That was Shaker to a T: he worried about his appearance but he didn't give a damn about his work.

'Where we headed, Easy?' he asked before he could slam the door shut.

'I tell ya when we get there.' I smiled at his consternation. It did me good to see an arrogant man like Shaker Jones go with an empty glass.

I drove north to Pasadena, where I picked up Route 66, called Foothill Boulevard in those days. That took us through the citrus-growing areas of Arcadia, Monrovia, and all the way down to Pomona and Ontario. The foothills were wild back then. White stone and sandy soil knotted with low shrubs and wild grasses. The citrus orchards were bright green and heavy with orange and yellow fruit. In the hills beyond roamed coyotes and wildcats.

The address for Linda and Andre was on a small dirt road called Turkel, just about four blocks off the main drag, Alessandro Boulevard. I stopped a few blocks away.

'Here we are,' I said in a cheery voice.

'Where are they?'

'Where them papers Mofass wanted?'

Shaker stared death at me for a minute, but then, when I didn't keel over, he put his hand into the worn brown briefcase and came out with a sheaf of about fifteen sheets of paper. He shoved the papers into my lap, turning a few pages back so he could point out a line that said 'Premiums'.

'That's what he wanted when we talked last December. Now where's Linda and Andre?'

I ignored him and started flipping through the documents.

Shaker was huffing but I took my time. Legal documents need a close perusal; I'd seen enough of them in my day.

'Man, what you doin'?' Shaker squealed at me. 'You cain't read that kinda document. You need to have law trainin' for that.'

Shaker was no lawyer. As a matter of fact, he hadn't finished the eighth grade. I had two part-time years of Los Angeles City College under my belt. But I scratched my head to show that I agreed with him.

I said, 'Maybe so, Shaker. Maybe. But I jus' got a question t'ask you here.'

'Don't you be callin' me Shaker, Easy,' he warned. 'That ain't my name no mo'. Now what is it you wanna know?'

I turned to the second to the last sheet and pointed to a blank line near the bottom of the page.

'Whas this here?'

'Nuthin',' he said quickly. Too quickly. 'The president of Vigilance gotta sign that.'

'It says, "the insurer or the insurer's agent." Thas you, ain't it?'

Shaker stared death at me a little more, then he snatched the papers and signed them.

'Where is she?' he demanded.

I didn't answer but I pulled back into the road and drove toward Andre and Linda's address.

Shaker's Plymouth was in the yard, hubcap-deep in mud.

'There you go,' I said, looking at the house.

'All right,' Shaker said. He got out of the car and so did I.

'Where you goin', Easy?'

'With you, Shaker.'

He bristled when I called him that again.

Then he said, 'You got what you want. It's my business here on out.'

I noticed that his jacket pocket hung low on the right side. That didn't bother me, though. I had a .25 hooked behind my back.

'I ain't gonna leave you t'kill nobody, Shaker. I ain't no lawyer, like you said, but I know that the police love what they call accessory before the fact.'

'Just stay outta my way,' he said. Then he turned toward the house, striding through the mud.

I stayed behind him, walking a little slower.

When he pushed through the front door I was seven, maybe eight, steps behind. I heard Linda scream and Andre make a noise something like a hydraulic lift engaging. The next thing I heard was crashing furniture. By that time I was going through the door myself.

It was a mess. A pink couch was turned on its back and big Linda was on the other side of it, sitting down and practicing how wide she could open her eyes. She was screaming too; loud, incoherent shrieks. Her wiry, straightened hair stood out from back of her head so that she resembled a monstrous chicken.

Shaker had a blackjack in one hand and he had Andre by the scruff of the neck with the other. Poor Andre sagged down trying to protect himself from the blows Shaker was throwing at him.

'Lemme go!' Andre kept shouting. Blood spouted from the center of his forehead.

Shaker obliged. He let Andre slump to the floor and dropped the sap. Then went for his jacket pocket. But by that time I was behind him. I grabbed his arm and pulled the pistol out of his pocket.

'What? What? What?' he asked.

I almost laughed.

'You ain't gonna kill nobody t'day, Shaker.'

'Get get get.' His eyes were glazed over, I don't think he had any idea of what was happening.

'You got some whiskey?' I asked Andre.

'In the kitchen.' Andre blinked his enormous eyes at me and made to rise. He was so shaken it took him two attempts to make it to his feet. Blood cascaded down his loose blue shirt. He was a mess.

'Get it,' I said.

Linda was still screaming. Her voice was already gone, though. Instead of a chicken she'd begun to sound like an old, hoarse dog barking at clouds.

I grabbed her by the shoulders and shouted, 'Shut up, woman!'

I heard something fall, and when I turned around I saw Shaker going at Andre again. He had him by the throat this time.

I boxed Shaker's ears, then I sapped him with the barrel of his gun. He hit the ground faster than if I had shot him.

'He was gonna kill me.' Andre sounded surprised.

'Yeah,' I said. 'You spendin' his money, drivin' his car, an' fuckin' his wife. He was gonna kill you.'

Andre looked like he didn't understand.

I went over to Linda and asked, 'How much of Shaker's money you got left?'

''Bout half.' The fear of death had knocked any lies she might have had right out of her head.

'How much is that?'

'Eighteen hundred.'

'Gimme sixteen.'

'What?'

'Gimme sixteen an' then you take two an' get outta here. That is, 'less you wanna go back with him?' I motioned my head toward Shaker's body.

Andre got the money. It was in a sock under the mattress.

While I counted out Linda's piece she was throwing clothes into a suitcase. She was scared because Shaker showed signs of coming to. It didn't fluster me, though. I would have liked to sap him again.

'Come on, baby,' Linda said to Andre once she was packed. She wore a rabbit fur and a red box hat.

'I just come from Juanita, Andre,' I said. 'Li'l Andre want you back, an' you know this trick is over.'

Andre hesitated. The side of his face was beginning to swell, it made him resemble his own infant son.

'You go on, Linda,' I said. 'Andre already got a family. And you cain't hardly take care of both of you on no two hundred dollars.'

'Andre!' Linda rasped.

He looked at his toes.

'Shit!' was the last word she said to him.

I said, 'There's a bus stop 'bout four blocks up, on Alessandro.'

She cursed me once and then she was gone.

'My car is the Ford out front,' I said to Andre after I watched Linda slog through the mud toward the end of their street. 'You go get in it an' I'll talk to the man here.'

Andre took a small bag from the closet. I laughed to myself that he was already packed to leave.

I sat and watched Shaker writhing on the floor and rolling his eyes. He wasn't aware yet. While enjoying the show I took three hundred dollars from the wad that Linda left. He came to his senses about fifteen minutes later. I was sitting in front of him, hugging the back of a folding chair. He looked up at me from his knees.

'Thirteen hundred was all they had left. Here you go,' I said, throwing the sock in his face.

'Where Linda?'

'She had somewhere to go.'

'Wit' Andre?'

'He's wit' me. I'ma take him home to his family.'

'I'ma kill that boy, Easy.'

'No you not, Shaker,' I said. ''Cause Andre is under my protection. You understand me? You best to understand, 'cause I will kill you if anything happens to him. I will kill you.'

'We had a deal, Easy.'

'An' I met it. You got your car, you got all the money that's left, an' you' wife don't want you; killin' Andre ain't gonna stop that. So leave it be or we gonna have it out, an' you know you ain't gonna win that one neither.'

Shaker believed me, I could see it in his eyes. As long as he thought I was a poor man he'd be scared of me. That's why I kept my wealth a secret. Everybody knows that a poor man's got nothing to lose; a poor man will kill you over a dime.

....

THE SECOND CURTAIN

Over a cup of tea in an Express Dairy Garner tried to recover the normal tempo of his life. He took out his notebook and unscrewed his fountain-pen, but these gestures no longer seemed to have meaning. He put the things away and inhaled the steam of his tea, staring into the distance. It was four-thirty: at seven o'clock he had a long-standing engagement to speak at the Centre of Contemporary Culture. He decided that he had time to go to the London Library. He drained his cup, recovered his hat, hold-all and raincoat, and thought how glad he would be when the pubs opened and he could take the edge off his weariness. He saw clearly how one became a boozer.

It was as he turned off Jermyn Street into Duke of York Street and stopped for a moment at the open window of the newsagent's shop to buy the *New Statesman* that he thought someone was following him. A man behind him had crossed the road and stood looking in the window of Herbert Jenkins: a man wearing a navy-blue raincoat or overcoat – Garner could not bring himself to turn his full gaze on the figure. Garner osten-tatiously read his copy of the *New Statesman* as he walked down to St James's Square and turned right past Chatham House. He tried to think what there had been in his interview with Chief

Inspector White that would make the police put a man on his tail.

At the top of the steps of the Library he pushed the door as he always did instead of pulling it, and while he fumbled he contrived to look back into the square. A few people were apparent among the parked cars but none of them was near. Garner went through the doors and up to one of the ladies sitting at the 'in' counter.

'Excuse me,' he said. 'I happen to have found a book belonging to the Library. I wonder if you could tell me easily who took it out?'

He had imagined that all that would be involved was a quick visit to the mysterious regions at the back of the entrance hall. But the lady looked puzzled.

'You are a subscriber?' she asked.

'Yes,' said Garner. 'But this isn't one of the books I've taken out myself. It's one that seems fortuitously to have come into my possession and I wondered whose it was.' He felt himself getting red: he should have come armed with a better story.

'Oh, I see,' said the lady. 'But I'm afraid we aren't allowed to disclose the names of subscribers. Of course, if you let me have the book we will ensure that the subscriber is advised that it has been returned to the Library.'

Garner was flummoxed. 'You *can* tell from your records, though,' he said, 'the name of the member who has a particular book out if one simply gives the name of the book.'

'Certainly, if there is only one copy of the book in the Library.' The lady looked at Garner rather oddly. 'But it is a strict rule that we mustn't divulge the member's name.'

'Yes,' said Garner. 'I appreciate that.'

'Have you the book with you?'

Garner's cheeks were burning. 'No, I haven't.' He could not leave behind an impression of complete dottiness. 'As a matter of fact,' he added, laughingly, 'I haven't *really* found a book belonging to another subscriber. I'm working out the plot of a murder story. I thought perhaps I could have a London Library book for a clue.'

'Oh, I see,' said the lady, dubiously.

'The amateur detective finds the book at the scene of the crime, gets the name of the man who borrowed it from the Library, and so is led to a vital witness. Only now I see that it wouldn't work.'

'No,' said the lady.

'Ah well,' said Garner. 'I must try to devise another clue. A pity.' He smiled ingratiatingly. 'So sorry to have wasted your time.'

'Oh, that is quite all right,' said the lady.

'Thank you,' said Garner, shuffling awkwardly away. 'Thank you very much.' As he escaped up the main staircase John Foster's clock tinkled out five o'clock. He would, he thought, have to return the bloody thing anonymously by post – and tell Viola of his ignominious defeat. And the Library had now become just one more place where he had reason for embarrassment, a metaphorical restaurant in which he had vomited.

On his way up to the Literature section he called in at the gentlemen's lavatory. He stood in the dark, single urinal, the acrid smell of the temple of Jupiter Ammon in his nostrils, and thought as he always thought what a splendid setting it would make for a Graham Greenesque spiritual crisis. Or the dumping ground for a body in a detective novel. And then he remembered the sense of pursuit he had had in Duke of York Street, and the hair-shirt of worry tickled him again.

He tried to reason clearly just why the police might be concerned about his movements, but the whole sequence of events since Widgery's disappearance seemed to lie under a fog of inexplicitness. Life was simply not like a detective novel: motives were not clear, events had not a single cause, things did not wholly explain themselves. And then, as usual, he looked into his own mind for the explanation.

Obviously, he was not in fact being followed: the dark figure opposite the Ladies' Turkish Bath was a product of his own sense of guilt. The Eumenides had no reality. He thought of his ambiguous relationship with Viola: the quietness, the increasing intimacy, the opportunities presenting themselves successively and his rejection of them one by one until his nerves were in shreds and he had been condemned to another sleepless night in that house. Had she been awake too? He shuddered at his inadequacies, and longed for the privacy and absorption he could find only in his own rooms, his own contrived life.

He emerged from the lavatory, continued up to Literature, found Humphry House's *The Dickens World* and came down the stairs again. While he was here, he thought, he might as well get the Bernard Van Dieren book. He was toying with the idea of writing an essay on Busoni, an essay that he might print in *Light*. He turned into the twilight of the rooms on the first floor and looked for the Music shelves. Here, only thick iron grids divided the rooms from the floor beneath. As he wandered along, switching the section lights on and off he became aware that underneath someone else was walking, following a parallel course. He stopped dead in the alley of books: in the comparative quiet that followed he heard a clank or two from the shoes of the man below on *his* grids, and then there was complete silence. At the Music shelves Garner crouched on his haunches, trying to peer, as he searched for *Down Among the Dead Men*, through the interstices of the iron floor. He was certain that somebody was down there, but that person could scarcely be looking for a book, for all was in darkness.

Garner found his book and stood up. The light he had switched on illuminated only a short section of the alley. On either side of him the tall shelves stretched into the increasing gloom. He felt a sudden compression in his chest, and an accession of childish fear. His hand hovered over the switch and then, with a wry gesture of concession to his folly, he left it on and walked back towards the main staircase.

He could not be sure whether or not he could hear those other footsteps. Perhaps there was some echo from his own. It was very late: the Library would shut at half-past five. In a momentary flurry of panic Garner wondered if it were not already that time, if the Library had not already closed its doors and left him marooned. He stopped again, switched on a light, and looked at his watch. It was five-fourteen. He pretended to examine the books on Medicine, straining his ears for sounds from below. And then he thought, with a clarity and conviction that brought him out in a sweat, that the police would never follow him *into* the Library: they would simply wait for him in that ideal waiting-place, St James's Square. The *Doppelgänger* underneath was someone who wished to harm him. As Widgery and Kershaw had been harmed, physically, cruelly.

Cunningly, his face taking on unconsciously an animal's expression, Garner walked without a sound *away* from the main staircase into the back store, and then tiptoed down two flights of wooden steps into the History basement. He came up another flight to the ground floor, and burst out, like a child from a dark corridor, into a lighted and populated room, into the main hall. It was almost with astonishment that he found everything normal – a bearded member glancing through the new foreign-language books in one of the cases in the middle of the floor, a member wearing a clergyman's collar having his books entered.

As his own books were being entered Garner kept looking back to the main staircase, but no one emerged from it. Really, he thought, his nerves were in extremely poor shape. He promised himself an early night: a long read in bed with the Dickens book and Van Dieren, a beaker of Ovaltine, and four aspirins.

....

PLAIN MURDER

On Sunday morning Morris woke at his usual time, and in response to what usually woke him – the noise of John and Molly playing in the next room. For a moment he experienced the usual depression, which turned to sleepy elation as he remembered that it was Sunday and that there was no need to get up immediately. With a murmured 'Bless those kids,' he turned over drowsily on to his other side to sleep again. It was a blessedly peaceful moment. He was just drifting off to sleep again when recollection came to him. He had to make a decision; the sudden shock of remembering this had him wide awake instantly. He began to go through his plan again, bit by bit, testing it, until he reached its consummation, and from there he proceeded onwards seeking out possible unpleasant consequences. In the end he decided that the plan was sound. Then in the laziness of Sunday morning he had to decide whether or not to carry it through.

Mary, dozing blissfully, suddenly began to appreciate the fact that her husband had turned towards her, and put out enquiring little hands to him under the bedclothes; but he ignored her, and when she persisted he hunched over again on to his other side so as to be free to think. For his plan to work really well called for the execution of it on a Sunday, so that if he did not act today he would have to wait a week, and a week might be too long.

Another essential part of the plan was the Sunday morning walk with the children, which would be a tiresome business. But on the other hand, in readiness for his decision, he had announced yesterday that he would take them, and it would be nearly as tiresome in its consequences to say that he had changed his mind. Young Reddy's life see-sawed in the balance as Morris lay idly in bed debating these factors for and against. Then the balance swayed down definitely and irrevocably as Morris arrived at a final decision. And having done so, Morris was able now to drift off again into a comfortable doze; he had that keen brain of his under better control now and he could restrain its activity better – largely, of course, because there was not so much exciting novelty about making plans now.

At breakfast it would have been difficult for anyone to discern any real difference in him. There might perhaps be an air of decision about him, a hard line or two round his mouth, which was not usually apparent. But he was not particularly abstracted to all seeming. Yet he may have appeared just a trifle anxious to start off in good time for that Sunday walk with the children.

'Where are we going, Daddy?' asked Molly as they left the house.

'Park,' replied Morris briefly. The air of decision was much more noticeable now, and he looked at his watch, and in consequence of the information gathered thereby he quickened his step, so that John in his push-chair felt he was really flying, while Molly had to trot beside him almost as fast as her short legs could carry her.

'Are we *really* goin' to the park, Daddy?' asked Molly. 'Oh, *Daddy!*'

For the park was a long way away, in a northerly direction (towards the district where Reddy lived), and it was so far away that Mrs Morris had rarely found time to take the children there. They had come to look upon it as a rarely attainable paradise.

Over the main road they went; they had to wait quite a long time before they could cross because there was so much traffic. There were plenty of motorcars setting out for the country, because this was a fine Sunday although a November one, and there were the usual trams and buses – the road was quite thick with traffic; and, although Morris fumed a little at the delay, he found the presence of so much traffic very gratifying somehow. Once across, they hurried by the side streets as fast as Morris could walk comfortably, and much faster than Molly could walk comfortably. But Morris strode along unheeding; he paid no attention and made no reply to the few conversational openings which Molly found breath to make. Then they came to another main road, and when they had crossed that and walked a few yards up the next road they reached a big iron gate with stone pillars, and, passing through, the whole wonderful view of the park was opened to them. John began to sing, and even Molly forgot how hot and tired she was.

But even in this lovely place Morris still appeared to be in a hurry, and he would not sit down on a seat and rest as Molly wanted him to do, nor would he go on to the grass and unstrap John from his chair as John wanted him to do. He hurried along the winding gravel paths, looking ahead as if he was seeking someone or something. Molly wanted to stop and look at the ducks being fed, but he did not bestow a glance upon them. They hurried round the lake with the rowing boats on it so fast that Molly could not see nearly as much as she wanted to see. The paths were full of Sunday morning people, and from every point of vantage Morris looked eagerly along the groups, as though searching for someone.

And then Morris ceased to hurry. He abandoned his rapid stride in favour of a gait much more leisurely and suitable for a fine Sunday morning.

'What did you say, dear?' he asked, bending down a little to catch Molly's childish comments on the beauties of the park.

Molly did not notice this magnificent condescension; she was merely pleased at at last having attention paid to her. Morris listened attentively; he took one hand off the back of the push-chair for Molly to hold, and the three of them went on very gently along the gravel path, with Molly holding her father's hand and chattering to him gaily. They made quite a pretty, leisurely picture; so it certainly appeared to the young fellow and his father who were approaching in the opposite direction.

'Why, it's Morris!' said Reddy suddenly. He turned a little pale at seeing him thus unexpectedly.

'Hello, old man,' said Morris. 'Good morning, Mr Reddy.'

He beamed at them in the pleasant winter sunshine.

'Good morning, sir,' said Mr Reddy. He had good old-fashioned ideas about being cordial towards his son's superior in the office.

'Isn't it a beautiful day?' said Morris. 'Taking the air, sir?'

'Yes, my son usually comes for a walk here with his old father on Sunday mornings,' said Mr Reddy, telling Morris exactly what he knew already.

'And I usually come for a walk here with my young son,' said Morris. 'John, Molly, say "How do you do" to Mr Reddy. And this is your Uncle John. That's your name, isn't it, Reddy?'

The children smiled shyly at the two strange men.

'And how old are you, Molly?' asked Mr Reddy.

'I'm nearly five,' whispered Molly.

The conversation followed stereotyped lines, with Reddy, rather pale and uneasy, in the background.

'Well, I must be moving on, I think,' announced Morris at length.

'Perhaps Mr Morris would come and have a cup of tea at home with us this afternoon, Johnny?' suggested Mr Reddy, still carefully cultivating a friendly attitude towards his son's official superior.

'Thank you,' said Morris; 'but I always spend Sunday afternoon with the wife and kiddies. Why don't you come over to tea, Reddy? Run over on the little mo'bike?'

Reddy did not specially want to; at the same time he had already learned by experience that an idle afternoon was terribly hard on his nerves. He hesitated visibly.

'You haven't got anything else to do, have you, Johnny?' asked Mr Reddy.

'No, Father.'

'Then of course you had better go.'

'That's fine,' said Morris. 'About four, old man?'

'All right,' said Reddy with an ill grace.

The party separated at the park gate, the children waving

goodbye to the two Reddys. Then Morris directed his way homeward again, striding out with the old vigour, Molly panting along at his side, and his pose as a kindly father completely vanished once more. He could picture the conversation going on at that moment between Reddy's father and Reddy; the old man accentuating the need for Reddy to be on the best of terms with Morris, and Reddy sulkily agreeing. The essential preliminaries of the plan had been accomplished marvellously well; now – there was roast mutton at home, and Morris was hungry. He did not even pause to leave the children outside a public-house while he went in for an appetizer. He hurried the children back along the side streets, over the main road and up the steep hill again to his home. A man of Morris's calculating and obstinate mind did not feel the stress of waiting very much. He ate his dinner with considerable appetite.

Mrs Morris was perfectly delighted with everything: with her husband's appetite, with the good food she had bought for her children and with the news that Reddy was coming to tea. He had paid flying visits once or twice before, and she was very struck with his nice gentlemanly manners and his cultivated accent. Mrs Morris did not know many men who would offer her a chair before sitting down themselves.

After dinner Morris was even able to doze for a time in his armchair, digesting his mutton and cabbage and baked potatoes, and stewed apples and synthetic custard. It was not merely that he was a man of steady nerve; it was largely because of a self-confidence amounting to vanity that he was able to await a crisis so calmly. But even he, once digestion was completed, grew just a little uneasy and restless and paced about the house for a while just before four o'clock. Then a motor-bicycle came roaring up the hill and stopped with a popping of the exhaust outside the gate, and Molly came running to her daddy with the announce-ment, 'He's come, Daddy.' Visitors to Morris's home were sufficiently rare to be exciting.

'Come on in, old man,' said Morris at the door. 'What about the old bus? Better not leave it in the road with all these kids about. That's the idea, stick it inside the gate. Here we are, then. You know Mrs Morris, don't you, old man?'

Morris's sham-bluff garrulity was not due to any nervous qualms about the immediate future. It was merely evidence of a conscious lack of good breeding. Reddy was brought into the sitting-room and the best chair was pushed forward for him, with Morris talking effusively, Mrs Morris wearing her best blouse, all of a pleased flutter, and the children, rather shy, standing near the door solemnly watching it all. All this fuss about a single visitor left Reddy rather bored and uncomfortable. He tried not to be snobbish, but he could not help noticing more than usual the traces of Morris's council school accent, and the unconsciously deferential tone in Mrs Morris's voice, and the awkward bad manners of the children. Tea, sitting up at the table, with thick bread and butter, and whispered reproofs darted at the children, who were reverting, as children will, from shyness to rowdiness, was more of an ordeal still. And when after tea Morris led him again to the fireside with the obvious intention of making further polite conversation Reddy was very bored and uncomfortable indeed.

It was even worse when Morris went out of the room and left him with Mrs Morris, who had no conversation at all. Morris was gone for quite ten minutes, and the interval seemed like hours to Reddy, while Mrs Morris sat opposite him painstakingly trying to make conversation and failing utterly. Some years of housekeeping on a four pounds ten a week income make a very poor training for acting as hostess to a good-looking young man twenty-one years of age and of good family. Mrs Morris was thoroughly uncomfortable as well by the time Morris came back into the sitting-room.

'You've been away a long time,' said Mrs Morris fretfully. 'What on earth have you been up to?'

'Oh, just looking after one or two things,' answered Morris, and the answer was deemed satisfactory, although anyone who paid serious consideration to the matter would have found it hard to have named any 'things' Morris might want to 'look after', or any particular reason why he should want to look after them just then. But Mrs Morris had long ago abandoned any attempt to account for her husband's actions.

Young Reddy rose to go, and Mrs Morris made no effort to

detain him. Although the prospect of a visit from a nice young man was always so stimulating, Mrs Morris found the actual event rather exhausting, and was glad when it came to an end. Morris himself was a little more pressing.

'Have you got to go, old man?' he said. 'That's a pity. I was looking forward to a long evening with you. It's a girl, I suppose, who demands your presence? No? We have to take your word for it, I suppose. Molly! John! Uncle John is going now.'

The two children came hurrying down the stairs; they were anxious not to miss the starting of that massive motor-bicycle which stood in the front garden and which savoured of hot oil in the most heavenly fashion.

It had fallen dark a little before. Reddy turned on his acetylene lamps and wheeled the machine out into the road at the corner, facing down the terrible slope. A new and delightful smell of acetylene came to the children's noses before Reddy struck a match and lighted his lamps. Everyone regarded him solemnly. Anyone who could have spared a glance for Morris might have seen hard lines round his tight-shut lips, giving him the same expression of savage resolution as he had worn at the moment when Harrison was shot.

Reddy said his farewells to the group; he shook hands with Mrs Morris, and he chucked Molly under the chin in the awkward fashion to be expected of a young man with no experience of children. He sought out John's hand and shook it.

'Goodbye, John,' he said.

'Goodbye,' piped John.

'Goodbye, old man,' said Morris. There was a flat kind of tone in his voice.

Reddy jerked up the stand to its catch, straddled the machine and thrust at the kick-starter. The engine broke into a roar. Reddy thrust once or twice with his feet, and as the bicycle began to run down the slope he put in his clutch. The clutch engaged for two or three yards while he adjusted the throttle controls, and then suddenly the note of the engine rose to a loud clamour which indicated that it was running free. Reddy's hand went automatically to the clutch. It hung curiously loose in its notch. It was a full two seconds before Reddy could realize that the drive to the back wheel was out of order. Actually the spring link of the driving chain had been weakened in some fashion – perhaps by unscrewing the nuts retaining it – and the chain now lay in the road fifty yards behind him. Reddy switched off the engine. He was already flying down that fearful hill; the manner in which the bicycle leaped at a bump in the road told him how fast he was travelling. He stretched out his fingers and gripped his brakes, first the rear one and then the front. And first the one lever and then the other came up at his touch without any show of resistance. The rods were pulling through the nuts at the points of adjustment; those nuts, too, must have worked loose somehow. By this time the bicycle was only a hundred yards from the main road, a hundred yards of steep hill in which to gather further velocity; and the main road across the foot of the hill was thronged with motorcars returning from a Sunday in the country, and with motor-buses, and with charabancs, and with tramcars. The bicycle covered that hundred yards in four seconds; just long enough for Reddy to realize with a gasp of fear the fate that lay before him. He felt icy cold; perhaps the strain of the last ten days had its effect on his nerve, too. He was sitting dazed and inert in the saddle as the motor-bicycle dashed silently and without warning into the mass of cross traffic. There was no possible hope for him; perhaps there would have been none had he kept his nerve. The bicycle rebounded with a crash from the side of a tramcar and a motorcar, although travelling at quite a moderate speed, pulled up too late. Several drivers had shouted in the flurry of the moment. They were silent now as they pulled up and got out to discover what damage had been done. A glance at the tangled mass of wreckage and the crumpled figure in the road told them that, almost instantly. But the rear wheel of the motor-bicycle, which somehow had escaped damage, stuck up grotesquely in the air and still revolved slowly.

ERNEST RAYMOND

....

WE, THE ACCUSED

The great pile of Trusted Church dreamed on its low hill. Even as its spire gazed over the green miles, and far away to the sea, so its spirit seemed to ponder on the centuries, and not on any momentary or transient activity at its foot.

But there was movement about the churchyard wall this sunny evening in July: a small movement and unobtrusive; almost stealthy. Three gates led through the wall into the churchyard: one at the westward corner, opening towards the great porch, one at the north, and one at the south-east, at the top of a tilted alley that ran its cobbles and gutters between the whitewashed cottages and the overhanging half-timbered houses. At each of these gates a policeman of the West Essex Constabulary quietly took up his stance, or quietly paced to and fro. The gates were sufficiently out of one another's sight for the policemen, at first, to excite but little attention. And their faces gave nothing away: from their expressions you might have thought them as little occupied with this present time, and as lost in the centuries, as the high spire above them. The house windows that looked upon the northern face of the church gave no heed to the two in their view; a tip-cart clattered past, and its driver did not turn his head; labourers turned into the bar of the Dun Horse Inn without a glance at the constable who paced before the western gate immediately opposite the bar door. The children of the village played farther down the hill, where the main street broadened into a wide market place; and from them the constable at the top of the cobbled alley was hidden. They went on with their play; and their voices, mingling with the birdsong in the churchyard trees, the clatter of a wagon round the corner, and the whistle of a far-off train, wove a texture that was more like silence than sound.

Nobody had noticed two very ordinary-looking men who had arrived in a car some time before, gone into the tobacconist's shop, come out again in about five minutes' time, and driven on to the rectory. There was no reason to notice them unless you remembered that Mr Neal, the tobacconist, was also the People's Warden up at the church. The two men had spent about a quarter of an hour in the rectory, and then come out and gone into the churchyard, just before the three constables walked up with their sergeant and diverged to their stations. They had walked through the gravestones to a white marble angel, the most conspicuous headstone of all, whose hand, stretched over her grave, seemed to be pointing whither to come. They stopped at the marble kerb about the grave and looked at the inscription. One of them drew the other's attention to the concluding text, as if he found it ironic in view of what they had come to do: 'Grant her Thy peace.' The other looked up to the battlemented wall of the church screening them on the right, and down to the row of lime trees at the foot of the slope, shutting out the meadows, and murmured, 'Good job it's on the south side and hidden from the houses. We shan't be disturbed here, I reckon.'

'Yes,' agreed his companion; 'and I tell you what, Clem; that angel's going to take some shifting.'

'You're right,' said the other. 'I'm glad they've got to do it, and not me.'

And both, since it didn't seem an occasion on which to talk much, lit up cigarettes and stood about with their hands in their pockets. Both were more interested than they pretended, for such a task as theirs this evening didn't come to them every day. The one addressed as Clem took from his pocket a typewritten sheet and read it again, his cigarette drooping from his lips. It was headed 'West Essex to wit' and proceeded:

Whereas I, Arnold Enfield Clarke, Coroner for the County of West Essex, have been informed that on the 15th day of October, 19— the body of one Elinor Presset was buried in the churchyard of your parish of Trusted in the said County and that there is reasonable ground to suspect that the said Elinor Presset died an unnatural death; and whereas I am of opinion that an inquest should be held upon the dead body: These are, therefore, by virtue of my office in His Majesty's name, to charge and command you that you forthwith cause the body of the said Elinor Presset to be taken up; And whereas I am satisfied that it is expedient to order the said body to be removed into the jurisdiction of Mr David Austen Home, Coroner for North Central London, who has consented to such removal: Now I hereby order that the said body shall be conveyed to the mortuary in the parish of Islington Vale in the County of London . . . Hereof, Fail not, as you will answer the contrary at your peril. Given under my hand and seal the —th day of July, One thousand and nine hundred and—

(*Signed*) Arnold Enfield Clarke.

To the Minister and Churchwardens of the said Parish of Trusted . . . To the Constables of the Metropolis and of the said County of West Essex.

Meantime a small blue motor van, coming from the direction of London, had stopped at the foot of the cobbled alley that led between its cottages to the churchyard gate. A large car following the van had not stopped but gone on, right round the bend of the street and past the north wall of the church and round into Battle Street, as if it had no part with the blue van nor interest in the church. A hundred yards up Battle Street it also stopped, and its doors swung open and four men stepped out.

The first was Dr Waterhall, in a suit darker and a hat at a less lively angle than usual. His manner was subdued and his voice low, to match a solemn occasion; but within he was thrilled and – well, 'happy' is perhaps an unfair word, but certainly he would rather have been in Battle Street, Trusted, this evening than anywhere else in England. No boredom tonight. In all his forty years of doctoring he had never had such an experience as was now to be his, and he was looking forward to it with deep interest. And how could he help hoping that they would ultimately find in the body that which they suspected: he *had* to hope it, both for his own justification and for the drama and excitement that would follow. These weighed more in the balance than the life of little Presset, because, dammit, if Presset had done the deed, he deserved all he'd get. One wasn't a sentimentalist about cold-blooded murderers.

He turned to murmur something to a thin, distinguished-looking, grey-moustached man who had stepped out after him, carrying a mackintosh on his arm. This man bore a very famous name; and he was plainly less impressed and less interested than Dr Waterhall, because he had attended at such a business many times before. With this man, in the journey from London, Dr Waterhall had been rather talkative, in a mixture of self-assertive equality and patent respect for a successful and well-known member of his own profession; and the grey-moustached man had been rather silent, for he was not deceived. He nodded now, as Dr Waterhall, feeling the church very close, spoke to him in a lowered tone; but he gave no other reply.

From the other door of the car Inspector Boltro had stepped out. He, like the doctor, was feeling his importance, and savouring to the full the interest of the hour. The word 'happy' must be given fearlessly to the Inspector's mood: he was engaged, he believed, on his greatest case and bringing it to a successful and ringing issue. Tomorrow the whole country would read of his activity in Trusted village this evening; his name would pass under the lintel of every house in the land. The old people in Wildean would be proud of their son and show the papers to their friends. And in the mean time he was enjoying all this secrecy which he himself had designed: it was spice in the hunter's game. He too hoped – hoped with all his heart – that the hunt would find what it sought; and the hope was as near a certainty as hope could be. It held only just enough of anxiety to make the moment thrilling.

After Inspector Boltro the undertaker stepped out; the same undertaker as we saw in this place before; keen featured, clean shaven and well tailored; moving on soft, considerate feet and speaking in low, reverent tones. He, perhaps, was more impressed with the evening's solemnity than they all; or, perhaps, he alone felt it incumbent on him to gather the solemnity between his folded hands and express it for them all in voice and movement and word.

'Well, gentlemen,' said the Inspector, who seemed to be in charge. 'We may as well go straight there, I think.'

'Right, Inspector,' agreed Dr Waterhall, who considered that, from his different professional angle, he also might be held to be in charge.

The grey-moustached analyst from the Home Office said nothing.

And the four men walked back down Battle Street towards the church: Dr Waterhall and the analyst in front, Inspector Boltro following, with the undertaker a respectful half-pace behind. They entered the churchyard by the western gate, the policeman on duty there saluting; and they walked round the great headland of the church till they saw the white angel in the midst of the tombs, with a little company of men about her.

'That is it,' said Dr Waterhall, pleased to take the lead. 'I was at the funeral;' and he went a few steps ahead, the analyst treading silently after him.

Through the untidy grass they picked their way towards the little company of people, which now contained, in addition to the two men from the Home Office, a party of gravediggers with planks and shovels and picks, a couple of stonemason's men, and the sergeant of the West Essex police. The four gentlemen took up positions at the grave's foot, and Inspector Boltro exchanged a few sentences with the sergeant, who then nodded to the stonemason's men and muttered, 'Right. Carry on.'

And the stonemason's men began. They separated the white kerbs and removed them to one side; they placed blocks of wood and rollers behind the statue and then, with mallet and chisel, they disconnected the statue from its brick foundation, prised it up, lowered it carefully on its back, and rolled it to a little distance away. There it lay, overthrown, its hand now pointing steadily and stupidly to the sky. They removed the brick foundations and stood back, leaving the diggers to continue the work.

The diggers went about their work with the quiet, whispering reverence of rough men. While the birds sang in the limes, fluttering the leaves as they hopped from branch to branch, and the voices of the children came up from the market place, and the flawless sky of a summer evening arched over their work, they opened the grave. The rest of the company stood watching without speaking, their eyes tranced into thought. So silent was it that one noticed many things which else had gone unremarked: the strong scent of carnations from a neighbouring grave, the overpowering scent of privet from a hedge to windward, and the scuttle of a rabbit down in the hollow under the limes. There was hardly a sound except the plat of the uplifted earth on to the mounting heap, and sometimes the rattle of a shovel on to a recumbent haft as the diggers tossed it down and took up a pick instead. The undertaker stood a yard or two behind the watching gentlemen, his hat in his hand and held against his breast. All were as reverent as if they were at a funeral; and indeed it was the scene of nine months before, reversed.

The operation was long, for the men had to excavate to a depth of nearly six feet. They paused often to wipe their brows with handkerchief or arm. The evening cooled, especially when a soft white cloud began to pass across the sun; and the grey-moustached gentleman put on the mackintosh which he had brought from London. Some of the watchers thought to themselves that they'd give anything to smoke, but none liked to be the first to do so; so they just stood, gazing in silence; or perhaps one of them walked a little way and looked at the other graves, their headstones and bright or faded flowers. But at length a spade's edge grated on the top of the coffin, and the digger, intending to refer only to the coffin, muttered, 'Here she is.'

Several heads craned forward, and the undertaker came with whispered apologies through the others to superintend the raising of the coffin; but suddenly the grey-moustached gentleman said 'Hold!' and instantly Inspector Boltro repeated, 'Hold a minute!' and all waited while the expert came and looked down.

Dr Waterhall also, as one with a right to do so, stepped forward and looked down. The analyst asked for some earth from the top of the coffin, and it was given him; and he walked away.

The diggers resumed their work; a spade scratched on the name-plate; and soon all was ready for the undertaker to instruct them how to get the webbing straps under the coffin. This was a task that gave them much difficulty, and for a time the quiet reverence was shattered by voices, and the birds seemed to chirrup louder, as if excited or alarmed by this new move. But after a while all was in order; and two men on each side of the grave stood on planks with the webbings in their hands.

'Right,' whispered the undertaker. 'Together now.'

The men pulled on the webbings, but the coffin came only an inch or two and stopped; and one of the men swung himself down into the grave and dislodged some more earth. His spade scraping along the lid of the coffin chafed the nerves. A fairway cleared, he swung himself above ground like a gymnast, and again the four men pulled on the webbings.

Slowly – ill balanced at first, then truly – the coffin came up . . . up . . . All the watchers bared their heads to salute this return of Elinor.

Its top rose above the lips of the grave; and Dr Waterhall watched with chin dropped Elinor rising again.

The coffin was now above ground, and all saw that the wood was in good condition but the metal fittings were rusted. The bearers were about to slide it on to the rollers, when the analyst said, 'Wait.'

'Wait!' repeated Inspector Boltro; and the men held it suspended.

Bending down and scraping with the edge of his hand, the analyst dislodged some earth from its side into a jar and took it away. The coffin slid on to the rollers.

Turning round, Dr Waterhall saw that the old verger of the church had wheeled up a trolley-bier. The men lifted the coffin on to this, covered it with a pall, and, at a nod from the Inspector and the undertaker, wheeled the trolley towards the western gate of the churchyard. Dr Waterhall and the analyst followed, leaving behind them a mound of upturned earth, a few men putting planks over a grave, and an overthrown angel whose guardianship had been violated.

At the western gate they saw the small blue van backed against the kerb, with a group of children and loafers standing by and gaping at the policeman. Across the road another little crowd had come to the door of the Dun Horse Inn. There was a movement of heads and a murmur of voices as the people saw another policeman, the sergeant, following behind the trolley. 'Keep back now; keep back,' begged the young policeman, as the trolley came through the gate and halted near the tail-board of the van.

'What is it? What's up?' demanded the people of one another.

'Looks as if the per-leace had been digging for trouble,' grunted one of the men.

'What's that? What's that you say?'

'Look's like an exhumation.'

'Will it be in the papers tomorrow?'

''Spect so.'

Inspector Boltro walked forward. Even before a little crowd of villagers he could not refrain from showing that he was really the man in authority. He issued directions, pointing with his arm; he talked importantly to the analyst and Dr Waterhall; he lifted his voice a little as he spoke to the sergeant. Here was the first ripple of that widening publicity. Tomorrow they would read of it, and say, 'That must have been Chief Inspector Boltro'; and for many months to come they would tell their friends that they had seen him. He stood there, the tallest figure of them all, watching the men as they slid the coffin, foot first, into the van.

'Right,' he said authoritatively as the door banged to.

He said a rather loud goodbye to the sergeant; and he, Dr Waterhall and the analyst, lighting up cigarettes, moved off to Battle Street, where their car waited – the undertaker staying behind with the van. A few curious children followed them and stood to gape, as they stepped into the car. The car which had been turned about drove off down Battle Street and Cutlers' Street, and, leaving the town behind, found the road to London. In a very little while Dr Waterhall, leaning back in his seat, saw the blue van ahead of them. They drew closer to it, but could not easily overtake and pass it by, because the road was winding and hilly. So for a time he sat staring at it, as it ran before them; and he thought, Thus Elinor returns to London. On past the green verges where the grass was high and the white of the cow-parsley lay like sea-spume; on between the hedgerows festooned and tangled with bindweed and tufted vetch, and aflower with dog-rose and bramble; down into a hollow where the bat willows stood silver-leaved and feathery, and then up again on to high ground where the fields of wheat and barley and winter oats stretched to either side; on beneath the chestnut, beech, and sycamore trees; on and on to London.

....

A DARK-ADAPTED EYE

On the morning Vera died I woke up very early. The birds had started, more of them and singing more loudly in our leafy suburb than in the country. They never sang like that outside Vera's windows in the Vale of Dedham. I lay there listening to something repeating itself monotonously. A thrush, it must have been, doing what Browning said it did and singing each song twice over. It was a Thursday in August, a hundred years ago. Not much more than a third of that, of course. It only feels so long.

In these circumstances alone one knows when someone is going to die. All other deaths can be predicted, conjectured, even anticipated with some certainty, but not to the hour, the minute, with no room for hope. Vera would die at eight o'clock and that was that. I began to feel sick. I lay there exaggeratedly still, listening for some sound from the next room. If I was awake my father would be. About my mother I was less sure. She had never made a secret of her dislike of both his sisters. It was one of the things which had made a rift between them, though there they were together in the next room, in the same bed still. People did not break a marriage, leave each other, so lightly in those days.

I thought of getting up but first I wanted to make sure where my father was. There was something terrible in the idea of encountering him in the passage, both of us dressing-gowned, thick-eyed wih sleeplessness, each seeking the bathroom and each politely giving way to the other. Before I saw him I needed to be washed and brushed and dressed, my loins girded. I could hear nothing but that thrush uttering its idiot phrase five or six times over, not twice.

To work he would go as usual, I was sure of that. And Vera's name would not be mentioned. None of it had been spoken about at all in our house since the last time my father went to see Vera. There was one crumb of comfort for him. No one knew. A man may be very close to his sister, his twin, without anyone knowing of the relationship, and none of our neighbours knew he was Vera Hillyard's brother. None of the bank's clients knew. If today the head cashier remarked upon Vera's death, as he very likely might, as people would by reason of her sex among other things, I knew my father would present to him a bland, mildly interested face and utter some suitable platitude. He had, after all, to survive.

A floorboard creaked in the passage. I heard the bedroom door close and then the door of the bathroom, so I got up and looked at the day. A clean white still morning, and no sun and no blue in the sky, a morning that seemed to me to be waiting because I was. Six-thirty. There was an angle you could stand at looking out of this window where you could see no other house, so plentiful were the trees and shrubs, so thick their foliage. It was like looking into a clearing in a rather elaborate wood. Vera used to sneer at where my parents lived, saying it was neither town nor country.

My mother was up now. We were all stupidly early, as if we were going away on holiday. When I used to go to Sindon I was sometimes up as early as this, excited and looking forward to it. How could I have looked forward to the society of Vera, an unreasonable carping scold when on her own with me, and when Eden was there the two of them closing ranks to exclude anyone who might try to penetrate their alliance? I hoped, I suppose. Each time I was older, and because of this she might change. She never did – until almost the end. And by then she was too desperate for an ally to be choosy.

I went to the bathroom. It was always possible to tell if my father had finished in the bathroom. He used an old-fashioned cut-throat razor and wiped the blade after each stroke on a small square of newspaper. The newspaper and the jug of hot water he fetched himself, but the remains were always left for my mother to clear away, the square of paper with its load of shaving soap full of stubble, the empty jug. I washed in cold water. In summer, we only lit the boiler once a week for baths. Vera and Eden bathed every day, and that was one of the things I *had* liked about Sindon, my daily bath, though Vera's attitude always was that I would have escaped it if I could.

The paper had come. It was tomorrow the announcement would appear, of course, a few bald lines. Today there was nothing about Vera. She was stale, forgotten, until this morning, when, in a brief flare-up, the whole country would talk of her, those who deplored and those who said it served her right. My father sat at the dining table, reading the paper. It was the *Daily Telegraph*, than which no other daily paper was ever read in our family. The crossword puzzle he would save for the evening, just as Vera had done, once only in all the years phoning my father for the solution to a clue that was driving her crazy. When Eden had a home of her own and was rich, she often rang him up and got him to finish the puzzle for her over the phone. She had never been as good at it as they.

He looked up and nodded to me. He didn't smile. The table had yesterday's cloth on it, yellow check not to show the egg stains. Food was still rationed, meat being very scarce, and we ate eggs all the time, laid by my mother's chickens. Hence the crowing cockerels in our garden suburb, the fowl runs concealed behind hedges of lonicera and laurel. We had no eggs that morning, though. No cornflakes either. My mother would have considered cornflakes frivolous, in their white-and-orange packet. She had disliked Vera, had no patience with my father's intense family love, but she had a strong sense of occasion, of what was fitting. Without a word, she brought us toast that, while hot, had been thinly spread with margarine, a jar of marrow and ginger jam, a pot of tea.

I knew I shouldn't be able to eat. He ate. Business was to be as usual with him, I could tell that. It was over, wiped away, a monstrous effort made, if not to forget, at least to behave as if all was forgotten. The silence was broken by his voice, harsh and stagey, reading aloud. It was something about the war in Korea. He read on and on, columns of it, and it became embarrassing to listen because no one reads like that without introduction, explanation, excuse. It must have gone on for ten minutes. He read to the foot of the page, to where presumably you were told the story was continued inside. He didn't turn over. He broke off in mid-sentence. 'In the Far,' he said, never getting to 'East' but laying the paper down, aligning the pages, folding it once, twice, and once more, so that it was back in the shape it had been when the boy pushed it through the letterbox.

'In the Far' hung in the air, taking on a curious significance, quite different from what the writer had intended. He took another piece of toast but got no further towards eating it. My mother watched him. I think she had been tender with him once but he had had no time for it or room for it and so her tenderness had withered for want of encouragement. I did not expect her to go to him and take his hand or put her arms round him. Would I have done so myself if she had not been there? Perhaps. That family's mutual love had not usually found its expression in outward show. In other words, there had not been embraces. The twins, for instance, did not kiss each other, though the women pecked the air around each other's faces.

It was a quarter to eight now. I kept repeating over and over to myself (like the thrush, now silent), 'In the Far, in the Far.' When first it happened, when he was told, he went into paraoxysms of rage, of disbelief, of impotent protest.

'Murdered, murdered!' he kept shouting, like someone in an Elizabethan tragedy, like someone who bursts into a castle hall with dreadful news. And then, 'My sister!' and 'My poor sister!' and 'My little sister!'

But silence and concealment fell like a shutter. It was lifted briefly, after Vera was dead, when, sitting in a closed room after dark, like conspirators, he and I heard from Josie what happened that April day. He never spoke of it again. His twin was erased from his mind and he even made himself – incredibly – into an only child. Once I heard him tell someone that he had never regretted having no brothers or sisters.

It was only when he was ill and not far from death himself that he resurrected memories of his sisters. And the stroke he had had, as if by some physiological action stripping away layers of reserve and inhibition, making him laugh sometimes and just as often cry, released an unrestrained gabbling about how he had felt that summer. His former love for Vera the repressive years had turned to repulsion and fear, his illusions broken as much by the tug-of-war and Eden's immorality – his word, not mine – as by the murder itself. My mother might have said, though she did not, that at last he was seeing his sisters as they really were.

He left the table, his tea half-drunk, his second piece of toast lying squarely in the middle of his plate, the *Telegraph* folded and lying with its edges compulsively lined up to the table corner. No word was spoken to my mother and me. He went upstairs, he came down, the front door closed behind him. He would walk the leafy roads, I thought, making detours, turning the half-mile to the station into two miles, hiding from the time in places where there were no clocks. It was then that I noticed he had left his watch on the table. I picked up the paper and there was the watch underneath.

'We should have gone away somewhere,' I said.

My mother said fiercely, 'Why should we? She hardly ever came here. Why should we let her drive us away?'

'Well, we haven't,' I said.

I wondered which was right, the clock on the wall that said five to eight or my father's watch that said three minutes to. My own watch was upstairs. Time passes so slowly over such points in it. There still seemed an aeon to wait. My mother loaded the tray and took it into the kitchen, making a noise about it, banging cups, a way of showing that it was no fault of hers. Innocent herself, she had been dragged into this family by marriage, all unknowing. It was another matter for me, who was of their blood.

I went upstairs. My watch was on the bedside table. It was new, a present bestowed by my parents for getting my degree. That, because of what had happened, it was a less good degree than everyone had expected, no one had commented upon. The watch face was small, not much larger than the cluster of little diamonds in my engagement ring that lay beside it, and you had to get close up to it to read the hands. I thought: In a moment the heavens will fall, there will be a great bolt of thunder. Nature could not simply ignore. There was nothing. Only the birds had become silent, which they would do anyway at this time, their territorial claims being made, their trees settled on, the business of their day begun. What would the business of my day be? One thing I thought I would do. I would phone Helen, I would talk to Helen. Symbolic of my attitude to my engagement, my future marriage, this was, that it was to Helen I meant to fly for comfort, not the man who had given me the ring with a diamond cluster as big as a watch face.

I walked over to the bedside table, stagily, self-consciously, like a bad actress in an amateur production. The director would have halted me and told me to do it again, to walk away and do it again. I nearly did walk away so as not to see the time. But I picked up the watch and looked and had a long, rolling, falling feeling through my body as I saw that I had missed the moment. It was all over now and she was dead. The hands of the watch stood at five past eight.

The only kind of death that can be accurately predicted to the minute had taken place, the death that takes its victim,

> . . . feet foremost through the floor,
> Into an empty space.

DOROTHY B. HUGHES

....

IN A LONELY PLACE

It was good standing there on the promontory overlooking the evening sea, the fog lifting itself like gauzy veils to touch his face. There was something in it akin to flying; the sense of being lifted high above crawling earth, of being a part of the wildness of air. Something, too, of being closed within an unknown and strange world of mist and cloud and wind. He'd liked flying at night; he'd missed it after the war had crashed to a finish and dribbled to an end. It wasn't the same flying a little private crate. He'd tried it; it was like returning to the stone ax after precision tools. He had found nothing yet to take the place of flying wild.

It wasn't often he could capture any part of that feeling of power and exhilaration and freedom that came with loneness in the sky. There was a touch of it here, looking down at the ocean rolling endlessly in from the horizon; here high above the beach road with its crawling traffic, its dotting of lights. The outline of beach houses zigzagged against the sky but did not obscure the pale waste of sand, the dark restless waters beyond.

He didn't know why he hadn't come out here before. It wasn't far. He didn't even know why he'd come tonight. When he got on the bus, he had no destination. Just the restlessness. And the bus brought him here.

He put out his hand to the mossy fog as if he would capture

it, but his hand went through the gauze and he smiled. That too was good, his hand was a plane passing through a cloud. The sea air was good to smell, the darkness was soft closed around him. He swooped his hand again through the restless fog.

He did not like it when on the street behind him a sudden bus spattered his peace with its ugly sound and smell and light. He was sharply angry at the intrusion. His head darted around to vent his scowl. As if the lumbering box had life as well as motion and would shrink from his displeasure. But as his head turned, he saw the girl. She was just stepping off the bus. She couldn't see him because he was no more than a figure in the fog and dark; she couldn't know he was drawing her on his mind as on a piece of paper.

She was small, dark haired, with a rounded face. She was more than pretty, she was nice looking, a nice girl. Sketched in browns, the brown hair, brown suit, brown pumps and bag, even a small brown felt hat. He started thinking about her as she was stepping off the bus; she wasn't coming home from shopping, no parcels; she wasn't going to a party, the tailored suit, sensible shoes. She must be coming from work; that meant she descended from the Brentwood bus at this lonely corner every night at – he glanced at the luminous dial of his watch – seven-twenty. Possibly she had worked late tonight, but that could be checked easily. More probably she was employed at a studio, close at six, an hour to get home.

While he was thinking of her, the bus had rumbled away and she was crossing the slant intersection, coming directly towards him. Not to him; she didn't know he was there in the high foggy dark. He saw her face again as she passed under the yellow fog light, saw that she didn't like the darkness and fog and loneness. She started down the California Incline; he could hear her heels striking hard on the warped pavement as if the sound brought her some reassurance.

He didn't follow her at once. Actually, he didn't intend to follow her. It was entirely without volition that he found himself moving down the slant, winding walk. He didn't walk hard, as she did, nor did he walk fast. Yet she heard him coming behind her. He knew she heard him for her heel struck an extra beat, as if she had half stumbled, and her steps went faster. He didn't walk faster, he continued to saunter but he lengthened his stride, smiling slightly. She was afraid.

He could have caught up to her with ease but he didn't. It was too soon. Better to hold back until he had passed the humped midsection of the walk, then to close in. She'd give a little scream, perhaps only a gasp, when he came up beside her. And he would say softly: 'Hello.' Only 'Hello,' but she would be more afraid.

She had just passed over the mid hump, she was on the final stretch of down grade. Walking fast. But as he reached that section, a car turned at the corner below, throwing its blatant light up on her, on him. Again anger plucked at his face; his steps slowed. The car speeded up the Incline, passed him, but the damage was done, the darkness had broken. As if it were a parade, the stream of cars followed the first car, scratching their light over the path and the road and the high earthern Palisades across. The girl was safe; he could feel the relaxation in her footsteps. Anger beat him like a drum.

When he reached the corner, she was already crossing the street, a brown figure under the yellow fog light marking the intersection. He watched her cross, reach the opposite pavement and disappear behind the dark gate of one of the three houses huddled together there. He could have followed but the houses were lighted, someone was waiting for her in the home light. He would have no excuse to follow to her door.

As he stood there, a pale blue bus slid up to the corner; a middle-aged woman got out. He boarded it. He didn't care where it was going; it would carry him away from the fog light. There were only a few passengers, all women, drab women. The driver was an angular, farm-looking man; he spun his change box with a ratcheting noise and looked into the night. The fare was a nickel.

Within the lighted box they slid past the dark cliffs. Across the width of the road were the massive beach houses and clubs, shutting away the sea. Fog stalked silently past the windows. The bus made no stops until it reached the end of that particular section of road where it turned an abrupt corner. He got out when it stopped. Obviously it was leaving the sea now, turning up into the dark canyon. He stepped out and he walked the short block to a little business section. He didn't know why until he reached that corner, looked up the street. There were several eating places, hamburger stands; there was a small drugstore and there was a bar. He wanted a drink.

It was a nice bar, from the ship's prow that jutted upon the sidewalk to the dim ship's interior. It was a man's bar, although there was a dark-haired, squawk-voiced woman in it. She was with two men and they were noisy. He didn't like them. But he liked the old man with the white chin whiskers behind the bar. The man had the quiet competent air of a sea captain.

He ordered straight rye but when the old man set it in front of him, he didn't want it. He drank it neat but he didn't want it. He hadn't needed a drink; he'd relaxed on the bus. He wasn't angry with anyone anymore. Not even with the three noisy sons of bitches up front at the bar.

The ship's bells behind the bar rang out the hour, eight bells. Eight o'clock. There was no place he wanted to go, nothing he wanted to do. He didn't care about the little brown girl anymore. He ordered another straight rye. He didn't drink it when it came, he left it there in front of him, not even wanting to drink it.

He could go across to the beach, sit in the sand, and smell the fog and sea. It would be quiet and dark there. The sea had appeared again just before the bus turned; there was open beach across. But he didn't move. He was comfortable where he was. He lit a cigarette and idly turned the jigger of rye upon the polished wood of the bar. Turned it without spilling a drop.

....

STRANGERS ON A TRAIN

'There's two kinds of guys!' Bruno announced in a roaring voice, and stopped.

Guy caught a glimpse of himself in a narrow panel mirror on the wall. His eyes looked frightened, he thought, his mouth grim, and deliberately he relaxed. A golf club nudged him in the back. He ran his fingertips over its cool varnished surface. The inlaid metal in the dark wood recalled the binnacle on Anne's sailboat.

'And essentially one kind of women!' Bruno went on. 'Two-timers. At one end it's two-timing and the other end it's a whore! Take your choice!'

'What about women like your mother?'

'I never seen another woman like my mother,' Bruno declared. 'I never seen a woman take so much. She's good-looking, too, lots of men friends, but she doesn't fool around with them.'

Silence.

Guy tapped another cigarette on his watch and saw it was ten-thirty. He must go in a moment.

'How'd you find out about your wife?' Bruno peered up at him.

Guy took his time with his cigarette.

'How many'd she have?'

'Quite a few. Before I found out.' And just as he assured himself it made no difference at all now to admit it, a sensation as of a tiny whirlpool inside him began to confuse him. Tiny, but realer than the memories somehow, because he had uttered it. Pride? Hatred? Or merely impatience with himself, because all that he kept feeling now was so useless? He turned the conversation from himself. 'Tell me what else you want to do before you die?'

'Die? Who said anything about dying? I got a few crack-proof rackets doped out. Could start one some day in Chicago or New York, or I might just sell my ideas. And I got a lot of ideas for perfect murders.' Bruno looked up again with that fixity that seemed to invite challenge.

'I hope your asking me here isn't part of one of your plans.' Guy sat down.

'Jesus Christ, I *like* you, Guy! I really do!'

The wistful face pled with Guy to say he liked him, too. The loneliness in those tiny, tortured eyes! Guy looked down embarrassedly at his hands. 'Do all your ideas run to crime?'

'Certainly not! Just things I want to do, like – I want to give a guy a thousand dollars some day. A beggar. When I get my own dough, that's one of the first things I'm gonna do. But didn't you ever feel you wanted to steal something? Or kill somebody? You must have. Everybody feels those things. Don't you think some people get quite a kick out of killing people in wars?'

'No,' Guy said.

Bruno hesitated. 'Oh, they'd never admit it, of course, they're afraid! But you've had people in your life you'd have liked out of the way, haven't you?'

'No.' Steve, he remembered suddenly. Once he had even thought of murdering him.

Bruno cocked his head. 'Sure you have. I see it. Why don't you admit it?'

'I may have had fleeting ideas, but I'd never have done anything about them. I'm not that kind of person.'

'That's exactly where you're wrong! Any kind of person can murder. Purely circumstances and not a thing to do with temperament! People get so far – and it takes just the least little thing to push them over the brink. Anybody. Even your grandmother. I know.'

'I don't happen to agree,' Guy said tersely.

'I tell you I came near murdering my father a thousand times! Who'd you ever feel like murdering? The guys with your wife?'

'One of them,' Guy murmured.

'How near did you come?'

'Not near at all. I merely thought of it.' He remembered the sleepless nights, hundreds of them, and the despair of peace unless he avenged himself. Could something have pushed him over the line then? He heard Bruno's voice mumbling, 'You were a hell of a lot nearer than you think, that's all I can say.' Guy gazed at him puzzledly. His figure had the sickly, nocturnal look of a croupier's, hunched on shirt-sleeved forearms over the table, thin head hanging. 'You read too many detective stories,' Guy said, and having heard himself, did not know where the words had come from.

'They're good. They show all kinds of people can murder.'

'I've always thought that's exactly why they're bad.'

'Wrong again!' Bruno said indignantly. 'Do you know what percentage of murders get put in the papers?'

'I don't know and I don't care.'

'One-twelfth. One-twelfth! Just imagine! Who do you think the other eleven-twelfths are? A lot of little people that don't matter. All the people the cops know they'll never catch.' He started to pour more scotch, found the bottle empty, and dragged himself up. A gold penknife flashed out of his trousers pocket on a gold chain fine as a string. It pleased Guy aesthetically, as a beautiful piece of jewelry might have. And he found himself thinking, as he watched Bruno slash round the top of a scotch bottle, that Bruno might murder one day with the little penknife, that he would probably go quite free, simply because he wouldn't much care whether he were caught or not.

Bruno turned, grinning, with the new bottle of scotch. 'Come to Santa Fe with me, huh? Relax for a couple of days.'

'Thanks, I can't.'

'I got plenty of dough. Be my guest, huh?' He spilled scotch on the table.

'Thanks,' Guy said. From his clothes, he supposed, Bruno thought he hadn't much money. They were his favorite trousers, these gray flannels. He was going to wear them in Metcalf and Palm Beach, too, if it wasn't too hot. Leaning back, he put his hands in his pockets and felt a hole at the bottom of the right one.

'Why not?' Bruno handed him his drink. 'I like you a lot, Guy.'

'Why?'

'Because you're a good guy. Decent, I mean. I meet a lot of guys – no pun – but not many like you. I admire you,' he blurted, and sank his lips into his glass.

'I like you, too,' said Guy.

'Come with me, huh? I got nothing to do for two or three days till my mother comes. We could have a swell time.'

'Pick up somebody else.'

'Cheeses, Guy, what d'you think I do, go around picking up travelling companions? I like you, so I ask you to come with me. One day even. I'll cut right over from Metcalf and not even go to El Paso. I'm supposed to see the Canyon.'

'Thanks, I've got a job as soon as I finish in Metcalf.'

'Oh.' The wistful, admiring smile again. 'Building something?'

'Yes, a country club.' It still sounded strange and unlike himself, the last thing he would have thought he'd be building, two months ago. 'The new Palmyra in Palm Beach.'

'Yeah?'

Bruno had heard of the Palmyra Club, of course. It was the biggest in Palm Beach. He had even heard they were going to build a new one. He had been to the old one a couple of times.

'You designed it?' He looked down at Guy like a hero-worshipping little boy. 'Can you draw me a picture of it?'

Guy drew a quick sketch of the buildings in the back of Bruno's address book and signed his name, as Bruno wanted. He explained the wall that would drop to make the lower floor one great ballroom extending on to the terrace, the louvre windows he hoped to get permission for that would eliminate air-conditioning. He grew happy as he talked, and tears of excitement came in his eyes, though he kept his voice low. How could he talk so intimately to Bruno, he wondered, reveal the very best of himself? Who was less likely to understand than Bruno?

'Sounds terrific,' Bruno said. 'You mean, you tell them how it's gonna look?'

'No. One has to please quite a lot of people.' Guy put his head back suddenly and laughed.

'You're gonna be famous, huh? Maybe you're famous now.'

There would be photographs in the news magazines, perhaps something in the newsreels. They hadn't passed on his sketches yet, he reminded himself, but he was so sure they would. Myers, the architect he shared an office with in New York was sure. Anne was positive. And so was Mr Brillhart. The biggest commission of his life. 'I might be famous after this. It's the kind of thing they publicize.'

Bruno began to tell him a long story about his life in college, how he would have became a photographer if something hadn't happened at a certain time with his father. Guy didn't listen. He sipped his drink absently, and thought of the commissions that would come after Palm Beach. Soon, perhaps, an office building in New York. He had an idea for an office building in New York, and he longed to see it come into being. Guy Daniel Haines. *A name*. No longer the irksome, never quite banished awareness that he had less money than Anne.

'Wouldn't it, Guy?' Bruno repeated.

'What?'

Bruno took a deep breath. 'If your wife made a stink now about the divorce. Say she fought about it while you were in Palm Beach and made them fire you, wouldn't that be motive enough for murder?'

'Of Miriam?'

'Sure.'

'No,' Guy said. But the question disturbed him. He was afraid Miriam had heard of the Palmyra job through his mother, that she might try to interfere for the sheer pleasure of hurting him.

'When she was two-timing you, didn't you feel like murdering her?'

'No. Can't you get off the subject?' For an instant Guy saw both halves of his life, his marriage and his career, side by side as he felt he had never seen them before. His brain swam sickeningly, trying to understand how he could be so stupid and helpless in one and so capable in the other. He glanced at Bruno, who still stared at him, and feeling slightly befuddled, set his glass on the table and pushed it fingers' length away.

'You must have wanted to once,' Bruno said with gentle, drunken persistence.

'No.' Guy wanted to get out and take a walk, but the train kept on and on in a straight line, like something that would never stop. Suppose Miriam did lose him the commission. He was going to live there several months, and he would be expected to keep on a social par with the directors. Bruno understood such things very well. He passed his hand across his moist forehead. The difficulty was, of course, that he wouldn't know what was in Miriam's mind until he saw her. He was tired, and when he was tired, Miriam could invade him like an army. It had happened so often in the two years it had taken him to burn loose of his love for her. It was happening now. He felt sick of Bruno. Bruno was smiling.

'Shall I tell you one of my ideas for murdering my father?'

'No,' Guy said. He put his hand over the glass Bruno was about to refill.

'Which do you want, the busted light socket in the bathroom or the carbon monoxide garage?'

'Do it and stop talking about it!'

'I'll do it, don't think I won't! Know what else I'll do some day? Commit suicide if I happen to feel like committing suicide, and fix it so it looks like my worst enemy murdered me.'

Guy looked at him in disgust. Bruno seemed to be growing indefinite at the edges, as if by some process of deliquescence. He seemed only a voice and a spirit now, the spirit of evil. All he despised, Guy thought, Bruno represented. All the things he would not want to be, Bruno was, or would become.

'Want me to dope out a perfect murder of your wife for you? You might want to use it some time.' Bruno squirmed with self-consciousness under Guy's scrutiny.

Guy stood up. 'I want to take a walk.'

Bruno slammed his palms together. 'Hey! Cheeses, what an idea! We murder for each other, see? I kill your wife and you kill my father! We meet on the train, see, and nobody knows we know each other! Perfect alibis! Catch?'

The wall before his eyes pulsed rhythmically, as if it were about to spring apart. *Murder*. The word sickened him, terrified him. He wanted to break away from Bruno, get out of the room, but a nightmarish heaviness held him. He tried to steady himself by straightening out the wall, by understanding what Bruno was saying, because he could feel there was logic in it somewhere, like a problem or a puzzle to be solved.

Bruno's tobacco-stained hands jumped and trembled on his knees. 'Air-tight alibis!' he shrieked. 'It's the idea of my life! Don't you get it? I could do it some time when you're out of town and you could do it when I was out of town.'

Guy understood. No one could ever, possibly, find out.

'It would give me a great pleasure to stop a career like Miriam's and to further a career like yours.' Bruno giggled. 'Don't you agree she ought to be stopped before she ruins a lot of other people? Sit down, Guy!'

She hasn't ruined me, Guy wanted to remind him, but Bruno gave him no time.

'I mean, just supposing the set-up was that. Could you do it? You could tell me all about where she lived, you know, and I could do the same for you, as good as if you lived there. We could leave fingerprints all over the place and only drive the dicks batty!' He snickered. 'Months apart, of course, and strictly no communication. Christ, it's a cinch!' He stood up and nearly toppled, getting his drink. Then he was saying, right in Guy's face, with suffocating confidence: 'You could do it, huh, Guy? Wouldn't be any hitches, I swear. I'd fix everything, I swear, Guy.'

Guy thrust him away, harder than he had intended. Bruno rose resiliently from the window seat. Guy glanced about for air, but the walls presented an unbroken surface. The room had become a little hell. What was he doing here? How and when had he drunk so much?

'I'm positive you *could*!' Bruno frowned.

Shut up with your damned theories, Guy wanted to shout back, but instead his voice came like a whisper: 'I'm sick of this.'

He saw Bruno's narrow face twist then in a queer way – in a smirk of surprise, a look that was eerily omniscient and hideous. Bruno shrugged affably.

'OK. I still say it's a good idea and we got the absolutely perfect set-up right here. It's the idea I'll use. With somebody else, of course. Where are you going?'

Guy had at last thought of the door. He went out and opened another door on to the platform where the cooler air smashed him like a reprimand and the train's voice rose to an upbraiding blare. He added his own curses of himself to the wind and the train, and longed to be sick.

'Guy?'

Turning, he saw Bruno slithering past the heavy door.

'Guy, I'm sorry.'

'That's all right,' Guy said at once, because Bruno's face shocked him. It was doglike in its self-abasement.

'Thanks, Guy.' Bruno bent his head, and at that instant the pound-pound-pound of the wheels began to die away, and Guy had to catch his balance.

He felt enormously grateful, because the train was stopping. He slapped Bruno's shoulder. 'Let's get off and get some air!'

They stepped out into a world of silence and total blackness.

'The hell's the idea?' Bruno shouted. 'No lights!'

Guy looked up. There was no moon either. The chill made his body rigid and alert. He heard the homely slap of a wooden door somewhere. A spark grew into a lantern ahead of them, and a man ran with it towards the rear of the train where a box-car door unrolled a square of light. Guy walked slowly towards the light, and Bruno followed him.

Far away on the flat black prairie a locomotive wailed, on

and on, and then again, farther away. It was a sound he remembered from childhood, beautiful, pure, lonely. Like a wild horse shaking a white man. In a burst of companionship, Guy linked his arm through Bruno's.

'I don't *wanna* walk!' Bruno yelled, wrenching away and stopping. The fresh air was wilting him like a fish.

The train was starting. Guy pushed Bruno's big loose body aboard.

'Nightcap?' Bruno said dispiritedly at his door, looking tired enough to drop.

'Thanks, I couldn't.'

Green curtains muffled their whispers.

'Don't forget to call me in the morning. I'll leave the door unlocked. If I don't answer, come on in, huh?'

Guy lurched against the walls of green curtains as he made his way to his berth.

Habit made him think of his book as he lay down. He had left it in Bruno's room. His Plato. He didn't like the idea of its spending the night in Bruno's room, or of Bruno's touching it and opening it.

···

PHANTOM LADY

She'd already been perched on the stool several minutes when he first became aware of her. And that was all the more unusual, in that there were only a scattering of others at the bar as yet; her arrival should have been that much more conspicuous. It only showed how unobtrusively she must have approached and settled into place.

It was at the very beginning of his turn of duty, so her arrival must have occurred only moments after his own taking up of position behind the bar, almost as though she had timed it that way: to arrive when he did. She had not yet been there when he first stepped out of the locker-room in freshly-starched jacket and glanced about his domain-to-be, that much he was sure of. At any rate, turning away from waiting on a man down at the other end, he became aware of her sitting there quiescently, and immediately approached.

'Yes, miss?'

Her eyes held his in a peculiarly sustained look, he thought. And then immediately thought, in postscript, that he must be mistaken, he must be only imagining it. All customers looked at him when they gave an order, for he was the means of bringing it to them.

In this gaze of hers there was a difference, though; the impression returned a second time, after having been discarded once. It was a personalized look. A look in its own right, with the giving of the order the adjunct, and not just an adjunct to the giving of the order. It was a look at *him*, the *man* to whom she was addressing the order, meant for him in his own right. It was a look that said: 'Take note of me. Mark me well.'

She asked for a little whiskey with water. As he turned away to get it, her eyes remained on him to the last. He had a trivial and fleeting feeling of being at a loss, of being unable to account for her bizarre scrutiny, that evaporated again almost as soon as it had risen. That did not bother him much, that was just there and gone again, at first.

Thus, the beginnings of it.

He brought her drink, and turned away immediately to wait on someone else.

An interval elapsed. An interval during which he did not think of her again, had forgotten her. An interval during which there should have been some slight alteration in her position, if only a shift of her hand, a raising or edging of her glass, a look elsewhere about the room. There wasn't. She sat there not moving. As still as a pasteboard cut-out of a girl seated on a bar-stool. Her drink was not touched, remained where he had left it, as he had left it. Only one thing moved: her eyes. They went wherever he went. They followed him about.

A pause came in his activities, and he encountered them again, for the first time since his original discovery of their peculiar fixity. He found now that they had been on him all the while, without his guessing it. It disconcerted him. He could find no meaning for it. He stole a look into the glass, to see if there was anything awry with his countenance or jacket. There wasn't, he was as other times, no one else was looking at him in that prolonged steadfast way but she. He could find no explanation for it.

It was intentional, of that there could be no doubt, for it moved about as he moved about. It was no glazed, dreamy, inward-mulling stare that just happened to be turned his way; there was intelligence behind it, directed at him.

Awareness of it having once entered his mind, it could not be dislodged again, it remained with him to stay, and trouble him.

He began watching her covertly from time to time himself now, each time thinking himself unobserved. Always he found her already looking at him when he did, always he left her continuing to look at him after he had already desisted. His sense of being at a loss deepened, became discomfort, little by little.

He had never seen a human being sit so still. Nothing about her moved. The drink remained as neglected as though he had not brought it at all. She sat there like a young, feminine Buddha, eyes gravely, uninterruptedly on him.

Discomfort was beginning to deepen into annoyance. He approached her at last, stopped before her.

'Don't you care for your drink, miss?'

This was meant to be a hint, a spur to get her to move on. It failed; she blunted it.

Her answer was toneless, told nothing. 'Leave it there.'

The circumstances were in her favor, for she was a girl, and girls are under no compulsion to be repetitious spenders at a bar, as a man customarily is if he expects to continue to be welcome. Moreover, she was not flirting, she was not seeking to have her check lifted, she was not behaving reprehensibly in any way, he was powerless against her.

He drew away from her again, worsted, looking back at her all the way down the curve of the bar, and her eyes followed him as persistently as ever.

Discomfort was settling into something chronic now. He tried to shrug it off with a squirming of the shoulders, an adjustment of his collar about the nape of his neck. He knew she was still looking, and he wouldn't look over himself any more to confirm it. Which only made it worse.

The demands of other customers, the thicker they came, instead of harassing him, were a relief now. The necessary manipulations they brought on gave him something to do, took his mind off that harrowing stare. But the lulls would keep coming back, when there was no one to attend to, nothing that needed polishing, no glass that needed filling, and it was then that her concentration on him would make itself felt the most. It was then that he didn't know what to do with his hands, or with his barcloth.

He upset a small chaser of beer as he was knifing it atop the sieve. He punched a wrong key in the cash-register.

At last, driven almost beyond endurance, he tackled her again, trying to come to grips with what she was doing to him.

'Is there anything I can do for you, miss?' he said with husky, choked resentment.

She spoke always without putting any clue into her voice. 'Have I said there is?'

He leaned heavily on the bar. 'Well, is there something you want from me?'

'Have I said I do?'

'Well, pardon me, but do I remind you of someone you know?'

'No one.'

He was beginning to flounder. 'I thought maybe there was, the way you keep looking at me –' he said unsteadily. It was meant to be a rebuke.

This time she didn't answer at all. Yet neither did her eyes leave him. He finally was the one who had to leave them again, withdraw as discomfited as ever.

She didn't smile, she didn't speak, she showed neither contrition nor yet outright hostility. She just sat and looked after him, with the inscrutable gravity of an owl.

It was a terrible weapon she had found and she was using. It does not ordinarily occur to people how utterly unbearable it can be to be looked at steadily over a protracted period of time, say an hour or two or three, simply because it is a thing that never happens to them, their fortitude is not put to the test.

It was happening to him now, and it was slowly unnerving him, fraying him. He was defenseless against it, both because he was confined within the semi-circle of the bar, couldn't walk away from it, and also because of its very nature. Each time he tried to buffet it back, he found that it was just a look, there was nothing there to seize hold of. The control of it rested with her. A beam, a ray, there was no way of warding it off, shunting it aside.

Symptoms that he had never noted in himself before, and would not have recognized by their clinical name of agoraphobia, began to assail him with increasing urgency; a longing to take cover, to seek refuge back within the locker-room, even a desire to squat down below the level of the bar-top where she could no longer see him readily. He mopped his brow furtively once or twice and fought them off. His eyes began to seek the clock overhead with increasing frequency, the clock that they had once told him a man's life depended on.

He longed to see her go. He began to pray for it. And yet it was obvious by now, had been for a long time past, that she had no intention of going of her own accord, would only go with the closing of the place. For none of the usual reasons that cause people to seek a bar were operating in her case, and therefore there was no reprieve to be expected of any of them. She was not there to wait for anyone, or she would have been met long ago. She was not there to drink, for that same untouched glass still sat just where he had set it hours ago. She was there for one purpose and one alone: to look at him.

Failing to be rid of her in any other way, he began to long for closing time to come, to find his escape through that. As the customers began to thin out, as the number of counter-attractions about him lessened, her power to bring herself to his notice rose accordingly. Presently there were large gaps around the semi-circle fronting him, and that only emphasized the remorseless fixity of that Medusa-like countenance all the more.

He dropped a glass, and that was a thing he hadn't done in months. She was shooting him to pieces. He glowered at her and cursed her in soundless lip-movement as he stooped to gather up the fragments.

And then finally, when he thought it was never coming any more, the minute-hand notched twelve, and it was four o'clock and closing-time had arrived. Two men engaged in earnest conversation, the last of all the other customers, rose unbidden and sauntered toward the entrance, without interrupting their flow of amicable, low-voiced talk. Not she. Not a muscle moved. The stagnant drink still sat before her, and she sat on with it. Looking, watching, eying, without even a blink.

'Good night, gentlemen,' he called out loudly after the other two, so that she would understand.

She didn't move.

He opened the control-box and threw a switch. The outer

perimeter of lights went out, leaving just an inner glow coming from behind the bar where he was, a hidden sunset creeping up the mirrors and the tiers of bottles ranged against the wall. He became a black silhouette against it, and she a disembodied faintly-luminous face peering in from the surrounding dimness.

He went up to her, took the hours-old drink away, and threw it out, with a violent downward fling of the hand that sent drops leaping up.

'We're closing up now,' he said in a grating voice.

She moved at last. Suddenly she was on her feet beside the stool, holding it for a moment to give the change of position time to work its way through her circulatory system.

His fingers worked deftly down the buttons of his jacket. He said cholerically, 'What was it? What was the game? What was on your mind?'

She moved quietly off through the darkened tavern toward the street-entrance without answering, as though she hadn't heard him. He had never dreamed that such a simple causative as the mere sight of a girl quitting a bar, could bring such utter, contrite, prostrate relief welling up in him. His jacket open all down the front, he supported himself there on one hand planted firmly down upon the bar, and leaned limply, exhaustedly out in the direction in which she had gone.

There was a night-light standing at the outer entrance, and she came back into view again when she had reached there. She stopped just short of the doorway, and turned, and looked back at him across the intervening distance, long and solemnly and with purposeful implication. As if to show that the whole thing had been no illusion; more than that, to show that this was not its end, that this was just an interruption.

He turned from keying the door locked, and she was standing there quietly on the sidewalk, only a few yards off. She was turned expectantly facing toward the doorway, as if waiting for him to emerge.

He was forced to go toward her, because it was in that direction his path lay on leaving here of a night. They passed within a foot of one another, for the sidewalk was fairly narrow and she was posted out in the middle of it, not skulking back against the wall. Though her face turned slowly in time with his passing, he saw that she would have let him go by without speaking, and goaded by this silent obstinacy, he spoke himself, although only a second before he had intended ignoring her.

'What is it ye want of me?' he rumbled truculently.

'Have I said I want anything of you?'

He made to go on, then swung around on his heel to face her accusingly. 'You sat in there just now, never once took your eyes off me! Never once the live-long night, d'ye hear me?' He pounded one hand within the other for outraged emphasis. 'And now I find you outside here waiting around—'

'Is it forbidden to stand here in the street?'

He shook a thick finger at her ponderously. 'I'm warning you, young woman! I'm telling you for your own good—!'

She didn't answer. She didn't open her mouth, and silence is always so victorious in argument. He turned and shambled off, breathing heavily with his own bafflement.

He didn't look back. Within twenty paces, even without looking back, he had become aware that she was advancing in turn behind him. It was not difficult to do so, for she was apparently making no effort to conceal the fact. The ticking-off of her small brittle shoes was clear-cut if subdued on the quiet night-pavement.

An up-and-down intersection glided by beneath him like a slightly-depressed asphalt stream-bed. Then presently another. Then still another. And through it all, as the town slowly veered over from west to east, came that unhurried *tick-chick, tick-chick*, behind him in the middle distance.

He turned his head, the first time simply to warn her off. She came on with maddening casualness, as though it were three in the afternoon. Her walk was slow, almost stately, as the feminine gait so often is when the figure is held erect and the pace is leisurely.

He went on again, briefly, then turned once more. This time his entire body, and flung himself back toward her in a sudden flurry of ungovernable exasperation.

She stopped advancing, but she held her ground, made no slightest retrograde move.

He closed in and bellowed full into her face: 'Turn back now, will ye? That's enough of this now, d'ye hear? Turn back, or I'll—'

'*I* am going this way too,' was all she said.

Again the circumstances were in her favor. Had their roles been reversed— But what man has sufficiently stout armor against ridicule to risk calling a policeman to complain that a solitary young girl is following him along the streets? She was not reviling him, she was not soliciting him, she was simply walking in the same direction he was; he was as helpless against her as he had been in the bar earlier.

He maintained his stance before her for a moment or two, but his defiance was of that face-saving kind that only marks time while it is waiting to extricate itself with the least possible embarrassment from a false situation. He spun around finally with a snort through his nose, meant to convey belligerence, but that somehow sounded a bit like windy helplessness. He drew away from her, resumed his homeward journeying.

Ten paces, fifteen, twenty. Behind him, as at a given signal, it recommenced again, steady as slow rain in a puddle. *Tick-chick, tick-chick, tick-chick.* She was coming after him once more.

He rounded the appointed corner, started up the roofed-over sidewalk stairway he used every night to reach his train. He halted up above, at the rear of the plank-floored station gallery that led through to the tracks, scanning the chute-like incline he had just emerged from for signs of her.

The oncoming tap of her footfalls took on a metallic ring as her feet clicked against the steel rims guarding the steps. In a moment her head came into view above the midway break in the stair-line.

A turnstile rumbled around after him, and he turned there on the other side of it, at bay, took up a defensive position.

She cleared the steps and came on, as matter-of-factly, as equably, as though he wasn't to be seen there at all in the gap fronting her. She already held the coin pinched between her fingers. She came on until there was just the width of the turnstile-arm between them.

He backed his arm at her, swinging it up all the way past its opposite shoulder, ready to fling it loose. It would have sent her spinning about the enclosure. His lip lifted in a canine snarl. 'Get outa here, now. Gawan down below where ye came from!' He reached down and quickly plugged the coin-slot with the ball of his thumb just ahead of her own move toward it.

She desisted, shifted over to the adjoining one. Instantly he was there before her again. She shifted back to the original one. He reversed himself once more, again blocked it. The superstructure began to vibrate with the approach of one of the infrequent night-trains.

This time he finally flung his arm out in the back-sweep he had been threatening at each confrontation. The blow would have been enough to fell her if it had caught her. She turned her head aside with the fastidious little quirk of someone detecting an unpleasant odor. It fanned her face.

Instantly there was a peremptory rapping on glass somewhere close at hand. The station-agent thrust head and shoulder out of the sideward door of his dingy little booth. 'Cut that out, you. Whaddye trying to do, keep people from using this station? I'll run you in!'

He turned to defend himself, the tabu partially lifted since this intercession wasn't of his own seeking. 'This girl's nuts or something, she ought to be sent to Bellevue. She's been follying me along the street, I can't get rid of her.'

She said in that same dispassionate voice, 'Are you the only one that can ride the Third Avenue El?'

He appealed to the agent once more, continuing to hang slant-wise out of the doorway as a sort of self-appointed arbiter. 'Ask her where she's going. She don't know herself!'

Her answer was addressed to the agent, but with an emphasis that could not have been meant for him, that must have had some purpose of its own. 'I'm going down to Twenty-seventh Street, Twenty-seventh Street between Second and Third Avenues. I have a right to use this station, haven't I?'

The face of the man blocking her way had suddenly grown white, as though the locality she had mentioned conveyed a shock of hidden meaning to him. It should have. It was his own.

She knew ahead of time where he was going. It was useless therefore to attempt to shake her off, outdistance her in any way.

The agent rendered his decision, with a majestic sweep of his hand. 'Come on through, miss.'

Her coin suddenly swelled up in the reflector and she had come through the next one over, without waiting for him to clear the way for her. A thing which he seemed incapable of doing at the moment, no longer through obstinacy so much as through a temporary paralysis of movement with which his discovery of her knowledge of his eventual destination seemed to have afflicted him.

The train had arrived, meanwhile, but it was on the opposite side, not theirs. It ebbed away again, and the station breastworks dimmed once more behind it.

She sauntered to the outer lip of the platform and stood there waiting, and presently he had come out in turn, but digressing so that he emerged two pillar-lengths to the rearward of her. Since both were looking the same way, in quest of a train, he had her in view but she did not have him.

Presently, without noticing what she was doing, she began to amble further rearward along the platform, relieving the monotony of the wait by aimless movement as most people are inclined to do at such a time. This had soon taken her beyond the agent's limited range of vision, and out to where the station roof ended and the platform itself narrowed to a single-file strip of runway. Here she came to a halt again, and would have eventually turned and retraced her steps back toward where she had come from. But while standing there, peering trainward and with her back still to him, an unaccountable tension, a sense of impending danger of some sort, began slowly to come over her.

It must have been something about the way his tread sounded to her on the planks. He too was straying now in turn, and toward her. He was moving sluggishly, just as she had. It wasn't that; it was that his tread, while distinct enough in the unnatural stillness that reigned over the station, had some sort of a furtive undertone to it. It was in the rhythm, rather than in any actual attempt to muffle it. It was somehow a leashed tread, a tread of calculated approach trying to disguise itself as a meaningless ramble. She could not know how she knew; she only knew, before she had even turned, that something had entered his mind in the few moments since her back had been turned. Something that had not been there before.

She turned, and rather sharply.

He was still little better than his original two stanchion-lengths away from her. It was not that that confirmed her impression. She caught him in the act of glancing down into the track-bed beside him, where the third rail lay, as he drifted along parallel to it. It was that.

She understood immediately. A jostle of the elbow, a deft, tripping side-swipe of the foot, as they made to pass one another. She took in at a glance the desperate position she had unwittingly strayed into. She was penned against the far end of the station. Without realizing it she had cut herself off from the agent's protective radius of vision altogether. His booth was set back inside to command the turnstiles, could not command the sweep of the platform.

The two of them were alone on the platform. She looked across the way, and the opposite side was altogether barren, had just been cleared by the northbound train. There was no downtown train in sight yet, either, offering that dubious deterrent.

To retreat still further would be suicidal; the platform ended completely only a few yards behind her back, she would only wedge herself into a cul-de-sac, be more at his mercy than ever. To get back to the midsection where the agent offered safety, she would have to go toward him, *pass* him, which was the very act he was seeking to achieve.

If she screamed now, without waiting for the overt act, in hopes of bringing the agent out onto the platform in time, she ran a very real risk of bringing on all the faster the very thing she was trying to prevent. He was in a keyed-up state, she could tell by the look on his face, on which a scream, more likely than not, would produce the opposite effect from that intended. This temporary aberration was due to sheer fright on his part more than rage, and a scream might frighten him still further.

She had frightened him badly, she had done her work only too well.

She edged warily inward, back as far as possible from the tracks, until she had come up close against the row of advertisements lining the guard-rail. She pressed her hips flat against them, began to sidle along them, turned watchfully outward toward him. Her dress rustled as it swept their surfaces one by one, so close did she cling.

As she drew within his orbit he began to veer in toward her on a diagonal, obviously to cut off her further advance. There was a slowness about both their movements that was horrible; they were like lazy fish swimming in a tank, on that deserted platform three stories above the street, with its tawny widely-spaced lights strung along overhead.

He still came on, and so did she, and they were bound to meet in another two or three paces.

The turnstile drummed unexpectedly, around out of sight from them, and a colored girl of dubious pursuits came out on the platform just a few short yards away from the two of them, bent almost lopsided as she moved to scratch herself far down the side of her leg.

They slowly melted into relaxation, each in the pose in which she had surprised them. The girl, with her back to the billboards, stayed that way, slumped a little lower, buckled at the knees now. He leaned deflatedly against a chewing-gum slot-machine at hand beside him. She could almost see the recent fell purpose oozing out of him at every pore. Finally he turned away from his nearness to her with a floundering movement. Nothing had been said, the whole thing had been in pantomime from beginning to end.

That would never come again. She had the upper hand once more.

INDEX

BIBLIOGRAPHY AND PERMISSIONS

....

Abella, Alex. Extract from *The Killing of the Saints*. First published by Serpent's Tail, 1991. Copyright © Alex Abella 1991. Reprinted with the permission of Alex Abella.

Armitage, Simon. Extract from *Book of Matches*. First published by Faber and Faber, 1993. Copyright © Simon Armitage 1993. Reprinted with permission.

Auden, W.H. 'Detective Story' from *W.H. Auden: Collected Poems*, edited by Edward Mendelson, copyright © 1976 by Edward Mendelson, William Meredith, and Monroe K. Spears, Executors of the Estate of W.H. Auden. Reprinted by permission of Random House, Inc.

Auster, Paul. Extract from *The New York Trilogy*. First published in the US by Sun and Moon Press, Los Angeles, 1985–6. First published in Great Britain by Faber and Faber, 1987, new paperback edition, 1988. Copyright © Paul Auster 1987. Reprinted with the permission of the Maggie Noach Literary Agency.

Benjamin, Paul. Extract from *Squeeze Play*. Copyright © 1991 by Paul Benjamin. Reprinted with the permission of The Carol Mann Agency.

Brecht, Bertolt. 'Über die Popularität des Kriminalromans' in *Gesammelte Werke*. Published by Suhrkamp Verlag, Frankfurt am Main, 1967. Translation © Jeff Morrison 1993.

Browning, Robert. 'Porphyria's Lover'. First published in *Dramatic Lyrics,* 1842. Collected editions of poems published by Oxford University Press (1971, 1983–), Penguin Books (1981), Longman (191–), and Ohio University Press (1988–).

Butor, Michel. Extract from *L'Emploi du temps*. First published by Editions de Minuit, Paris, 1951. Published in English as *Passing Time*. Translated by J. Stewart. First published by Faber and Faber, 1961, new impression, Jupiter Books (John Calder), 1965. Reprinted with the permission of Editions de Minuit.

Cain, James M. Extract from *The Postman Always Rings Twice,* copyright 1934 and renewed 1962 by James M. Cain. Reprinted by permission of Alfred A. Knopf, Inc.

Cain, Paul. Extract from *The Fast One*. First published in the US by Doubleday, Doran and Co., 1933. First published in Great Britain by Constable, 1936. Published by Oldcastle Books, 1987, and by No Exit Press, Harpenden, as a graphic novel, 1990. Reproduced with the permission of No Exit Press.

Chandler, Raymond. 'Casual Notes on the Mystery Novel' from *Raymond Chandler Speaking,* edited by Dorothy Gardiner and Kathrine Sorley Walker. Copyright © 1997 The Regents of the University of California. Reprinted with the permission of the University of California.

—Extract from *The Lady in the Lake,* copyright 1934 by Raymond Chandler and renewed 1971 by Helga Greene, Executrix of the Estate of Raymond Chandler. Reprinted by permission of Alfred A. Knopf, Inc.

—Extract from 'Pick-Up on Noon Street' from *The Simple Art of Murder,* copyright 1950 by Raymond Chandler and renewed 1978 by Helga Greene. All rights reserved. Reprinted by permission of Houghton Mifflin Co.

Chekhov, Anton. Extract from *The Shooting Party*. Translated by A.E. Chamot, and revised by Julian Symons. Published by Andre Deutsch, 1964, 1986.

Chesterton, G.K. 'How to write a detective story' in *The Spice of Life, and Other Essays*. Edited by D. Collins. Published by Darwen Finlayson, Beaconsfield, 1964.

Cole, G.D.H. and M. Extract from *Murder at the Munition Works*. First published by Collins, 1940. Published by Lythway Press, Bath, 1974. Reprinted with the permission of David Higham Associates.

Conrad, Joseph. Letter to R.B. Cunninghame Graham, 8 February 1899, in *The Collected Letters of Joseph Conrad,* Volume 2. Edited by F.R. Karl and L. Davies. Published by Cambridge University Press, 1986.

Dubus, Andre. Extract from 'Killings' in *Selected Stories*. First published in the US by David R. Godine Publishers, 1991. First published in Great Britain in Picador by Pan Books, 1990, with a new paperback edition, 1991. Copyright © Andre Dubus 1991. Reproduced with permission.

Duffy, Carol Ann. Extract from 'Model Village' in *Selling Manhattan*. First published by Anvil Press Poetry, 1987. Reprinted with permission.

Dürrenmatt, Friedrich. Extract from *Das Versprechen: Requiem auf den Kriminalroman*. First published by Die Arche, Zürich, 1958. Published in English as *The Pledge*. Translated by R. and C. Winston. First published by Jonathan Cape, 1959. Reprinted with permission of Tessa Sayle Agency and Pan Macmillan Ltd.

Eco, Umberto. Extract from *The Name of the Rose,* reprinted in the US by kind permission of Fabbri Editori, Bompiani, a division of RCS Libri, translated by Michael Dibdin.

Eliot, T.S. Extract from *The Criterion,* June 1927.

—Extract from *Selected Essays*. First published by Faber and Faber, 1951; published in the US by Harcourt Brace. Reprinted by permission.

Faulkner, William. Extract from 'Smoke' from *Knight's Gambit,* copyright 1932 and renewed 1960 by William Faulkner. Reprinted by permission of Random House, Inc.

Fenton, James. Extract from 'A Staffordshire Murderer' in *The Memory of War.* First published by Salamander Press, Edinburgh, 1982. Published as *The Memory of War, and Children in Exile: poems 1968–1983* by Penguin, 1983, and in a new paperback edition in the Penguin International Poets series, 1992. Copyright © James Fenton 1972, 1978, 1980, 1981, 1982, 1983. Reprinted with the permission of Peters Fraser & Dunlop Group Ltd.

Forester, C.S. Extract from *Plain Murder.* First published by John Lane, 1930. New edition published by the Bodley Head, 1968. Reprinted with the permission of the Random Century Group and the estate of C.S. Forester.

Frye, Northrop. Extract from *The Anatomy of Criticism: Four Essays.* First published by Princeton University Press, 1957. New paperback editions published by Princeton University Press, 1971, and Penguin Books, 1990. Reprinted with permission.

Fuller, Roy. Extract from *The Second Curtain.* First published by Derek Verschoyle, 1953. Published by Penguin, 1962. Copyright © Estate of Roy Fuller. Reprinted with the permission of the estate of Roy Fuller.

Gide, André. Entry for 13 January 1948 in *The Journals of André Gide.* Translated by J. O'Brien. First published in 3 volumes by Secker and Warburg, 1947–9. Published as *Journals 1889–1949* by Penguin, 1967 and in a new paperback edition in the Twentieth Century Classics series, 1991.

—Extract from 'The Vatican Cellars' from *Lafcadio's Adventures,* translated by Dorothy Bussy, copyright 1925 and renewed 1953 by Alfred A. Knopf, Inc. Reprinted by permission of Alfred A. Knopf, Inc.

Gramsci, Antonio. Letter of 6 October 1930 in *Lettere dal carcere.* First published by G. Einaudi, Turin, 1947. Published in English as *Letters from Prison*. Translated by L. Lawner. First published by Harper and Row, 1973. Copyright © 1973 by Lynne Lawner. Reprinted by permission of Georges Borchardt, Inc. On behalf of Lynne Lawner. Published in Great Britain in *Prison Letters: Lettere dal Carcere*. Translated by H. Henderson. Published by Pluto Press, 1988.

Grierson, Edward. Extract from *Reputation for a Song*. First published by Chatto and Windus, 1952. Published by Penguin, 1955. Reprinted with the permission of the Random Century Group and the estate of Edward Grierson.

Hammett, Dashiell. Extract from *The Glass Key,* copyright 1931 by Alfred A. Knopf, Inc., and renewed 1959 by Dashiell Hammett. Reprinted by permission of Alfred A. Knopf, Inc.

Hare, David. Extract from the Introduction to *The History Plays*. First published by Faber and Faber, 1984.

Haycraft, H. (ed.) Extract from *The Art of the Mystery Story: A Collection of Critical Essays*. First published by Grosset and Dunlap, 1961.

Heath-Stubbs, John. Extract from 'Send for Lord Timothy' in *Collected Poems 1943–1987*. Published by Carcanet, 1988. Copyright © John Heath-Stubbs 1988. Reproduced with permission.

Hemingway, Ernest. 'The Killers', reprinted with permission of Scribner, a division of Simon and Schuster, Inc. From *The Complete Short Stories of Ernest Hemingway*. Copyright © 1927 by Charles Scribner's Sons and renewed 1955 by Ernest Hemingway.

Higgins, George V. Extract from *Trust*. First published by Andre Deutsch, 1989. Copyright © George V. Higgins 1989. Reproduced by permission. New paperback editions published by Abacus Books, 1990, and Sphere, 1991.

Highsmith, Patricia. Extract from *Strangers on the Train*. First published by Cresset Press, 1950. Published by Heinemann 1966. New paperback edition published by Penguin Books, 1974.

—Extract from *The Talented Mr. Ripley*. First published by Cresset Press, 1957. Published by Heinemann, 1966, and a new paperback edition by Penguin, 1977.

Hughes, Dorothy B. Extract from *In a Lonely Place*. First published by Nicholson and Watson, 1950. New paperback edition published by No Exit Press, 1990. Reprinted with the permission of Blanche C. Gregory, Inc.

Iles, Francis. Extract from *Malice Aforethought: the Story of a Commonplace Crime*. First published by Victor Gollancz, 1931. Copyright © The Society of Authors 1931. Published by Dent (Mastercrime series), 1986. Reprinted with the permission of Campbell Thompson & McLaughlin Limited.

James, P.D. and Critchley, T.A. Extract from *The Maul and the Pear Tree: the Ratcliffe Highway Murders,* 1811. First published by Penguin, 1971. New paperback edition published by Penguin, 1990. Copyright © P. D. James and T. A. Critchley 1971. Reprinted with the permission of Elaine Greene Ltd.

Jesse, F. Tennyson. Extract from *A Pin to See the Peepshow*. First published by Heinemann, 1934. New paperback edition published by Virago, 1979. Reprinted with the permission of Reed International Books.

Joyce, James. Extract from *Finnegans Wake*. First published by Faber and Faber, 1939. New paperback editions published by Faber and Faber 1975, Paladin (1992), Minerva (1992), and Penguin in the Twentieth Century Classics series, 1992.

Kafka, Franz. Extract from 'A Case of Fratricide' in *Short Stories 1904–1924*. Translated by J.A. Underwood. First published by Macdonald Books, 1981. Reprinted with permission of J.A. Underwood. New paperback edition published by Cardinal, 1990. Complete editions of the short stories are published by Penguin (1989) and Minerva (1992).

King, Francis. Extract from *Act of Darkness*. First published by Hutchinson Books, 1983. Reprinted with the permission of Francis King.

Krutch, Joseph Wood. Extract from 'Only a Detective Story' in *The Nation*, 25 November 1944. Copyright © 1944, The National Company Inc. Reproduced with permission.

Lawrence, D.H. Extract from *Women in Love*. First published by Secker, 1921. Copyright © 1920, 1922 David Herbert Lawrence. Copyright © 1948, 1950 by Frieda Lawrence. New editions published by Cambridge University Press (edited by D. Farmer, 1987) and Everyman's Library (1992) and in paperback by Penguin (1969), Cambridge University Press (1987), Penguin (Twentieth Century Classics series, 1990), and Wordsworth Classics (edited by Marcus Clapham and Clive Reynard, 1992).

Leonard, Elmore. Extract from *Freaky Deaky*. First published by Viking Penguin, 1988. New paperback edition published by Penguin, 1989. Copyright © Elmore Leonard 1988. Reprinted with the permission of Penguin Books Ltd.

Levin, Ira. Extract from *A Kiss Before Dying*. First published by Michael Joseph, 1954. Copyright © Ira Levin 1954. Reprinted with the permission of Penguin Books Ltd.

Lowndes, Marie Belloc. Extract from *The Lodger*. First published by Methuen, 1913. New edition published by Hutchinson in the Black Dagger Crime series, 1991.

McCabe, Cameron. Extract from *The Face on the Cutting-Room Floor*. First published by Victor Gollancz, 1937. Reprinted with the permission of the author.

McClure, James. Extract from *The Steam Pig*. First published by Victor Gollancz, 1971. Copyright © James McClure 1971.

Mosley, Walter. Extract from *A Red Death: An Easy Rawlins Mystery*. Copyright © 1991 by Walter Mosley. Reprinted by permission of W.W. Norton & Company, Inc.

Newman, G.F. Extract from *Sir, You Bastard*. First published by W.H. Allen, 1970. Revised for this edition by G.F. Newman. Copyright © G.F. Newman 1993.

Nicholson, Harold. Extract from 'Marginal Comment' in *The Spectator*, 23 March 1951. Reprinted with the permission of *The Spectator*.

Partridge, R. Extract from *New Statesman*, 10 August 1940.

Perelman, S.J. 'Somewhere a Roscoe', copyright © 1959 by S.J. Perelman. Reprinted with the permission of Harold Ober Associates, Inc.

Poe, Edgar Allan. 'The Tell-Tale Heart' in *Tales of Mystery and Imagination*. First published by Milner and Sowerby, 1955. New paperback edition published by Dent, 1990; it can also be found in *Complete Tales and Poems*, edited by Arthur Holson Quinn, Penguin, 1987. Story first published in *The Works of the late Edgar Allan Poe*, 4 volumes, by J.S. Redfield, 1850–56.

Postgate, Raymond. Extract from *The Verdict of Twelve*. First published by Collins, 1940.

Pritchett, V.S. Extract from *New Statesman*, 16 June 1951.

Queneau, Raymond. Entry for 15 September 1945 in *Batons, chiffres et lettres*. First published by Gallimard, Paris, 1950. Copyright © Editions Gallimard 1950. Translated for this collection by Michael Dibdin. Reprinted with permission.

Raymond, Ernest. Extract from *We, the Accused*. First published by Cassell, 1935. Reproduced with the permission of A.P. Watt Ltd and the estate of Ernest Raymond.

Robbe-Grillet, Alain. Extract from *Les gommes*. First published by Editions de Minuit, Paris, 1953. Published in English as *The Erasers*. Translated by R. Howard. First published by John Calder, 1966. Copyright © this translation Grove Press Inc., New York, 1964. New paperback edition published by Calder, 1987. Reprinted by permission of the Calder Educational Trust, London.

Rycroft, Charles. Extract from 'The Analysis of a Detective Story' in *Imagination and Reality: Psychoanalytic Essays 1951–1961*. First published by the Hogarth Press, 1968. New paperback edition published by Maresfield Library, 1987. Reprinted with the permission of the Random Century Group.

Sartre, Jean-Paul. Extract from *Les mots*. Reprinted by permission of Editions Gallimard, represented by Georges Borchardt, Inc., in an English translation copyright © George Braziller, Inc. Reprinted by permission.

Simenon, Georges. Extract from *L'Homme qui regardait passer les trains*. First published by Fayard, Paris, 1938. Published in English as *The Man Who Watched the Trains Go By*. Translated by S. Gilbert. First published by S. G. Routledge and Sons, 1942. New paperback edition published by Penguin, 1986.

—Extract from *Maigret's Memoirs*, translated from *Les Memoires de Maigret* by Georges Simenon, copyright © 1950 by the Estate of Georges Simenon, all rights reserved. First published in Paris by Fayard.

Singer, Isaac Bashevis. 'Under the Knife' from *Short Friday and Other Stories*. Copyright © 1964 by Isaac Bashevis Singer and renewed 1992 by Alma Singer.

Sjöwall, Maj and Wahlöö, Per. Extract from *The Copkiller*. Translated by Thomas Teal. First published by Victor Gollancz, 1975, as by Maj Sjöwall and Peter Wahloo. Copyright for this translation © Random House Inc. 1975. Reprinted with permission.

Snow, C.P. Extract from *A Coat of Varnish*. First published by Macmillan, 1979. New paperback edition published by Penguin, 1980. Copyright © C.P. Snow 1979. Reproduced with permission.

Steeves, H.A. Extract from 'A Sober Word on the Detective Story' in Haycraft (ed.), op. cit.

Stern, P. Van Doren. Extract from 'The Case of the Corpse in the Blind Alley' in Haycraft (ed.), op. cit.

Stevenson, Robert Louis and Osbourne, Lloyd. Extract from 'Epilogue: to Will H. Low' in *The Wreckers*. First published by Cassell, 1892.

Symons, Julian. Extract from *The Man who Killed Himself*. First published by Collins, 1967. Copyright © Julian Symons 1967. Reprinted by permission Curtis Group Ltd.

—Extract from *The Thirty-First of February: a mystery novel*. First published by Victor Gollancz, 1950. New paperback edition published as *The Advertising Murders: 'The Thirty-First of February' and 'The Man Called Jones'* by Pan Books, 1992. Copyright © Julian Symons 1950.

Thompson, Hunter S. Extract from *Fear and Loathing in Las Vegas*. Copyright © 1972 by Hunter S. Thompson. Reprinted by permission of International Creative Management, Inc.

Thurber, James. Extract from 'The Wings of Henry James' in *Lanterns and Lances*. First published by Hamish Hamilton, 1961. New paperback edition published by Penguin, 1963. Copyright © 1959 by James Thurber and renewed 1989 by Rosemary A. Thurber. Reprinted by arrangement with Rosemary A. Thurber and The Barbara Hogenson Agency.

Togawa, Masako. Extract from *A Kiss of Fire*. Translated by S. Grove. First published by Dodd Mead & Company, 1988.

Vine, Barbara. Extract from *A Dark-Adapted Eye*. First published by Viking Penguin, 1986. New paperback edition published by Penguin, 1987. Copyright © 1986 by Kingsmarkham Enterprises Ltd. Used by permission of Bantam Books, a division of Bantam Doubleday Dell Publishing Group, Inc.

Weisz, P. Extract from 'Simenon and "Le Commissaire"' in *Essays on detective fiction*. Edited by Bernard Benstock. First published by Macmillan, 1983. Reprinted with permission.

Wilde, Oscar. Extract from *The Picture of Dorian Gray*. First published by Ward Lock, 1891. New paperback editions published by Oxford University Press (World's Classics), 1981, Collins: Nelson (edited by K.R. Cripwell), 1985, W.W. Norton (critical edition, edited by Donald Lawlor), 1988, Oxford University Press in the Oxford Bookworms series, 1989, Penguin (edited by David Crystal and Derek Strange), 1991, and Wordsworth Classics (edited by Marcus Clapham and Clive Reynard), 1992.

Wilson, Edmund. Extracts from 'Why do people read detective stories?' and '"Mr. Holmes, they were the footprints of a gigantic hound!"' in *Classics and Commercials*. First published by Farrar, Straus, 1950.

Woolrich, Cornell. Extract from *Phantom Lady* by Cornell Woolrich writing as William Irish. Reprinted by permission of The Claire Woolrich Memorial Trust, administered by The Chase Manhattan Bank, Trustee.

Zola, Émile. Extract from *Thérèse Raquin*. First published by Lacroix, Verboeckhoven & Cie., Paris, 1867. Translations by L. Tancock, published by Penguin, 1977, by P. Broughton, published by Absolute Classics, 1988, and by A. Rothwell, published by Oxford University Press in the World's Classics series, 1992.

THE TALENTED MR. RIPLEY
by Patricia Highsmith

Tom Ripley is sent to Italy with the commission to coax Dickie Greenleaf back to his wealthy father. But Ripley finds himself very fond of this prodigal young American. He wants to be like him—exactly like him. Ripley will stop at nothing to achieve his goal—not even murder.

"[Highsmith] has created a world of her own—a world claustrophobic and irrational which we enter each time with a sense of personal danger."   —Graham Greene

Fiction/Crime/0-679-74229-8

THE CHILL
by Ross Macdonald

A distraught young man hires Archer to track down his runaway bride, but no sooner has he found her than Archer finds himself entangled in two murders, one twenty years old, the other so recent that the blood is still warm.

"The American private eye, immortalized by Hammett, refined by Chandler, brought to its zenith by Macdonald."
—*The New York Times Book Review*

Fiction/Crime/0-679-76807-6

THE KILLER INSIDE ME
by Jim Thompson

Lou Ford is the deputy sheriff of a small town in Texas. The worst thing most people can say against him is that he's a little slow and a little boring. But then, most people don't know about the sickness.

"Probably the most chilling and believable first-person story of a criminally warped mind I have ever encountered."   —Stanley Kubrick

Fiction/Crime/0-679-73397-3

VINTAGE CRIME/BLACK LIZARD
Available at your local bookstore, or call toll-free to order:
1-800-793-2665 (credit cards only).